THE TRIALS OF OPHELIA

THE CURSE OF OPHELIA SERIES

NICOLE PLATANIA

The

Trials

of

Ophelia

Nicole Platania

Stars Inked Press, Inc.

6320 Topanga Cyn Blvd. Ste. 1630 #1033

Woodland Hills, CA 91367

First paperback edition March 2024

© Cover design: Franziska Stern - www.coverdungeon.com - Instagram: @coverdungeonrabbit

Developmental Edit by Kelley Frodel

Copyedited by Grey Moth Editing

Proofread by K. Morton Editing Services

Map design by Abigail Hair

ISBN 979-8-9862704-7-0 (Paperback)

ISBN 979-8-9862704-6-3 (ebook)

www.nicoleplatania.com

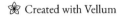 Created with Vellum

*To those who feel torn and broken inside
and worry that they're not good enough.
You are more than enough, just as you are.*

Author's Note

This book contains depictions of alcohol/drug dependency; blood, gore, and violence; discussion of sexual assault (not on page); recounted child abuse; torture; PTSD; and some sexual content. If any of these may be triggering for you, please read carefully or feel free to contact the author for further explanation.

PRONUNCIATION GUIDE
CHARACTERS WHO ARE CROSSED OUT WERE DECEASED PRIOR TO THE BEGINNING OF THE TRIALS OF OPHELIA.

Mystique Warriors

Ophelia Alabath (she/her), Mystique Revered: *Oh-feel-eeya Al-uh-bath*
Malakai Blastwood (he/him): *Mal-uh-kye Blast-wood*
Tolek Vincienzo (he/him): *Tole-ick Vin-chin-zoh*
Cypherion Kastroff (he/him): *Sci-fear-ee-on Cast-Rahf*
Jezebel Alabath (she/her): *Jez-uh-bell Al-uh-bath*
Akalain Blastwood (she/her): *Ah-kuh-lane Blast-wood*
~~Alvaron (he/him), Master of Coin: *Al-vuh-ron*~~
Annellius Alabath, (he/him): *Uh-nell-ee-us Al-uh-bath*
~~Bacaran Alabath (he/him), Second to the Revered: *Bah-kuh-ron Al-uh-bath*~~
~~Collins (he/him): *Call-ins*~~
~~Danya (she/her), Master of Weapons & Warfare: *Dawn-yuh*~~
~~Larcen (he/him), Master of Trade: *Lare-sen*~~
~~Lucidius Blastwood (he/him), Revered: *Loo-sid-ee-yus Blast-wood*~~
Lyria Vincienzo (she/her), Master of Weapons and Warfare: *Leer-ee-uh Vin-chin-zoh*
Marxian (he/him): *Mark-shen*
Mila Lovall (she/her), Mystique General: *Mee-lah Love-all*

Missyneth (she/her), Master of Rites: *Mis-sin-ith*
Tavania Alabath (she/her): *Tuh-vahn-yuh Al-uh-bath*

Engrossian Warriors

Kakias (she/her), Engrossian Queen: *Kuh-kye-yus*
Barrett (he/him), Engrossian Prince: *Bair-it*
Dax (he/him): *Dax*
~~Victious: *Vik-shuss*~~

Mindshapers

~~Aird (he/him), Mindshaper Chancellor: *Air-d*~~
Ricordan (he/him): *Rik-kor-din*
Trevaneth (he/him): *Treh-vuh-neh-th*
Zaina (she/her): *Zay-nuh*

Bodymelders

Brigiet (she/her), Bodymelder Chancellor: *Bri-jeet*
Esmond (he/him), apprentice: *Ez-min-d*
Gatrielle (he/him): *Gah-tree-elle*

Starsearchers

Titus (he/him), Starsearcher Chancellor: *Tie-tuhs*
Vale (she/her), apprentice: *Veil*
Cyren Marvana (they/them), Starsearcher General: *Sci-ren Mar-vaw-nuh*

Seawatchers

Ezalia Ridgebrook (she/her), Seawatcher Chancellor: *Eh-zale-ee-uh Ridg-brook*
Amara Ridgebrook (she/her), Seawatcher General: *Uh-mar-uh Ridg-brook*
Andrenas (they/them): *An-dreh-nuss*

Chorid (he/him): *Core-ihd*
Leo Ridgebrook (he/him): *Lee-oh*
Seron Ridgebrook (he/him): *Sair-on Ridg-brook*

Soulguiders

Meridat (she/her), Soulguider Chancellor: *Mare-ih-daat*
Erista Locke (she/her), apprentice: *Eh-ris-tuh Lock*
Quilian Locke (he/him), Soulguider General: *Quil-ee-
en Lock*

Non-warrior characters

Santorina Cordelian (she/her), human: *San-tor-ee-nuh
Kor-dee-lee-in*
Aimee (she/her), Storyteller: *Ay-me*
Lancaster (he/him), fae: *Lan-kaster*
Mora (she/her), not specified: *Mor-uh*

Animals and Creatures

Astania, *Uh-ston-ya*
Calista: *Kuh-liss-tuh*
Elektra: *Ill-ectra*
Erini: *Ih-ree-nee*
Ombratta: *Ahm-brah-tuh*
Sapphire: *Sah-fire*

Places

Ambrisk: *Am-brisk*
Banix: *Ban-ix*
Brontain: *Brawn-tane*
Caprecion: *Kuh-pree-shun*
Damenal: *Dom-in-all*
Fytar Trench: *Fie-tar Trehn-ch*
Gallantia: *Guh-lawn-shuh*

Gaveral: *Gav-er-all*
Palerman: *Powl-er-min*
Pthole: *Tholl*
Thorentil: *Thor-in-till*
Turren: *Tur-in*
Valyn: *Val-in*
Vercuella: *Vair-kwella*
Xenovia: *Zin-oh-vee-yuh*

Angels of the Gallantian Warriors

Bant (he/him), Prime Engrossian Warrior: *Bant*
Damien (he/him), Prime Mystique Warrior: *Day-mee-in*
Gaveny (he/him), Prime Seawatcher: *Gav-in-ee*
Ptholenix (he/him), Prime Bodymelder: *Tholl-en-icks*
Thorn (he/him), Prime Mindshaper: *Thorn*
Valyrie (she/her), Prime Starsearcher: *Val-er-ee*
Xenique (she/her), Prime Soulguider: *Zen-eek*

Gods of Ambrisk's Pantheon

Aoiflyn (she/her), Fae Goddess: *Eef-lyn*
Artale (she/her), Goddess of Death: *Are-tall*
Gerenth (he/him), God of Nature: *Gair-inth*
Lynxenon (he/him), God of Mythical Beasts: *Leen-zih-non*
Moirenna (she/her), Goddess of Fate & Celestial Movements: *Moy-ren-uh*
Thallia (she/her), Witch Goddess of Sorcia: *Thall-ee-uh*

PROLOGUE
DAMIEN

Many centuries ago

"What have you done?" Fear turned my words low and gravelly, the night nearly swallowing them.

One moment, I was trapped in that Spirits-forsaken chamber that reeked of stifled power. The next, I was greedily gulping down the scent of rain-soaked rock, blooming cyphers, and *freedom*.

The chosen warrior stood before me, eyes swarming with a rage so fresh and burning—swarming with a betrayal-spawning defiance. One unlocked by ancient truths and whirls of secrets, irises blending from calm brown to burning pinks.

He did it, then. He found and took the agent.

This should have been a moment of victory, but his next words dripped with vitriol. "I've learned the truth."

Four words that splintered my entire mission, unleashing a tidal wave of failure. The key had been dragged on a rope before me. But every time I took a step toward it, it was yanked back again. Elusive and wanting, but I had it.

I. Had. it.

Had him.

I had allowed my own feathers to shed because I was so certain. He was supposed to be the resolution, the absolution of sins stacked against us. Instead, he chose to become our greedy undoing.

As I clenched my hand at my side, my power flourishing within me, I realized that left me with an atrocious choice. It went against everything my eternal presence signified, but things had been altered by the hands of fate, that brutal mist of being.

At the thought, my unbeating heart pulsed with remorse. *Imagined*, I reminded myself. *Your heart does not beat.*

Was there a way I would not have to do this?

But he said he knew the truth and declared it with such disdain. His fate was already sealed, then.

"You are certain the rumors you have heard hold true?" Worry gnawed behind my ribs, tightening my lungs. Though I did not need breath, it was restrictive. If the chosen did not know everything, though, maybe we could reignite the path. Maybe I could convince him otherwise...

But when he lifted his chin, that magenta promise glinted. He knew it all.

"I wish the wars of eternal beings were mere rumors," he said.

And prophecy shattered around us with the weight of a thousand bursting stars. His skin glowed, subtle and faint, reminding me of a light I had not seen in centuries as it poured forth. Grief clawed through me, shrinking my vision, but this power was not nearly as potent, untainted, or burning as that lost source.

This was the sacrificed essence of the seven, locked away for millennia.

Wind whipped around our shoulders, the breeze burnished with failure and imbued with the energy of my mountains, singing a disjointed melody along my bones. I gritted my teeth against it. The shift of ether smothered the desperation mounting within me.

Discordant magic ripped through me.

Shredding.

Tearing.

Taking all I was.

I fought it, bearing down on the long dormant power that tried to wrench from me. This was not as planned...this was not...

Panting, I crashed to the ground across from him, two

promised beings on their knees at the bequest of magic. I willed the force breaking from me back where it belonged.

But it was a stranger beneath my own skin.

As it trickled from my grasp, I made that last move. I shot it out, wrapped it around the greedy warrior. And I pulled.

Pulled until sinew and tendons, blood and bones bent to my will.

Crimson leaked from his nose, his ears.

"I am not your puppet," he spat, voice caught in the wind. It swirled around us with dying leaves and flowers and signs of how close we had been. *Puppet, puppet, puppet.* "Nor am I a fool."

"You are no puppet," I said through clenched teeth, "but you become a greater fool each day." Gods, it should not have been this way. If I had only seen the signs.

Blood poured over his chin, the stream growing thicker. His skin paled, but it was not fear entering his eyes. It was triumph. And that chilled me enough to loosen the grasp on his being.

"What have you done?" I gasped. My light dimmed.

"Brother..." A hoarse whisper. Sad eyes. "What have *you*?"

First, an echoing silence filled my mind. Then—an explosion.

With a roar, I ripped back the reins of my magic. Rocks shattered, peaks trembled, trees swayed. The domain bent to my will.

The warrior's palms slapped into dirt. His coughs wracked the air, each puncturing the force of wind around us until all that was audible was those dragging, wet heaves.

Blood splattered earth.

Promise seeped into dust.

And he collapsed before me, still in a pool of his own sacred blood. The light we had both been emitting flickered out until only the ghostly-silver glow of the moon remained.

I toiled through the shocked grief that swarmed me as I stared at those sightless magenta eyes. I had no choice. This was not my fault. The warrior brought about this end.

Pressing my palms into the dug-up earth, I inhaled the iron-tinged air, reminding myself he had done this, not me. The warrior had been greedy, and that was the story legends would spread.

As I worked to persuade myself of it, the wind calmed. The

earth began restoring itself, and I convinced myself he had been a ruin of Angels.

But accusatory magenta eyes swam behind my lids.

What have you?

I failed, that was what I had done. I would not fail with the next chosen.

PART ONE
BIA

CHAPTER ONE
OPHELIA

MY HEART HAD BROKEN SO MANY TIMES, I THOUGHT IT would have stopped beating by now. Surely one organ could only take so much pain before it decided to quit. In the two months since the Battle of Damenal, a hole had formed behind my ribs, widening each day, swallowing up pieces of me. That cavity echoed with a dark void, a blade swiped clean between my bones.

Slice. Puncture. Bleed.

It was the rhythm I operated to, and I masked my pain with work. Restoring what had been damaged throughout Damenal when Queen Kakias had launched an attack on the city atop the peaks. On that midnight when she defied the bounds of magic and used my blood for an unnatural immortality ritual.

That rhythm was how I found myself at the grand set of stone stairs that used to lead to the Sacra Temple, the largest in Damenal, located in the Sacred Quarter in the western quadrant of our divine city. The site of the blast that killed my father and the rest of the Mystique Council on Daminius.

The explosion meant for *me.*

Because I was supposed to be in the temple that day.

I knelt before the cracked stone, brushing my fingers across the dusty edge of the lowest stair. Scraping my nail against one of the divots where a chunk had been blown away. Not to clear it, just to *feel* it. To absorb a touch of the vibrant lives this spot had seen—

7

the stories the temple had contained. My knees dug into the gravel sprinkled at the base, and I let each piece imprint itself against my skin like those losses imprinted themselves on my soul.

Much of the debris had been cleaned away. I'd organized the restoration myself, but it was leagues from being complete. Still, there was a method to the chaos now.

Stacks of stone had been gathered based on their usability. Some would be carted off to the battlefront. At the border of the southern mountains, between Mystique and Mindshaper territory, a war mounted. Lyria Vincienzo had taken up the position of Master of Weapons and Warfare, having been the former commander, Danya's, only apprentice. She now led our alliance forces against the barrage from the Engrossian-Mindshaper army.

The supplies we sent would be used for catapults and securing trails through the snow winter would bring. My friends and I would leave Damenal to join them in a few days, despite my heart remaining in this city.

Shoving aside the thought, I rose from my crouch and crossed to the piles of smaller rocks and pebbles. I didn't know what to do with them. My gaze dragged across each individual stone. Where had it belonged before the temple was destroyed? How had each small crumb supported the whole?

I grabbed a shovel and walked around the side of the temple. The spot I'd been working on yesterday was no more than a sweep of gravel hazardously littering the ground, but I began scooping. It was tedious, walking each shovelful to the organized piles. My hands ached around the wooden handle, splinters piercing the skin, but I continued the work. As sweat beaded across my forehead and under my leathers, I worked.

As the echoes of blasts that shattered my entire world resounded in my head, I worked.

As my heart continued to crack within my chest, I worked.

Until a hand rested gently on my shoulder, and even then I kept working.

"Ophelia," Jezebel said softly.

"Just a little longer," I mumbled, voice flat.

"You've been out here for hours," she answered, squeezing my arm once, a reminder that she was with me, that I wasn't alone. "You're going to be late."

I paused, looking to the sky. When had the sun risen so high? It had to be nearly midday now, meaning I only had two hours until the ceremony.

I'd barely accomplished anything, but I sighed and rested the shovel against the work table. My hands were dirt-streaked, blisters of blood forming beneath the skin.

Gloves. I'd forgotten gloves. How careless of me.

"Come on," Jezebel said, leading me away from the ghost of a structure. "Santorina and I will help you clean up." Even her voice was dull. It had been since the battle. Dark shadows lined her eyes daily.

I often found her loitering in corridors, staring out windows, entranced. Every time I snapped her out of it, she seemed like a bit more life had been taken from her. My once animated, sparkling sister, now hollow.

Except when it came to me. She channeled every remaining dash of her vivacity into our bond, into lifting me up as I guided our people through heartache and warfare. I squeezed her hand tighter as we walked silently through our city.

Ruins.

Ruined homes.

Ruined families.

Ruined hearts.

We'd made progress over the last two months, but gaping holes remained. Windows shattered and boarded up. Unstable buildings abandoned.

We rounded a corner and passed where the largest library, save the archives in the palace, had been taken out and strode down another alley, where a cluster of unassuming homes had been raided and vacated. And every time I closed my eyes, I saw the spot where the Sacra Temple once stood, where the first blast had rocked the foundation of my world.

That moment would haunt me for eternity. The jarring snap to a horrid reality when I'd been lost in a bubble of blissful naivety, believing maybe I could have beautiful things, like stolen moments in that bathing room with Tolek. Until the life-changing explosion had grabbed hold of reality and shaken it, flipped it, broken it, taking out a structure that stood for millennia and my father with it—my father who had been the most resolute structure in *my* life.

As if she read my mind, Jezebel passed through the gleaming palace gates and said, "The temple..."

"Yes?" I asked when she did not continue.

"You've done good work there."

"Thank you," I said. "It's for him."

"I think"—Jezebel worried her lip—"Father would be overcome with gratitude at what you're doing to honor him, but he would want you to keep moving. To say the Spirits' blessings for the fallen but give your heart to the living."

I stopped walking. "How can you know that?" How could anyone know what the dead wished for? It was one of the cruelest parts of them leaving. Had any of them been ready? Had they died with regrets? With final messages?

Even if I gave my heart to those still here, there would always be a piece lost on Daminius.

Jezebel gnawed her lip again as I walked up the stairs alongside her. Sitting on the highest point of the city, in the Northern Quarter, our home was one of the few places where you could see all of Damenal. The view was now bittersweet.

"I suppose I can't know," Jez finally said, her shoulders sinking. "But you're draining yourself by trying to restore this city. I don't want to see the end result of that."

It was the only way I was keeping myself together these days because my father and the council had died in my stead—hundreds of warriors fell that night—and Tolek still had not—

No.

My fingers shot to my emblem necklace, locking around the shard that had broken from my spear months ago. One of the seven tokens of fossilized Angel power I was meant to unite, thanks to an ancient prophecy from the Prime Warriors themselves.

I breathed over the pain, summoning strength from the emblem. Restoration aside, we'd spent every spare moment these past two months searching the archives for what these tokens might be and where they were hidden. The chancellors of the minor clans were doing the same in their territories.

What did we have to show for it? A pile of history on the Angels and no hint of answers. It made my fingers twitch. That was how I'd ended up at the Sacra Temple this morning, needing to do *something* besides thinking of all we did not know.

The metal heated beneath my hand. It once burned and blistered my skin, but now, it steadied me. It soothed the thoughts I couldn't handle today.

I swallowed all those feelings bubbling up within me. All the grief that split my chest right open. The memory of a smirk I missed so deeply, the longing for a hug from my father, and the fear for what came next.

"I don't want you to worry over me," I told my sister as we turned down the corridor to my suite. Marble floors gleamed and artwork framed the walls, beautifully out of place. "I'm doing what has to be done."

"Maybe," Jez countered. "Or maybe you're sacrificing pieces of yourself each day. You only have so many."

Pressing my hand to the door, I froze. My nails curved into the wood. Maybe it was because of what today signified or a wound dug open by the Sacra Temple, but I admitted what I'd been hiding for weeks, "I'm running out of pieces, Jez. I—I know there are more of them. I can feel all these desires and dreams buried within me, but it's like I don't know how to reach them beyond this pain. Every time I try, they all blur together."

And there was so much to be done. A war to fight and a prophecy to decode, emblems to hunt for and a city to rebuild. How could I focus on my own pieces when the external ones were so much bigger?

Jezebel removed my hand from the door and held it between her own. "I know how it feels. *I know* how dark our minds can get. Today is a day to celebrate, though. It is a day about *you* and this magnificent future you're going to have. You've waited for this— you made incredibly hard decisions to get here. Don't let it pass by because you're digging up those pieces." And though her words were encouraging, her voice was flat. Like she had to say it but did not believe it for herself.

Knowing that only added to the devastation wringing my bones. If I wasn't careful, I'd exist solely of it soon.

The door to my suite swung open before us, and Santorina propped a hand on her hip.

"There you two are." Her eyes dropped to the already healing blisters on my hands and back to my face. "Come on, I'll have those good as new faster than a god's breath."

Rina's hair was braided—two small plaits stopping halfway back, the rest falling in a sleek onyx sheet—and she'd applied a modest amount of products to her eyes.

Ready. She was already ready for today. I could be ready, too.

As I quickly bathed and sat before the mirror in the dressing chamber, gratitude welled in me for Jezebel and Santorina. For them helping me stand before our people each day, my sister even through her own loss.

And Rina had supported us both, being the focused guidance we needed when the grief became too much. Like now, as she ensured we both looked presentable. As she tightly laced the corset of my leathers and fastened on my sky-blue cloak. As she flurried around the room, maintaining grace despite the cloud of melancholy Jezebel and I were trying to stifle.

My mind was somewhere else entirely as they prepared me, my body limp and doll-like. Until suddenly, I was standing before a mirror, waves cascading around my shoulders and matching the gold lining my eyes. Leathers pristine—not the worn set I donned earlier—and pale scars catching the light.

The darker one Kakias had left on my forearm at the battle pulsed, but I didn't react. Didn't care enough to. I'd become used to the dull, radiating pain.

Another worry I would not indulge today. Another piece shoved down as a knock sounded on the door to my bedchamber, and Cypherion and Malakai appeared. The former held my spear, Angelborn, and short sword, Starfire, both freshly polished.

"Thank you," I said. Sliding my sword into my belt and slinging Angelborn across my back, I released a slow breath. Their weight rested against my hip and shoulders, and some of my tension eased. It was not only due to the defense they offered, but also because my weapons were like limbs I was incomplete without.

"You're welcome," Cyph said, but he did not return my forced smile.

If Jezebel and I had been swimming through our grief these months, Cyph was battling a different kind of loss. The kind when you allowed yourself to want something you never had—something that slipped through your fingers. He refused to talk about it with any of us, but finding out Vale, the Starsearcher apprentice, had been lying to us all summer by suppressing her readings had flipped something in his heart, like he'd been a current flowing south and was unnaturally redirected north.

Since then, Vale had conducted sessions to assist us, seeing nothing helpful. She resided in the palace still, somewhere between prisoner and guest to all except Cypherion. He had yet to speak with her.

I exchanged a fleeting glance with Malakai, and he shook his head. Cypherion wouldn't budge.

Gratitude to Malakai for being here lifted my spirit. How did he feel today? Where I'd once been able to read his emotions like my favorite book, the pages were now worn and faded.

We'd spent time together since the battle, both with our friends and alone, reviving the lessons we'd undergone as children. Diplomacy, finances, history. With those goals, we were able to take steps toward friendship. Even though Malakai would rather be anywhere than a council meeting, we understood each other in a way no one else ever would.

And the Bind still tied us together. We didn't know how to remove the tattoos and were left with threaded souls indefinitely. Every so often, hints of emotion slipped across the North Star, but it was a haunting echo rather than an intentional message. There was a beat of something resembling warm pride in it today, but it could have been my imagination.

Looking around at our group, there was an obvious hole among us. Tolek's absence was *felt*, a gaping lack of someone so woven into our lives that at times it was like we didn't know how to act anymore. We were still us, but occasionally, someone would speak, and a beat of silence would answer, like we all knew Tolek would have been the first to respond.

It reminded me of when Malakai first left, and one steadfast pillar of our lives was taken. We were stronger now than we were then. We'd fought to keep our family together, leaning on each other, but dammit it was agonizing.

Before we left, I gripped Rina's hand. "Did you see him?"

The others stilled.

Santorina's eyes softened, and the sadness she hid for us all broke through. "I did, Ophelia. And I'm so sorry. I thought he'd be awake by now. I thought we lifted the draught early enough. I thought—"

"It's okay," I said, forcing my shoulders back and lifting my chin. The lie twisted through me, but what I said next was true. "It's not your fault, Rina. You're the only reason Tolek is still alive, in some form."

Because we thought we lost him once.

About three weeks into his coma, something changed. He'd thrashed and thrashed in his sleep. The screaming—Spirits, it was worse than I'd heard when he was captured over the summer by the Mindshapers or when he'd had a nightmare in that cave. It was tortured, guttural, and so very *broken*.

And then he fell silent.

And his heartbeat had been so faint.

"We can prolong the coma," Rina had blurted. All tear-streaked eyes in the room shifted to her. "I can give him a potion that will keep him under but continue to heal his body. We can lift it in a month and see if he's stable enough to wake."

A month, I'd thought. A guaranteed month longer without him. *But it could save his life.*

"Do it," I'd told Rina.

And I'd watched as she poured the clear liquid down his throat. Listened as his heartbeat leveled out again. Watched over the next month as healers continued with treatments for muscular repair that ensured he'd be able to walk and fight when he woke, after a bit of practice.

When we lifted the draught—nearly two weeks ago—he had been more stable. Whatever magic Santorina had worked with the Bodymelders had strengthened him.

But he had not woken.

He should have within hours or days with the rate his body was recovering. Yet I was still counting the moments until I heard his voice again, until his breath tickled my skin and his jokes inflated my heart.

Santorina squeezed my hand, pulling me back to the present.

"I wanted him to be here for this," I admitted.

"We all did," Malakai said.

"But we're proud of you," Rina added.

If I was being honest, I was proud of myself, too. I wasn't letting the void inside of me hold me back. I'd postponed this ceremony for weeks, hoping Tolek would wake, but even though the memory of his lips against mine heated the hollows inside my chest, I couldn't wait any longer. War was raging at the southern border of the mountains, a queen wanted my blood, and an angelic prophecy haunted my future.

While I had a plethora of support in this very room and more beyond the walls, to an extent I was doing this alone.

I was doing this for me.

"Today will be a good day," I announced. Meeting each of their eyes, I laced my stare with the hope of the Mystique Warriors. When I continued, it was words I thought Tolek might say if he saw how we were all behaving. "We deserve to celebrate, no matter what has happened these past months. For today, let's set aside our pain because I was chosen by the damn Angels, and a new age is dawning. Let's choose the good in honor of those who cannot be with us, because you know damn well he'd yell at us all if he saw us moping."

It was a forced speech, but if it encouraged my friends to set aside their burdens, I could try, too. And I wasn't lying—it was what Tolek would want for us.

"You're right," Cypherion finally said. "I'm sorry, Ophelia."

"Me, too," Jezebel muttered.

"You don't need to be sorry," I assured, though I swore I heard Tol's voice saying, *Yes, they do.* I wasn't sure whether it made me want to laugh or scream. Instead, I swallowed the lump in my throat and said, "Let's just do our best."

Jezebel, Cypherion, and Malakai led the way to the stables. As Rina and I followed, she leaned in to whisper, "I may have kept him alive physically, Ophelia, but Tolek's heart is beating because of you."

And in a way, she was right.

Not a day had gone by since the battle that I hadn't felt Tolek's spirit. It was such an intrinsic part of me, like it outlined the frame of my bones. It was the shell of my ribs that protected my cavernous heart.

I'd carried it with me my entire life and continued to do so as I mounted Sapphire and traveled to the city limits, ready to be inducted as the next Revered of the Mystique Warriors.

Chapter Two
Ophelia

Sapphire's steady pace lulled me into a sense of calm as we approached the mountainside clearing where the ceremony would be. A spot away from the city. Away from the loss and destruction and echoing holes of grief.

The path below her hooves widened the closer we got to the entrance. In the distance, a low hum of voices carried on the crisp autumn breezes. Since Malakai and Santorina weren't ascended warriors and couldn't officially be part of the procession, they went ahead to join the crowd.

"Cypherion," I said, stopping him from leading my sister and me onto the path. My voice was casual, pretending nonchalance, though my fingers fluttered over the reins. "You should enter after Jezebel, just before me."

Cyph's jaw tightened, shoulders stiff. Deep blue eyes flicked between Jezebel and me, marred with doubt and annoyance. Licking his lips, considering his opponents, Cyph finally sighed. "Fine."

It was a small win, but one I'd take. The tiniest signs meant everything in ritualistic ceremonies, and having Cypherion before the Revered was a step in the direction I hoped he would take.

My heart rioted as Jezebel led our line into the ceremony site. A hush fell across the crowd, all eyes landing first on my sister and her silver mare, then on Cypherion, and finally finding me, perched atop my sapphire-maned warrior horse, adorned in leathers and a sky-blue cloak, weapons catching the sun.

As we passed, I met the eyes of every warrior I could. Flowers were crushed in fists, but they were clad in leathers and quiet awe. There were hundreds present—all those who were unable to join the war effort due to age, injury, or choice. Young and old, they stretched deep across the mountainside, but I *had* to etch their stares into my mind. To remember who placed me on the pedestal. The Spirits may have appointed me Revered, the Angels may have fed their blood into my veins, but I was nothing without the warriors surrounding me.

I committed both the hope and hurt in their expressions to memory. Let them carve places across my heart as I made my way to the dais in the center of the crowd.

With a stroke down Sapphire's mane after I dismounted, I said a silent thank you for being my steadfast companion these months. Then, I turned.

And my eyes landed on my mother—on the Bind on the fourth finger of her left hand. My eyes stung, but I lifted my gaze to hers.

I'm proud of you, she mouthed.

I inhaled that sentiment, holding the air in my lungs until I was certain I wouldn't cry. We'd never seen eye to eye, my mother and I, but we set aside our differences following the loss of my father.

Thank you, I mouthed back, and I ascended the dais.

Missyneth, the Master of Rites and the only surviving member of the former Mystique Council, waited for me. She'd shrunk to a withered shadow of her former self since Daminius, mourning the loss of her fellow masters and warring with a guilt I understood. But today she stood beneath an arch of peonies and eucalyptus, smaller blossoms and sprigs of baby's breath tucked between them, and the sheen in her eyes spoke of promises.

"Ophelia Alabath," she began as I removed my spear.

A ring of seven candles lined the platform, each etched with a sigil of an Angel. Beside Missyneth, a worn ledger was propped on a medal podium, the thin stand woven of florals much like the

Mystique Band tattoos that declared rank. And beside that, a folded pile of blue silk and a halo of golden vines awaited me.

"Master of Rites," I greeted.

"You stand before the Mystique Warriors today, prepared to swear the Oath of Reverent Guard, a historic vow. The words the Prime Warrior, Damien, bequeathed unto his successor prior to his ascension to Angel. The promise passed hand to hand, mouth to mouth, among Revereds for millennia."

"I do." I projected so every warrior present would feel my oath along their bones, even those who were not here. This vow stood for those Spirits already called away, too.

I tightened my grip on Angelborn, swallowed my sorrows, and slipped into the countenance of Revered, the memories of those gone holding my bones upright.

Missyneth bowed her head. "Please kneel." My knees pressed into the white velvet cushion she'd set before me. "Extend your weapon of severance." I balanced Angelborn in my palms. Starfire remained at my hip, and a piece of me longed to swear the oath with both, but the spear was the gift of the Revered, forged in the fire of the Spirit Volcano and, until recently, carried a piece of Damien himself. Angelborn was the clear choice.

Missyneth picked up Damien's candle. "As Mystique Warriors are forged in flame and delivered to it upon their death, so their ruler shall be affirmed."

The book's leather spine cracked as Missyneth opened it, the century since the last induction weighing it down. Tattered edges lined the center—a ghost of the last used page having been torn out.

Flame from the Spirit Fire itself melted Damien's candle. Missyneth held an elthem flower from a cypher tree up to that heat, burning its petals until ash coated the page of the book where my induction would be recorded for all of history. She dipped her thumb in the remnants and anointed me with it.

An *X* on each palm. "May these hands that bear weapons guide true." One on my chest. "May this heart that beats for its brethren stand strong."

Missyneth spread the remaining ash over the blank page in the book, then lifted a pen. Dipping it in a well of imbued ink, she held it over the gray surface. "Please recite the oath you have memorized for the occasion."

A tingling sensation slithered through my body. The Bond on the back of my neck hummed.

"On my spirit," I proclaimed, and Missyneth recorded my promise in the ledger. As she did, wax from Damien's candle dripped onto the page, languid as only the magic of our Spirit Volcano could make it. The white shimmered with gold veins in the sun, spreading across the ledger, and sealing my vow with an impossibly thin sheen. It was a tangling of magics gifted from the Spirits.

"And on those who have carried this honor before me, I swear to uphold the promises of the Mystique Warriors. To guard the range and all hereby contained within, to protect and serve the Mystique Warriors, and to honor the Angel, Damien, in all I do."

As I finished, a bead of that higher power snapped through my body. My blood quickened, my chest seizing. Head pounding.

The scar Kakias left on my arm *throbbed*.

Missyneth scratched the final letters of my vow in ink and wax, holding the fire over the paper until it caught flame, solidifying the oath.

And something within my body exploded.

A burst of light poured forth from my emblem necklace, there and gone in a flash like lightning, coating me with a familiar warmth. Shock rippled through the crowd, a low murmur of awe and uncertainty.

Panting, I found the Master of Rites' eyes. Most present had never seen an induction before, but she had conducted the last two. In her timeworn stare, questions shone. Though she didn't voice them, it was clear: that was not supposed to happen.

I laid a hand over the necklace. Metal warm but not searing, it pulsed against my palm.

Missyneth watched the movement, lips pulled tight. Our gazes caught, silence yawning between us. *What do you know?* I wanted to ask her. But her own suspicion glared back: *What do you?*

The murmurs of the crowd grew. Instead of letting it run wild,

Missyneth moved to the final items on the dais. She exchanged my cloak for the Spirit shroud—a swath of silk passed from Revered to Revered—then lifted the halo from its cushion, hands trembling slightly. Shining gold vines twisted around each other, a sigil of both the power nature gifted warriors and those we honored above us.

While the halo symbolized nature, it was reminiscent of veins, and I thought of those carrying my Angelblood. Ever since Damien had visited after the battle and confirmed the Angelcurse meant I needed to seek an emblem from each Angel, I'd seen reminders of them everywhere.

Even today, during my induction, the thoughts followed me.

My heart pounded as Missyneth placed the halo on my head, and a weight of responsibility settled in its place.

"*Believe in the Angels,*" she began.

And the crowd answered, "*Be guided by the Spirits, and align with the stars.*"

"Rise, Ophelia Alabath," Missyneth said. "Revered of the Mystique Warriors, Chosen by Spirits, Child of Angels."

A storm of applause followed her words, led by my friends. I found my mother's eyes and looked past the arguments we'd had, beyond the heartache we shared, and found a sense of peace between us. Beside her, my Soulguider grandmother smiled wide and knowingly at me, as if today wasn't a surprise to her at all.

My heart beat with the title I'd just claimed. The one I'd never expected. The one I still sometimes doubted I was good enough for but would do anything to fulfill.

I swore my oath, lacing it with the blood of those I'd lost and the breath of those standing beside me, their lives on my shoulders, futures balanced in the palm of my hand, and safety poised on the end of my blade.

And though not everyone I loved was physically here, their spirits bolstered me, and I held myself up through this divine moment.

Chapter Three
Ophelia

"Thank you for today," I said, finding Cypherion lingering at the banquet table as the sun was setting on the induction party. The celebration was understated—no elaborate decor. Just music, refreshments, and the gates open to guests.

I'd been a prized possession thus far, passed from hand to hand, as the halo upon my head glinted. Exhaustion was beginning to weigh on my limbs, my stomach grumbling, but I wouldn't give up the smiles on my people's faces for anything.

It was the first genuine joy I'd seen from them since Daminius, and it nurtured a seed of hope in my gut.

"I know you didn't want to participate," I continued. "But it's where you belong."

"You're welcome." He only half faced me, looking intently over the rows of cured meats and cheeses.

Impatience burst my seams. "How long are you going to avoid the topic?"

"How long are you going to insist on discussing it?" he snapped.

My eyes narrowed. "I know you think because you're not a full-blooded Mystique you're unfit."

"I am."

"I am not even a full-blooded Mystique!" I whispered harshly.

"Neither is Malakai or Jezebel. Do you think they are unworthy of anything?"

He was quiet for a long moment, fingers drumming on the table. The most contemplative response he'd shown since I approached him weeks ago with the offer.

"Cypherion, you are the only one right—"

"Not today, Ophelia." He looked at me then, vulnerability cracking the surface, blue eyes swimming with pain. "I don't want to fight with you tonight. We should be celebrating."

I'd been giving him space for weeks, and we were approaching the time when I couldn't put off the decision. Now that I was officially inducted as Revered, I needed to formally name my Second. There was no one better suited than Cypherion.

But his damn false reservations about his upbringing stopped him.

By the ever-loving Angels, Cypherion was the most worthy. With a truly good heart, and a natural instinct for strategy, he effortlessly achieved the balance of caring and calculation so many strived for. Not only a powerful warrior, but a naturally investigative and fair mind, he tried to understand others. Spirits knew that was something politics often lacked.

Since Daminius—since Vale—he'd allowed that tendency to slip, but it didn't make him any less. Those emotions truly only made him more fit. We were all complex, and those who embraced all sides of themselves were often the strongest.

But I would lay aside the argument for tonight. He couldn't be forced into a position he didn't think he was qualified for. I'd have to *show* him how wrong he was.

"For tonight, we'll celebrate," I confirmed, raising my glass to him. "To me, the Revered of the Mystique Warriors, and to my friend, who will one day stop being so blind and see the greatness within himself."

He rolled his eyes, but tapped his glass to mine, a small smile lifting his lips behind the rim.

Sipping the sparkling wine, I settled for that.

"Now," I said, my eye catching a sweeping blue robe across the room, "I have another matter to attend."

Cypherion sighed. "You should really learn to relax."

"Perhaps one day," I muttered, setting my nearly-full glass on the banquet table and heading to the edge of the dance floor.

"I thought you would at least wait until tomorrow," Missyneth greeted me.

"We leave for the war front soon," I said, ignoring the swirling in my gut and lowering my voice, keeping feigned interest on the crowd moving with the flow of the music and nature's magic in their blood. "I figured we could talk while everyone is distracted."

Missyneth nodded with the far-off stare of a scholar lost in thought. "I've never seen it before," she finally said. "In neither of the two induction ceremonies I performed did Angellight appear."

"How did you—"

"Please, Revered." She smirked, cocky, and it reminded me of Damien himself. "I may have never been graced by the Angel, but I've studied enough to recognize his gift when I see it."

"And in those studies, did you ever find hints of what could cause his light to come from something...else?" I knew the emblem at my neck held a bud of his power, but I didn't share that. Something had to ignite it. Before, it had been my blood, but now...

Missyneth twisted the sleeve of her robe, leathers peeking out beneath it. Most acolytes stuck only to the draping cloth rather than having official leathers crafted, but Missyneth had carved her own path. I admired that.

She always had a comforting yet aloof presence. Perhaps it was the familiarity. She stood in every meeting, attended every ceremony, and though she only spoke when necessary, there was a certain reliability I'd grown to expect with her.

"Typically, it takes a lot to be touched by an Angel, Ophelia." Her eyes swept over me. Over the scars on display between my leathers and the necklace beating against my sternum. "You've seen him haven't you?"

"Yes," I admitted.

Missyneth nodded, watching the dancers and letting that soak in. "Angellight is a substance of pure power. It can do miraculous and dangerous things when wielded by a true source."

"A true source?"

"An Angel," Missyneth clarified. "From what I've learned in my studies, nothing else retains that power."

Amid the music and revelry, the unspoken question settled between us, heating my emblem necklace: *why now?*

Missyneth cleared her throat, turning toward me. "I can offer you two pieces of information." Goosebumps prickled along my skin. "The first, after all the time I've spent honoring the Spirits, it is clear to me that yours sits differently on the plane among us. I don't know what, but I know it means something."

A chill gathered at the Bond and trickled down my spine.

"The second is advice." Her voice was far off now. "Always inquire, Revered. Motivations—as you've learned with the Engrossian Queen—tell a variant story from one's actions. They often complete the picture. Whatever is within you, whatever drew that light from your soul, it has a motive as well."

She didn't know about the active Angelblood in my veins, yet her blue eyes burrowed into mine as if they could *see* it. That agent within me squirmed—riled until I thought the snap of power I'd felt at the induction ceremony would crack again.

But nothing came.

Instead, a throbbing pushed against it, centered in Kakias's scar. It battled my Angelblood, twisting painfully through my arm.

"Oh, and Revered." I blinked to focus on Missyneth. Worry creased her brow. "Keep an eye on your sister. The Spirits send tidings."

"Thank you," I bit out, stifling a cry as the scar pulsed again. "I have to go."

With her warning about Jezebel echoing in my head, I fled the ballroom, stumbling onto an empty balcony and gripping the railing. The metal was cold beneath my palms, but I wrapped my fingers tighter. Took deep breaths.

Keep an eye on your sister. I would always watch over Jezebel.

My arm flared with pain again.

And my spirit sitting differently on the plane? I didn't have the capacity to determine what that meant, but foreboding resounded through my gut, and my body hummed with the taint of ancient wars.

~

Eventually, the pain subsided, but I was still out on the balcony, trying to decipher what Missyneth could have meant, when my mother found me.

I shoved aside the thoughts and focused on her. "Enjoying yourself?"

"It's been a beautiful day, darling. We're so proud of you." Her red-rimmed eyes tore at me. They were always like that these days, even when she hadn't been crying. A permanent reminder of her loss.

"Thank you."

"You know he would be, too." Those words were small, but I recalled my father's stare across the Sunquist Ball, pride glinting in his eyes. The memory ached, but it was the good kind of pain, the reminder that while he was gone, I had pieces of him to hold close.

"He is, I know it," I assured my mother, swallowing my own grief. *Keep pushing*, I reminded myself. "How long will you be staying with us?"

"Grandmother and I head back to Palerman tomorrow with Akalain." Malakai's mother had accompanied them to the mountains for the ceremony. She'd looked happier than when I'd last seen her. She'd even given me playful grief over no longer being with her son, before squeezing me to her and whispering she wanted me to find true happiness.

"I'm glad you came." I stepped forward and wrapped my arms around my mother's neck. Hers came around my waist, and in that embrace, years of hostility unfolded between us. The weight sitting on my chest dissolved.

My mother and I had been adversaries for much of my life, different ideas of what and whom I should be pulling us apart. But recently, I'd come to understand all she ever wanted was to keep me from the loss I'd suffered. To protect me, even if she showed it through regulations.

When my father died, we lost the buffer between us and had been forced to face those differences head on. Though I'd rather have my father alive and happy, arms wrapped around us now, these past two months sharing grief with my mother had healed wounds unspoken between us.

Pushing back, she whispered, "Keep an eye on your sister, wherever you go next." Worry wavered her voice, but she knew by now she couldn't keep us from the war. It was of our own making, the very breath in our lungs. Instilled in our blood and building our bones.

"Always, Mother."

We stood outside for a few minutes, and I inhaled all of the silent healing bonding us. Apologies and regrets, new starts and forgiveness. There was beauty to be found in loss, I supposed. It was a cruel kind, wrought of unfair circumstances, but it existed. This entire day, from the choice to pursue the induction to the peace of the night over a ruined city, spoke of the strength of surviving horrors and forging forward.

As I rested my head on my mother's shoulder, I understood the necessity of that type of warped elegance in life.

"Ophelia!" Santorina shouted. She ran up to us, eyes flaring wide and a Bodymelder I didn't recognize on her heels. "You have to come quickly. Something's happened."

Chapter Four
Malakai

We'd all developed vices since Damenal was ransacked. They kept us going. Ophelia ran around fixing things until she swayed on her feet and her words slurred. Cypherion had found his way into a new realm of organized fighting, dens popping up around the city each week. It was where he headed now as we split on the path toward the merchant quarter.

"See you at home," he mumbled and turned down the block, unbuttoning his cuffs and rolling them as he disappeared.

"Show no mercy!" I called after him, though it was unnecessary. Cypherion rarely lost a fight.

Some may have said it's unhealthy, how we chose to cope, but as I knocked on a creaking door of the locked apothecary deep in the Merchant Quarter, I chose to ignore the less approving opinions on vices. Verana opened the door, leaning against the frame in nothing more than a silk robe.

"Mr. Blastwood," she greeted, voice sultry. "Same as usual?"

Sliding my hands into my pockets, I nodded and followed her inside. "I'll be quick." The click of the door closing was loud in the quiet night, though at the palace, the party was still reveling. "I have somewhere I need to be."

It had become too much for me up there. Too much noise, too many people. Overwhelming in every sense.

The apothecary owner strolled around her work table, bare feet padding against brown tile floors, and placed both hands flat against the wooden surface. Bundles of dried flowers and herbs hung from the low ceiling, a shelf overflowing with tiny glass jars taking up the entirety of one wall. Anything a warrior could need, from pain remedies to meditative incense, could be found between these stone walls.

Verana tilted her head, dark hair lit by moonlight cascading over her shoulder, and she studied me for a moment longer. She seemed to decide not to voice whatever she thought of me being here every week, instead, turning to her shelves and digging.

"Here you are," she said finally and pushed two pouches into my hands. "You know the deal. Dissolve these in water, a small pinch—no more. They should last you a while."

"Thank you," I said, slipping them into my pocket and handing her the coins.

Her eyes bore into me as I left, but I ignored the questions in them and continued back toward the palace, well aware of the fact that I was late but not caring tonight.

The induction had been flawless. Ophelia most of all. Then again, anyone who expected less from her would be a sorry soul.

Ophelia wasn't perfect. I'd once seen her as such, but in the months since our reunion, I'd learned perfect wasn't real—ideals were only dreams. Yet while she wasn't perfect, she fit her position perfectly. Effortlessly. Transforming it to fit her mold.

When citizens of Damenal looked to her these past months, she'd shown unfaltering strength, through what some might look at as weaknesses. Through tears for her father and fury-fueled promises of protection, she became the pillar holding them up.

Spirits, how did she do it? My chest ached with only the consideration, my own demons rising at my shoulders. Gripping the pouches in my pocket, I brushed them off. I'd put these in water, and the numbing effect would sink in.

Ophelia Alabath was made for the position of Revered—quite literally born for it. When I imagined myself dawning the shroud and halo in her place, taking that vow, the image blurred. It was... wrong. A memory of what *could* have been but never *should* have been.

But that wasn't what plagued me. Ruling, having people relying on me, dammit I was glad to be rid of the pressure. The shadows were a welcome reprieve to my life, one I'd grown comfortable with. Recently though, I'd started to question what else may be out there.

The darkness was retreating—the progress slow and fucking terrifying if I was honest. Every step I took into the light, a beast rose before me.

Inadequate.

Failure.

Useless.

They screamed the faults at me, my own misgivings working their way out of my caged heart to form bars around my body, paralyzing me. It was ironic, but if you kept a beast caged too long, it turned feral.

I didn't know the way past it, but I'd realized one thing. In order to move forward, I needed to look back. There was a hole somewhere in me. One my father's lies had dug out. A slow excavation of my entire life—one I'd barely realized until the pit was so deep I couldn't avoid falling into it.

There'd be no way forward until I filled that hole. So that's what I'd been doing these past months since the battle. That's how I found myself swinging open the door to my father's office as I had most nights.

Only one person understood why.

"You disappeared early." Barrett turned from the shelves, balancing journals in each hand, weighing which to start with. "Thought you'd beat me here."

"Had somewhere to stop first," I grunted. I strode to the desk and dumped a generous pinch of herbs in a glass of water for later, then poured a measure of whiskey to have on hand in case the shadows rose too high or the flickering light of the fire reflected off a piece of metal or glass at the right angle. Like moonlight on an ax.

I poured one for Barrett, too.

Lucidius's office was a long gallery space with shelves stretching to the ceiling, artifacts and books weighing down the wood. When mystlight fell through the open door and my footsteps echoed on the marble, I was struck again by how vast the research was. How much more we had to sort through.

We'd cleared three shelves near the desk, beside the door to the balcony covering the back wall. The top for priority research, the middle for current, and the bottom for what came next. The rest...towering above us, it overwhelmed me.

But while I may be battling my demons internally, in this fight I wasn't alone for once.

"Right where we left off, then?" Barrett extended one notebook to me. I handed him a whiskey glass in exchange, and we fell to our usual seats to begin reading.

The disarray had been cleared, books reorganized into a method that only made sense to us as we picked apart Lucidius's secrets. Journals of untidy, half-mad scrawl and drawers packed with jumbled theories.

The pieces of his life I studied were stones across the chasm within me. Answers building a bridge of understanding and acceptance, forgiveness of my sins the dirt packing below it.

I didn't know if it was healthy. Cypherion had seemed skeptical when he found me pouring over notes about Angels and curses and prisons, Alabaths and Mystiques and mountains. But there were so many answers to find and if I'd learned one thing from this work, it was that knowing satisfied something within me.

I wasn't doing this to justify Lucidius's actions. It was for closure and to help in any way I could. Fighting was a challenge—I hadn't completed the Undertaking—and one ill-timed attack would send me spiraling back to my cell. Meetings were easier but still dragged up harsh memories of Lucidius standing in the Revered's spot, secrets beneath his smile. Maybe if I could figure out what those secrets were, I could move forward.

The night was quiet, a breeze drifting in through the balcony door, and for a while we worked. Two scorned sons, pawns in a game we never asked for, finding a bit of solidarity between us.

"Are you ready for the journey to camp?" Barrett asked.

"Are you?" I redirected, because, no—I wasn't. Though there were reasons I was interested in traveling to the battlefront in a few days, there were a thousand reasons not to be.

"Yes," Barrett said, though his eyes dipped. "If the Engrossians are fighting—if they're dying—I deserve to be there." Remorse twisted his words, rattled my heart.

I cleared my throat. "We should get back to work. Who knows how much spare time we'll have once we're there."

Barrett nodded. A twinge of guilt flooded my system at shutting him down, but I shoved it aside. I wasn't ready to talk about any of it.

Though Barrett would be fighting *against* his people, they weren't truly his people. They fell to a dark magic his mother forced upon her troops, and the grief he suffered over that was palpable.

But if he was there, I should follow his example. Set aside my personal reluctance and do what was needed of me.

I didn't tell him that, though. The bastard didn't need me to inflate his ego.

Besides, this had become our routine, barely speaking unless necessary, the father we shared forging a twisted fucking union with the man I once—sometimes still—thought the symbol of everything I wasn't. He was wanted while I was a burden, an accident—

No. I reminded myself, crinkling the edge of the paper in my hand. Barrett had been used, too. Kakias tried to dictate his life and manipulate his people as she had mine.

Pushing aside that mess of thoughts, I forced myself to focus on the words before me. My father's personal diary from forty years prior. The handwriting was nearly-illegible, but it was becoming easier to decipher. The way his letters gathered when he was writing quickly, but the bottoms of his *j*'s and *g*'s and *y*'s always looped big and exaggerated, crossing through half the word below.

This was the journal I'd been picking through for the past week. My skin prickled as I read an entry from the middle of summer, the tattoo on my chest weirdly warming when I saw—

"He was trying to call on the Angel," I gasped, slapping the journal down in front of Barrett. Papers lifted across the desk with the force. "Lucidius—he was contacting Damien."

"That's unheard of..." Barrett leaned forward, extending a hand to trace the words I'd just read, his sigil ring catching the light, the Engrossian Angel emblem glinting. When he saw the words in Lucidius's own hand, Barrett's eyes widened.

Tonight, I'll call him from the highest mountain, the site I read about. Elthem flower of the cypher trees burned in lava of the volcano. The confrontation will be enthralling.

There was a manic overtone to his glee, but the entry faded into a tangential monologue of Lucidius's greatest thrills, the script wavering as he rattled on. But that second sentence, those two ingredients, it was certain. The flower pulled from branches of the trees that were magical conduits across Gallantia incinerated in fire from our most reverent site. Every clan had a rumored ritual to summon their Angel, but they were considered sacrilegious.

Even Barrett, born of our enemy clan, knew.

"I wonder..." He trailed off.

"What?" I pushed.

He evaluated the shelves. "Nothing, that just reminded me of something." He dismissed it, but it was obvious whatever the tangent was, it continued poking at his mind.

Finally, he gestured back to Lucidius's journal. "What did he want?" Barrett flipped through the journal, but the entry didn't continue. "He goes on about the time he camped in the Engrossian Valleys for a week undetected..."

"It isn't as tedious as the tour of the Starsearcher temples we sat through three weeks ago." I attempted a joke, and Barrett gaped at me for a moment before releasing a laugh, shaking his head. "I'm guessing it didn't work, whatever he tried to do. That's why he never wrote about it."

Barrett brushed a thumb over his lips, thinking. "Or it did work...and whatever he found out was too distracting to write."

I considered, brows drawn together as I read and reread those words until they blurred together before me.

"The only record of an Angel appearance to a Mystique that any of us have found is Ophelia." Granted, Damien had shown himself to her four times now, but there was no evidence he'd done so with any warrior in recent history.

"It's possible," Barrett continued, "Lucidius's ritual worked, your Angel appeared, and he delivered a secret or a prophecy. That whatever it was, it was too personal to write down or too jarring. Maybe he didn't want the words to reach other ears, or maybe Damien was angry. Calling on an Angel is a risk—it could have ended with Lucidius's death if Damien didn't deem him worthy."

"We know that didn't happen." Fucking Spirits. Though neither of us would be here now, it would have saved the continent plenty of pain. "Maybe that's why..."

"What's why?"

I pushed my chair back and paced before the fire, hands rolling around my whiskey glass, the amber liquid sloshing inside. "What if...what if this was the start of him becoming so warped? What if Damien told him something that drove him mad and everything else came after? There's a reason no mere warrior sees the Angels. Their power is...strong."

We'd all briefly seen Damien appear to Ophelia after the battle, and while she'd been fine, fed even by his presence, the rest of us had *felt* the consumption of it.

My boots pounded against the floor, every sixth step cushioned by carpet as I pivoted. My heart raced, tattoo tingling. This could be an explanation, a hint as to what happened to turn Lucidius into the bastard he'd grown into.

He'd claimed it was his mother's lies about his heritage and the nurturing of the Engrossians that swayed his allegiance, but what if that was only the start of a kinship, an opportunity to learn things he shouldn't have, and there was a circumstance that turned him truly evil.

If that was true, maybe there was hope for me, and I wasn't a lost cause because of my father's blood in my veins.

But Barrett hadn't moved.

Straightening, I looked across the office at him, ghosts of our shared past littering the space between us. "Malakai," he said softly. Pity weighed my name. My chest seized under the pressure.

"It's possible," I argued.

Barrett pursed his lips. "It is. But it's not likely. And it's probably better for us both if we don't look for reasons Lucidius was evil and accept it was his nature."

His nature. Those words threw me off balance.

"If it's his, then it's ours."

"Not necessarily," Barrett hummed. "Despite what resides in our past, only we get to shape our future, brother."

But my past wasn't *residing,* it was consuming. I didn't want to be a victim to the fucked-up circumstances I'd been put through, nor to the truth of my existence, but it was heavy. The facts weighed me down further each day, and though I actively fought them, I wasn't sure how much longer I could outrun the shadows.

"Come on," Barrett said, taking my glass from my white-knuckled grip and placing it on the mantle. "We've done enough tonight. We can go over these new theories tomorrow."

I nodded, voice stuck in my throat. Silently, we tucked away the papers and journals we'd been working with, filing them into the pile of current projects on the middle shelf of the bookcase. Before we left, I swiped up my water glass. It was earthy as I downed it in one go and ignored Barrett's pressing gaze.

When the door shut behind us, I already felt a bit lighter, the drugs working to ease the tension and shut off my mind.

"This confirms one thing, though."

"What's that?" Barrett asked, brows raising.

"This mess we're in with the Angels...Lucidius knew something about it."

And for the first time, I wondered if maybe my father's death wasn't entirely good.

CHAPTER FIVE
OPHELIA

SHOUTS ECHOED FROM THE INFIRMARY, AND MY BOOTS pounded harder against the palace's marble corridors.

I knew that scream. Had been haunted by it for weeks.

Rounding the corner, I skidded to a halt, Santorina and my mother on either side of me.

"What's happening?" I gasped.

Sweat coated Tolek's body, the sheets were damp, his eyes closed, and those guttural shouts scraped up his throat again and again. Rough, like scratching a sword against jagged stone.

"Why are you holding his arms and legs?" My words were panicked, my chest flaying wide open as he shouted, like the sound ripped out pieces of me one by one.

Two Bodymelders stood on either side of Tol, trying to keep him still so he wouldn't hurt himself, but he bucked wildly. The scars littering the right side of his torso where his bones had shattered caught the light. The large one across his shoulder and second around his hip tore pieces of me out further.

"He started thrashing again," Rina said in the soothing voice she always used around patients. It didn't help. "We can give him another—"

"No!" I cut in, rushing to the bedside and placing gentle hands on his shoulders. Putting only enough pressure to let him know I was there but not cage him. My mother's presence was steady

36

beside me, an unexpected cloud of comfort. "We cannot keep drugging him like that."

"Ophelia, he can't—"

"STOP," Tolek shouted, and everyone froze. "No, no *no!*" His body bucked again.

"He's talking, Rina!" Sobs caught in my chest as I whipped around to face my friend. I shoved them down. Now was not the time for me to fall apart. "He wasn't doing that before."

"Not-not—I CAN'T!" His scream echoed off the high stone ceilings, head turning from side to side and brow creasing.

"Tol," I whispered, a bit broken and a bit desperate. "Tol, wake up." I cradled his face to keep him steady.

Did he lean into my touch, or was I imagining it?

"Tolek, Tolek...please," I begged, tears slipping free. My chest was empty, a void, not even pain residing there anymore. "Tolek, please come back to me."

My words were so low, no one else in the room would hear. Words meant only to cast a rope into the darkness and pull my best friend back into the world.

But he fell still, and what was left of my world shattered.

"NO!" The shout was jagged up my throat. "You made me a promise, damn it, Tolek!"

I kept my hands against his cheeks, trying not to shake, and dropped my forehead to his, my eyes squeezing against the tears.

His heart was still beating—that lifeline I'd clung to every day still tethering me down. My breathing turned slow and meditative, willing him to follow suit. Willing his heart to keep trying, to not stall in the silence that haunted me.

And as I sat there, every memory of our childhood played through my mind. The games through Palerman and broken curfews. The taunts when he grew taller than me and the wooden-sword duels it resulted in. The tears I shed for various reasons and the simple fact that he had *always* been there to catch them.

Followed by every future we hadn't had a chance to experience yet. Of us strolling through Damenal under the moonlight and racing our horses around the city limits. Of every nook and alcove of this palace being filled with the type of unyielding love he inflated my heart with. Of one day, laughter and the patter of small warrior feet bursting through the halls.

I wanted all of them. I listened to his breathing, clinging to him now, and made promises on every Angel that we'd have them if he would only come back to me.

Then, there was a weak brush against my shoulder.

A faint tickle down one arm.

My eyes shot open, meeting a pair of dazed chocolate-brown ones that all my dreams and worlds and anguish unfolded within, stretching from the beginning to the end of time.

Infinitely.

That weak flutter of a touch lifted to my cheek, catching an errant tear.

"Is my beauty really that devastating?" Tol barely croaked, voice hoarse from shouting and disuse.

And fucking Angels, I laughed like I hadn't in a long time, the heaves mingling with sobs I finally allowed free. They were a tangle of relief and awe and desperation, of all the grief that had been hanging over my head for two months and the fears that this moment would never come.

I locked my arms around his neck, and though he was weak, Tolek held me to him, inhaling against my hair. Like he needed this as much as I did. For an endless moment, we remained like that, imprinting the feel of each other back into our memories.

I had to let him go for Santorina and the Bodymelders to do an assessment and give him strength remedies to continue the progress they'd made while he was unconscious, but I stood right there, never leaving him.

"You'll need a new workout regimen, and a cane might be necessary," Rina instructed, and my stare stayed on Tolek as he rolled his eyes.

I barely looked away when Cypherion and Malakai—the former sporting a split lip and the latter's eyes fighting to stay open —tore into the room.

And Tolek kept his fingers entwined with mine.

My mother remained the entire time, too, save for when she

left to get Jezebel.

Finally, it was only Tolek and me and the remnants of the moon as dawn approached.

"Come here," he whispered, tugging my hand and scooting to the edge of the small bed.

I curled into his side, careful not to jostle his injuries.

"It's been two months," he said, "I'm healed."

Physically, his injuries had been healed for well over a month, but he was still weak, still hurting. And if the way he'd screamed earlier said anything, there was more going on within his mind.

"Two months." I exhaled. Tears leaked from my eyes to his bare chest as I listened to the steady—strong—beat of his heart. So much stronger than it had been even hours ago.

Tolek placed a finger beneath my chin, tilting it upward.

"Miss me, Alabath?" he teased, stroking a hand down my back, but there was a shadow to his usual playfulness.

"I thought I lost you." And a piece of me truly had believed it.

"Nothing would keep me from you. Infinitely yours, remember?"

My chest nearly caved in at those words. "You heard?"

He'd heard me when I spoke to him. Every desperate plea for him to return. He heard my vow that he was it for me, though I needed time to build this slowly—and he'd come back.

"Every word. It was like I was trapped within my own body, but I heard everything you said to me, and I've waited months to hold you like this and reassure you." Tol kissed my forehead, tucking me back into his side and resting his cheek against my head.

A future just like this stretched before me, of peaceful moments easily found. Locking our fingers together, I sealed the thoughts in my mind, a promise to us both of a safe future after the Angelic prophecies and mortal war awaiting us.

"Now, tell me what I've missed outside of this room," Tolek said. Spirits, every time I heard his voice it was like a shredded piece inside of me was stitched back together.

"There's a lot..."

"Start at the beginning."

And I did. I'd told him of the Battle of Damenal while he was out, but now I answered his questions about Kakias's ritual and the Angellight I displayed at the induction ceremony, and how I was trying to figure out what it all meant. He leveled a murderous stare at the scar the queen left on my arm, throbbing pain shooting through it.

I told him of how the chancellors were assisting in the hunt for the emblems, but we had made little progress aside from research on the Angels. And I told him how Vale had offered her sessions—though inconclusive—and how I thought she might become a true ally if Titus was not controlling her.

Tolek held me when I spoke of my father, not saying anything for a long stretch, and simply letting me get out the emotions I hadn't shared with anyone else. The anger I'd been suppressing over it all. He let me indulge in each feeling, the good and the bad, catching every single one I couldn't carry.

By the time the sun was fully risen, exhaustion lined both our frames.

"You should sleep, Tolek," I said. At the suggestion, his eyes flared wide. Terrified.

His nightmares.

I desperately wanted to ask what plagued him. To help him overcome them. But when I opened my mouth to ask, he cut me off.

"Will you stay here?" The words were small and vulnerable, his fingers tracing aimless patterns across my palm.

"Of course," I whispered. "I don't want to be anywhere else."

"Thank you," he muttered, and leaning his head against mine, he tried to sleep.

There was a darkness in his words, though. A haunting he wasn't speaking of, perhaps wasn't ready to share. I wouldn't push him, but I'd be here however he needed. As long as he needed.

Because my infinite tether had come back to me, and I wasn't letting him leave again.

CHAPTER SIX
TOLEK

✳✳✳✳✳

"SPIRITS, TOLEK!" MALAKAI BARKED AS HE EMERGED from the bathing chamber with a towel around his waist. "Knock first."

"In the mood for an outing?" I asked, leaning against the door frame, the damn cane Santorina bullied me into using beneath my hand.

"Sit down," Malakai instructed. Once I obliged—because he was stern and not at all because my leg muscles were aching—he narrowed his eyes at me. "Where are you trying to go?"

I pulled a pouch from my side and tossed it in the air, the coins within jingling.

"Shouldn't you be resting?" Malakai proposed, but he disappeared into his dressing chamber and emerged a moment later with a shirt and pants in hand.

"I told him the same," Cyph grumbled from the doorway.

"Yes, but you were already on your way into the city, so really there's no argument there," I said.

"I didn't wake three days ago from a two-month coma!" Cyph challenged.

A chill swept across the back of my neck at the reminder. At the slightest memory of what I'd seen while in that coma, of the images that played on a loop in my mind.

"I've slept enough, then," I forced out, attempting to be cheerful. "Let's go."

I pretended not to notice the look Malakai and Cypherion exchanged as I led the way, cane supporting my weight. I needed a fucking distraction.

∼

"Fighting?" Not that I judged Cypherion's choice of activity, but it wouldn't have been what I expected him to choose.

Then again, as we walked through Damenal and dusk faded to night, I supposed a lot had changed while I was...gone. The setting sun stretched ruined shadows across cobblestones, leaving the city with a morphed imprint of what it should look like.

My friends had explained what happened, had detailed how they'd spent their days trying to restore the city atop the peaks, but it hit a spot in my gut to actually see the devastation. To feel the quiet of nights once so raucous settle across my skin. The moment Santorina had cleared me today, I wanted out of the infirmary, but still, a part of me had been unprepared.

"Fighting works out the tension," Cypherion answered, hands flexing like he was mentally already in the ring.

"Tension?" I asked. Malakai elbowed me, shaking his head to warn me to stop, but I continued, "Have you truly not spoken to Vale?"

"Spirits," Mali huffed.

"No, and I don't approve of the way Ophelia is using her now either. How can we trust any information she's giving us?"

"I don't think she's truly given us anything," I said. Based on what Ophelia told me, Vale had been attempting to read, but when it came to the Angel prophecies and the darkness surrounding Ophelia from Vale's previous sessions, the Starsearcher saw nothing.

Ophelia seemed to think she was being honest, and that was enough for me, but I was wary of her after the way whatever she'd done had broken Cypherion. He was a different person than before Daminius. We all were, I supposed.

He was harsher, though, lines tightly drawn that not even I was allowed to cross.

"Is that why you've been rejecting Ophelia's request?" Malakai asked, as if only now putting those pieces together. "You don't approve of partnering with Vale, so you're withholding on the appointment?"

That wasn't it. Cyph was too noble to let his pain interfere with the role of Second. "CK, do you truly think you aren't fit for it?"

He chewed his words as we walked. "Why wouldn't she offer it to you?"

"Because you're the better man for it." It was true, and it didn't hurt to admit. Cypherion was best suited for the role of Second.

Besides, I had too much messing with me to be in a leadership role, even if Cypherion wasn't an option. Day and night, remnants of the Mindshaper torture from last summer echoed through my thoughts.

Failure, incapable, worthless.

Words that had been spewed at me during my childhood had plagued me while unconscious. Now, as I crossed the ruined streets of Damenal, they hung in the shadows. I'd been a failure in that battle. I was incapable of any role on the council. I wouldn't be able to take care of Ophelia.

Those sentiments had dug their claws in much deeper than I realized as a child. When the Mindshapers had directed their twisted power at me, those emotions had latched on to whatever was available. To the instability the Undertaking wrought within me. To the recollections of my father blaming me for nearly losing my mother when I was born. To the nightmares of me being guilty for the death of someone else I loved, blade in my hand and blood pouring over her skin—

"Good luck," Malakai said, pulling me from my thoughts outside a dark alley.

"We'll see you at home," I said to Cyph. He nodded and disappeared into the shadows.

"He doesn't do it every night," Malakai told me as we continued. "More so since we're heading to the war front soon."

They'd been planning to leave today, but had postponed until I was fit to ride. Something I was determined to master soon.

Truthfully, I was ready for the thrill of it. For the battle cries as our united front tore through the enemy, for the slice of my sword against those who had driven the city around me into such ruin, for the blood of the queen who threatened Ophelia.

But I didn't know how that drove Cypherion into organized fights. One look at Malakai said he didn't either.

"Here," I said, stopping outside the tavern a staff member at the palace had told me about. "Should I wait for you after?"

Malakai shook his head and flashed a journal. "I sent a note to Barrett to meet me."

He entered the dimly-lit establishment through the front door while I went around back. Down a staircase nearly hidden in the dark, the light above intentionally off, and through a purple curtain.

And as I entered the gambling den, a bit of the tension rolled off my body. Games had always been a habit I fell into as easily as swinging a sword. The way a victory pumped my blood faster and encouraged my desire to prove I could win. My opponent's coin falling into my hand a silent seal of approval.

"What are we playing tonight?" I asked, dropping into a seat at the table as if I belonged there.

A glass with cheap liquor was placed before me by a barmaid. The warriors around the table observed me.

"Sanctifiers," a man grumbled, not unkindly.

Quickly, I flashed through the rules in my head. Seven suits, one for each Angel, two cards per player, the objective to put together the strongest hand of five cards using the two in your hand and ones in the center.

And I grinned.

"Deal me in."

~

"WHAT'S ALL THIS?" I asked, walking into my suite hours later to find the office door thrown wide open, an array of papers and books spread over the table I rarely used. I kept my most important books in my bed chamber.

"Tol," Ophelia said, hopping up from her lazy sprawl in one of my chairs, her cheeks flushed. Spirits, I loved that glow. "Come sit."

She gestured from my cane to the available seats. As I crossed the room and took the one beside her, I hid how my leg was nearly shaking. The hike from the city to the palace was more strenuous than I remembered.

"How was the rehabilitation this evening?" she asked.

Before I could answer, Rina said, "He's doing well." Her dark eyes cut to mine. "I'm certain he's hiding how much pain he's in right now, but that's to be expected. He'll be fighting and riding in no time."

Pride warmed my chest. "That I will. In time to join the first line of our army." A mix of admiration and wariness swept through Ophelia's eyes, but just as those full lips I wanted to taste so desperately parted, I asked, "Now, what's going on here?"

"We're working," Ophelia answered, fidgeting as if she knew exactly where my mind went. Spirits, seeing her flustered around me was still so new and alluring.

Rina broke my attention, admonishing, "And you should have been in bed hours ago, Tolek."

"Yes, my kind and lovely healer, but I'm not. And it looks like you've been in here for some time."

Santorina's gaze flicked to Ophelia, who said, "I set up in here shortly after...I was more comfortable here." *Because it was closer to you*, she didn't add, but her stare did, and the urge to kiss her nearly stole control of me.

Did she want that, though? Would it make her uncomfortable? The past few days had been hectic, and we had yet to address us. She wanted this. I'd heard that much while unconscious. But how fast, I wasn't sure.

So instead of doing one of the many things I'd dreamed of doing to her, I settled for tucking a piece of hair behind her ear and relishing in her answering shiver.

"You're always welcome here," I said.

She scooted her chair closer, cheeks a soft pink. "We're going over the plans for Rina to build a training program for humans. The acting Masters of Trade have been helping, and we've been in touch with the chancellors about it."

I glanced over the papers—lists of cities and contacts most likely to participate. Where the largest populations of humans resided, and how the training would be executed. It was only the foundation, but it was roots. Damn strong ones at that.

"This is impressive," I said thoughtfully, flipping the pages.

"And we've done enough on it for the evening," Santorina said, stacking her papers and pushing them to the organized end of the table. "I'll see you both tomorrow."

As Santorina left, Ophelia rose and walked to the other end of the table—the one with pages haphazardly lying about and books marked with random objects to hold the page. Was that truly a dagger in one?

I followed her, my leg rested a bit, and observed her as she pulled a file toward her and unwound the tie. Took note of the heavy bags beneath her eyes and the weight I could practically *see* pressing on her shoulders.

She was more stoic these days. It twisted my heart to know she'd been battling this grief for two months, alone. Sure, she had people around, but she carried the burden of everyone's safety, everyone's happiness, everyone's anger.

She hadn't said that in the infirmary the first night I woke, but she might as well have. It was clear in each shaking breath, in each tear she tried to blink back. Ophelia had been catering to everyone else without wanting to divulge her own pain for fear of it taking away from their own. She thought they'd all been going through enough and put this city on her back to carry.

She didn't have to anymore now that I was here. We'd support each other, and that spark would return to her eyes.

"It's late," I started. "You should—"

"Did you win tonight?" Ophelia asked, taking me by surprise.

"Three games of Sanctifiers, actually." I smiled proudly.

She was quiet for a moment, mind spiraling through all those magnificent thoughts she held.

"Is something wrong?"

"No," she blurted, but it wasn't the whole truth. This timid side of her tightened my stomach.

"You can tell me, Alabath. Whatever is concerning you, we'll talk about it."

Her brow furrowed as those words sank in, like they surprised her a little. Like she wasn't used to them.

Though I had always supported her most reckless ideas, she'd been pushed so many times in her last relationship, she now had this wall up that allowed her to stand entirely on her own. It was admirable, but Angels, I wanted to know the fears hiding behind it.

"I worry," she started, "for the purpose of it."

Ah, there it was. When Malakai had disappeared, Ophelia used alcohol to blur her pain. She was worried I was using gambling the same way.

"Come here." I took her hand and propped myself against the table, pulling her to stand between my legs. "After...everything, I have things I'm not ready to face, I can admit it. A lot of things I don't quite understand yet. And when those things press in, I need a distraction. I need to do something I'm good at."

Marble rushing toward me...

A dagger piercing flesh and bone...

Blood, warm and cursed, slipping across my hand...

I blinked away the thoughts, gripping Ophelia's hip to ground my racing heart. Here. I was here. Not in that haunted landscape.

She was safe.

I swallowed the fears. "There's a high I feel when winning a hand, and it helps remind me what I'm capable of."

Ophelia blinked slowly a few times, letting those words sink in and choosing her own carefully. "Thank you for being honest about it."

It wasn't what I expected her to say. I could tell there were questions bursting the seams of her mind. About my nightmares, about my childhood. She didn't know how deeply it ran—I didn't think I did either—but I didn't know how to talk about those yet.

Before I could respond, she continued, "For every day I

breathe, Tolek, I'm going to convince you how wrong your beliefs of yourself are. You're so much more than you've been taught to see, and I wish to watch you realize it."

Spirits, she saw straight past my words to the heart of the pain my father had caused. A pain I was still coming to terms with, yet she understood. The desire to kiss her was an ache in my chest. Spread along my body. I *needed* her.

Was she ready, though?

Her tongue flicked over her bottom lip, and I wanted it to be mine. She was pressing up onto her toes, hands braced against my chest. Each inch she leaned closer, my hand slid further around her back, pressing her to me.

The scent of lemon and jasmine washed over me. *Fuck.* I wanted to know what every inch of her tasted like.

No, I wanted to wipe this table clean and lie her down on it while I showed her exactly how much I missed her. To touch, taste, coax those decadent little moans out of her that had haunted my unconscious mind.

She pressed so close, it was evident how hard my cock was, and a gasp escaped her.

"Tol..." She exhaled.

Fuck it.

My lips were so close to hers, they brushed when I asked, "How do *you* feel about games, Alabath?"

I knew the answer. Knew this fucking girl better than myself.

Her breath fanned across my lips as she breathed, "Games?"

There was a teasing gleam in her eye. I *knew* that look. We'd challenged each other so many times in our lives, but this one was different. This one held a tinge of lust that told me she was hungry for this. For something between us that filled the void that had grown in her these months—something carefree and lively and ours.

"How do you feel about this?" I slowly walked around her, brushing her hair over one shoulder, making sure to let my fingertips ghost down her neck.

Ophelia shivered. "I love that."

I ducked my head, lips against the shell of her ear, flicking my tongue out. "And this?" I hovered my mouth down her neck and grazed her collarbone with my teeth. It was a tease for both of us, the taste of her so close, but I couldn't have it.

"Please," she breathed, voice nearly cracking on a whimper as her fingers curled against the table. I smiled, resting my forehead against her temple.

"And if there are other people in the room?" I pressed a slow kiss to her jaw, moving back in front of her and drifting my lips to the corner of her mouth. Not kissing her. Not yet. "I can do this?"

At that question, her eyes snapped open. "I'm not keeping you a secret, Tolek," she whispered against my jaw. "I'm not ashamed or hiding—if anything, it's the opposite."

I pulled back an inch, unsure what she meant by that.

Ophelia took a breath, steadying herself with her hands on my chest. "We should talk about this."

"Mm-hmm," I hummed. "Talk." My fingers drifted down her spine, and she arched into me.

"Slowly." She barely forced the word out. Lifting my head, I met her clouded magenta eyes. "I want to go slowly." Her tone firmed a touch, like she was trying to remember what she wanted to say. That had me pretending I had any blood left in my head.

I forgot sometimes that while I'd been dreaming about this for years, we were new to her. We were in different places, but I'd wait for her to catch up.

Concern averted her stare, but I turned her chin toward me, and she looked up from beneath dark lashes. Ophelia's past was littered with delicate scars, ones she fought every day to keep from prying open. Together, we'd heal those wounds.

"If time is what you need, then that's what we'll do," I agreed. "We have centuries ahead of us, Alabath, and I'm a patient man."

She sighed, the sound a release of a fear I wasn't sure she was aware she held. One grown from long fights and hurled accusations.

"I want those centuries," she affirmed. "But first, I want to...heal."

When I first woke in the infirmary and saw her waiting for me, those first moments had been the most dizzying, most fucking *horrifying*, and somehow the most breathtaking of my life. Her being there had fixed it all. I'd wait as long as she needed.

"I'd love to heal with you, Alabath." I kissed her forehead, but an ache echoed in my chest at the thought of all the time I'd missed. I pulled back and brushed a piece of hair behind her ear. "Spirits, I wish I'd been there."

She tilted her head. "Where?"

"At your induction ceremony." When I'd realized I'd missed it, my chest caved in. This life-changing moment for Ophelia, and I hadn't been there to support her. She'd stood on her own, though, and for that I was proud of her. But selfishly, I wanted to *see* it. See that burst of Angellight she'd explained, too. "I'm sure you were radiant. The Angels will write sonnets about you."

"I don't think they're my biggest fans currently," she said, eyes trailing over the books.

"Then I'll write them," I promised and gestured to the table. "Now, show me what you've been working on here."

She cleared her throat, taking a minute to steady herself, and I hid my smirk. I loved knowing I could do that to her. Then, she walked around the table, waving a hand. Probably for the best if we sat on opposite sides.

"This is all about the prophecy and what Damien said when he visited after the battle."

"Which was?"

She slid a piece of paper across the table to me and placed a finger on the words underlined at the top. "Paint the shards with vengeance. Awaken the answering presence."

Chills broke out along my arms. I dropped into a chair, pulling a spare journal toward me and scribbling down the Angel's words.

"Shards refers to the emblems?" I tried to remember the details I'd been told since waking, ignoring the disappointment clenching my chest.

"Yes," she said, toying with the piece of metal strung along her necklace. "One token for each Angel, strewn about the continent somewhere, that I'm meant to find." She sighed, exasperation weighing her frame.

"We have two already," I reminded her.

"Yes, but there are still five more. Those two came to us easily."

"We'll find them," I assured her, locking my stare to hers. "We'll find them and end whatever this damn Angelcurse is." Before it wreaked any more havoc over her.

"There's also the prophecies," Ophelia said, flipping to another page in her notebook.

Born again through the shade of heart,
The Angelcurse claims its start.
Seek the seven of ancient promise.
Blood of fate, spilled in sacrifice.
Strive, yield, unite,
Or follow the last's lost fight.

That was the one Damien had revealed last spring when we'd already been in Damenal. But there was another—the first he'd ever delivered to Ophelia. That one I hadn't read before, and it was recorded in snippets rather than in full:

The time of thy reckoning...twentieth year...warrior with blood of two...try thy spirit...

The pages were crowded with notes of her musings.

"We know what some of this means," Ophelia said as I copied everything down into my own journal.

"Shade of heart and seek the seven," I said. It had to mean her eyes and the Angel emblems, respectively.

"Blood of fate likely means my Angelblood." The rare substance threading through Alabath blood that needed an agent to activate it—one that, somehow, Ophelia had and Jezebel didn't.

That wasn't the part concerning me, though. It was what came next: spilled in sacrifice. Anger was a riled beast in my chest, but I swallowed it down.

"And these are the files on Annellius?" I asked, grabbing a stack. Flipping through them, I scanned the pages documenting the life of her ancestor, the only other warrior known to carry the Angelcurse.

"All right," I said, pulling my notebook and a book Rina had found that addressed the Angelcurse toward me, "I'll work on these since you've been staring at them for weeks. Is there anything else I can help with?"

Ophelia blinked at me, surprised. "No. I'll..." She searched the table. "I'll go over these notes from your sister."

I wished she wouldn't. Wished she would get some sleep, but I knew better than to push her. "Tell her I say hello."

I'd exchanged a letter with Lyria to assure her I was okay, though, truthfully, I was surprised she'd written. Surprised she had shown up here when I was captured, too. I was beginning to think our father had poisoned that relationship more than I'd realized.

"I will," Ophelia said, sitting down. "And thank you, Tol." A bit of the weight already seemed to lift off of her.

"Of course."

We'd been working for nearly an hour when I caught myself unable to look away from her, taking in the harshness of her face that hadn't been there before. Still as beautiful as ever, but the lines had shifted these past few months as her grief and the pressure she'd put on her shoulders had settled. Like the final strings of the innocence we all retained when this began were wiped clean during the battle.

"Why are you staring at me?" Ophelia asked without looking up.

"I'm only appreciating you, Alabath. I missed you."

Her eyes lifted, and for a moment she bit her lip, fidgeting with her papers as if unsure what to say. Then she said, "Yes, well, I was told the Angels would write sonnets about me."

"I've changed my mind about that." Her brows shot up. "Nothing they write would do you justice."

Ophelia sucked in a breath, lips parted, and again I couldn't look away. Boundaries. She needed boundaries. I'd respect that, but damn did the air thicken between us. This was going to be more difficult than I expected.

There was a slight stir of the air, and a small piece of paper appeared before Ophelia. Mystique ink.

"What's that?" I asked, my voice low even to my own ears.

And Ophelia's face lit up as she read the note, eyes glowing as bright as Angellight. "You're going to need to get in riding shape quickly."

CHAPTER SEVEN
OPHELIA

WE'VE FOUND IT.

Three words. Three words that offered the thing I'd been needing these past two months: progress. Action that would demonstrate my purpose and capability. Answers in this fight for retribution stirring beneath my skin.

As the sun crested the mountains, Rina stood on my left in the Mystique Council chamber, Jezebel on my right. The boys lined the table across from us, pale dawn light warming the dark wood and brightening the map-covered walls like it was pointing us toward those wild lands.

"Nothing else," Tolek commented.

"I told Ezalia not to write too much when we last spoke." Though the bottles of Mystique ink I'd given the Seawatcher Chancellor should ensure the message was delivered to me, we couldn't risk information falling into the wrong hands. "But she has it—or she knows where it is."

An Angel emblem. Wings of anticipation fluttered through my chest.

The first of the five we needed to find. As I curled my hand around the one I wore at my neck, a weightless sensation stole through my limbs.

"And where is it?" Cypherion asked.

I flipped the slip of parchment over and held it to the light. There—faint but evident with the rays of sun—was a lone word, as if written by a Spirit. *Brontain.*

"The cliffs," Santorina breathed.

"The cliffs," I repeated.

The stretch of coast along the northern region of the Seawatchers' eastern territory was treacherous. Waves slapped threateningly against rock on a good day, storms riling the seas with a godly vengeance on the worst. Legends of what lay beneath those waves painted nightmares for children, warding off adventurous warriors before they wound up with their lives taken too early.

"Sounds like we're going on a vacation, boys," Tolek said, wrapping his arms around Cypherion's and Malakai's shoulders.

"Cursed Spirits..." Cyph rolled his eyes, but I exchanged a laugh with Santorina, anticipation clearing a bit of the gloom I'd fallen into.

"What about the war front?" Malakai asked, but he didn't pull out of Tol's grip. For that I was grateful, that he'd set aside his animosity for his friend despite what brewed between Tolek and me.

"We'll go to the cliffs first, find whatever Ezalia has, then head to camp." I turned to Tolek. "Can you write to Lyria?"

He nodded, walking steadily with his cane to the sideboard where we kept supplies of ink and parchment and scribbling a hasty message to his sister. Dark hair fell over his forehead as he bent over, and my fingers twitched to push it back.

"Actually," Malakai said over the scratching of the pen, pulling my attention from those faded honeyed highlights. My cheeks flushed at his tight expression. "I think I'd like to go to the border."

"What?" Cypherion blurted.

"I can be a point of contact there. Help Lyria and maybe talk to some of our allies in person about their Angels." I met Malakai's eyes, and though he was no longer mine to read, I couldn't help myself from digging through the ghosts lurking within, turning pages of my old favorite book. There was determination there, even though he was often sent into his darkest places during battles.

"Are you sure?" I asked for good measure. "You're not..." He hadn't ascended in the Undertaking; surely, Lyria would not allow him to fight.

But Malakai said six words that, when combined with the edge in his voice, nearly broke my heart: "It's where I need to be."

The sentiment flooded the chamber, threatening to entomb us with the words he didn't say. Shaking it off, I dared to find the fluttering in my chest again and claim the bit of joy that found me.

"Everyone may go where they wish."

"I'm with you," Tolek said without hesitation. At his low tone, the memory of the way he'd teased me last night had me biting my lip. The glint in his eye said he was thinking of it, too.

Spirits, I'd been so close to giving in. To kissing him recklessly, senselessly. But I was still damaged. Still broken. I wanted to figure out how to heal before giving myself over to him.

"Well, I suppose I am, too, then," Rina agreed. As I snapped back to the present, my cheeks flared with heat.

"You'll certainly be needed more on the frontlines," Tolek huffed, arms crossed. I almost laughed at his exasperation.

"I'm the healer here." Rina braced her hands on her hips. "And I'm still monitoring your progress. If I say I'm needed, then that's what goes." Her tone brokered no argument, but her stare flashed to Kakias's writhing scar on my arm, the line red and angry today. "Besides, the Bodymelders have a sufficient infirmary set up at the camp without me."

Tol opened his mouth, but I shook my head, and his jaw snapped closed.

"Jez?" I asked. She'd been quiet all morning, standing at my shoulder, gaze cast over the mountains. Chewing her lip, she toyed with the charm around her neck—

No. She held the place where it should be. The necklace—the one Erista had given her when their relationship was still a secret—was gone. She'd had it on at the induction, and Erista had been here for the ceremony. I didn't know what had happened between now and then. Rina and I exchanged confused glances.

"I'll go to the cliffs," Jezzie finally said.

It was the defeat in her voice and clenching of her fist over her chest that had me opening my mouth. "You can go—"

"The cliffs." She took a deep breath, eyes shut. "I need to be with you."

Secretly, I was torn. Happy to have Jezebel beside me, but terrified of the hollow look behind her eyes—dead and poisoned by a fate I didn't understand. She didn't appear ready to talk about it, but we all watched her with concerned stares.

"Good," Tolek said, squeezing Jezebel's shoulder as he walked back around the table. "We need you, Jez." And they exchanged a smile in their own secret language.

"Cyph?" I asked. "I'd like you with us, but if you insist on going to camp, I'll understand."

Let him make his own choice.

Cypherion's voice was as void as Jezebel's stare. "What will we do with her?"

Every spine in the room stiffened. The *her* he referred to wasn't my sister, nor was it Santorina, or me.

"What would you suggest?" I had my preference.

Cypherion chewed over the question for a moment, a battle playing out behind his eyes. "She should come, too."

"Really?" Tolek asked, a bit skeptical, searching for a hint of feeling in his friend's expression, but Cypherion had shut it all down. In return, loss darkened the amber specks in Tol's eyes, adrift without being able to decipher his friend's thoughts.

Cyph nodded. "I don't trust her with anyone else as her guard. When we leave, she comes with us."

It was a half truth, I supposed. Perhaps he truly did not want Vale guarded by anyone else—he certainly didn't trust her—but I suspected there was more to his decision. Regardless, it didn't matter to me. I wanted Vale with us, as well.

"She comes to Brontain, then." I looked around at the five of them, my family through it all, and a thrill for the journey we were about to embark on tangled with the slightest bit of uncertainty. I didn't know what lay before me, and too much death and destruction lay behind me, but with them beside me, I had the strength to keep moving forward.

"Will you tell the council where we're going?" Rina asked.

"I'll have to. In case they need to reach me and can't write for whatever reason." We didn't share details of the emblems with the newly-appointed Mystique Council members. I didn't trust many outside of this room and our allies with that information, but they knew there was a task at hand when I took over rule and that it would require us leaving Damenal.

I once would have balked at the idea of entrusting my city to an untried council, but these past two months had sprouted something within me. The new Masters of Trade and Coin, along with Missyneth, would see to the protection and guidance of the Mystiques in my stead. They'd been the strongest candidates for the positions before Larcen and Alvaron had—

Guilt slammed a rope around that thought. I breathed deeply around the rock lodged in my lungs.

The Masters of Trade and Coin each had an expanding network of apprentice branches beneath them. The new system was established for many to rule, distributing power and pressure. That made leaving slightly more palatable, though we still had not found a Master of Communication.

While I was wary of abandoning Damenal, I wanted to lead by example, not locked up in my golden tower.

"The five of us will head to Brontain with Vale," I said. "And Malakai, you'll head straight to the border with Barrett and Dax to meet Lyria. Pack what you can carry—"

"Plenty of food," Jezebel instructed.

"Yes," I agreed, wrapping an arm around her shoulder. "Whatever you deem necessary. We don't know when we'll be back."

"This all feels a bit familiar," Tolek whispered to Cypherion.

"We'll never get a chance to rest," Cyph grumbled in return.

For a moment, I remembered rain pounding rusted gutters and wind shuddering the wooden walls of the Cub's Tavern. Rina's worn carpet swam with shadows of the crackling fire. I believed myself alone then, the Curse burrowing into my skin, eating at my blood each day. The need to escape, to get moving and find Malakai before time ran out, choked me.

But now—I had the five people surrounding me. I hadn't been alone then, though I didn't realize it. And I certainly wasn't now.

"Okay." I cleared my throat. "We'll leave as soon as Tolek can ride—"

"Immediately, then," he interrupted, looking pointedly at Rina.

She sighed. "He dragged me to the stables this morning to see Astania and prove he could remain seated."

I raised my brows at Tolek, who shrugged. "This is important. We can't wait."

We *would* wait if it meant his safety, but I read the sentiment between his words, *I want to go on this adventure with you,* and my heart pattered against my ribs.

"And?" I asked, turning back to Rina.

"It seems the muscular repair work we did while he was unconscious worked better than I hoped. His thighs are strong enough to keep him up and Astania is intuitive, catering to him." A hint of pride warmed her voice, then she added, "I wish he'd wait longer—"

"No need," he interrupted. "We leave today."

"Tolek," Rina lectured, "You really shouldn't risk—"

The door slammed open, and Barrett rushed in, Dax on his heels.

"Good morning to you, too," Tolek said.

"It's so much easier when you're all already gathered," Barrett observed, lacking his usual energy.

"It's barely dawn. I don't know how you knew where they were," Dax grumbled, but he followed his prince to the table. They were both half-dressed, Barrett's tunic untied and the lieutenant shirtless as if just pulled from bed.

"I figured something out," Barrett said, without any prelude.

The queen's scar writhed. "What?" I asked.

"Since your induction, I've been thinking about how my mother reacted to the Angellight you showed on Daminius." When he and I had faced Kakias down and she'd done her immortality ritual, my blood had spilled on my necklace and Barrett's ring. It was the first time it had happened, and the burst of light was shocking. I'd been close to unconsciousness, though. I barely recalled Kakias's reaction.

"It's always bothered me that she fled," Barrett continued. "Why would she?"

Dax added, "She nearly had you, Ophelia. Wouldn't it have been easier to end it there?"

They were right. It seemed odd she left. I'd thought it was some effect of the Angellight dulling her powers, but maybe—

"You think she recognized it?" Cypherion asked.

"I think it's entirely possible." Barrett leaned against the table. "So, I wrote to Lyria late last night and asked where her network of spies reported my mother was last." The Master of Warfare had a private legion specifically ordered to keep tabs on Kakias. One we knew little about.

"Where is she?" I hissed, hand tightening over my scar. Tolek came around the table to stand by me.

"She's been moving west, toward Seawatcher Territory." The note from Ezalia burned.

"She can't cross into their land," Cypherion reminded us.

Dax's expression was grave. "I don't think she cares much about alliances and territories she doesn't have a right to. And Lyria reports she's moving quietly."

"You think she's after the emblems?" I asked, blood chilling. "That she knows about them?"

"Lucidius might have known," Malakai blurted, and every head swung toward him. "His journals make it seem like he was trying to summon an Angel. There's no mention of emblems, but he was working on something. Traveling all over the continent. If he knew, who's to say Kakias doesn't?"

"We don't know for sure," Tolek said, trying to soothe me, but his eyes burned with hatred for the queen.

"But we can't rule it out either," I argued. "We have to assume Kakias knows about the emblems and can use them. And she's heading right toward the only one we know of."

"What does that mean?" Jezebel asked.

"It means Tolek gets his way," Rina answered. "We *are* leaving today."

"We have to get to them before her," I said, eyes on that one, barely-visible word on Ezalia's note. *Brontain*. And as I pictured wind whipping against cliffs and Angellight burning through my veins, Kakias's scarred face swam across it all.

~

FOUR HOURS LATER, I was steadied, packed, and seated atop Sapphire. Kakias's presence followed my mare's swishing blue tail as we exited the palace grounds; as we wound our way through the city and to the eastern limit; as we parted ways with Malakai, Barrett, and Dax.

"We'll take care of him," the prince whispered as I dismounted my horse, and he hugged me goodbye.

"Thank you," I said. "But take care of yourself, too, Barrett. Please."

He blinked those familiar eyes, wound with pain his mother placed there, and gently touched the scar she'd left on my arm.

"We're going to find her," he swore.

"We are."

"And promise me this, Ophelia." Barrett paused, waiting for my nod. "It will be my blade that ends her."

I swallowed the venom in that statement and searched his expression for a flicker of vulnerability.

There was none.

The former Engrossian Prince had been hardened in this war.

"I promise." I wouldn't hold him to it when the time came, but I'd offer the chance.

"And here"—he paused, tugging his sigil ring from his finger and holding it to me—"I think it's best if you take this."

I slid the Engrossian Angel emblem on my thumb, my second pulse riling in recognition and heat gathering in both my necklace and, oddly, Kakias's scar.

Barrett moved down the line to continue his goodbyes and I exchanged a quick hug with Dax.

"Thank you," he said.

"For what?"

His eyes landed on the man he loved. "He'll never admit it, but he needed the acceptance you offered us. What she did to him—how empty she left him when she took his throne...his entire life's purpose was gone in a blink, and I don't think I could have healed him alone."

Kakias had denied Barrett a lot throughout his lifetime. She'd imprisoned him in his own room when he rebelled, locked Dax away from him, and tried to force him as her puppet. She never gave him a voice of his own. No, she did not physically torture him as she did Malakai, but that treatment left wounds beneath the skin.

"You kept him standing, Dax." I squeezed his arm. "You got him here. You're his guiding light."

Dax smirked, running a head over his shorn hair. "We'll see you soon."

Saying goodbye to the prince and his consort who had become irreplaceable pieces of my small circle in the past months had nerves twisting my gut. Placing a kiss to my cheek, Dax stepped aside.

Then, it was only Malakai.

"I'm proud of you," I told him. Whether or not I was supposed to be, I was. In going to the camp, he wasn't only fulfilling whatever self-appointed mission steeled his stare, but he was assuming responsibility he didn't want. Representing my core guard when the rest of us hunted Angel emblems. That he was able to do so after everything he'd been through was nothing short of impressive.

"Thank you." He ran a hand over the back of his neck. "I'm proud of you, too."

A beat passed, gratitude for those years we spent as one nearly spilling out of me. Not regret or longing, but satisfaction at where we ended up and a damn fierce hope we'd still be standing here when this was all over. Green eyes against magenta, empty tattoos tying us together until the stars stopped shining.

I smiled at him as a bit of the tension between us dissolved. "Do you think we'll always be saying goodbye to each other?"

Malakai blew out a breath. "If you asked me five years ago, I'd have said never. But now...We have our own paths to walk."

His words calmed my soul as they once always had, starting with the part we shared. We'd always have those pieces of each other, and the natural friendship we'd started building back since our shared heartbreak was comforting after so much loss.

It meant even more that Tolek wasn't bothered by it. He understood I'd always hold love for Malakai, just as he did.

So when I stepped forward and hugged the man I once thought was my forever, my North Star, I did so without hesitation. And he embraced me back without reluctance.

"Take care, Malakai," I said.

"You, too."

We watched the trio leave, then mounted our warrior horses. The four friends I'd left Palerman with and Vale, who wouldn't meet my eye. Despair shrouded her, hair hanging limp around her shoulders and eyes glued to her hands.

We'd given her a horse of her own, and maybe that was foolish, but I didn't think she'd run. We were her source of sustenance in a territory she didn't know, and she'd been trying to help.

In a way, Vale sat between us as a reminder that we were not the same five naive trainees leaving Palerman. It was not the same dawn breaking around us, air heavy with the unknown. Cursed blood in my veins and a veil over my eyes, searching for one last adventure and justice, blind to the unraveling threads of the world around me.

Now, my eyes were open.

Leaving Damenal was different than Palerman. That had been where we'd *grown*. Endless, blissful nights and long days beneath the sun. A war and the people we'd suffered beside.

Damenal was the city we'd *claimed*; where we restarted our lives and transformed into more than warriors; where I suffered the deepest losses of my short life but also reveled in the most addictive highs; where I said goodbyes to some loves and hello to others.

The city I'd always dreamed of became so much more. The Bond on the back of my neck prickled as we walked away, getting farther from its purpose. How would it feel when we were gone?

An instinct nagged at me that I was leaving something important behind.

A true home.

I only hoped I'd see it again soon, free of curses and war and death.

CHAPTER EIGHT
MALAKAI

"WHY DID YOU CHOOSE US?" DAX RODE UP BESIDE ME when Barrett went ahead to scout the path.

We were traveling along the eastern side of the mountains, cutting south. If all went to plan, we'd reach the first outpost at the border of the Mystique and Bodymelder Territories in a few days and spend a couple nights there to assist however we could. The stations were mainly responsible for shepherding supplies between territories and the border camp.

From there, we'd stop at villages in Bodymelder Territory to move supplies, hopefully reaching the main camp within a few weeks. The battles surrounded the southern border of the mountains, and Lyria had stationed our troops in the range, using the natural valleys as upper ground. We'd kept the Engrossians and Mindshapers out of the mountains so far.

I'd made the journey down from Damenal in near silence, and dammit, I thought I might get to stay that way. I should've known better with these two as my companions. Though Dax was much quieter than Barrett, calm countenance tempering the former heir's wild tendencies, he was just as observant. Neither relented when it came to intruding on my thoughts and feelings.

"I didn't choose *you*."

"You sort of did," Dax said, laughing at my unamused scowl.

"Fine, if you didn't choose us...why did you choose the war? I'd have thought..."

He didn't need to finish *what he thought*. I knew it didn't make sense. Why I—the former heir to the Mystiques, the boy who had been tortured by the Engrossians, the man who refused the Undertaking—would want to be anywhere near a battlefield.

Still, I looked over my shoulder at the jagged peaks of the Mystique Mountain Range cutting into clouds streaked fuchsia and pale pink as the sun set on our first day of travel, and felt...empty.

"There's nothing there for me anymore."

"You could have gone with your friends, though."

"If you really wish to be rid of me, Dax, you'll have to try harder." I nudged my mare, Ombratta, so she quickened her step, sticking to our shelter between the mountains and trees.

Dax laughed. "So, he does have a bite. Barrett said as much, but I'd yet to see it."

"I like you better than him," I said.

"Most do."

"*Hey!*" Barrett's offended scoff echoed from ahead, the prince having circled back.

Dax waved him off. "But truly, Malakai, why didn't you go with them?"

I'd asked myself the same question, but when Ophelia shared that note, nothing stirred inside of me. No sense of urgency, no hint of excitement at the challenge. Not even a sense of relief at one of her precious tokens being located.

Though happy for her...I felt nothing. Numb and fucking void. An emptiness I'd grown accustomed to.

It wasn't something I wanted to discuss.

"They're chasing Angels and curses, the unknown and impossible. I've had enough of that volatility in my life." I sighed, the sound nearly a growl, and rubbed my chest to soothe the tight sensation this vulnerability dragged up. "I may be a lousy fighter since...But at least at camp, I'll have a clear task. War is fickle, nothing guaranteed. I'm not naive enough to think I've chosen a less tumultuous path. Just one that's easier to conceptualize."

I could bracket the trials and triumphs of war. Count the losses, divide the provisions, and organize the battles. It was a stability I'd been craving, one that felt more right than chasing some unknown prophecy.

"Beautifully put," Dax muttered, warm serenity saturating his voice again.

"You deserve to choose what you prefer," Barrett added.

"I know." My lips pulled into a tight line. "I don't know what, but there's something more out there for me."

As I said it, the tattoo on my chest heated ever so slightly. I rubbed the heel of my palm against it.

"Come on," Barrett said, inclining his head. "I found a spot that will work for a camp tonight."

The odd heat dissipated as I followed him through the weeping cypher branches, but the memory of it stuck with me.

∽

DAX FELL ASLEEP QUICKLY, his boots coming within inches of the mystlight lantern as he stretched and rolled over.

"Idiot," Barrett murmured, shaking his head and scooting the lantern out of Dax's sleeping reach. He brushed a hand across his consort's hair, pulling his cloak up higher.

"At least someone can sleep," I said, searching the branches curtaining our small shelter, ears perked for any aberrant noises. Chills crept up my neck. "We have to be alert while we're out here."

My gaze remained glued to the dark spaces between the branches, so narrow it barely mattered where I was looking.

"Fae and winged creatures and soured beasts," Barrett drawled. His voice was flat, though, lacking his usual careless teasing, and his hands shifted toward the weapons beside him. He trained with both swords and axes now.

"Supposedly," I muttered. Barrett leveled me a harsh stare, though.

Ophelia had beaten the threats of Gallantia's corruption into us before we'd left, recapping each encounter she'd had between her journey to the Undertaking and her quest to rescue Tolek over the summer. Still, I struggled with the facts. What possible reason was there that not only one but multiple wild beasts of Gallantia would be roaming the continent with corruption in their systems? And the fae she'd bargained with? We were no closer to discovering what the bastard was doing on our land.

We were out of other options, though. We had to charge forward without answers.

Barrett stood and crept around the clearing. For a moment, I observed him. In the months since the Battle of Damenal, I'd come to see more sides of this prince than I'd allowed myself to previously.

Former prince. I had to correct myself often. It was still hard to reconcile who I thought the Engrossian heir was with this man before me, securing our campsite. His claim to the throne had been revoked. I didn't know where that left him when this was all over—didn't think he knew either.

Honestly, most of us weren't thinking that far ahead. I didn't dare to hope for a future beyond this war, had no idea what I even wanted it to look like.

If we didn't win—if Kakias wrapped her cruel power and twisted intentions around the continent—I didn't know if I wanted to be around to see it.

"What happens if you get her?" I mumbled.

Barrett stiffened. "Hmm?"

"If your mother is killed—"

"When I kill her, you mean." Barrett continued his slow prowl along the tree line, eyes flicking to Dax briefly to ensure he was still asleep. "Because make no mistakes, brother, only one of us will live to see the end of this war. Bant guide me, I hope it's me." He tacked on the last sentence like a silent confession given to the night, exposing that vulnerability in him I kept trying to overlook.

"And when that happens—when she's gone—what happens to your people?" I pulled my knees up, draping my arms across them and studying him. "Will you lead?"

"I relinquished my crown," he snapped, starting a second loop of the clearing, pacing more than seeking now.

"Under a corrupt regime," I reminded him. As the future Revered, I'd been schooled in the political traditions of each clan. There was no provision for this situation in Engrossian law. Why would there be? Most leaders did not expect their reign to be corrupt, and those who did would never establish a rule against their own supremacy.

"A verdict is a verdict. Law upholds the monarch's word unless formally challenged, and I—" Barrett stilled, leaning a hand against a cypher. "I knew what I was doing when I left. I knew I was abandoning the seat I should one day hold, but I was doing so to save my people so there would even be a population to lead." His fingers curled against the bark. "I thought it through. Promised I knew what it meant. But sometimes I wonder if I didn't think about how it would *feel*."

"To no longer be fit for the one thing you always expected?"

Barrett gave me a tight smile over his shoulder. "If we do win, and my mother is gone, who's to say I'd even be welcomed back?"

On this side of the war, we knew why Barrett made his choice. We understood the vision he had for his people. It was admirable he was willing to remove himself from that future in order to give it a chance to bloom.

To the Engrossians, though...an Angel could flip a coin on how they would react.

"Who's to say you wouldn't?" I challenged.

While Barrett and I shared the same sense of misdirection about our futures, there was one stark contrast: he still mourned his title.

Barrett wanted to see his people thrive and be the one leading them to peace. It was clear in the tension rolling off his shoulders. Where I had turned my back on title, happily handed it over to Ophelia as rightful Revered, Barrett held onto a different kind of hope, whether he wanted to or not.

"She tried to turn me into a monster." His eyes squeezed shut. "The roots are there. A part of me is afraid of how they'll grow if I have power."

And I told him something it had taken me months to recognize. Something Ophelia and my friends had proposed the day he first arrived in Damenal, bleeding and chained and so damn snarky. "You are not your mother."

A beat of understanding passed between us. A silent acknowledgment of how far we'd come since that first introduction and a wary tremor of concern for where we might go.

"Thank you." He studied me for a long moment, those eyes, twin to mine, introspective and personal. "I'm going to sweep the perimeter and take watch. Send a message to Lyria updating her of our progress, then get some rest, brother."

I huffed at his continued use of the name, but pulled my cloak around myself and huddled against a trunk. Quickly, I scribbled a letter:

Lyria,

A few days until post one. Send word of what is needed from the villages.

- M

We kept our letters brief and without explicit detail. A list of supplies Esmond and the other healers needed most from the Bodymelder villages, but no routes. We trusted our allies surrounding her at camp, but we'd been burned before.

And with us traversing the territories, it was possible the responses would take time to arrive or could even misjudge a location if we were mobile while it was sent. Still, I sealed up the inkwell and tossed the folded letter over the mystlight lantern where it vanished.

Taking a canteen from my bag, I took a long drag of the herb-infused water I'd packed. Then, I flipped through Lucidius's journal to reread his plan to summon an Angel and the tangents that followed.

There was a reason these were here—there had to be. Unless Lucidius had been overtaken by some power that night he attempted to summon the Angel—which I supposed could have happened—these next entries had to be important. With my own ink and pen, I underlined words that jumped out to me. Which clans he referenced, which legends. Even mundane hints like the weather patterns. Anything that woke the churning feeling in my gut, until my worries were soothed by the monotonous scratch of ink on paper and the hum of docile forest creatures.

Not long later, I received a message, but it wasn't from Lyria.

M,

How good of you to let us know. List from Es is below. Safe travels, and we'll welcome your royal envoy soon.

- Mila

I sat up straighter, rereading her message and trying to calm the shot of adrenaline in my veins. I'd thought about Lyria Vincienzo's best friend since she left with our commander to secure the border. Thought about the soothing words of hope and reasons to fight she'd given me at the Battle of Damenal, when Cypherion was injured and I was caving to my mind's torture, and she'd shown up at the last moment to save us.

I'd wondered a few times how she was faring, remembering those scars that covered her legs.

There was a joke woven in Mila's words now that chased away those inquiries. Pulling out the inkwell, I scrawled a response:

A royal envoy? You seem to think highly of us.

The next letter appeared quickly, in her handwriting.

Perhaps some of your party has grown on me.

The drugs I'd ingested were turning my head heavy, so I set the note aside and shut my eyes rather than decipher her words. And when I drifted to sleep, visions of clashing weapons outside a fog-filled temple chased me.

CHAPTER NINE
OPHELIA

"Do you suppose they'll allow us to train with them?"

"I'm sure they will, Tolek," Cypherion deadpanned, their mares walking alongside each other.

"Finally, you'll all see my potential with a bow and arrow," Tolek said dreamily.

"You don't need to exert yourself any more than is necessary," Santorina added.

"My dear, Rina, I understand you believe I need doting care, but while I appreciate the fawning, you need not worry."

They'd had varying forms of the same conversation in the four days since we'd left Damenal. Tol, eagerly debating the various archery techniques he'd practice while we visited the Seawatchers. Cyph, placating his infatuation with the weapons, though he showed little enthusiasm for his friend's fancies. And Rina, continuing to dissuade.

No matter how often we reminded Tolek we weren't staying for long, he insisted he'd find time and was well enough to do so.

Admittedly, he was riding better than I expected, and he only needed the cane at the end of the day. He never told us when he required a break, but we read his exhaustion and stopped more than was likely necessary or smart, given the fact that Kakias was pursuing the emblems, too. But we weren't willing to risk him.

Rina conducted assessments and exercised with him while the rest of us tended to the horses or trained. Their constant chatter was a welcome monotony amid the uncertainty of the task ahead. There was a buzz of anticipation in the air that heightened with every step. It had me leaning forward in the saddle, fidgeting.

"Eager, Alabath?" Tolek said, bringing Astania up next to us. I swept my gaze over him; he leaned a bit to the left, compensating for the side of his body that had been hurt. I tucked away that knowledge.

"I feel on the brink of something important," I explained. "I don't know what Ezalia has for us, but it feels like a door is about to spring open to the answers we've been searching for."

Tolek smiled at me, full and brilliant, and his stare scorched all the way to my toes.

"What?"

"Nothing." He shook his head. "It's just been a while since I've seen you so enthralled. This hunt we're on—you're glowing. I missed it."

My cheeks warmed. "Me, too."

I missed you, I thought we both meant.

I looked over the landscape, up to the heavens. We were entering the Wild Plains of the Mystique Territory, the land the majority of our trek would consist of between cities. Rolling hills and clouds floating like whispered kisses along the soft blue skin of the sky. But when my gaze dropped, it didn't find the lush grasses and wildflowers our territory was known for.

"Why is everything dead?" I mourned. I'd noticed it when we descended the mountains, but thought it was a fluke. Told myself it was only the one patch. But after days of travel, I couldn't deny it.

"The mountains..." Tol's gaze narrowed on the hills before us. As far as the eye stretched, tans and browns rose and fell where greens normally greeted travelers. "The magic isn't keeping everything healthy as it should."

I swallowed that truth; I hadn't wanted to admit it to myself, but I'd been suspecting it for a while now. Every time I left the mountains, it seemed the earth was a little more dull. Sad. Dying.

"Why, though? Magic is a pillar of our lives." Of Ambrisk. It fueled nature as it did living beings.

"Look at me," Tol demanded. The moment our eyes met, I fell into him a bit more. The lulling sway of Sapphire's steps no longer held me down—he did. "We'll find answers. As you said, we're on our way now. This is the first step, and whatever is going wrong, we'll resolve it."

I nodded, fidgeting in the saddle again. Tolek's certainty reignited that hope in me, too. One that had dimmed those two months without him but was now back.

And that spark between us returned, too. The simmering fire that wanted to roar sent my heart pounding as I remained locked in his gaze and my skin heated. Now that I knew what Tolek's lips felt like against mine, how his hands fit my body, it took everything in me not to abandon Sapphire immediately.

How desperately I wanted to cast aside my rules and indulge in him. But I had walls for a reason, and I was afraid of blowing through them rashly and hurting us with the debris—of failing before we'd begun.

"Let's sleep beneath the stars tonight," I breathed, fighting the urge. "If something is amiss, I want to be at the forefront."

"Whatever you wish," Tol promised, voice hoarse enough to make me think he felt that fire, too.

Dismounting as the sunset faded into dusk, fabled constellations winked into existence carrying endless tales. Our group gathered, and though we hadn't found healthier land as we traveled, a little piece of my worry soothed with the sweeping night.

Six sleeping mats circled a fire, smoke curling into the heavens. Normally, we'd use lanterns to avoid screaming our location, but the plains were entirely open. If we circled up, we could see any threats coming.

Tolek lay on his mat, Santorina's gentle hands assessing his legs. "How does that feel?"

"Wonderful," he gushed, teeth only slightly gritted.

"Tolek, you need to be honest with me," she said.

"I am," he shot back. "I am truly fine, Santorina. The salves are welcome after hours of riding, and the stretching is necessary, but I feel okay."

Their voices faded as I sat before the fire, fiddling with my necklace. Beside me, my sister twisted a ring around her finger, a bright pink gem catching the light.

"Jez?" I asked, and she hummed in response. "What happened with Erista?"

Jezebel's spine straightened as she was pulled from her thoughts. Her eyes flickered across our group, over Cyph and Vale staunchly ignoring each other and Tol and Rina bickering vividly.

"We had a fight." She spoke slowly, like she didn't want to admit it. "We fought a lot in the days leading up to her return to their territory. She wanted me to go with her. I wanted her to stay with me. Both of us knew it wasn't really a choice."

Duty came before love in times like these. It was the standard excuse. But it shouldn't be.

"You could have gone with her," I encouraged.

"No," she denied, shaking her head, but it was clear her heart was in the desert. "After father...I wanted to be with you. I wanted to see through what we've started and uphold my promise to protect each other."

I wasn't quite sure what she meant by that, but I knew one thing. "He'd want you to be happy, Jez. And I'm sorry, but I can tell you aren't without her."

"We've written," she clarified. "It's...tense. After so long of being apart, then finally being together, going back to the distance is hard. And I don't know if we'd be writing at all if it weren't for the emblems." A non-committal nod of her head. "But it's something."

Spirits, I wanted more for her than strained communication. I wanted her to bask in the love I'd seen between them. The one I thought was bringing her back from her dark place, with the girl who'd stood by her all those years during the war.

"Why did she have to return?"

"To prepare. Their Animasse is approaching." The Soulguider version of our Undertaking. "It's imperative for the potential heirs of the noble families to prepare and conquer."

The only thing I could see coming between two warriors as fierce as my sister and Erista was loyalty to their families. Hopefully they'd reconcile because I knew they each considered the other to be a true piece of that family. Spirits, I missed Erista, and not only for the way she helped my sister.

"You'll be okay," I said, pulling her into my side. "I promise."

She looked up at me with large tawny eyes bathed in uncertainty, and it tore at my heart. Her mouth opened on a thought, but she seemed to reconsider and closed it.

Behind us, Tolek cursed colorfully, and I shook my head.

"What's going on with you two?" Jezebel asked.

My head tilted. "What do you mean?"

She leaned away, giving me a look as she pulled her knees in, rested her elbow on one, and propped her chin in her hand. A picture of innocent curiosity.

"We've set...boundaries," I explained carefully, and Jezebel released a small laugh. "What?"

"Boundaries?" Jezebel's brows raised.

I cast her a glare. She rolled her eyes in return, and for a moment it felt normal. Like we were back to our old, undamaged selves, bickering in the family sparring circuit.

"Ophelia, subtlety has never been Tolek's strong suit, and patience has never been yours. It's clear how you feel. You move like a string ties you together. Why boundaries?"

It was such a blatant question, such a boiled down explanation of what Tolek and I were, I almost felt foolish for my reservations. But my chest was crowded, a pressure mounting between my ribs.

I wasn't ready to give that part of myself to him. Not because I didn't trust him or didn't want to—cursed Spirits, I wanted to more than anything—but I didn't feel whole after everything I'd been through. I'd rushed it in the bathing chamber on Daminius, consumed by our isolation from the world, and the battle had changed everything. Had been an alarm in my head reminding me how fragile we all were. That healing was worth the wait.

And something was haunting Tolek, something in those nightmares had been amplified after his coma. He deserved every good thing the world had to offer, and I wouldn't force broken pieces of myself into his hands when he was facing so much. Intimacy was something I'd used as a crutch before. I wanted better than escapism for us.

A piece of me was scared to voice my feelings, to make them matter that way when everyone was dealing with their own troubles. I was still trying to find the right words to explain the pain I went through after Malakai. Trying to understand why I was afraid now. So instead, I stretched a hand to that ring Jezebel fiddled with.

"That's beautiful," I said. "Is it new?"

When her eyes met mine, it was clear she heard what I didn't say. That I was figuring things out. That I needed support. She curled her fingers around mine in answer.

"It's from Grandmother. For my birthday."

"Wait," Tolek barked from behind us, having finished Rina's evaluation. "I missed Jezebel's eighteenth birthday." He blew out a breath as if he had just realized and the knowledge punched him in the gut.

"I completed the Undertaking six months ago now," Jezebel argued, reaching for a canteen. "Eighteen doesn't matter for me."

"That's a load of Angelshit, and you know it." Tolek ripped the water from her hand and held it above his head. Jez jumped to her feet, stretching up for it. "Baby Alabath isn't a baby anymore. That's something to celebrate."

"Don't call me baby Alabath," Jez grumbled, tugging his arm so she could reach her canteen. Once she retrieved it, she sat back beside me.

Tolek sat on my other side, a grin bursting his cheeks, and I had a feeling he'd refer to her as Baby Alabath exclusively from now on.

Beneath that smile, though, his discomfort was evident. Maybe not to everyone else, but the slight crease of his brow and roll of his shoulders told me how much it unsettled him that he'd missed these important moments in our lives.

Still, he allowed Jezebel to drop the argument—for now—and slung an arm around my shoulder, tucking me into his side. "You know," Tol whispered in my ear, "we could certainly play some games out here."

Our taunting *games* from his office came back to me. The brush of his fingers along my spine, his lips nipping at my ear, and the feel of his length through his leathers had my own arousal stirring. I fidgeted, fighting the urge to squeeze my thighs together.

Tol chuckled, pulling a deck of cards from his pack. "Get your mind out of the mud, Alabath." With a wink, he placed a quick kiss on my cheek, and turned to the group. "Sanctifiers?"

I waited.

Waited for the fleeting looks from our friends. For the amused laughs or wide-eyed inquisitions. They knew things had shifted between Tolek and me, but they had rarely *seen* us together. Everything so far had belonged to the two of us. Intimate and private.

Not a secret—I meant it when I told Tolek I would not hide us.

But how would everyone react? Would they be concerned for our group dynamic? For our hearts? They'd watched Malakai and me fall apart; did they think this was a repeat of that cursed fate?

But Tolek shuffled the deck, and still I waited for comments that didn't come. As if Tolek and I being together was not only natural to me, but to our friends, as well. And that soothed a piece of the concerns I hadn't realized I'd grown.

Santorina grinned as she looked at her hand. "We haven't played much since Cub's."

"I miss those nights." An ache beat through me at the wistful memories. Shaking them off, I looked at my cards: a Soulguider four and a Mystique five, nothing matching of the two.

"My offer of games still stands," Tolek teased low against my ear, teeth grazing my skin.

"Don't know what you mean, Vincenzo." I did a terrible job hiding my interest, my voice low and breathy. Tolek smirked.

Jezebel exhaled a small laugh, quiet as she took her cards and shrewdly evaluated the hand.

"Thank you," Vale said, taking hers, too.

Cypherion rolled his shoulders and pushed up from the ground. "I'm going to get more firewood."

Liar. We had plenty.

Folding my hand, I stood. "I'll help you."

Cyph wanted to tell me not to—I could see it. But instead, he huffed across the plain.

When we'd gotten far enough away from the group, I turned on him. "I won't force you to help me—"

"Cursed fucking Spirits," he mumbled, trying to step back.

"*However*," I continued, grabbing his arm, "I have a plan for Vale, and I'd like your input if you'll give it."

If he wanted no part of it, I'd respect that wish, but I couldn't placate his feelings to the point of harming others. Vale was trying to help us, and though I still was not entirely sure of her story, that earned a level of trust.

Cypherion worked his jaw. "What is it?"

I sighed, relieved to see the rational side of Cyph that I loved. "I want Vale to train with us, starting tomorrow." He opened his mouth to argue, but I held up a hand. "We tried it your way, but it's been two months, and nothing has changed."

We'd had an explosive argument over it—our first in the history of our friendship. I told him how I felt about Vale's position, and in his pain, he lashed out, claiming I was being reckless with my strategy.

It had hurt, and I told him as much, but I was too beaten down by my father's death to care. Too busy taking care of Mystiques, I didn't have time to push. Instead, I allowed Vale to be a different kind of prisoner. She may not have been in chains, but she held no power.

But now, with the crisp air of the plains clearing the grieving fog I'd been trapped in, I had to put an end to it.

"We need to treat her like a warrior, not a prisoner," I started. "Think about it, Cypherion. What happened to Malakai when he was imprisoned?"

He didn't answer, but his eyes betrayed his understanding. We weren't torturing Vale, but we were demeaning her. Trapping her.

"She's been a prisoner her entire life, in one sense or another,

Cyph." The more tension slipped from his shoulders, the more my voice softened.

"She doesn't think so," he said. "She thinks her cage was her haven."

Sadness welled in my chest. "Maybe if we put a weapon back in her hand, she'll feel stronger again. If we unlock that door, she may finally look for freedom." And perhaps then we'd get some progress out of her.

Cyph sighed, running his hand over his face, leaving a smear of dirt behind.

"All right," he relented. "I don't want to help. I don't want to be around her any more than necessary. But I won't interfere."

It was something. A negotiation between two level-headed warriors. Cypherion and I truly did make a good team, balancing out each other's instincts.

"Thank you."

"By the way," Cyph said as I turned back toward the group. I looked over my shoulder at him. "You two." He nodded toward Tolek who was boasting over the hand he'd won. My breath lodged in my throat as I waited for some kind of warning, but Cypherion only cracked a smile that had become so rare. "It's about fucking time."

Relief swept through me. Though I was still afraid of hurting Tolek, Cypherion trusted me with his friend's heart.

And that had to mean something, right?

~

THE NEXT DAY, and every day after as we marched closer to the Seawatcher village at the Cliffs of Brontain, Vale stood before me with a sword in her hand.

It was on the last day of our journey that she finally snapped.

A ferocity had been burning closer to the surface with every session. Each time I knocked her weapon—or her body—to the ground, she seethed, cheeks flushed and eyes heated. Life came back to her steps and her movements. Her voice rang out like a bell again.

"Why do you keep fighting so dirty?" she yelled. Everyone else stopped, watching us.

I held my hand out to help her up, but she pushed it aside, grabbing her short sword and shoving herself up, brushing her brown waves from her face. "I'm trying to teach you, Vale. In a real battle, your opponent won't play fair."

"But I—"

"If you're going to learn to fight, you may as well learn the right way. You're behind on training, and—"

"I am *not* behind!" Vale stormed, the bell of her voice a lightning strike. "I've been training my entire life!"

"What do you mean?" I smiled victoriously at her admission. I'd told Cyph Vale needed to be pushed. Here was the proof.

"I lied when I told you all I hadn't been trained. At the temples"—she panted as she prowled forward—"they insisted we learn. Not a damn day went by where a sword, a dagger, or triple blade wasn't shoved into my hand." She swiped out at me with her borrowed weapon, and I met the attack.

"I was honed into a weapon in defense of the sacred sites, whether I wanted to be or not." Another clash of blades. "It didn't matter if my readings were strong—I had to be strong in this way, too." I ducked her sword and twirled around her. She spun to meet me with impressive precision. "So stop your dirty tricks and fight fair if you expect me to do the same."

"Why lie to us, Vale?" I fired back, shoving my weight against her so she staggered. "Why hide your skill when you first arrived?"

"Because it's all I know." The hysterical cry broke through her lips.

The ragged sound of it shocked me, my blade falling.

Defenses torn down, she dropped hers, too. I had the distinct feeling she was admitting this truth to herself for the first time.

"The temple. The readings. Titus. My—Secrets are all I've ever known." I wasn't entirely sure what she meant or what else she was hiding. "Never the kinship and protection you have. Never the belief in my own promise. Weapons and mental defenses were what I had. Being told what lies to feed others, harsh obedience, and being *used*."

She was shackled to a life she'd never wanted, a future beyond her control, and though resentment tattered her voice, fear widened her olive eyes. A fear I'd wager was fueled when she considered maybe her future didn't have to look that way.

"Don't you want to know what else is out there?" I asked.

The fear staring at me solidified, a wall shooting up where a moment before there had been clarity.

"No," she whispered. "No, I don't."

Vale threw her sword at my feet and stormed away, readying her horse for the rest of our journey.

I turned to my friends. While Tolek, Santorina, and Jezebel, shot me encouraging looks, Cypherion only stared after the Starsearcher. Dumbfounded.

CHAPTER TEN
MALAKAI

TWO WEEKS INTO OUR JOURNEY, AND MY BACK, THIGHS, and ass fucking ached from riding. I'd missed Ombratta, but Spirits, I'd forgotten how exhausting long journeys were. And it had been years since I'd made one this tough.

At least we'd stopped at numerous villages along the way once we entered Bodymelder territory. Their land was rife with fields of wildflowers and herbs, bunches of trees coated with orange and red leaves, green vines poking through the fire. Instead of large cities, the minor clan spread themselves among villages built of the land, huts and cottages with thatched roofs above clay and rock walls. Ivy and flowers cascaded around them, crawling up the sides.

The minor clan territories were all influenced by their power. Bodymelder land was not only flooded with supplies to be harvested for healing, but it was lush with forests. All except the Fytar Trench east of the capital, which cracked the ground like a delicate egg shell and stretched to Spirits knew what depths.

I admired it—how even their homes represented their dedication to their guiding magic.

Each village we stopped at welcomed us for a night, slowing our progress, but I didn't mind. We were doing something useful here. As I collapsed beside a fire in our current host's home, the warmth worked into the tightness of my body. My muscles thanked me.

"Here's supper." A small golden-haired girl no older than six handed me a bowl, amber eyes wide.

"Thank you."

She gave me a sheepish smile and fled, following her mother from the room. Her father and the leader of the village, Darell, chuckled as she went.

"She's infatuated with you. Can't believe it—a Mystique," he scoffed. His terra-cotta skin and joking smile caught the light, broad shoulders sinking into the couch as he relaxed.

"She's a good kid." The soup warmed my throat on the way down, the burn welcome. A folded parchment appeared at my side; curiosity and something else flared within me, but I gave Darell my attention. "The whole village is."

"We've been lucky to be assigned aloe collection." Darell brushed a hand down the sleeve of his thick moss-colored tunic. The Bodymelder sigil glinted in gold thread on the chest: an olive branch, a stalk of wheat, and a feather crossed with the letters *K L P* above them. Knowledge, logic, precision—the pillars of his clan. The same three letters tattooed on his knuckles.

"Why's that?"

Every Bodymelder village had a task. Whether they gathered a healing agent, mixed tonics, or worked textiles for injuries, each was given an imperative responsibility, and nomads traveled between villages exchanging the goods. It was a complex network, but the leaders in each town made it appear effortless. Darell's village bordered a large aloe field, green stalks jutting up from the soil and painting the hillsides, looking down on the cottages.

"Many are finding their supplies dwindling this season. It's caused a lot of economic uncertainty."

"I don't recall Brigiet mentioning that at the Rapture." Granted, I'd been distracted, not listening to every word. Or most words.

"It's been rapid." Darell shook his head, brushing his dark hair behind his ear. "The decay was there, only just, but recently it's spread. It hasn't hit the aloe fields yet, so my people are safe, but…" He didn't need to finish that sentence.

"I'm sorry." I set my bowl aside, thinking of the contaminated creatures and wondering if it all connected. "If there's anything we can do, please let me know."

"It's not your responsibility, but thank you." Genuine gratitude thickened his voice. That was why I liked the man. He didn't look at me and see a fallen Revered's son, tainted with the blood of my enemies. The Bodymelders were neutral in alliances, operating more on logic than anything else, and Darell's acceptance of me in his home, around his people, reflected that.

The fire crackled behind me as I sipped a mug of ale. With the warmth at my back and the drink in my stomach, tension leaked from my muscles. Perhaps getting out of Damenal, away from Lucidius's legacy, was good for me.

Barrett and Dax returned from their own day of loading wagons to cart supplies to the mountain camp.

"We'll be heading out early," Dax reminded me. "Are you going to bed?"

"In a bit," I said.

Barrett narrowed his eyes on the parchment beside me. "Still saving ink for emergencies?"

They'd been raising their brows at the letters Mila and I exchanged since the first one, given that Mystique ink was supposed to be conserved. Something about writing to her was comforting, though. To share a few of the monotonous pieces of my day and reveal a little bit of what I was working through. It was easier to put things in writing than to look someone in the face.

Not that I was exchanging any deep-ridden secrets. The letters were quick. Mainly updates about our progress and whatever she could share from camp. But they offered consistency. Whenever I considered not responding and retreating into my mind again, I remembered her words in the temple: *You have to retain a belief in yourself*, and I tried to loosen the cage in my chest.

"Go to bed," I commanded. Barrett shook his head with a laugh, running a ringed hand through his curls. He slung an arm around Dax's shoulders and dragged him down the hall.

Darrell followed shortly, but I wasn't ready to return to my empty room and stare at the ceiling with a head full of questions.

Instead, I pulled out Mila's latest letter. I'd written this morning asking how things were progressing.

Same as before.

She couldn't say more than that, but I understood. The Engrossian-Mindshaper infantry continued to hammer the southern border.

How are you? I wrote back, though I wasn't sure why. What I'd wanted to ask was what being back in a war camp was like. Was it the same as last time? What was different? Better or worse or equally as horrific? I wanted—*needed*—to know every detail of the war Lucidius imposed on the continent and the terrors it inflicted on the survivors. Maybe if I knew, I could help resolve it.

Or maybe I wanted to carry the guilt.

Her response was prompt this time.

Tired. And you?

Before I could respond, a second note appeared. An afterthought.

Your father?

The pen tumbled from my hand. I'd told her Barrett and I had been reading his journals, but why was she asking now?

Hand shaking slightly, I wrote back:

Going to spend some time with him.

When her last reply said only, *Good luck,* I set aside the note and tried to rid myself of the many questions the dichotomy of Mila rose in my head, instead diving deeper into the past.

In Lucidius's journal, I flipped to the entry on wildflowers, tilting the book toward the fire. Rambling words stared back, most crowded together in his looping script.

Fields stretched on endlessly and I felt small a tiny dot in the map of the world whose purpose was to make an impact and I would make that impact that was what drove me to the spot

Bushels of overgrown weeds that's what all this was I didn't understand why they favored this spot so much

Field of birds marking it they had a name for its roar of yellow and orange poppies and spirits knew what else but this was where I needed to be besides the pointless view and the way it made me feel

I had to be here

He went on to dissect every flower he could find, all in the same nearly-unintelligible ramble. The words faded before my eyes. Blinking furiously, I rubbed a hand down my face. Another page of pointless thoughts, another night spent wondering if I was wasting my time with Lucidius. But if someone like Mila, a direct victim of his actions, could set aside her scars to ask about him, I couldn't give up.

～

"WHAT'S THAT?" Dax asked, eyes locked on a spot between the trees in the camp we'd made in the mountains. The small fleet of Bodymelders accompanying us chattered away, not having heard the lieutenant.

Following Dax's sightline, I found two glowing orbs in the night. My mind flicked back to winged beasts, nemaxese, fae, and every other warning Ophelia had given as I gripped my sword against the cool earth.

"Stay still," I warned.

But Barrett was already up, taking sure but slow steps toward the trees. Dax pushed to his feet, watching closely.

"*Barrett*," I growled.

"Relax," the former prince said. "I don't think it's anything to worry about."

He disappeared into shadow for a moment, and then a light laugh drifted from the trees. Dax was striding after him before I could respond. With a groan and a quick look around to confirm no one was paying us any attention, I tucked Lucidius's journal into my pocket and ran after them.

"What in the Spirits are you think—"

There, spread on the floor with his stomach to the sky was a *wolf*. He couldn't be older than a pup, large enough to be over half a year, but still all floppy legs and ears. Barrett was crouched beside him scratching his belly affectionately.

"Why are you touching it?" I reached for Barrett's shoulder but Dax grabbed my wrist.

"He's fine." Dax's warning glare was much harsher than his tone. "He likes animals."

"And this one seems harmless," Barrett added.

Dax observed them. "He probably wandered over from Mind-shaper Territory for warmth."

"And now he'll have plenty traveling with us." Barrett scooped the wolf into his arms.

"What do you mean *traveling with us?*" I looked between the Engrossians. "He can't stay with us."

"He can, and he will," Barrett said, a hopeful gleam in his eye as he stared down at the wolf.

"Barrett," I sighed. "We're going to war. You cannot have a pet."

"He'll be trained and helpful. We can't leave him alone out here." Both the prince and the damn wolf turned sad looks on me, all dark eyes and floppy hair on the both of them. And I swore to Damien, that wolf seemed to evaluate me. His large blue eyes were knowing, more understanding than any animal should be. It sent a wave of unease through my stomach.

With a gleeful little yelp I wouldn't admit was cute, the wolf flipped out of Barrett's arms and bounded to me. He placed his too-large paws on my chest and stretched up. Did his eyes look human? They dug into me, begging me to let him stay with us.

I staggered back, and Lucidius's journal went tumbling to the ground. The wolf's jaw clamped around it, and with a sly wiggle of his tail, he took off into the forest.

"Rebel, no!" Barrett shouted as we all ran off after the animal. Spirits, those gangly legs were quick.

"Rebel?" I panted.

"It was either that or Exile, and the latter simply isn't cute at all," Barrett said, shaking his head as if that was obvious.

As the three of us chased down the wolf, I considered Barrett's names. Rebel or Exile—two that could define him, but one much more favorable than the other. Which way did he view himself?

Something within me softened at this prince who missed his people, his title. Who now clung to one random pup in the woods, desperate to care for it and give it a home.

My resolve softened. "Rebel can stay with us."

Chapter Eleven
Ophelia

The Cliffs of Brontain were wrapped in harsh winds that had me wishing I hadn't tucked my cloak away in my pack when the sun beat overhead this afternoon. Gray waves slapped against dark rock. The flat ground was covered in a thin layer of bright-green grass, blades rifling in the wind, but beyond the plateau, the drop off was sharp.

White caps unfurled more peacefully the further out I looked, but right here, against the cliffs, the water was choppy and rough, biting into the sides of the land like a predator ready to attack.

A large wave slammed into the surface. Water shot up around us, small droplets briny as they flecked my hair and skin. Next to me, Ezalia breathed it in, serenity smoothing out the lines around her eyes and mouth.

"This is one of my favorite views," the Seawatcher Chancellor said, eyes closed. There was a hint of protectiveness in her voice, like she wanted to guard this place.

The breeze lifted her hair, brown strands swirling around her pointed chin and shoulders. Though my arms peppered with goosebumps, hers remained smooth, as if the wind sank right into the bare olive skin on display around her tan leathers.

"You like it better here than the capital? Or the Western Outposts?" The two other major civilizations in the split Seawatcher territory. The capital, Gaveral, I'd been to. A thriving city of brightly-colored stucco buildings on the southeast coast. Palm trees shadowed every corner of worn white stone, fronds like fingertips stretching to the sky. Canals ran through the land, small bridges dotting the streets to hold it all together.

I'd spent one summer there when we were fourteen, and it was a dream. Perhaps my second favorite territory besides my mountains. And the Western Outposts were said to be comprised of white sand beaches and turquoise waters so clear you could see the fish swimming beneath and the great expanse of coral fields lining the ocean bottom.

This, though, the Cliffs of Brontain, I wasn't sure I understood.

"Yes," Ezalia answered. "The others are gorgeous, but this is raw nature at its finest. It's the kind where you have to really look beneath the surface to find the charm." The wind whipped around us again, emphasizing her words. She tucked a strand of hair behind an ear lined with coral and sea-green gems matching the ones on her bangles and stitched into her leathers. "Even beautiful things are more rewarding when you work for them."

Her words struck a chord in me. The views in the mountains were undoubtedly exquisite. The way the sunset reflected off the peaks and the clouds toyed with them, like all of the world's different entities were living beings greeting each other. How one breath of the clear air, one moment of silence, could still the most riling emotions within me. It was effortless to find the beauty there.

But Damenal, after being ruined and currently being rebuilt, was spectacular. It was easy to get lost in the rubble, but to pick through the calamity, to see the work poured into shops and homes, and the warriors who tirelessly gave every effort—it held an allure that motivated me each day.

"The same can be said of people," I mused. "Sometimes beauty is buried. It takes a sharper eye to discover it."

One corner of Ezalia's lips lifted, and I had a feeling that was what she'd meant all along.

"Come on, let's start the tour," she said. "The heart of the village is a bit of a walk."

Ezalia had been waiting for us on the outskirts of Brontain. A few of her warriors took our horses and packs to the inn she'd cleared out for us for the duration of our stay. The only buildings out here were small weapon sheds and huts for warriors to sleep and bathe in on longer shifts. They all appeared to be made of driftwood, yet somehow stood strong against the battering winds.

Ezalia led me to where the rest of my group was waiting with three Seawatchers. Santorina and Vale stood to the side, speaking in hushed tones as Rina assessed a minor wound Vale had received in training this morning.

Cypherion was in conversation with Seron, Ezalia's partner; Jezebel and Tolek with the remaining Seawatchers.

Seron held his hand out to me, large and covered in rings matching Ezalia's bangles. "It's a pleasure to finally meet you, Revered Alabath. Congratulations on the official title."

"Thank you. I'm sorry it's taken us this long to be introduced." The only time Seron was in Damenal since I'd moved there was during the battle when the Seawatchers saved our lives. When I was unconscious.

"As am I, but someone has to remain in the territory to watch over things while my partner dazzles the Rapture." He placed a hand on Ezalia's shoulder, and for the first time, the chancellor blushed.

"Dazzles is a word for it." She smirked, sea-glass eyes shining.

"I'd say it was dazzling when you told Aird off," Tolek chimed in.

"Oh, I quite liked that." Jezebel nodded in approval.

"Yes, well, it's best he's gone now." Ezalia's nose wrinkled at the mention of the former Mindshaper Chancellor. She didn't know I'd been the one to kill him. Avoiding eye contact, I looked at the two other Seawatchers.

"Oh," Ezalia blurted, tracking my stare. "These are two of my top-ranking advisors. Chorid specializes in navigation"—she gestured to the man with dirty blond hair braided down his back and green eyes that wrinkled when he smiled—"and Andrenas. They're an expert in sacred studies." The tall warrior beside Chorid waved a dark-brown hand and brushed their braids over their shoulder. Each Seawatcher, save Ezalia, had a quiver of arrows across their back. Bows rested against the nearest hut. I didn't have to look to know Tolek was studying them.

"Pleasure to meet you all," I said. My eyes went back to the Seawatcher Chancellor, unsure how much I should say.

Understanding my thoughts, Ezalia continued, "These three are the only ones who know why you're here."

"She hasn't told us much," Chorid added, crossing his arms. His frustrated tone was countered by a gentle grin, like he knew his leader had reasons for keeping pertinent information from him.

"We know you are looking for something that has to do with an Angel?" Andrenas annunciated each word, as if our language wasn't their first. Tolek perked up at the sound. "And we found—"

"Why don't we speak about it once we get to the inn," Seron said. Were those nerves in his voice?

"Good idea," Cyph agreed. I tried to catch his eye, but he shook his head.

When we rounded the edge of the hut, though, the concern fled my mind.

"Holy dead Spirits," Tolek blurted, awe turning his words airy, and I thought he may have stumbled if it wasn't for the cane in his hand. I realized why Ezalia had wanted to begin our tour here.

"Cannons," I gasped. Lining the edge of the cliff as if they'd stood there for centuries—which they probably had—was a series of huge iron weapons. Noses pointed to the sea, warriors stationed at each, it was clear what they were for: defending the continent. It was also clear from the easy lean of the Seawatchers against their posts that the weapons were rarely used. Precautions from an era when our coasts were ravaged by enemies.

"By the ever-loving Angels." Tolek started forward, but I grabbed his wrist.

"No..." I shook my head, wide-eyed.

His jaw popped open, and he looked frantically between me and the new toys. "Come on, Alabath—"

Ezalia laughed, the sound mixing with the breeze again. "We can provide a demonstration later."

"That would be excellent." Tol's face lit up. "Thank you,

Chancellor. See?" He dropped a kiss to my cheek, the unexpected fire swirling in me and melting my worries. "Nothing to fret about."

"You have no idea what obsession you've planted in his head," Cypherion told the Seawatcher.

Tolek was going to love it here.

"Expanding your expertise can never hurt." Ezalia smiled, but kept walking, leading us past the rows of canons and the storage shed behind them. Tolek laced his fingers through mine and followed on her heels with the most satisfied smirk I'd ever seen.

As we got closer to the inhabited part of town, the buildings were made of the same ashy driftwood, but they became slightly larger. Flat and elongated, as if it was quicker and easier to build out rather than up. Warmth fell from their windows, pouring over the dirt-lined streets, families within preparing for dinner.

This wasn't a city like Palerman or even Gaveral. This was an outpost. Warriors lived here, but it was evident from the architecture that it served a purpose: defense. Besides homes, there were two small inns for travelers—one of which Ezalia cleared out for our party—and a handful of shops and stables.

It was peaceful, though. Not desolate like one might expect. A steady hum of life filled the air, and it was clear while it may be a small village lifestyle, hundreds of warriors still proudly call Brontain home.

As we approached the inn, a small building with its front almost entirely covered by green stalks of ocean-yarrow, I gripped Cyph's wrist.

"Why did you and Seron want to move back here?" I hadn't missed the way they both surveyed the area when the Angel task came up.

Cyph watched the rest of our group disappear inside, crickets chirping out a tune that set my nerves on edge. Then, he ran a hand through his hair. "He said they've been having trouble with wildlife out there. That the cliffs have been attacked twice recently —once by land and once by sea."

My breath caught in my throat. "Was it Kakias's doing? Searching for the emblems?" I'd been relieved we made the trek here without a hint of her, but perhaps that was because she was ahead of us.

"Not warriors," he said. "The land creature came in the night. Long limbs and wild screeches."

Concerns of the queen vanished.

"Wings?" I whispered.

He shook his head. "The sea one, though." He shivered. "It sounded horrific. Jumped thirty feet out of the water and collided with the rock, taking a chunk of cliff with it. It was there and gone so quickly, they barely had a chance to take note, but they think it was an alpheous."

"Those haven't been seen in centuries," I gasped. Giant sea serpents legend told were born out of sediment of ocean depths, alpheous were believed extinct. Or at least kept themselves far enough from warriors to not be seen in nearly a millennium.

"I know." Cyph nodded. "But it sounds like one. Large scaled body with rows of spikes along the spine and gullet. Nearly thirty feet long." There was something in his voice I didn't recognize.

"What else?" I asked.

"Nothing, but..." He looked up at the wooden overhang, searching the planks for an answer. "I'm worried. Why are all of these creatures surfacing? It can't be good, and I'm afraid we're in way over our heads."

I swallowed the honesty and realized what the tremor in his voice had been: fear. Cypherion rarely showed it, but dammit did it scare me when he did.

"You might be right," I answered just as honestly, but I didn't tack on I was afraid, too.

~

Ezalia directed us to three rooms, taking the two remaining for herself and her warriors. As our group of six stood outside the closed doors with shells carved into their frames, the warm yellow mystlight illuminated our averted glances and awkward shuffling.

Three rooms, each with two beds.

My sister couldn't hide her grin as she watched the rest of us. I could share with Tolek, but I was already resisting temptation by a fragment of a thread. It didn't matter there were two beds instead of one.

And if we shared, where did that leave Cypherion? With Santorina or Jezebel, I supposed. He wouldn't be alone with Vale, that was for certain. But—

"Oh, for the love of the Angels." Jezebel finally threw her hands up and swung one of the doors open. "Boys—in here." She strode down the hall to the next. "Rina and Vale—that way if you need to rewrap that wound." She crossed to the last room. "Sister, we'll take this one. Now, we're meeting in the dining room in twenty minutes. I suggest you all wash up quickly."

"Thank you, Jezebel," Rina said. "At least someone is still thinking with their head."

I hated the two of them a bit for blatantly laughing at the rest of us, but I couldn't blame them.

Cypherion stalked into the room he'd been appointed, keeping up his habit of pretending not to watch our Starsearcher. Tolek pursed his lips, looking over my shoulder after Jezebel. The consideration of an argument furrowed his brow.

"Next time, Vincienzo," I teased, reaching up to straighten my pin that still adorned his leathers.

Catching my hand, he brought it to his lips wordlessly. That one small, innocent motion burned right through me, and truly I considered abandoning my intentions and telling Jezebel to go room with Cyph.

After Tolek released my hand, I stood frozen for a moment. Then, I backed away from the fire in his eyes and shut the door.

When I exhaled, Jezebel laughed behind me. "Oh, you two aren't going to last another week."

CHAPTER TWELVE
TOLEK

I'D NEVER LIKED SEAFOOD. I COULDN'T STOMACH THE texture. But when the Seawatchers prepared it—with an abundance of rich spices to please every palate, from smokey to citrusy, lemongrass to dill—it was divine.

The innkeeper placed the trays in the center of the round table set for ten and finished off the presentation with a large bottle of rum, freshly uncorked. That syrupy sweet scent wafted over as I pulled out Ophelia's chair, and she flashed me a small smile.

I collected those, her little grins and winks and smirks. Since I'd woken up, I'd taken to tucking away each to battle back the nightmares.

As the keeper poured everyone a measure of rum, I kept one eye on Ophelia. She didn't turn him down, but she also didn't raise the glass to her lips. I wouldn't blame her if she had stumbled back into old habits after her father's death—it would have been easy for anyone to do—but she left the glass untouched.

"Thank you, Leo," Ezalia said to the keeper as he left, addressing him by his first name as if she truly knew him.

Once the door closed behind Leo with a snap, every spine around the table stiffened. Eyes shifted as bowls were passed. Utensils clicked against plates, doling out helpings of white fish with lemon and basil, roasted greens and sea-salted potatoes.

Ophelia speared Ezalia with a look, body practically buzzing. "You've found it?" One hand clutched her emblem necklace.

"We believe so," the chancellor said, "but we won't be certain until you go to the site."

"Which is where?" I asked, scooping the flaky fish onto my fork.

"There's a series of three rocks jutting out of the water in the Neptitian Sea. Too far to see clearly from the shore but not too great of a distance to reach by boat. They're like tiny islands. That's where we think your answer is."

As Ezalia spoke, I pulled out a journal and noted every word. Wrote it all down in case a day came when we needed to look back in order to go forward. It had been Malakai and Barrett's request after spending so many hours on Lucidius's journals.

"Why do you think it's there?" Cyph asked. He leaned back in his chair and brushed a hand over his jaw.

"There's a story." Ezalia sipped her rum, fidgeting with the glass. Ophelia and I exchanged a look that confirmed we were thinking the same thing: whatever this story said, it was a Seawatcher secret.

"About your Angel?" Ophelia prodded gently. "About Gaveny?"

Every Seawatcher sat a bit taller at his name.

"Was it a visitation?" Vale's voice drifted through the room, that soothing tone calming all but Cypherion, who gripped his knife tighter. The metal screeched across his plate as he harshly sliced the buttery-smooth fish. His agitation had me grimacing, too.

"Not particularly," Ezalia continued, ignoring the tension. "But these platforms were...important to him."

"Gaveny was legendary for his adventurous spirit," Andrenas explained. "Never stalled, always seeking among the tides. I have been exploring each of his greatest feats."

Ophelia's magenta eyes glowed. "And why do you think this location in particular is the one we're looking for?"

"Markings," Seron said gruffly.

"Markings?" I repeated, scribbling the details.

"We scouted it three weeks ago. We'd been searching these

types of sites since you told us. Any place that appeared...significant."

It made sense. If one was looking for an emblem from an Angel, it was only logical they might be in locations special to their mortal selves. Damien had delivered Ophelia's spear, but that didn't mean the others would be as blatantly exposed.

Seron brushed a hand across his jaw. "This one was different. The stones were—"

"Burned." Andrenas's subtle accent was harsh. "The stone was burned."

"Stone doesn't burn." Santorina's brows pulled in.

"Exactly," Seron answered. "Whatever happened there left deep scorch marks. They had to have been centuries old, but they were still warm to the touch."

"They were hot?" Ophelia's hand wrapped around her necklace again.

"Not hot, no," Seron said. "But not as cool as stone islands in the ocean should be. The water evaporated right off of them."

Ophelia turned to me, and fears screamed through her gaze. The two emblems we already had burned her when she first touched them. Only her.

"It's supposed to be me," she muttered. The shattering behind her eyes was a hammer to my chest. She took all of this on her own shoulders—didn't want this pain caused by the Angels to touch anyone else.

"Maybe each one is different," I offered.

Her eyes dropped from mine, my stomach clenching, but I tucked my arm around her, and she quickly recovered herself.

"When do we go?" Ophelia asked the chancellor.

"We can be ready in three days." Ezalia smiled, and it was the same smile she'd worn during the Rapture. A flash of full teeth that said she was ready for a challenge. "We'll finish preparations."

She placed a hand over Seron's on the table and squeezed. Cresting wave tattoos aligned on the backs of their hands, forming one endless swipe of water. My jaw ground as I watched it, the back of my neck sweating. Tattoos and their commitments—

A cool hand tangled in the hair at my nape, and I blinked out of the trance, meeting Ophelia's raised brows. *Are you okay?* she silently asked.

Tangling my fingers with hers, I kissed her palm. *Perfect.*

Across the table, Jezebel laughed, shaking her head.

Low muttering started around the table now that a plan had begun to take shape, but Ophelia stared at her plate, brows scrunched. I ducked down, brushing my lips against her shoulder, and muttered, "Your thoughts are awfully loud, Alabath."

"Something Barrett told me..." The uncertain bob of her voice had me shutting everyone else out, being here for her as I hadn't been for two months. "Shortly after the battle, I asked him where he got his sigil ring."

"He stole it from his mother, correct?"

"It was passed down through his family, and he doesn't think his mother ever intended to give it to him, but if it's an Angel emblem, where did it *truly* come from? Before his family..." She sighed. "According to him, the ancestor who first found the ring rescued it from"—she hesitated, and I squeezed her shoulder to encourage her—"a seven-headed swamp monster."

When I didn't answer immediately, Ophelia looked up warily, like she was expecting me to laugh.

"Do you believe it?" she asked.

"Am I crazy to say sort of? Perhaps the original story has gotten warped over time. Most legends do. Maybe it was simply a reptile or even a very angry jungle cat, but maybe the ring *was* found in a swamp. Look at the big picture rather than the details."

She mulled over that for a moment, the dull hum of conversation surrounding us. Somewhere in the distance, waves crashed against three landforms that had once been very important to an Angel.

"So, why the swamp, then?" she asked.

"And why the islands?"

"And how can these help us find the locations of the others?"

"Or the purpose of the entire task?"

"I'll write to Barrett tonight," Ophelia said, fire returning to her voice.

"That's my girl." I kissed her forehead.

Then, Rina's voice broke through the din. "Do any humans happen to live in Brontain?"

"We have human towns all throughout the territory, but mostly in the south," Ezalia responded.

Santorina flashed a look at Ophelia who nodded proudly at her friend. "I'm hoping to progress the training program for humans as we tour different territories," Rina explained.

"Is it not our responsibility to protect Gallantia?" Andrenas asked kindly.

"The land, yes, and yourselves," Rina answered. "But humans are a free people in Gallantia, so does it not stand that they should also be able to take up arms should they choose?" Andrenas smiled understandingly at Santorina, and Rina turned back to Ezalia with restored confidence. "I know Ophelia wrote to you already, but is there anyone I can speak to while here?"

"There is." She smiled, then opened her mouth and bellowed, "LEO!"

The innkeeper came jogging back in. "Aye, do you always have to be so loud, Ez?"

"Yes," she deadpanned. "But you know that already, brother."

Brother? I looked between the two and found the same shade of dark-brown hair and sea-glass eyes. The same crooked smirk and straight noses and annoyed scoffs, but also an easy affection I didn't quite understand.

Lyria and I had never been...*She came to Damenal for me,* I reminded myself. *She had said she was proud of me.*

"Santorina would like to speak with you about organizing a project of sorts," Ezalia told Leo. "I'd like you to help her by writing to whoever you think would be an asset. Form an organizational chart, please, and we'll look at it after our business is taken care of this week."

Rina and Leo disappeared to the bar where she animatedly dove into her reasoning for the program, and the Seawatcher listened dutifully. When she was done, he pulled out ink and parchment, and Spirits damn me, there was a glimmer in his eye.

"Your brother?" I asked Ezalia.

"Ten years elder and abundantly more patient." Her voice was layered with adoration that stung.

"If he's the oldest of your family, why is he not chancellor?" I asked.

She aimlessly moved food around her plate with her fork. "The Spirits chose me. They showed it to me during my Isla Trysva." Their ritual, like our Undertaking. My hand fisted atop the table at the reminder. I rolled my neck to dispel the sudden tension.

"Was it ever competitive between you two, then?"

Ezalia watched her brother. "Never. He didn't want this position. He would have taken it—would have excelled at it, too. But Leo always wanted something simpler. A different kind of life that most in our family aren't allowed." She looked at me. "I've had this position for thirty years now, since I was only fifty, and not a day goes by where I don't think he would do a better job. But I wanted it more. I'm happier with it than he ever would have been."

Next to me, Ophelia listened quietly, but her eyes were intent on my face. When I did not answer the chancellor, she said, "I suppose just because two people share the same blood, doesn't mean they're destined for the same future."

I wasn't sure if she meant her sister or my own.

MARBLE SURGED TOWARD ME, the veins as familiar as if etched on my own body.

I'd been here before. Sharp edges and hard surfaces all cold against my skin.

Bruises and blood and bones cracking.

"A fucking disgrace." Those words echoed as I fell. As hands left my back, and no one screamed but me. Except this time—

I turned to save my shoulder and stumbled through the world.

When I landed, a knife was in my hand, piercing flesh. Grating through bone, and a small gasp followed.

Blood bloomed. Horror bloomed faster. How did I let this happen? How did I do this? I was born a mess, meant to destroy.

"No...no, no, no." It was all I could think as I pressed my hand to the wound, trying to force that life source back in.

But it didn't work that way. It coated tan skin, quickly paling, my own hands burning crimson, too.

A fucking disgrace.

No, no, no...

"Tolek!"

So much blood. All my fault.

"Tolek, wake up!"

No, no, no...

Something warm met my cheeks. Was I crying? Fuck, I should be. No, this was soft and firm, and then—

Lips against mine. Hot and full, coaxing me to meet their rhythm.

I rocked upright, eyes shooting open as I panted. Sweat-stained sheets tangled around me, and two magenta eyes met mine, only inches away. Ophelia's hands cupped my face. She searched my gaze as we both caught our breath, verifying I was really with her.

"You wouldn't wake," she admitted, swallowing.

I rushed forward, taking her lips again. *She is here. She is okay. She is here.* The sheet fell around my waist, my hands roving over her goosebump-coated arms and silk-clad back, gripping her thighs to pull her closer. Just to be sure.

She is here. She is okay.

I repeated the reassurances to myself as I bent her back until she was flat on the mattress, her legs bending to bracket my hips. My tongue flicked against hers, teasing and tasting and trying to fucking forget the fear I'd been buried in and bury myself in her instead. She tasted like magic laced with temptation, and Angels, could I stay here forever?

Her hands dug greedily into my hair as I explored her neck with my lips, and a small moan slipped up her throat. I dragged my fingers from her ankle, up her calf, and back down her thigh, grabbing on to her waist as my hips ground against hers.

"Wait," she said softly. Then, a bit more assured, "Tol, stop."

I shot back.

Ophelia followed me, eyes hesitant. I was silent as she brought one hand to my cheek, brushing my damp hair from my eyes with the other. Then, she laced our fingers and brought the back of my hand to her lips.

For a moment, we sat in the stillness, crickets chirping and waves crashing in the distance. Cypherion had yet to return to our room, so it was only us—my eyes glued to her swollen lips, and Ophelia, waiting for me to speak.

"First kiss," I finally said, breathless, unable to find other words with the feel of her still everywhere.

"Not technically." Ophelia smirked. "I think about that bathing chamber a lot. What would have happened..."

Spirits, was she trying to undo me right here before I even got a chance to watch her come, to memorize every sound she made? It would work. Even the thought—

No. What happened after that bathing chamber had changed everything for both of us. And we needed to work through that.

"Our first should have been better than that," I said. "It will be."

Ophelia crawled into my lap, looping her arms around my neck and resting her head on my bare chest.

"I'm sweaty," I reminded her, my voice still raw.

"I've held you bruised and bloodied, Vincatzo." I flinched at her choice of words, but didn't say anything. She didn't know what the nightmares held; to her it was only a figure of speech. "I can handle sweat."

As if to prove it, she placed a kiss to my chest, right over my heart. When her eyes flashed up to me from beneath dark lashes, I wasn't sure if they were heated or if it was a trick of the moonlight. Either way, all my blood flooded south.

This was why we couldn't share a room. Every look she gave me was a temptation. I couldn't wait for those nights, but I wouldn't push. I adjusted her on my lap so she didn't think I was trying to take this somewhere she wasn't ready for.

"I don't mind being woken up that way."

Ophelia blinked up at me, not giving into my joke. "They're getting worse."

"Yeah." I swallowed. "They are."

She waited after my confirmation, giving me the space to share more without pressure.

"They're better when you're here," I whispered, running a hand down her hair. When I reached the gap between her silk top and shorts, I absentmindedly ran my thumb across her spine, and she shuddered. I kept doing it. "You get through to me, Alabath." I sighed, pressing a kiss to her head. "You save me."

A small smile cracked her lips, though I wasn't sure why. It was only the truth.

Pushing out of my lap and laughing at my disgruntled groan, Ophelia pulled me to my feet.

"Where are we going?" I asked.

"I have an idea."

As Ophelia led me from the room, I swiped up a special book, having an idea of my own.

I FOLLOWED HER BLINDLY—WOULD follow her anywhere—down to a black-sand crescent of beach tucked beneath the bluffs. The waves roared in the distance, but in this secluded spot, the tide washed up gently.

"I noticed it earlier," she explained, shrugging. Moonlight dripped over her long hair and all that exposed skin—sweetest temptation I'd ever seen and so damn hard to look away from.

I dropped the book to the sand.

"And what did you bring me here for?" I gripped her hips and walked her backward—toward the water.

Her eyes widened, lips parting on a smile.

I didn't wait for her to answer. I tightened my hold on her, and threw her over my shoulder, taking off for the waves, my injuries feeling good as new with Ophelia so close. Her threats and my laughter echoed around us.

We plunged into that icy water and came up gasping. It stung the bones in my right knee, but I shoved it away. Ophelia's eyes locked on mine, revenge burning beautifully in her gaze, and it took every shred of self-control not to stare at where silk clung to her peaked nipples.

"You'll regret that, Vincienzo," she promised, beaming as she leaped at me.

I ran, but her arms wrapped around my neck, legs around my waist as she stuck to my back.

For a while, we stayed in the waves, chasing each other as we had as children, like our lives weren't now shredded by warfare and vindictive Angels. Stealing kisses when she talked back to me, running my hands over her body beneath the water, and allowing the ocean's melody to steal our worries.

When we finally collapsed on our backs in the sand, both panting, Ophelia rolled her head to look at me. "Do you remember your fourteenth birthday?"

Reaching over, I brushed away the wet strands of hair sticking to her face, tangled with grains of sand. The soft smile it elicited from her was one of my favorites. I tucked it in my memory. "Our summer exchange in Gaveral," I said. "You convinced me we should sneak out to celebrate."

"Malakai and Cypherion thought we'd get in trouble so they didn't come."

"We raced through the waves for hours, and you got mad at me every time I won."

"Your legs were longer!" she argued. Even now, so many years later, she argued.

I laughed, pushing onto my elbow. "That's one of my most cherished memories, Alabath."

"Mine, too, Vincienzo." She fell silent for a moment, eyes searching mine. "Do you want to talk about it?"

No.

But I did want her to know. One piece at a time.

"You know that I nearly didn't finish the Undertaking." I'd admitted that to her the first time she heard my nightmares, in a cave hidden in the mountains where we were completely alone. Safe. "And the Mindshapers dragged up those feelings. All of those things—I think it stems from my father."

"Your father?"

"Because of how he treated me growing up." I'd always hid how my father felt toward me. Hid the scars it caused within me—

and a few without—until we'd first traveled to the Undertaking. Leaving Palerman had given me perspective.

"When my mother nearly died giving birth to me, I think something changed in him. He became so desperate to hold on to her. I think..." This was the part I was still attempting to figure out. "I always felt like I was meant to do horrible things because of my mother."

"That's not true, Tolek," Ophelia said, sitting up.

"That disdain was always what I'd known, though. When I was younger, I didn't realize it was wrong."

I hadn't understood a parent should not make you feel unworthy, like you'd fail at everything you attempted. That those lessons weren't supposed to be imprinted on your soul.

And they followed me, Mindshaper torture latching on to those memories and generating horrifying images of whom else I might kill.

I wasn't ready to voice the rest of it, yet. To bring the memories of what my father did to me to life or tell her about the haunting possibilities my mind conjured because of it.

"You are meant for great things," Ophelia whispered. "Do you want to know how I know?"

"How?" I humored her.

"Because you've continued to fight for everyone around you despite the lies your father fed you. Only someone truly strong could do that. You're the brightest star in my life, Tolek Vincienzo. Truthfully, some days you're the only reason I can face all of this."

That confession was like lead in my chest.

"Come here," I said, pulling her into a seated position between my legs. "I want to show you something." Grabbing the book I'd dropped in the sand when we arrived, I angled the cover so the words stamped in the leather caught the light.

Ophelia squinted. "This isn't our language."

"I've been studying others."

"Since when?"

"Since we moved to the capital. Not *every* night I can't sleep is spent winning other warriors' coin."

Her brow creased, but I'd tried to avoid her often when we first arrived in Damenal, and forcing ancient languages into my head had been a helpful distraction when my drug of choice was in another man's bed. I considered myself a scholar of many arts, and language was one of the most beautiful.

Laughing softly, I kissed that line between her brows. "I figured it was a good thing to know," I said, flipping to the story I wanted. "This is Endasi. It's practically a dead tongue now, but it was once—"

"The language of the Angels." She flashed a satisfied smirk. I tucked that one away, too. "You aren't the only one who's studied, Vincienzo." The little attitude flipping up her words had me hard again. Dammit, I loved when she displayed that confidence.

"My apologies." I pointed to the scrawl titling the story. "Do you know what this says?"

Ophelia shook her head. "I know what Endasi is, but I can't translate it."

This time I let out a satisfied hum, and she gently smacked my arm in return. I caught her hand in mine and pointed our clasped fingers to the page. "This word in particular has a few translations. In short, it means forever, but it also means eternal saving grace or a promise unto the heart and earth."

"That's lovely," she said, studying the word.

"That's what you are to me, Alabath. My saving grace, my promise." Her eyes softened as she inhaled sharply, and those lips popped open. "My infinity, *apeagna.*"

Ophelia was still for a moment, my words sinking in one syllable at a time. Then, her arms were around my neck, and she was turning in my lap to straddle my hips. Her fingers drifted absently across my collarbone, and I had to chase off the fear that she was searching for a tattoo she'd never find there.

"You're mine, too, Tolek. I may not know ancient languages to repeat it in, but you are."

I didn't need fancy words to know she meant it. She was slower to understand it than I was—I'd been settled into these feelings for years—but it was in the way her body relaxed in my arms, the way her eyes studied me, and how she gently pressed her lips to mine.

If *I* could be good enough, we'd get there.

CHAPTER THIRTEEN
MALAKAI

"I'LL SHOW YOU MINE IF YOU SHOW ME YOURS."
Barrett's voice snaked through the opening to the tent I'd claimed
at the war camp. We'd only been here for a night, but when I
returned after breakfast, a note had been resting on my cot.

I crossed the small tent space that wasn't crowded with unnecessary belongings. A trunk for clothing, my pack from the travels
here, a mystlight to ward off the crisp chill, and a cot. Aside from
my weapons, it was all I needed.

I held up the crumbled bit of parchment bearing Ophelia's
familiar tidy scrawl: *Found it.*

"She's not one to waste words, is she?" Barrett said, stepping
aside so I could join him and Dax outside and handing me his own
note.

What tale does the swamp tell, Prince?

"What does she mean?" I pulled my cloak tighter around my
shoulders. Rebel trotted alongside, floppy ears bouncing. It was
hard not to notice the wary looks warriors cast us as we walked
through camp.

A tiny village—with only a smattering of cabin-style homes—
had been vacated for the army, the families relocating north.
They'd given their houses to the highest-ranking warriors. Barrett,
Dax, and I had been offered one upon our arrival, but we took
tents instead.

The further south you went in the range, the closer to Mind-shaper Territory, the colder it got despite the fact that it was still autumn. The land surrounding the range, officially across the border, was icy and frigid. Here it was unpleasant but tolerable.

"Likely about my ring." Barrett dropped his voice as we passed a huddle of warriors who fell silent, and proceeded to spin an unlikely tale of a seven-headed swamp monster guarding the family heirloom.

"It's only a story, though." Barrett mindlessly massaged the spot on his index finger where the ring used to be. Now there was only a white band of skin, even paler than the rest of him.

"Is it?" Dax asked. We both looked at him. "It could be true."

"Those monsters don't exist," I began—that wasn't what she'd asked, though. "But she wants to know of the swamp."

"The location," Barrett said, running a gem-covered hand over his jaw. As we reached our destination, the cabin's windows warm and inviting, he put a hand on each of our arms, halting us. "The story of the swamp...the why. I think we have some questions to ask."

They'd have to wait, though. War was on our doorstep.

Still, as we knocked and entered Lyria's home, I considered that proposition. Why would an ancient, sacred piece of metal containing a sliver of Angel power be hidden within a swamp? And was there any way my father's inquiries as to the Angels could be connected?

"Welcome to your first official briefing," Lyria said, straightening from where she hunched over a polished wood table strewn with plans. Mystlight lanterns cast a gold glow across maps, lists, and coordinates, but I looked at the warriors around the table instead.

"This is the council we'll be working with," Lyria explained, catching my eye. Her long brown hair was braided back, and she wore her usual leathers. Dark circles framed her eyes. "Five generals total. And Esmond, our lead healer."

The Bodymelder stepped away from the kitchen taking up the entire right side of the open first floor, dressed in a thick brown tunic accented with maroon and gold. Beyond him, the counter was littered with tonics, plants, and supplies I'd seen in Santorina's office but wasn't an expert on. We exchanged a brief hello, and Rebel trotted over to the fire, curling into a ball.

"That's Rebel," Barrett said, offering no more of an explanation.

"Right." Lyria's brow creased as she studied the wolf. "Anyway, this is Cyren Marvana. They're mainly in charge of sessions." A Starsearcher with long dark hair and triple-bladed daggers at their hip stepped forward. "And Amara Ridgebrook. Special forces. Archery." This woman was clearly a Seawatcher based on the tan leathers and aquamarine studs woven into her sandy-blonde braids. I pulled out the history of the ruling families I'd been forced to memorize as a child.

"You're related to Ezalia, right?" I asked.

"Her older and wiser cousin," Amara retorted. She had those same sea-glass eyes as the chancellor.

"And Quilian Locke. He's one of our Infantry Leads." The final general waved cheerfully. When the deep-purple shawl over his leathers caught the light, bronze thread gleaming, I realized the strategy here. One from each minor clan.

That was only three generals, though, and Lyria had said—

The door slammed open, wood shuddering against the wall, and a laugh slipped from Lyria. Clanking metal and aggrieved grumbles filled the silence as a flurry of cold air lifted the maps spread before us.

Head snapping around, something in my chest stuttered.

Mila stood with her back to us, removing her twin swords from her back and tossing them on the couch.

"Everything all right?" Lyria asked, not bothering to hide her smirk at her friend.

"More fucking bigots in the training circuit," Mila snapped, finally spinning to face us. Her platinum braid whipped through the air, and the anger fell from her expression, amusement replacing it. Her lips pursed, head tilting, as ice blue eyes bore right into me.

"Well," she said, sauntering toward the table, "look who decided to show up."

Had her voice always had that lilt to it? I couldn't be sure. After exchanging letters the last few weeks, I'd forgotten the smooth sound of it. Instead, I heard everything in a warm whisper, like one spoken in a ruined temple.

It stirred something beneath my skin—a curiosity maybe. One that made my heart beat faster and my throat feel thick.

"I'm sure you've been waiting impatiently," I quipped as Mila took up a position across the table, unbraiding her hair with long, steady fingers.

She smirked and dropped her eyes to Lyria's plans. Just like that, she slipped into the controlled mind of a soldier.

"Our fourth general," Lyria confirmed. "I believe you three know Mila Lovall."

"That we do." Barrett draped an arm around my shoulder.

I ignored him. "You said five generals?"

"I suppose I should correct myself." Lyria's eyes went to Dax. "I hope to have five, if you'll accept the position."

"Me?" Dax balked. Lyria nodded, exchanging a smirk with Mila. "But I'm Engrossian. And you two don't even like me."

At that, Lyria laughed. Full and hearty, like her brother. "We didn't trust an Engrossian when we first met, you're correct. But given recent events"—she paused, her eyes flashing to Barrett—"you two deserve our trust. You were a lieutenant in our enemy's army. We can't overlook that. It might take a while for some of the warriors to understand your intentions as we do, but it also makes you one of the most important pieces of this team."

Dax let that sink in for a moment, then brought his fist to his heart in a show of appreciation. "I'd be honored to serve in this army, Master of Warfare."

Sincerity blazed through his words.

"Update us, then," I said. "How's the development of the blended army?" Asking questions, being involved, had my chest unwinding. A direction—it was what I'd been lacking.

"They're starting to meld. It's been a long few months." Lyria sighed, twirling her braid around a finger. "First, getting the troops here following the last war and the Battle of Damenal took time. Many were invigorated..."

"And the rest?" Barrett prompted.

"The rest were scared to see exactly what happened to their loved ones last time happen again." She rubbed her eyes, releasing a groan and letting herself slip for a brief moment before straightening up and falling back into her role. "Rightfully so. They've suffered enough, and asking them to rush back to a battlefield after only a couple years...it doesn't matter if we're warriors. That's pressure on anyone."

"But they'll do it," I finished for her.

She nodded. "Every clan will."

"And we'll do it damn well," Quil encouraged. His confident, warm demeanor shed reassurance on the room.

"The ones who were more eager were hard to delay," Mila interjected. "After many long nights, we convinced them it wouldn't help to launch an unprepared attack. Once they cooled from the injustice of Daminius, they knew we were right."

"There have been almost constant attacks on the southern border," Cyren offered quietly. "Our first host, composed of the most fit of all of our clans, has thwarted them, but it's been two-to-one in terms of numbers."

"They've got twice as many as we have?" My eyes widened.

"No," Amara corrected, voice severe. "We've had to send twice as many as they had in order to hold the line."

My stomach plummeted to my feet. Forget launching a larger attack, if this kept happening, they'd chip away at our forces before we even met them.

"And my spy network reports they have a growing force." Lyria's eyes flashed to Rebel, curled before the fire, then she continued, "Besides that we've been focusing our efforts on cohesion."

She pointed to a series of charts pinned up on one wall. Lists of the legions from the four clans we were uniting under our banners. Seawatchers being the smallest, Mystiques the largest. Then, it paired off the different troops into strategic groups based on skill set and advantages. Noted which had been tried, which worked, which hadn't, and why.

They weren't only rebuilding the Mystique force; they were

incorporating an inclusive army among all the clans. Sending them out as one. It was a genius plan. One I didn't think had been done in Gallantian history.

"This is good," Dax observed.

"It's revolutionary," I said.

"It was Danya's goal," Lyria explained, her tone softer than I'd heard all evening when she spoke of the former Master of Weapons and Warfare. "It was what we were working on before..." She cleared her throat. "I only put it to work."

"She'd be proud." We exchanged a small smile.

"Which of these have been tested?" Dax asked, gesturing to the lists.

Lyria walked over and pointed to the second from the right. "These were successes." Then, the one on the far right. "These could be improved."

"The successes are who has held the border?" I clarified.

Lyria nodded, pride lifting her chin. "They haven't breached the range. But there's a problem with the Mindshapers."

"Problem?"

"That power of theirs is a dangerous weapon. Only a few of them have harnessed it in a destructive way, but I expect more will. Especially if Kakias is controlling them with dark magic. I don't know the extent of it, but we need a defense against them."

"In the meantime"—Mila stepped forward—"you all join us for training tomorrow."

THE WIND WAS bitter against my skin bright and early the next morning, but Barrett, Dax, and I donned leathers and weapons and wound through the tents and cabins until we arrived at the makeshift training yard.

Warriors of all four alliance clans were there.

"Right on time," Mila called, jogging over. "Are you ready?" She looked all three of us over, but the question seemed more for me than it was them.

"Of course," I answered, meeting the challenge.

"Good." She nodded. "General Goverick," she addressed Dax, then signaled over her shoulder to where Amara, Cyren, and Quilian stood. The five generals had met for hours last night, reviewing strategy. "You can observe the regular routine with the others. We'll adjust as we all see necessary over the coming days."

"Thank you," Dax dismissed himself.

"You two want to pair up?" Mila asked Barrett and me.

We exchanged a look. Barrett's lips quirked into a smile. "Let's go, brother."

"Fucking Spirits." I laughed, removing my sword from my belt. The Engrossian ax I'd taken from the Battle of Damenal hung opposite it, and Lucidius's dagger with that. I shoved the prince's shoulder. "Come on."

Mila barked out orders to the warriors. The first training shift was the smallest, but even then there were more of us than I'd expected. Barrett and I fell among them, some giving us a wide berth. I gritted my teeth and pretended not to notice. We were fighting beside them, weren't we?

Setting my stance, I flexed my fingers around the leather grip of my sword once, twice. Tried to focus on only the blade in my hand and the opponent before me. I breathed as deeply as possible as we circled, the clangs of weapons around us dulling to a muted hum.

It was one of the first times I'd really trained since the Battle of Damenal, having spent weeks avoiding arenas. Cypherion pulled me in occasionally, seeing through my bullshit excuses, but normally I was *busy*.

When Barrett struck and I successfully countered the attack, I was surprised by the satisfied warmth spreading through my chest.

I pushed him back, lunging to the left when he swung again. I rebounded and met his next strike. He danced toward the arena railing with light steps, our weapons repeatedly clashing between us.

Barrett was a surprisingly good swordsman—a graceful and fluid threat. Should he unleash the ax at his side, he'd be brutally skilled.

"That's it, Malakai!" Dax cheered from the sideline as I nearly got my sword around Barrett who threw a curse his consort's way.

Rebel barked on the sidelines. Spirits, that wolf was eerily everywhere.

We wove between warriors, dodging not only each other's strikes but limbs and weapons of the pairs as if we could sense them before they struck. Was this what it was like to be in a cohesive army? The energy buzzing between us all was palpable. Lyria had said they were still learning to move as one, but if this was a taste of the inclusion to come, I wanted to be a part of it.

It called to that purpose I'd wanted—

Pain lashed through my side, warmth trickling over my ribs. I cursed, pressed my hand to the spot. When I pulled it back, my gloves were crimson.

I met Barrett's fear-stricken eyes. "I'm so sorry!" he blurted, hand to his mouth. "Fuck, that wasn't supposed to hit you."

"It's okay," I whispered, but I couldn't get the words out at full volume. My throat was tightening. I dropped my weapons and tore off my gloves, air crisp against my slick palms.

Pulling aside my tunic, the chill rose goosebumps as I looked at the spot where an old scar had reopened. One from those days. That cell.

Sweat cascaded down my back, sticking my leathers to my skin. Taunts and jeers echoed. My muscles slackened.

My knees met the dirt one at a time in a shattered rhythm.

I fell onto my hands. Cool earth grounded me. Sharp rocks dug indents into my palms.

"Malakai," a calm, impossibly steady voice said. Not a hint of the torment I toiled through showing. Blue eyes swam before me.

I couldn't look, though. Couldn't face anyone.

Instead, I gathered whatever strength I had remaining, pushed to my full height, and fled from the arena.

I STORMED INTO MY TENT, the flaps slapping shut behind me. As the clashes of training echoed in my mind, I dug into the trunk storing my belongings until my fingers locked around the canteen with herb-infused water. I downed the last few drops and dropped it to the floor, breathing heavily.

Silence wrapped around me.

"Fuck!" I growled, kicking my cot. The metal frame rattled in the quiet tent. I pressed my hand to my side; the blood had stopped flowing, the wound already healing. A sticky mess remained.

There was no world in which I'd be fit to be on a battlefield. At least it made the decision easier. Still, when I'd first started fighting, I thought, maybe I could do it, despite not completing the Undertaking. For a few minutes, it had felt right.

I thought maybe I could be the warrior everyone wanted me to be.

It was all I'd ever known anyway, being that man. I'd prepared for it all my life, worked to fulfill everyone else's expectations until the day I found out about that damned treaty and the world unraveled at my feet.

"Malakai." The one voice I didn't want to hear echoed from the doorway.

"You don't have to say it." I didn't face Mila. "I don't want to fight anyway." Then why was my heart stuttering so desperately?

"What?" Mila asked. She moved into the tent and made herself at home in the small space. It felt so full with her—with her scent, something sweet but strong like cinnamon—and the sound of her voice. It overwhelmed me.

"Why else would you be here?"

"To help," she said baldly.

I scoffed, looking over my shoulder. "How could *you* help?"

She straightened. Eyes turning icy and arms crossing her chest. "I'm going to pretend you didn't say that given everything you're going through and the fact that you know very little about me."

"Everything I'm going through?"

"The fear in the yard, and the—"

"I'm not afraid," I spat, crossing the tent with two steps so we were face-to-face. "I'm not."

Mila's brows shot up, but she didn't back down. She was quiet for a moment, maybe giving me a chance to admit the truth.

"Fine." She stepped away. "You're not afraid. But I was going to offer to help you overcome the mental block you're obviously not struggling with. Clearly, you're fine on your own."

She didn't give me a chance to respond before sweeping from the tent, leaving me with an uncomfortable guilt swarming my chest.

Chapter Fourteen
Malakai

I couldn't fucking believe myself. Mila hadn't deserved that. She responded well in leaving—that was for sure. Honestly, the way she stood up to me and called me on my bullshit had been enticing, letting me stew on my mistakes rather than forcing me to listen. Seemed I was doing that often lately.

But Mila had only been trying to help.

Now, after sleeping off the drugs I'd downed for the majority of the day, I was stuck in the freezing night, stomping to her and Lyria's cabin to fall on my damn sword and admit things I didn't want to admit to anyone, let alone her.

"Mila?" I called, pounding on the door. I didn't want to intrude. Hopefully she was alone—

I hadn't thought about the fact that she might not be. I hadn't seen her with any men in the day since we'd arrived, though, so she hopefully wasn't...entertaining any guests. If she was, well, I couldn't look more pathetic than I already did. Interrupting couldn't hurt. Give her more ammunition for me.

There was no sound through the door. A rush of relief went through me.

"Mila?" I huffed again, louder this time. My breath fogged in front of me. My fucking balls were gonna freeze off if I kept waiting out here. Mystiques weren't made for this weather. At least inside our tents we had the warmth of mystlight.

"Mila, if you're in there, answer so I can fucking apologize, or else I'm going to come inside."

The door swung open, but it wasn't Mila.

"Lyria."

"Malakai." The commander leaned against the frame. "To what do we owe your aggrieved presence?"

So Mila hadn't told her. Maybe she wasn't angry with me, then. Or maybe she truly didn't care that I'd been an ass.

"Is Mila here?"

Lyria stepped aside. "Up the stairs, second door on the right."

"Thanks." Clenching my hands beneath my cloak, I swept past the war room and kitchen and up the rickety staircase against the wall, wood groaning beneath my feet.

Mila's door was cracked. I rapped my knuckles on the wood and waited, but she didn't say a thing.

"Mila?" Spirits, she had to be able to hear me. The walls were thin for Damien's sake.

I'd never been patient, though. "Mila?" I knocked again, harder this time, and the door swung open a few inches, hinges squeaking.

Peering through, I caught what I thought were maps pinned to the walls and an assortment of weapons lining the dresser.

But I barely saw any of it because across the room, water drops glistening on her golden-tan skin after bathing, was Mila. Her back was to me, and she wore nothing more than white lace undergarments and—

Those fucking scars.

I'd seen them on Daminius, crisscrossing her legs and carving out a place in my mind. They froze me now. My vision went red, pale jagged marks all that filtered through.

And because of all the frustration already vying to get out of me, the question I'd been dying to ask but had told myself was prying broke free without a thought: "Who did that to you?"

Spirits, I sounded like a fucking animal.

She whirled, eyes wide, but there wasn't a hint of embarrassment at me seeing her. Not even anger. Only a brief flash of alarm and then that infuriating but admirably calm demeanor she commanded, like everything else was locked away. She was a damn fortress.

Mila crossed her arms, tucking her hands around herself. All I saw was white lace, golden skin, and those scars calling for payment.

"What are you doing here?" At her voice, my head snapped up. She didn't sound mad—merely curious. Like this happened every day. And—

Shit.

I'd walked in on her nearly naked. I averted my eyes, but her scars were everywhere. Plastered on the damn ceiling and wooden beams spanning it.

"I—I called and you didn't answer. The door swung open on its own—"

"You should probably wait outside."

"You're right, sorry." I ducked out before she could say anything else, my back flattening against the wall on the other side of the door.

My breathing came quicker as I waited, short gasps through tight lungs.

When I closed my eyes, I saw Mila's scars, but I also saw my own. A warped history and the casualties committed through it. Had hers damaged her mind the way mine had? Maybe they had. I couldn't know.

I did know one thing: scars equaled pain and torture and betrayals. And seeing them—especially ones so horrible—on anyone put me right back into that haunted place where I existed to be beaten. Where I was a tool for their entertainment. Where I learned not to feel the physical pain but every damn second was seared into my mind.

I tried to breathe deeper and force the memories away.

Dragging my hands through my hair, my head thumped back against the wall. Fucking Spirits, I shouldn't have asked her about them. What had I been thinking? I didn't want to know. Even the thought of it...

My chest tightened. I rubbed the heel of my hand against it. *Breathe*, I coached myself.

How do you breathe again?

Useless, incapable, Warrior Prince.

One hand was braced on my knee, the other on my chest. I tried to focus through blurry vision, counting the cracks in the floorboards.

By the time I got to eight, my lungs had loosened a bit, air working its way back in at a normal pace.

I ran my hand across my jaw—across the small scar my father had left. It was one of the more innocent ones I had, yet it plagued me the most. Funny how that worked, how the bigger moments— the whips, the hot knives—dulled compared to the one slap that left me marked forever, where I had to see it every damn day.

And then there was the thought I'd been avoiding. Wet skin and pristine white lace. It was branded into my brain after one look, and if I hadn't been so panicked about the scars, it likely would have been my only thought.

I'd been with women since Ophelia and I broke up. Meaningless physical connection to distract myself.

But I hadn't felt that desire with anyone since her. Not the way my blood was pumping as I pictured what I wasn't supposed to have seen. I hadn't looked at someone's body with the same addiction as when I'd seen Mila, scars and lace and temptation for my own depraved sake.

I wanted to see more. And based on the fact that my cock was stiff, the rest of me did, too.

It was the scars, I told myself. It was my sick fascination with Lucidius's actions and my own trauma. That was why I cared.

Finally, her voice drifted through the crack in the door. "You can come back."

I adjusted myself and did my best to act normal—as if I even knew what normal was now.

Mila was leaning against the dresser holding her weapons, now fully dressed. Those golden cuffs were back around her wrists, a navy silk robe falling to her knees.

"Sorry about that," I muttered.

Now that I wasn't as distracted, I looked around. With a double bed on one wall and overflowing bookshelves on another, the tiny room was crowded. Made more so by the thoughts screaming through my mind.

"To what do I owe the honor?" Her gently joking tone rolled off the walls and down my spine as I took a seat.

White lace, white lace, white lace, fuck. Would that be the death of me? Her propped against the dresser, robe falling open around her thighs, certainly wasn't helping.

"Malakai." She snapped for my attention, a teasing smile on her face. "Eyes up here."

Fuck me again.

"Right. Yeah." I leaned forward and braced my elbows on my knees. "I have an offer for you."

"An offer?" She raised a brow.

"It's more of a request, I suppose." I ran my hand through my hair, gathering every scattered thought. "What you said earlier. That you'd teach me."

Her brows shot up. "You want me to help you train?"

"Yes." I nodded. "To shut off my emotions. To not let...any of it affect me when it matters."

"That wasn't my offer."

"That's what I'm asking of you, though."

Mila assessed me, those turquoise eyes sweeping over my body from head to toe. "All right."

My heart stuttered at how easy that had been, until she held up a finger.

"On one condition."

I sank into the chair, feet planted firmly. "I'm listening."

Mila unfolded herself from the dresser and crossed the room until she was standing before me. "I'll train you, with whichever weapons you choose, and help you beat these freezing episodes. But you also have to work with me on your emotional control." She bent down until we were nose to nose and lifted her finger to tap the side of my head. "To stop avoiding what's happening in here"—she lowered her hand to my chest—"and in here."

Stop avoiding it? I ran my tongue over my teeth, considering. That didn't sound like a good idea. I'd fought hard to cage up everything I was feeling, and though the panic still gripped me, most days I was fine. Unleashing it...that would set me back.

How the fuck did she know what was going through my head, anyway?

"You can't just teach me how to fight without looking pathetic?"

Her eyes softened. Voice, too. "No, Malakai. It runs deeper."

There was something to her tone. A *you know this already* implication that had a scoff building in my throat. But deep down, I knew she was right. The source of my incapability on a battlefield was linked to everything else that was fucked up in my mind.

I swallowed. "Fine."

"Then you have a deal, Warrior Prince." Mila straightened and held her hand out to me.

"Don't call me that," I growled, pushing to my feet so I towered over her, not taking her hand.

But she gripped my palm and pulled me forward. "Lesson number one: don't let their useless words hurt you."

I tightened my grip, forcing her to step into me. Where her hands had been smooth upon our first meeting, they were now rough and calloused. "Got it, General."

Mila released a small hum of contemplation, then turned, walking toward the door.

"What?" I asked, standing there like an idiot.

She turned over her shoulder, lifted it. "I liked the sound of that." Her hips swayed dangerously as she continued toward the door. "Your second lesson starts tomorrow, Warrior Prince. See you at sunrise."

And as she left, I wasn't sure if I had just made the greatest deal of my life or the stupidest. One thing I did know—I needed to think with my head and not my fucking cock.

Chapter Fifteen
Ophelia

A THUNDEROUS BOOM SHOOK THE DRIFTWOOD WALLS of the inn. I shot from my bed, tearing back the curtain around the room's small window.

"What in the Spirits?" Jezebel mumbled, blinking grouchy eyes up at me. Starfire was in my hand. Dawn light filtered in, dimmed gray from the ocean fog rolling across the ground.

A second *boom* followed, close enough to rattle the entire building. And I realized what it was.

"Those fucking cannons," Jezebel groaned, falling back into bed, and pulling the cover tighter over her head.

I let her be. The Seawatchers had hosted us at a bonfire last night which Tolek deemed Jezebel's belated birthday celebration. She'd danced and drank well into the night, and though my chest squeezed at the realization that she was grown, contentment stilled my racing heart.

I pulled on my leathers and prepared for the day, quietly shutting the door on my sleeping sister. The town was still at this hour. The warriors who lived here or were stationed temporarily were likely used to the echoing blasts and hadn't sprung from bed as I had.

It was calming as I crossed sand paths lined with fronds and crane flowers. They were an unusual combination, but something about it made this small town uniquely beautiful. After speaking with Ezalia when we first arrived, I tried to pick out those pieces, seeing the threads weaving the tapestry of this small gray outpost into a work of art. The air prickled with something akin to anticipation.

As the buildings thinned and the sand and dirt stretched out to the cliff's edge, thin blades of grass peaking weakly through, a deep voice called, "Test six!" And another blast echoed.

I followed the voice around a bend in the cliff, and the world poured before me. Endless gray ocean sparkled silver in the rising sun. As I walked closer, I realized it wasn't a sleet-colored sheet as I'd thought. It was arrays of deep navy and indigo, swipes of cerulean shimmering like brushstrokes with the rippling tide. Each color melted together as the clouds parted.

And on the cliff's edge, looking over that expanse of world teeming for us to explore, Tolek sat at a cannon.

Seron stood beside him, doling out instructions, and a number of Seawatchers surrounded them. Tolek's eyes were wild as he soaked in each word, hands exploring the different levers used to turn and aim the massive weapon.

My heart squeezed in my chest at the exhilaration in his gaze. After what he'd told me about how his father's treatment had manifested within him and how the Mindshaper torture and the Undertaking had warped his thoughts further, each of his laughs was something to cherish, even more so than before.

Cypherion stood on the outskirts of the group, listening with his arms crossed but eyes bright and intrigued.

"You allowed this, then?" I asked as I approached.

"He was awake before the sun, throwing a pillow at me and saying Seron arranged this for us." Cypherion shook his head. "There was no stopping him."

"Test seven!" Seron's booming voice carried along the cliff again. It seemed amplified, and I wondered if it was an effect of the acoustics or some trick their Angel gave them.

Cyph and I watched as Tolek restocked some kind of powder in the next cannon, ignited a fuse, and—*BOOM*.

This one shook my entire frame, the blast ringing in my ears.

"Should have warned you," Chorid laughed, brushing his

blond hair back with a soot-streaked hand. It was unbound around his shoulders this morning. He patted my arm before following the Seawatchers to the next weapon, stationed fifty feet down the cliff.

"They test them once a month," Cyph explained. "The next was supposed to be in a week, but they moved it up since we're here."

And hopefully by next week, we'd be gone. Off to the war front with an Angel emblem in hand, before Kakias sniffed out this one.

"Good morning," Tolek said, rushing over to place a kiss on my cheek. It was so effortless, the way he did that now. I supposed that ease had always existed between us, in words and gestures, but the small ones like that kiss that were becoming more frequent were my favorite. The little ways he showed he cared for me no matter what terrors were going on around us, as if he simply couldn't resist.

I was craving them more and more.

"Did you see that?" he asked, placing a hand on my lower back to guide me to the next weapon.

"It was incredible," I answered. The way it had arched through the air once fired, the distance and precision a weapon so massive could achieve. It was a marvel. But what I really loved about it was the energy it gave Tolek. As he gushed about the process he'd learned this morning during the next two tests, there was a tangible buzz to his voice. It dulled the haunting shadows of his nightmares.

Tol always felt his emotions so deeply I thought I could reach out and touch them. *Life*, I thought. *Tolek is so full of life.* And places like this brought it out in him. Constantly seeking the next adventure, the next challenge.

Spirits, I wanted to bottle up his vivacity and drink it, if only so I could feel it with him. After all the grief and guilt I'd been wading through, I wanted to *live* with Tolek.

I gazed up at him as he explained the powder was pulverized rocks that fell from the mountains, and their residual magic, when burned, powered the cannons. His happiness was contagious, bubbling over into me until I thought my own might drown me.

When Cypherion left us to go test one of the cannons himself, I stretched up onto my toes and placed a kiss on Tolek's cheek.

"What was that for?" he asked, but even that one touch ignited the fire in his eyes.

I shrugged. "I'm feeling very grateful this morning."

He slung an arm around me and kept a hand on my skin— shoulder, waist, or even entwined with my own—for the remaining twenty cannon tests.

It was as the last one boomed that Ezalia's voice sliced through the morning.

Seron was at her side immediately, Cypherion, Tolek, and I joining them. "Change of plans," the chancellor panted, a frantic edge to her words.

Andrenas ran up, Jezebel and Vale on their heels. They were both dressed in leathers, weapons strapped to their bodies. I looked Ezalia over, tan dress cut to mid-thigh with a thick belt and sleeves. Coral cuffs around her wrists held small vials, and knives were strapped across her chest. Andrenas had similar garb and a long stretch of rope gathered at their waist.

Unease roiled through my gut.

"What's wrong?" I asked.

"A storm is rolling in from the south," Ezalia said.

Seron sprang into action, calling for Chorid. That prickling I'd felt in the air—it was the earliest hints of a squall.

"It's going to be a rough one," Ezalia added, lips pulling into a grim line. "Those islands are going to be buried under choppy waves and who knows what sediment after the storm. And the seas will be too rough to reach them during."

My stomach sank. If the platforms they'd singled out as an important spot to Gaveny were gone, if the emblem really was out there, we could lose our one chance.

Unite them.

"How long do we have?" I rushed.

"If we leave immediately, we might beat the storm," Ezalia said.

"We didn't finish charting our route," Andrenas commented with the only uneasy swallow I'd seen since meeting them. "But we'll have to trust in Gaveny now."

Follow the Angels, to death and dismay, or glory and grace.

"Where's Santorina?" Tolek asked, and I froze.

"She left with Leo this morning," Vale responded, braiding back her hair. "They're riding to a nearby town to work on her human training agenda and said they'd be back tonight."

"Spirits," I cursed. "We go without her, then. I'll leave a note."

"Nine is a good number," Ezalia encouraged, whispering something to Andrenas. She sent the warrior on their way to prepare the ship. "Three for each platform."

"Eight, you mean," Cypherion said, looking around and counting.

"I'm coming with you," Vale objected, understanding who he'd intended to leave behind.

Cyph's jaw ticked. "No, you're not."

"You're not the one who gets to decide that," the Starsearcher growled.

"It's not safe." I didn't know whether Cyph meant it because he didn't trust her and didn't want to have her on our team or if there was something else. He ground his teeth together, hands flexing as if that sentence wasn't what he'd actually wanted to say.

"For you or for me?" And Vale's stare—narrowed and daring—was layered with accusations.

"All right, we don't have time for this," I interrupted whatever Cypherion was about to snap. He closed his mouth, seeing my reason. "Vale, if you want to come, you may come."

In that moment, I didn't care about their feud. I admired her for wanting to help when we were charging into a storm, path uncharted.

"You three grab the rest of your weapons," Ezalia instructed Cypherion, Tolek, and me as she walked away. "Meet us at the south end of the cliffs as soon as you're ready."

Out over the sea, thunder boomed. As the storm rolled from the east, my own fearful clouds formed over my head.

~

PLUMES of deep gray formed on the horizon as we followed the Seawatchers down a set of narrow notches carved into the cliffside and leading to a black sand cove below. A small dock jutted out into the water. Our boots echoed hollowly against worn wood as we dutifully marched to the ship waiting for us.

"This is the only one ready on such short notice that can also withstand a harsher storm," Ezalia explained as she led us across the dock and up the ramp.

I helped Chorid untie the clean hitch knots securing the boat rocking in the water as tempests brewed across the horizon.

Standing at the bow minutes later, the wind whipped my hair around my face. I breathed steadily over the waves slapping wood below, muscles locked to battle the rolling sea beneath us. Tolek, Cypherion, and Jezebel stood beside me.

"You're all sure of the plan?" I asked. "We get to those platforms and follow any scorch marks or signs of heat we can detect." I didn't know if only the Seawatchers would feel the lingering Angel presence or if we could, too. "Once we find it, we get back to the ship as quickly as possible. All of us. Together."

It was as straightforward of a plan as we could have, but I couldn't dissuade the curling of my stomach as those islands rose into view, clouds hanging in the distance. The three land masses appeared made of piled rock, like an Angel's hand had precariously placed them there, and centuries had melded those boulders together.

"We'll be fine," Cypherion assured me. At my stare that argued we'd uttered that phrase so many times now and nearly hadn't been, he amended, "We'll be smart."

I took a deep breath. It was all I could ask when we didn't even know what we were searching for.

"What about her?" Jez asked, flicking a hesitant gaze at Cyph before tilting her head toward Vale. She stood at the rail, hands white-knuckled and eyes closed.

"She's reading," Cypherion muttered, distastefully.

"She's with you two," I said. Cyph opened his mouth to argue, but I held up a hand. "Ezalia said she's with Tolek and me on the center platform given it's the largest. I need you with her, though, Cypherion."

At that, he quieted and nodded.

Before I felt ready, the Seawatchers were dropping a heavy anchor. Three row boats lowered into the water, and we split into our teams.

As she was about to descend, I grabbed Vale's wrist. "Anything?"

"It's hard out here—so far from the temples." She chewed her lip, a flash of emotion I couldn't place in her olive eyes. "I saw a lot of successful paths, and some..." Her voice trailed off. "Searing light. Effervescent and burning with promise."

And that was what I needed.

"It's here then." My pulses kicked up at the confirmation. Knowing this mission might be worth it made climbing into the boat between Ezalia and Tolek easier.

Three rowboats speared out from the ship, each carrying three warriors with hearts pounding and weapons poised. Looking over the side of the boat, fish scurried beneath us. A few with long flicking tails jumped, hopping in and out of the water. One soared toward us, coming within inches of my face in a shock of rows of sharp, snapping teeth.

Ezalia pulled me back, using her oar to slap the fish back to the water.

"Those are pygmites," she said. "Do *not* get near them. They're small but those teeth can shred through human flesh in a matter of minutes."

A shiver crawled down my spine, and we paddled ahead in silence, with only the roaring waves to calm my nerves. With each stroke, I pulled out the mask of Revered that now felt vintage. The one that absorbed my inhibitions—didn't allow room for emotion.

For this, I needed it.

My blood roared in my ears as we narrowed in on the center island. It wasn't even the size of my family home in Palerman. Moss and seaweed draped across the boulders, like lace on a woman's figure.

Where it met the water, the rocks got smaller, turning to pebbles and eventually tiny grains of sand disappearing beneath lapping waves. The shores ebbed with prophetic secrets, wood scraping over them and drowning out the whispers as we pulled the rowboat ashore.

Before I could go further, Tolek turned me toward him, his hand gripping the back of my neck. His eyes searched my face, peeling apart every layer I'd hidden away. Every concern I was too afraid to voice. He saw it all, despite my mask. Took it all in so it balanced between us, rather than on my shoulders.

"It's going to be all right," he whispered, bending to press his lips to my forehead. "In and out."

"We get in, we get out," I said.

"I meant your breathing, but that, too." He smirked as he pulled away, earning a roll of my eyes. "Now let's go show the Angels what you've got."

Giving him my own appreciative smirk, I pulled Starfire from her sheath and walked up the beach to where Ezalia was waiting.

We started climbing, and halfway up, I gasped. Gouges cleaved some of the boulders. Large, immovable rocks that had somehow been sliced through.

"What did that?" I wondered aloud.

"I don't want to know," Tol said. "Come on."

Placing a hand on my lower back, he led me away from the site. But not before I quickly pressed my fingers to the rock. And felt the warmth within.

My second pulse was racing by the time we reached the plateaued top, and the rest of the small island spread before us. More of those scorch marks lined the stone, and each time I touched one, it flared with a dull heat. Like a wick after a flame had been extinguished.

The islands were evenly spaced out. Close enough that you could swim the distance if you had to, but with the pygmites' razor-sharp teeth prowling beneath the waves, I wasn't willing to try. Still, using the shell horns Ezalia had given us, we were able to call to the others.

To our right, Cypherion helped Jezebel and Vale up. The three turned to face us. Fifty feet of choppy, predator-infested water. That's all that separated these land masses. But they felt so much further.

"Ready?" I called through the mouth of the horn.

"We are," Cypherion's deep voice answered as if he was right next to me.

I looked over my shoulder to the third platform. Seron, Andrenas, and Chorid stood proud atop the ridge, looking like a unit of ocean warriors, bows and arrows ready to write a legend. Ezalia watched them with pride shining in her eyes.

"May the tides hold true and the farers find their way home," Seron called through his horn. Chills spread over my skin, and not because of the salty ocean spray off the rocks.

"Stay true," I called to my own warriors.

I tightened my hands around Starfire. Angelborn's encouragement beat at my back.

Tolek had his sword in hand and the Vincienzo dagger ready at his hip.

Ezalia's bow was loaded.

A seven-headed swamp monster guarded it, Barrett's voice said in my head. *Maybe it was simply a reptile.* I gritted my teeth against the fear.

With one deep breath that felt timed by the heavens, we stepped forward.

And the island on our left exploded.

Chapter Sixteen
Ophelia

Ezalia's scream could shatter glass.

Dust plumed in the air from the spot where the island had stood—Seron, Chorid, and Andrenas atop it. Rocks tumbled through the waves as the thing sank.

Sank. Like one wave had crested over it and swallowed the land with a massive maw of watery death.

It was gone. And in the place where it stood, crimson bloomed within the water.

The pygmites.

"What's happening?" Cypherion's voice echoed from the horn.

Ezalia was clamoring down the rock, weapons cast aside. Tolek ripped the horn from my grasp as I ran after her, telling the others what we were seeing.

Where the Seawatcher Chancellor scampered nimbly over seaweed clad rocks, I slipped on their strands, slicing my palms on stone. Spirits, please let her retrace our steps. I didn't know what set off that exploding whirlpool, but I didn't want to risk our island succumbing to one as well.

Had they triggered something without realizing?

And Ezalia was frantic, limbs moving impossibly fast to reach the shoreline.

When I finally caught up with her, she was on hands and knees, dragging in ragged breaths. Eyes glued to the horizon, fingers dug into the rocky sand. Salt water lapped at her knees as she screamed.

And screamed.

And screamed.

One name: Seron.

It tore through me. And I sank beside her on the beach, telling the Angels to wait a fucking minute and stop toying with our lives as if they didn't matter.

I wrapped an arm around this warrior whom I'd come to admire in so many ways, letting her loss bleed into me. And I swore the Angels would answer for these injustices.

"Seron," she breathed what could have been minutes later, I wasn't sure. And she pushed onto her knees. "Seron!" She took off running into the tide.

Following her desperate stare, I saw it.

In the waves between our island and where the third had stood, Seron clung to a piece of driftwood. His other hand clutched something. The water was washed with scarlet around him as each ebb brought him closer.

Ezalia tried to dive into the current, but I snatched her around the waist.

"Let go of me!" She thrashed.

"If you go in there, the pygmites will get you."

"I don't care—"

"You can't help him if you're dead."

She fell still at that.

Agonizingly, we waited until he was close enough we could risk the short swim, and then dove in. Sharp teeth nipped at my legs, but they couldn't break through my boots.

The harsh, stormy current slammed against my cheeks. I kicked pygmites without remorse. One shot out of the waves, arcing over my head. Treading water, I ripped my dagger from my thigh and jammed the creature through the gullet as it aimed for Ezalia's shoulder.

She had one vision right now: Seron. And I protected her back.

He was muttering something as she reached him. *He was alive.*

But the red in the water was darkening every second. I didn't know how much longer he'd stay that way.

Ezalia pulled something from Seron's grasp. A rope. She looped it around him and tugged to tighten it. Then, with a wide-eyed nod at me, we began the short swim back to shore. We'd only gone about twenty feet out—but it felt so much further with the weight of Seron's life weighing us down.

My throat and the pygmite bites burned from salt water, limbs straining and body water-logged. Tolek was on the beach as we trudged from the waves.

He pulled me up, hissing at the marks covering my skin. They weren't severe, though, already sealing over.

"Seron," I breathed.

Tolek pulled Seron from the water, and—

Spirits.

His legs were shredded.

From right above the knee, they were nothing more than strips of flesh and scraped bones. Whether it was from the blast, the pygmites, or both, I didn't know.

Ezalia ripped two vials from her wrist strap, pulled the corks free with her teeth, and dumped blue liquids over what was left of her partner's legs. He writhed beneath the sizzling tonics, smoke curling up from the injuries. Ezalia only bent over him, pressing her lips to his head, and muttered, "*I'm sorry,*" repeatedly.

When the steam cleared, the blood had staunched. It didn't have to be said—Seron wouldn't walk again.

He was breathing, though. Clammy skin sweat-soaked and pale, eyes fogged over. But alive.

Lifting a limp hand, Seron tugged on the rope he'd been dragging.

It was only then that I realized where it had come from.

Andrenas. The rope they'd had on their belt when we left.

They'd thrown it out to him when the island went down, so they could remain together. I didn't know what happened to Chorid, but these two had at least tried to stay intact. And now...

I followed the rope to the tide.

Found a ragged lump of flesh at its end, victim to the beasts in the water after the explosion.

They didn't even look like a person anymore. Didn't resemble anything that had once lived.

I fell to my knees in the waves and silently screamed a violent prayer. I didn't know who it was to—certainly not the Angels— but I asked someone for the revenge these warriors deserved for taking on a battle that shouldn't have been their own. For Chorid and Andrenas and all those who had died too soon to be given their peace.

And I swore I'd see to it.

I curled my hands in the sand for one last grounding moment, then shot to my feet and raced back up the beach.

"Ophelia." Tolek grabbed my elbow and swung me around to face him. I had my mask sealed up tighter than ever, though. Wouldn't even let him in.

"Ezalia," I said softly, looking at the chancellor where she lay over her partner. Tolek's stare burned into the side of my face, but I wouldn't break. I couldn't. We still had a task to complete. "Let us help you take him back to the ship."

"No," she responded, wiping her eyes. "He's okay, he's sleeping." She'd wrapped his wounds with seaweed. I didn't know what it did. A Seawatcher tactic, I supposed. "He's better here, by the water."

"You don't have to come with us," I offered.

Her answering stare was determined. "I do."

Tolek carried a sleeping Seron away from the tide, resting his limp but breathing body against the rocks. As long as our island stood, he'd be safe here.

And if it didn't...then we were all at the Angel's dismay.

"Let's go," I said, turning before I could let fear work its way any further within me.

When we got back to the top of the ridge, Cypherion, Jezebel, and Vale were waiting anxiously on their island.

"Seron's alive," I said into the horn. They knew what it meant for the others.

"Sticking to the plan?" Angels bless Cypherion for knowing

we needed to stay focused in this moment. We'd already lost so much time, the clouds on the horizon now rolling above us.

"Yes. But move carefully."

I didn't let myself say any more than that. I didn't want to think about what could happen. Couldn't say goodbyes.

Hesitantly, I stretched a foot out. Tapped a toe on the rock ahead. Nothing happened.

I chanced a jump forward, landing lightly on my feet. No reaction.

Looking over my shoulder, I nodded at Tolek and Ezalia for them to follow in my steps. And I trailed the subtle residue of scorch marks as they painted a blackened pattern across the rocky surface.

With each step, I sank further into Angelborn's pulse. It wasn't hers, though. It was the shard of Damien that swung on my neck. The piece of fossilized Angel power that reckoned with my own beating heart and instilled a second strain of life. I didn't know how it worked, another piece in this great puzzle, but I allowed it to take over my instincts now.

It was a part of me, a part of the Angels. It could guide me to one of its missing seven.

There wasn't any vegetation or soil for roots on this small island. You could see clear over the circumference from the center. And when we got there, a starburst of burn marks radiated from it.

"There's something," I breathed, standing in the central point of the island and watching my feet. Slick gray rock stood impenetrable beneath my boots, but something was alive here. It called to me.

"Do you guys see or feel anything?" Tolek called through the horn.

"There's indentations in some of the rocks," Cyph yelled back. "And those burn marks on the side of the island facing yours. But nothing else."

"Is anything warm?" Ezalia asked. They volleyed questions back and forth, but I studied the pattern of burn marks beneath my feet.

Spikes burst out from the center where I stood. Eight in total, every second one longer than the first.

Like a four-pointed star with smaller ones between them.

The longest stretched to my right and up diagonally. Crouching down, I pressed a palm to the ground. I cursed when the rock burned me.

"It's here." I lifted my palm to show Tolek and Ezalia the already healing blisters.

Bending back down, I traced the star again, relishing in the heat this time. But—

I screamed out, the sound rough and from the depths of me.

Something writhed beneath the flesh of my arm. Squirmed along that scar from Kakias's dagger and pulled at my skin. As I clutched my arm to my chest, something else shot toward the pain, an opposing force within me.

"What is it?" Tolek's eyes were frantic.

I clenched my teeth, forced the words out. "I—don't know. It's—it's...Spirits, it fucking *hurts*."

This hadn't happened before. The scar had plagued me—had been painful—but this was excruciating. Was Kakias closer? Was this her power digging into me?

Tenderly, Tolek took my arm. The edges of the scar were red, little tendrils of black dancing out from it like tiny fissures. That certainly had not happened before. It reminded me of the dark veins on the inside of my wrist from my Curse.

"Holy Angels," I panted. Without thinking, I grabbed my emblem necklace and held it tight. Willed whatever power resided in it into my body, to target the taint in that scar as it had with Kakias's power during the Battle of Damenal and *push it out*.

Just get it fucking out.

Slowly, the pain began ebbing away. The Angelblood in my veins stifled it. But the sensation stayed imprinted on my memory.

"It's okay," I shakily reassured Tolek.

We didn't have time to question any of it right now. Instead, I focused on the second pulse thrumming within me and tried to collect myself. The Angel emblem was somewhere on this land mass.

"Tell Cyph—"

An ear-splitting screech drowned my words as a giant creature reared up out of the water.

Not any creature.

An alpheous.

CHAPTER SEVENTEEN
OPHELIA

THE SERPENTINE BODY SHOT TWENTY FEET ABOVE US, navy scales glistening with the sea. When it roared a second time, its spiked fan flared around its face. Fangs gleamed, and solid dark eyes searched.

Then, it dove. Straight for the rock—spearing for us.

Ezalia and I rolled to one side, Tolek to the other. The alpheous slammed straight into the island, then reared up again.

It splashed back into the water, diving, diving, diving. Silence echoed. We waited, stood back-to-back to watch our surroundings.

On the other platform, our friends did the same.

The hair on the back of my neck rose, a chill slithering up my spine. And the alpheous sprang from the water behind me.

We dodged, and this time, when its fangs hit the rock, it left deep grooves.

I looked at Tolek, brows raised. "There's our answer."

"I didn't really want to know," he panted. Lifting his sword toward the giant serpent, he waited for it to attack again.

I held Starfire tightly. Behind us, Ezalia fired off an arrow. It landed in the fan around its face, but the creature barely flinched. Instead, it looked down. I didn't know how I knew it was searching us, but somehow I did.

And when its solid onyx eyes landed on me, I swore it grinned.

And I grinned right back.

Thunder cracked, and the skies opened, a patter of rain falling on us and sizzling against heated stone. The storm was here, in both beast and nature.

Whether this thing was a creature of the gods or a wild, tainted beast like those we'd seen before, I didn't care. I vowed I'd beat it if it tried to stand in my way.

So when it shot back toward me, it's maw dripping, forked tongue lashing, I ducked and rolled beneath it. The rock seared right into my skin, blistering around my leathers. But I swung Starfire up and across the underside of its throat.

Its scales were impossibly thick. My sword only left a scratch.

"Fucking Spirits," I growled, pushing to my feet. I wiped rain from my eyes.

"We don't need your damn sacrifices right now, Alabath," Tolek yelled, and I swore there was actual anger in his voice. "We need to get out of here in one piece."

"That's the plan, Vincienzo," I called back, dodging another attempt of the alpheous.

Then, a second shriek pierced the air.

Another serpent, this one silver and larger than the first, emerged from the water, slamming into the other platform.

My heart almost beat right out of my chest as my sister was nearly impaled on those foot-long fangs. As she—

Something crashed into my gut. I flew backward, air cascading from my lungs as I hit the rock. The world spun for a moment, my lungs clenching as the alpheous's shadow rose over me.

It had flung me back with the underside of its tail. At least it hadn't been the spiked top, or I'd be bleeding out now.

Head spinning, I blinked rapidly and caught my breath. Ezalia continued to fire arrows at the beast, crimson now shining against its navy scales.

Throwing a hand on the rock beside me, I rolled as that spiked tail battered the rock where I'd been a moment before.

And something in my palm sparked like pure *fire*.

My hand pressed into the largest point of the starburst scorch mark. And the outline *glowed*. A gold radiance that called to my blood and bones, turquoise fringing the edges.

I followed the river of Angellight through the rock with my eyes. It trickled down a barely imperceptible path and landed feet away among a smooth pile of rocks.

Both alpheous were still attacking, still desperate and hungry for us, but I pushed up and ran to that source.

I scraped my palms across it, ignoring the burning, and searched for an opening, a piece that may come off. Anything that could be the emblem.

Tolek appeared at my side.

"It's in there, I know it is," I panted. "We need—"

"I have an idea," Tolek said, watching the alpheous rise above Ezalia. He whistled, and the beast snapped his attention to us like an obedient pet. Thunder cracked overhead, lightning splitting the gray sky.

Picking up a rock, Tolek squared his feet before the hiding spot and chucked it at the giant serpent. Lured the thing to chase us.

And at the very last moment, we dove.

The alpheous went snout first into the rock, shattering it. It's tail thrashed, fully on land now, and I thought I heard Tolek grunt, but when I looked, he was glaring at the serpent.

Before the alpheous could shake off the impact, an arrow went through the soft flesh at the back of its neck, piercing deep enough to kill.

A roar echoed from the other island. We all spun to see Cypherion's scythe brace across the second creature's open jaw.

Those fangs were an inch from snapping his body in half. My heart lurched into my throat.

But Vale was running up one of the rocky inclines. Without pause, she jumped. Launched herself right onto the creature's back, narrowly missing the spikes along its spine, and used a small dagger to repeatedly stab it.

It didn't die—those wounds were too small to kill it, but it roared, hot rancid breath blowing through Cyph's hair as it pulled back and writhed, trying to dislodge the unwelcome rider on its back.

Cypherion stood, shocked, trying to make sense of who had saved him.

The alpheous thrashed enough that Vale flew from its back, landing on a bed of seaweed near the shore. Cyph screamed like a feral creature, running toward it.

And as that silver serpent tried to rise again, the dead one on our island moved. Arrow still in its neck, wound bleeding, its limp body dragged across rock and slid upwards, as if carried by another entity or a wind.

Up, up, up it went, still dead but controlled by something, until it was hanging above the water.

And it swung with the force of a thousand warriors toward its friend. Toward—

Jezebel.

My sister stood with her hands raised, her fingers splayed. And where she turned, the alpheous turned, too. Where she directed, the lifeless body spun and hurled into the attacking serpent in a head-to-head collision.

Two scaled bodies tangled and splashed back into the water. Jezebel dropped her arms to her sides.

From here, it was clear her small frame was quaking. Whatever power she had displayed weakened her knees.

The rest of us stared.

No more attacks came. Rain lashed down around us.

Finally, Jezebel's tired voice came through the horn. "Get your Spirits-damned emblem so we can get out of here, Ophelia."

With the navy alpheous gone, the rubble of the rock it had crushed was easier to pick through. I followed that heated shard pulse within me, throwing aside chunks of stone until I found it nestled between soft layers of moss like a treasure within an oyster.

A tiny, sea-foam-green piece of glass. Round and smooth, it burned where it rolled across my palm. I grasped it tighter, relief washing over me, loosening my joints.

We'd found it.

We had a third emblem.

The storm was picking up around us, rain falling in fat drops. Puddles formed in the rocky crevices, and waves slapped the shores.

"We need to go." Ezalia was already on her way down the platform to her partner.

Together, we heaved Seron into the rowboat. Ezalia held him as Tolek and I battled rough waters to get back to the ship. The others beat us there and helped get the injured Seawatcher inside the captain's quarters, protected from the storm.

Vale collapsed beside him, telling us she'd watch over him as she nursed the ankle she'd sprained jumping on the alpheous's back.

Tolek, Cypherion, and I followed Ezalia's expert instructions as she guided the ship ahead of the storm to get us back to Brontain safely.

But standing at the stern, quiet and contemplative and refusing to speak, was Jezebel. As I watched her, I thought of what she'd done—the demonstration of power over that sea serpent.

And fear dug its nails into my gut.

Still, it had saved us. Had ensured no one else got injured or worse.

Removing the pearl from the pocket of my leathers, I held it tight within my fist. The heat embedded itself in my skin.

And as I clenched this tiny shard of power, I couldn't help the realizations from beating down on me. That had been a trial unlike any other—unpredictable and deadly. There were four more of these tokens to be found, each likely guarded as fiercely as this one had been. Why, though?

What were they for?

Why did they require such strong protection? Who *didn't* want them found? And why had the spear come so easily, then?

Finding the Seawatcher emblem only raised another world of unknowns, but one thing was certain: this was going to be a hunt harsher than what we'd assumed.

So, we had one more emblem, one more shard of Angel power that I needed to unite, but at what cost?

PART TWO
NIKE

CHAPTER EIGHTEEN
TOLEK

"You can have the room," Jezebel said. "I need an hour to myself."

She hadn't spoken to any of us on the way back from the platforms. Now, she insisted on a walk, and Ophelia had shut herself in their bathing chamber.

Baby Alabath looked at me with this vulnerable expression that made me feel like a boulder was sitting on my chest. I wanted to protect her, even if space was what she needed.

Selfishly, it worked for my plan anyway.

"Not a minute more," I swore.

The spot on my side where the alpheous' snout had rammed into me ached as I twisted to shut the door to Ophelia's room after Jez left. I had an hour, though, and I wouldn't waste it on my damn ribs or the pain in my right knee.

But when I turned to the two beds in the center of the room, a small bottle waited on the one I knew was Ophelia's—neatly made where Jezebel's had rumpled sheets. Dark green glass reflected the moonlight streaming in through the window, a piece of wrinkled parchment beneath it.

Contraceptive tonic—you're welcome.

-J

Fucking, Jezzie. She found it within herself to mess with me despite whatever power she'd displayed today. A shiver worked down my spine at the memory, and damn was I curious about it, but I'd let Ophelia talk to her first.

Throwing the note in the fire, I stormed back to the door. A small click sounded through the room as the handle locked. Perhaps I'd have more than an hour—if she couldn't get in.

I tucked the tonic under the bed and checked it couldn't be seen. Jezebel loved to joke with *me*, but I didn't want Ophelia to think I'd brought that. Didn't want her to think I would pressure her into anything when we'd set clear boundaries.

I was forward, didn't hide much from that girl ever since I poured my heart out on her sleeve, but that was the point. She knew *all* of my intentions for her. Maybe I didn't tell her about the ones that kept me up at night imagining every different way I could have her, but she knew it.

And I laid them out before her to take when she was ready. To walk across and leave footprints on my soul. As long as she was coming toward me, I'd gladly suffer all those imprints.

I'd wait an eternity if she wanted.

Tonight, though, I didn't have an eternity. That lock wouldn't hold an angry, sleep-deprived Alabath for long. Particularly not one who held...well, whatever it was Jezzie had been keeping secret.

I settled down on the neatly-made bed, untied my boots, and leaned back against the pillows. The orange glow of the fire cast a wavering circle on the floor, dancing shadows piercing the circumference. Where it crept across the dark wood and met moonlight, the two bled together, hot flame and icy night contrasting and conflicting, but somehow fitting. How two things could be so opposite, made of entirely differing properties, and still be made for one another, was beautiful—

The bathing chamber door finally swung open and every poetic thought fled from my mind.

"By the ever-damned Angels, Vincienzo!" Ophelia gasped as she strode out, long legs on display under maroon silk. "What are you doing in here?"

She finished tying her robe, crossing her arms in a way that only pushed her breasts up and had my attention in an instant.

By the Spirits, I scolded myself, *get it together, Vincienzo*. It wasn't like I hadn't seen her in less before…and always had the same damn reaction. Been hiding it for as long as I could remember.

So I tucked my hands behind my head, kicked off my boots, and crossed my feet on her bed, plastering on the smirk she was weak for. "Just waiting to say goodnight."

"You let yourself in?" Her brows flicked up, eyes flitting toward the door she'd come out of. I could practically read the thoughts coursing through her magnificent mind.

"Surprised I didn't run right in there while you were in the bath?" I laughed.

"Well, truthfully, yes." Her arms fell to her sides, and it was an effort to not laugh again at the adorably confused crease in her brow. Ophelia wasn't often caught unaware. Any time I was one step ahead of her, I cherished it.

"I may jokingly test boundaries, Alabath, but I'm always going to respect your wishes."

"I know that." Her face softened, losing the rest of that mask she wore for the world so often, sometimes she forgot to take it off. "Things seemed to have"—a shrug—"progressed."

She ran a hand up the scar from Kakias that twisted my fucking gut every time I saw her flinch over it. Magenta eyes went to the three items on the dresser: her emblem necklace, Barrett's ring, and the new pearl we'd acquired today.

And those walls tumbled down within her tightly built frame.

"Ophelia," I whispered. Scooting to the edge of her bed, I held out an arm.

The wrong arm, stupidly. Because when she curled into my side, I winced, and those shrewd eyes caught it.

"What's wrong?" she asked, pushing away from me.

Not in the Spirit-guarded hell.

I pulled her back. I'd spent too long not being able to act like I wanted to hold her—no way was I letting go now.

But she kept her narrowed stare on me, picking apart my tells.

I sighed. "I got hit today. The alpheous—straight to the ribs."

"Tol!" She shot up, unbuttoning my shirt and pulling it aside with hands wracked by tremors so slight, others might not notice.

She gasped at the mottled, dark purple bruise spread across my ribs.

Shit, it did look worse than I remembered. Maybe it was her worried eyes on it making the pain flare—another flaw I needed to hide.

Ophelia was up before I could respond, tugging her robe tighter and padding around the foot of the bed. "I'll get Rina."

"Hang on there, Alabath." I grabbed her wrist, careful not to react to the flare of pain through my side at the sharp movement. She was probably right—I should see Santorina. But... "Sit for a second."

I tugged her closer; her steps were reluctant. Angels, she was so gentle—a word I had never associated with Ophelia until I woke up in the infirmary. Grabbing her hips, sinking my fingers into the cool maroon silk, I pulled her closer again until her hands were braced on my shoulders.

"Tol," she murmured, her eyes glued on that bruise.

Absolutely not.

"All right, then," I sighed, and slid my hands down her body. Wrapping them around her bare thighs, I lifted her. She clasped my neck as she squealed, but I sat her across my hips. With her thighs bracing mine, I settled back against the pillows. "These smell good," I said, sniffing the sheets. "They smell like you."

She rolled her eyes. "You need to take care of this." Touch featherlight, she ran fingertips over my bruise. She eyed it as if a look that searing would erase any pain I'd ever felt. Didn't she know she did that just by existing?

"I will. After. Jezebel only gave me an hour, and we've already wasted time."

"For what?" Her eyes narrowed.

I brushed a strand of hair behind her ear, cupped her cheek. "I wanted to make sure you're okay after everything today. You snapped those walls up pretty quickly out there."

Her head cocked to the side for a second, but she shook it quickly. "I'm fine. Physically at least." We both looked at the scar on her arm.

The scream she'd released echoed in my ears, and dammit, I

never wanted to hear that sound again. *I won't*, I swore. She'd never feel pain like that again. The images from my nightmares tried to rear up, but I forced them away. My fingers curled tighter around her hip as if they could sear that promise right through the silk and into her skin. Mark her with it.

"And not physically?"

She sighed and finally met my eyes. "I'm fucking terrified, Tolek."

And it was the way her voice cracked on my name that tore down the rest of those shields she kept up for the world. Ophelia took coaxing, and I'd always done—would always do—that for her so she could work through the emotions she kept bottled up, too stubborn to lay them bare.

"Terrified of what?" I ran a hand up and down her arm, softly over the scar as if it wasn't even there. Didn't change a piece of her.

"Terrified because you all could have died today. Because two people *did* die today, and Seron will never walk again, and it was by pure coincidence none of our family was on that platform." Her voice was rising now, words heated and torn. "And it was for me! You're all searching for these emblems because I carry an Angelcurse. This—this—I don't even know what it is because I haven't gotten any answers!"

She was breathing quickly now, hands gripping my shoulders.

"We all knew what we were getting ourselves into," I soothed. "We would never let you risk your life alone."

"But I'm the one that's destined for it," she shrieked. "I'm the one meant to, so none of you should have to!"

"If you're destined for it, then we are, too." I kept my voice calm, not stoking the fire she was barely controlling. That wasn't what she needed this time. Now, she needed to be tempered.

"No, that's not—"

"Don't you dare argue with me, Alabath, or I'll find a different use for that mouth of yours." That stunned her into silence. Then, a quick laugh escaped her. "This Angelcurse is your destiny? Fine. Then write it into my fate, too. Because *you're* my destiny." I gripped her by the back of the neck, tugging her until our foreheads were pressed together. "You're my destiny, Alabath.

Infinitely yours, and for whatever waits beyond. And though they may not mean it in the same way—or I hope they don't—your sister, Cypherion, Santorina...they'd all say the same. This fight is all of ours."

Ophelia's eyes dropped to her scar again, and I whispered, "She won't get you." I would be strong enough to protect her.

Visions of marble stairs and sharp daggers and blood—so much blood—filtered through my mind again.

Failure.

"I know." Ophelia brushed off my comment, walls snapping back up.

All of my fear vanished at her dismissive tone. She truly didn't get what I'd do for her, did she?

"No. Listen to me, Alabath. *Nothing* will happen to you, so long as my heart beats." Unless I—no, my mind couldn't go there right now. "That queen will die long before you do, and you will get the long, happy life you deserve."

For a beat of silence, we sat there, looking at each other. Every word I'd said sat between us as she took them in one by one. As she counted the amber specks in my eyes she said she loved so much, and I counted her breaths. As she picked apart each syllable I'd spoken, testing them for holes, for a hint of weakness.

Keep looking, Alabath, I blinked at her. *I dare you to find a lie.*

She leaned a little closer and did what she did when she didn't know what else to say—pressed her lips to mine and said everything with that little touch. Except this time, her hands slipped up my shoulders, tightening behind my neck. Her fingers curled in my hair, and—fucking Angels—she rolled her hips against me; every good intention I had went out the window.

A few more seconds—

My hand tightened on her waist on its own, grinding her against me, and the other tangled in her hair. A small moan slipped up her throat. Damn Spirits, that nearly undid me.

"Okay," I breathed against her lips. "Let's calm down." I needed to, because it would only take the slightest touch from her to push me to the point of no return, and she was scared and worrying right now. I wouldn't have her like this for the first time.

"Calm down?" she asked through swollen lips and lust-filled eyes I'd be thinking about later.

"Alabath," I groaned, falling back against the pillow.

"I'm...not ready." Dammit—the apology in her voice? She had *nothing* to be sorry for.

"Look at me." I slipped a finger beneath her chin, drawing her eyes. "You never have to explain yourself with me." She was tunneling into her past. Restless energy had her fingers toying with her pin on my leathers, so, I added, "If we don't stop now, I won't be able to stop at all, and leaving tomorrow will be a lot harder if *you* can't walk."

Her eyes lit up—hungry and desiring. Damn me if it wasn't one of the most beautiful sights.

Leaning forward, I gave her one more kiss, let this one linger, then lifted her off my lap as the door handle rattled.

"Tolek!" Jezebel shouted, banging on the door. "You weren't supposed to lock me out."

"You locked it?" Ophelia laughed, pulling her robe tighter.

I shrugged. "She deserved it." My eyes flicked to where the contraceptive tonic hid under Ophelia's bed, but it wasn't visible.

"You're leaving?" she asked as I shoved my feet into my boots.

"I need to go take care of this." I waved a hand at the evident bulge straining against my leathers as Jezzie pounded on the door again, wood shuddering. Damn, her fists were strong. *Remember to never fight her, especially with that chilling death power.* "And you need to go take care of that."

The shadow of everything that had happened with her sister passed over her face, taking the little joy we'd found with it. I'd have to get better at keeping it away longer. Or never leave her side.

"Hey." I stepped forward, kissing her forehead one more time. "Talk to her. I bet she has a lot of answers." Starting with how she wielded that power and where the fuck it came from.

"I'm worried about her."

"She's as tough as you are. She learned from the best—takes about as long to open up as the best, too." She glared at me briefly for that one. "My point is, she's going through something. She'll talk about it eventually."

"Tolek!" Another series of pounding. "You better not be in my bed!"

"Now there's an idea." I swung the door open. "I'll have to remember that for next time."

Jezebel shoved past me. Eyes sweeping over the room and finding it safe, she climbed onto her bed and crossed her arms, a wine bottle dangling from her hand. The pink silk nightgown she already wore was almost identical to her sister's.

"I did you a favor," she growled.

"We'll discuss your *favor* later," I swore, eyes flicking under the bed again. Before Ophelia could ask, I added, "Good night, Alabaths."

"Go see Santorina!" Ophelia called after me.

Sticking my head through the door at the last second, I winked. "Whatever you say."

Chapter Nineteen
Ophelia

The door clicked closed after Tolek, and the easy joy carrying me a moment ago went with him. I collected myself as quickly as possible, dragging in a long breath and releasing it. The heat budding within me cooled just as slowly.

Tolek Vincienzo really was going to kill me. In a head rush of my own lust-filled dreams—that's how I'd go. And I didn't think I'd mind. Utter black out, all that would be left was desire and thoughts of his lips against mine.

I couldn't let my thoughts go down that path right now, though. Couldn't use him to avoid what was happening with Jezebel. Instead, I stifled them for later as I toyed with the pillows on my bed.

Jezebel's baiting tone followed Tolek out the door, and a heaviness settled between us. Clearing her throat, she unfolded her legs and drifted to the writing desk, shuffling papers out of the way.

"Drink?" Jezebel asked. She held up a bottle I hadn't noticed, crisp white wine sloshing behind the condensation on the glass. She poured two without waiting for my response.

"You don't like when I drink," I reminded her as she handed me one.

"I'd rather you have one for this conversation." It was the avoidance of her tawny eyes and the nervous purse of her lips that convinced me—as if there was more she longed to let out, but she wasn't ready yet.

I took a small sip, waiting for her to settle again. Her hand went to her collarbone absently, falling when it didn't find her necklace.

Takes about as long to open up as the best, too, Tolek had claimed. He was right; my sister and I were two sides of the same coin, outwardly presenting—defending—in different ways, but deep down, that need to smother what we didn't understand was intrinsic and toxic within us both. I'd be damned if I let her make my mistakes.

What had worked to get me to start opening up, though?

Space and safety.

Tolek thought he was smart with his gentle prodding—and I'd give him credit because it worked—but it worked *because* he didn't pressure me. He allowed me to come to terms with things in my own way, on my own time. And that made me want to do it always, I'd realized. Because with him, I was comfortable. I wasn't judged. I was *safe.*

I'd sit here all night if Jezzie needed time to form her words.

Luckily, it was only a few minutes of the crackling fire filling the silence until she opened her mouth. "So today..."

"Thank the Spirits." I sighed.

She laughed. "I was trying to see if I could outlast you. You're learning patience, sister."

"Trying." I rolled my eyes. Then, we both turned serious once more, facing each other from our respective beds. "What was that, Jezzie?"

"I don't know." She ran a finger around the rim of her glass. "Not entirely."

It was the same hollow voice she'd adopted after the winged beast attacked us on our journey to the Undertaking all those months ago. The one she'd been shaking off through the months in Damenal but that had taken over again after the battle.

"Tell me what you do know, and we'll figure the rest out together." I scooted to the edge of my bed and gave her my undivided attention.

"It's going to sound ridiculous—I thought it was for years."

Years?

"I've been cursed by the Angels and can create Angellight with my blood and pieces of metal, Jezzie. I think the concept of ridiculousness is relative."

She tilted her head, considering. Why *had* both of us been gifted these powers?

Finally, she said, voice strong and sure, "I can communicate with spirits."

My glass nearly slipped from my hand, because of all the things she could have admitted, that wasn't one I'd expected. But I tried not to show my surprise, taking a long sip of wine. Cool notes of pears and summer berries lingered on my tongue as I decided what to say next.

Ease into it, I figured.

"Like a Soulguider?" It could make sense. We both had the blood of the minor clan from our grandmother. Granted, her line was weak, but it was there.

"Not exactly." With a surge of confidence, she leaned forward. "I can't guide them. I only *hear* them. It first happened during the war, when the battles moved closer to Palerman. Spirits, when they tore through the city...they took out so many of our people, so close, so loud—they were *so loud.*" She swallowed, eyes clenching shut as the horrors played out in her memory, voices likely rushing through her ears.

Angels, my own blood chilled watching her like this. Hastily, I clamored to her bed and pulled her into my arms.

"There were so many of them," she whispered against my shoulder. "So many dying, shouting, asking for one last minute, for their families."

With trembling hands, one still holding her glass, she tried to cover her ears. Smother those memories. She'd only been fourteen. *Fourteen years old.* Barely of age to train formally—not an adult by any means. And she'd been drowning in the voices of the desperate and dying.

"I'm so sorry." I kissed her hair, running a hand down her spine. Slowly, tension leaked from her body.

When she sat up, her eyes were bloodshot, but she didn't shed a single tear. It almost unsettled me.

"I hadn't noticed it before then. I think it always happened, but that was the first time it was so heavy I couldn't excuse it as an odd draft of wind or whisper from a stranger."

"Why didn't you say something?"

She gave me a look that broke a bit of the tension between us. Right—secrets. That's what we used to do.

"I told Erista," she continued. "We were already together, so I asked her more about Soulguider experiences. I thought maybe it was the magic developing and, for some reason, my blood tended toward Grandmother's instead of Mystique."

It was possible, I supposed. To have a minority bloodline overshadow the majority. I didn't know much about it, but with the magic comprising warriors, I assumed there was a way.

"It isn't, though." Jezebel finished her wine and set the glass on the side table. "E said there's no division of Soulguider power that functions like mine. She dug through history and couldn't find a single mention of it."

"Maybe it wasn't recorded?" I offered.

A shrug. "That's possible. If it's atypical, it could mean whoever else had it didn't want to report it. Maybe they thought it would label them as an outcast." Her brows pulled together, eyes dropping to the array of decorative shells on the side table. She picked up a small gray-streaked one and twirled it between her fingers.

"It doesn't make you an outcast." I turned her chin to face me. "It makes you powerful, Jez."

"Power can create unintended boundaries." That small voice was back.

"It can." I nodded. I wouldn't lie to her. Power was delicate. How it was handled, even more so. "But if we're aware of that, and work against it, we can ensure it does not happen."

She nodded, closing her grip around the shell. I scooted back to give her space, crossing my legs.

"Is there more you know?"

She brushed a strand of hair behind her ear. "You remember that winged creature from before the Undertaking?"

"Do I remember the terrifying, strange beast that nearly killed my sister? Can't say I do."

Jezebel hit my arm lightly, lips pulling into a line when she realized she'd nearly hit my scar from Kakias. After looking at it for a long moment, she said, "That's the reason it didn't kill me. I could hear it."

"Its spirit?"

"I think so." She nodded. "It was the first time I'd ever communicated with a *living* thing, though. Before it had only been the dying. Before their spirits crossed over, when the barrier was weakest."

Realization crashed into me. That beast had *looked* at Jezebel. Truly looked at her—recognized her unlike any of us. And then, it had fled. And she sank into herself, unraveling a power none of us knew about.

This opened up so many more questions. I picked one to start. "Did it say anything?"

"It was screaming—roaring—like it was as surprised as we were and couldn't get its bearings. And then it kept saying one thing: *I wake, I wake, I wake.*"

"I wake," I mumbled.

She nodded. "I haven't been able to figure out what it means. When Erista was in Damenal, we searched for answers every day." Another kernel of understanding—where she kept disappearing to all those weeks. "I even went to the Spirit Volcano a few times, trying to find answers."

"Jezebel, you can't," I gasped. A warrior could only go into the volcano twice: once for the Undertaking, and once for their death.

"I didn't go in." She shook her head. "Just...listened. Tried to speak to them."

"Could you?"

"Only the dying." I saw the Palerman memories shudder behind her eyes, again. And then, my heart cracked with another realization.

"The Battle of Damenal?" I asked quietly.

"The worst day of my life." She swallowed, lips trembling. "I heard...all of them." A deep breath, like she was gathering confidence. "Father..."

My chest caved under what she'd had to experience that day. Hearing our father's spirit as it left him.

"He said goodbye," she continued, and I didn't know how she wasn't sobbing in my arms at the memory. "He said he loves us and he's proud of us. Reminded us to protect each other."

That nearly undid the last restraint I had on my own tears, but I forced them back. For him, for her, I held myself together.

"I'm glad I got to hear it," she admitted, and there was a peaceful smile playing at the corners of her lips. "I got to hear him say goodbye. To promise him we would protect each other."

I supposed that was the blessing in it.

"Did he know?"

She shook her head. "I never told him. I wanted to, but there was never a time. Or...that's what I kept telling myself." I understood; I had done the same with my own curse. "I regret it now."

"Me, too," I said quietly, gripping her hand.

"I told Grandmother, though." Jezebel livened a bit, voice pitching up. "When she was in Damenal for the induction, I told her everything."

"Did she have any sage advice?"

"No, but"—her brows creased—"I think she already knew."

A shiver worked through me, but I understood. Our grandmother's predictions devolved sporadically with age, but still, some of them had to hold true. Her clan could see where a person's soul would end up. If Jezebel could communicate with spirits, it was safe to say this power would hold influence on her life's path.

I only hoped, if our grandmother saw it, it didn't mean it would lead to an early end.

Shoving aside the morbid thought, I asked, "So, what happened today?"

"I...reached for the serpent." Jezebel frowned, brows pinching. "Everything was going wrong. That thing nearly killed you and Tolek, the Seawatchers were gone, and the second one was about to take out both Cyph and Vale. I didn't even think; I lashed out and grabbed on to the alpheous's spirit."

"But it was already dead." She'd said she could only speak to those who were dying.

"It takes a while for a spirit to leave a body," she explained. "Even longer because that thing was so large. I could still hear it."

"And you told it to attack the other?"

She shook her head. "No, I did that. Somehow—and I can promise you this has never happened before—I controlled the dying alpheous and used it to attack its friend."

I tilted my head. That added a new layer to her power. Nerves slipped into her voice as she explained it.

"Are you worried?" I prodded.

"I wasn't until today, because I thought I had a handle on it, even if I couldn't understand why it happened. But now"—she sat straighter—"I'm curious. I want to find answers."

It wasn't nerves in her voice—it was anticipation. An eager swirl through her stomach that straightened her spine and caused her to squirm.

"We'll find answers for you, Jez. I promise."

She beamed.

"In the meantime, though—"

"No," she snapped. "I don't know what you're about to say, but you have your protective sister expression on your face. So, no."

"Jezzie." I sighed. Selfishly, reluctance almost stole my words, because what I was going to say was the last thing I wanted. "I don't know if you should go to the war front. There are so many people dying there, and that would be so traumatic for you. When we head there next, maybe it will be better for you if you don't come. I don't want you to have to live through it again."

Having to hear their final thoughts, the regrets and last hopes. I wouldn't wish it on anyone.

She considered for a moment, and again her hand went to where her necklace should be. "I don't know where else I'd go."

My heart crumbled. For a moment, nothing else mattered. Not the alpheous or the emblems, not my own curse or scar. Nothing but the defeated look in my sister's eyes admitting she didn't know where her place was in the world.

This girl who had always been strong, who carried more burdens than the rest of us ever guessed, who had said she knew her destiny would carry her somewhere grand, was confessing she was lost.

I pulled her to me. "Everything is going to be okay." I tried to believe it, but as I rubbed a hand down my sister's hair, my scar caught my eye, and I hoped I hadn't just lied.

We sat like that for a few minutes, sinking into the comfort of secrets spilled between us, until finally Jezebel pushed back. There was a teasing gleam to her eye I knew I wouldn't like. "Now can I ask you about Tolek?"

"What about Tolek?" I rolled my eyes, but I'd known she wouldn't let the conversation from the plains rest.

"I realized I hadn't asked before. Are you happy?"

It was greedy after everything she'd said, but I couldn't fight the smile splitting my lips. "I am."

And she beamed back at me.

Wings fluttered through my chest at only the thought of him. And because Jez had shared so much, I offered a piece of what I hadn't admitted to anyone. "I'm so scared I'm going to mess it up, though."

"Mess it up?"

I sighed, getting up on the pretense of pouring her another glass of wine, but truly needing to avoid looking at her.

"When I think of being happy with Tolek, it feels too good to be true. As if it will crash to earth like a fallen Angel if I'm not careful." As most good things had. "I screwed things up spectacularly with my last attempt at love."

Broken goodbyes and a whispered *until the stars stop shining* echoed in my mind from the last time Malakai and I had been together. I clenched my hand around Jez's glass, turning to give it back before I could shatter the thing. Spirits, it was warm in here. I moved closer to the window to gulp down the briny sea air.

It wasn't missing Malakai that caused that pain; it was the fear of my bad patterns repeating themselves. I wanted Tolek more than I wanted air to breathe, but not at the cost of hurting him.

"That wasn't your fault, sister. It wasn't his either. It just...was. Is. That's how things happen sometimes."

"I know you're right, but I *was* at fault for some things."

"We all are. You and Tolek, though, it's different."

"How so?" I curled up on my bed, pulling a throw blanket around my shoulders and toying with the loose strings. The sounds of waves echoed off the coast in the distance.

"The change in you—It's like the sun shining after a storm. Like the first buds of spring pushing through the frozen ground. Tolek brings out those pieces of you."

Tolek made me want to be a better person, *to live.*

"Don't hold back with him," Jezebel encouraged, reclining against her pillows.

"I'm not." I paused. "Well, I am with some things."

Jezebel tilted her head. "You mean..." She sprang to her feet. "Wait a minute."

Then, she was tearing open drawers and the armoire, even disappearing into the bathing chamber for a moment.

"What are you doing?"

"Where did he put it?" She crawled across the ground, ducking beneath her bed first, then mine. "Ah!" Retreating out, she held up a small bottle full of a deep green liquid I recognized.

"How did that get there?" I gasped, snatching the contraceptive tonic from her.

"I left it in here for you two. I figured when he asked for time, that was what he meant." She wiggled her brows. "And you were at the beach for hours the other night."

"That was your *favor*? Jezebel even if you'd been right, you know it doesn't work that quickly!" I nearly scolded my sister, but then stopped. Brow furrowed, I watched the emerald liquid absorb the firelight. "And he hid it. Instead of asking about it?"

I didn't know why it surprised me. Tolek had eagerly accepted my boundaries.

"I've never seen anyone as in love as that man is with you, Ophelia. He looks at you like you wove the constellations in the sky. Like you spun the Angels' wings and carved the mountains. He'd turn the world to ash if you asked him to, hoisting you above the ruins." My heart beat a little quicker—because I would, too.

For me, he didn't only string the constellations in the sky at night. He was the reason I saw them shine. "So a request as simple as waiting? I believe that was an easy answer for him."

And it was the divine feeling of knowing no matter what you did, with that one person in the world, you would always be accepted, always be comforted and at home, always be *safe*, that wrapped itself around my bones as Jezebel and I tucked ourselves into bed, and dreams of Angels' wings and constellations battled off thoughts of spirit voices and monsters.

Chapter Twenty
Malakai

Sunrise came quickly, not like I slept much. All I saw every time I tried were scars and lace. A sinful combination of torture and temptation.

I rose before the sun was even up, shoved my feet into my boots, slung my sword across my back, and grabbed a quick breakfast from the mess hall. It was still all I saw. By the time I met Mila, the sun was starting to filter through gray clouds, a foggy haze coating the peaks of the mountains.

"Where's everyone else?" The training arena was empty, not a warrior in sight.

Mila looked up from where she was tightening her gold cuffs, leather covering her hands and the rest of her body around them. "Likely still sleeping."

"What?"

"You wanted private training. I can't postpone everyone else's practice time."

"I didn't mean it had to be private," I grumbled.

"What was that?" She tilted her head closer as if she couldn't hear me.

"I said it doesn't have to be private. We can work around all the others, can't we?" This didn't need to be a big deal. I wanted the connection I'd briefly felt with the other warriors. It had been a buzz of unity, tiny and fickle, but with potential to grow.

"Trust me, Malakai." Mila's voice was softer now, all hints of teasing gone. "For this, we want privacy."

She strapped her swords across her back and jerked her head to tell me to follow her. Stewing, wondering what she'd meant by that last comment, I did.

Mila led us around the back of what was serving as the armory, to a large building next to the stables. Most horses were tethered near their owners' tents. Only a handful were kept here, so the space was mostly quiet.

Shoving the heavy rolling door open, Mila walked inside. Our boots echoed against aged wooden floors, flurries drifting in to stick to them. High ceilings and dusty windows looked down on us.

"Here?" I asked.

"Here," she answered. "Let's get to work, Warrior Prince."

And we did.

At a much more grueling pace than I'd expected. Mila instructed me on a work out circuit that had me panting on the floor in a puddle of my own sweat not an hour later, all without touching a weapon.

"By the fucking Angels," I swore at her. "What was that for?"

"How's your mind?" She sat down beside me and crossed her legs.

"What?" I shoved my damp hair out of my face.

"Your mind? Is it racing like normal?"

I narrowed my eyes, lifting my head to assess her. "How do you know what my mind normally does?"

A shrug and no response.

Flopping my head back against the floorboards, I counted dust specks floating through the sun beams and dug into my mind. Oddly, it was calm.

"It's...slower." I caught her nod out of the corner of my eye. "The thoughts aren't as loud."

Like a roaring stream had slowed to a trickle, the patronizing memories had ceased. For that hour when I was paying attention to where my body was placed and how my muscles contracted and making sure I remembered to breathe through each set, my mind calmed for the first time in months.

I'd grown so used to the constant hum—could feel it mounting again as I lay there, but it had *stopped*.

"Because you focused," Mila explained. "You spent the past hour giving every scrap of your attention to your physical fight rather than your mental one. I can guarantee the opposite happened yesterday, and it distracted you. Rightfully so, given what you've been through."

My brow quirked. She'd said it in such an offhand manner, as if it was something I obviously already knew. Like my memories and the scars I bore were all valid and real, and I did not have to hide from them.

I sat up, abdominal muscles already groaning, and leaned my weight on my palms. "So, I have to be exerting myself in order to escape?"

"You won't always," Mila reassured. "But I wanted you to see you could. When there weren't distractions and blades clashing around you, I wanted you to see what you were capable of."

"But there *will* be distractions if I ever make it onto a battlefield."

"Small steps win races, Warrior Prince." Pushing to her feet, Mila extended a hand and pulled me to my feet. "That's what my very first instructor told me. I was eager and wanted to train with my older brother's class. Mind you, I wasn't even thirteen." As she talked, I poured us both glasses of water and handed one to her. "That instructor let me practice in small increments, with children my own age, and when I complained, he reminded me that the smallest lessons would one day serve me."

"Where's your brother now?" I asked.

Mila spun her water glass between her hands. "I have four, but I lost that one during the first war." Her words rattled the cage around my heart. When she lifted her eyes to mine, there was steel within the blues. An admirable strength that I wanted to study. "I learned a lot of lessons from that day, too."

I didn't ask what they were; I could imagine how raw and vulnerable they must be. Instead, I searched for her original meaning and considered all the lessons I'd learned—from the brutally honest to the crushing losses to the hopeful attempts—and thought about how they'd all gotten me to where I was today. To a place where I had a calm head for once after months of roaring thoughts.

"I'm sure he'd be proud of the little girl who relentlessly trained and the general she's become," I said, tapping my glass against hers.

And I wondered about the boy I once was, who thought his dreams were crushed with the signing of a treaty. Perhaps there was hope for him yet.

Mila smiled. "Today you saw that you *could* take steps forward. Tomorrow we'll work on controlling how."

And for days, that's what we did. The two of us in an abandoned stable reeking of stale hay and must. Before the sun rose fully and until voices drifted to us from the proper training yard. We compared the different methods we'd grown up with, exchanged stories of summer exchanges and techniques we'd learned from the minor clans. Truthfully, in those sessions, my mind quieted and I forgot the world outside.

First, it was only workouts. Each morning of that week, she never allowed me to raise a weapon. There were raids almost daily and a few close breaches of the border, though I was kept from the fighting.

Evenings were spent with us and at least a few other members of Lyria's council in their cabin, planning the next move. Whoever was not stationed with our soldiers at that moment was within those walls. There, I was more helpful, relying on the leadership training I'd undergone my entire life.

Every time the horns sounded through camp and Mila was called away, I remained where I was instructed like a well-behaved soldier and awaited her return. I hated it, but I was dedicated to the structure. Grateful for it.

And after days that felt endless with sweat and the stench of death in the air, Mila and I moved to the basics of sparring with wooden swords. Things about footing and grip my instructors had drilled into my muscle memory when I was six.

We were two weeks into our arrangement when I found myself grumbling, "I already know how to slash." And where to do it based on my opponent's strengths and weaknesses, assessed quickly and covertly.

"You learned these techniques as a child, yes," Mila agreed, pouring herself a glass of water. She may be a ruthless trainer, but at least she was working right beside me.

"Then why am I learning them again?"

Her hair was braided down her back, but a few strands stuck to her face. It happened every day, I'd realized. Little pieces of her fortress coming undone when she was focused. I wondered what she looked like when she came completely undone.

I pulled myself from those thoughts.

"It's going to help you." Mila brushed her hair aside with a smirk that grated on my confidence and tightened my chest.

"Is this funny to you?"

Her face fell. With an icy grace, she set her glass down. "You think I find what you've been through funny?" I shrugged. "Nothing about this is funny. This is war. You may not have been there the first time, but I was. I remember the cries of the dying on every battlefield I stepped on. I remember learning field healing to get them back to camp and holding them when I couldn't fix their wounds. I remember—" She sucked in a breath, her eyes closing. Her hands gripped her wrists.

Should I do something? Soothe her somehow? Nothing I could do would be enough, because she was right—everything she'd been through was horrific. I may have my own scars, but I couldn't imagine living with her memories.

Though, I supposed I'd find out before this was over if I could learn to keep myself on a battlefield.

"None of it is funny," she said. "But forgive me for trying to ease the pain we're both about to face."

"I'm sorry," I mumbled. "You're right. Starting at the beginning is helping me." And maybe being able to talk about what I'd been through so casually was, too.

Her shoulders dropped a bit at my apology. Not disappointment, I realized after a slight moment of panic. *Relief.*

"I'm starting with the basics of your training because I want you to relearn how to move with your new mentality. After everything you went through, Malakai, you're a new person. You're going to be a new fighter. I don't want you to rely on the instincts honed by your former self."

Angels, she was brilliant. How did she know so much about this?

"Okay," I conceded, not reluctantly. "Let's get back to footwork, then."

And when I picked up a sparring sword and resumed my place, the smile she flashed me made the long days a little easier.

~

"THEY'RE CALLED THE BLACKFYRE," Barrett said about the journal entry he'd just read. Something about Lucidius in Engrossian Territory.

The prince had been lounging on the couch across from me in Lyria's cabin, the journal propped open on his chest and Rebel curled on the floor beside him, when all of a sudden, he shot to his feet.

"It's as pungent and powerful as the fire in your Spirit Volcano, but it was controlled by Bant when he lived." Rebel bounced onto the couch, pressing his nose to Barrett's shoulder for attention, feeding off that energy.

"And you think that is the swamp where the Engrossian emblem was found?" I asked.

"I think it's most likely. There's a wealth of legends surrounding them. I'll have to go through them all again." Barrett scratched between his wolf's ears. The animal watched him with an eerie attentiveness. "I've studied Bant for years, and I can't believe I haven't thought of this, yet. Bant and Damien feuded in their mortal lives, and one source of contention was the Blackfyre and Bant's connection to it."

Warring Angel powers, and the two strongest at that. It was something to note.

"Why does it matter? The Engrossian emblem is already

secured," Cyren chimed from where they sat at the table besides a quiet Lyria.

We'd told the generals of the emblem search recently and had started combing through Lucidius's journals in the main cabin during our spare time, getting their input. As she did most nights, Lyria mumbled to herself as she hunched over documents. A soft bubbling filled the air from where Esmond prepared tonics in the kitchen along with herbal scents and steam. I wasn't sure why he tended to do so here instead of in the infirmary, but it had become a steady presence for us all.

"Because Lucidius visited these swamps on one of his galli-vanting missions around the continent," I explained.

"So it really does seem he was visiting Angel sites," Barrett added. "Whether or not he knew of the emblems is still unclear, but the locations hold powerful magic regardless."

"And Ophelia's letter said the Seawatcher emblem was found in a site sacred to Gaveny," I said.

"So you need to know the locations important to all Angels?" Cyren asked, tilting their head in thought. Mystlight gilded their braided coronet like an eerie halo. "There are numerous for each clan."

There were. And that was only one problem.

It had taken the Seawatchers two months to narrow down where they thought the emblem was, and they'd only begun to focus on locations because Gaveny was an adventurous spirit. But with the locations of Bant's emblem possibly being this Blackfyre —a sacred site according to Barrett's expansive knowledge on the Angel—we were starting to refocus our interpretation of Lucid-ius's journals.

"There are endless possibilities, and we need to figure them out before my mother does," Barrett confirmed. His voice was heavy with exhaustion.

"She's back in Mindshaper territory," Lyria interjected, head finally snapping up from her maps.

"She is?" I asked. What made Kakias retreat? Last we heard, she was seeking the emblems. Had she found Thorn's?

"My spies sent a letter today." The commander eyed Rebel,

then ducked back down, as if she'd never been speaking to us in the first place.

Barrett and I exchanged a confused glance.

"She can't get Thorn's emblem before Ophelia," I said. "I don't know what your mother can do with these pieces of metal, but it can't be good."

The prince nodded. "Our best bet is still Lucidius. His wanderings seem to indicate he knew *something*." We just did not know what that something was.

I flopped back against the couch, breathing out a harsh breath.

"There's this one," I said, grabbing one of the journals and roughly flipping through the pages. So much incoherent scrawling, so many useless tales of a dead man's life.

I found the passage from back in Bodymelder Territory and read aloud:

"Fields stretched on endlessly and I felt small a tiny dot in the map of the world whose purpose was to make an impact and I would make that impact that was what drove me to the spot

Bushels of overgrown weeds that's what all this was I didn't understand why they favored this spot so much

Field of birds marking it they had a name for its roar of yellow and orange poppies and spirits knew what else but this was where I needed to be besides the pointless view and the way it made me feel

I had to be here"

Esmond's voice cut through. "Are you talking about Firebird's Field?"

Our attention snapped toward the kitchen. "What's Firebird's Field?" I asked.

"It's near the capital." Esmond wiped his hands on a rag and rounded the counter, coming to stand behind the couch. I tossed him the journal. As he leafed through it, he explained, "It's a wild-flower field overflowing with gold and orange flowers, and it's tied to Ptholenix—hence the name. There's a long drawn-out history of the place, but nowadays it's used for an array of offerings."

Tied to the Bodymelder Prime Warrior. Their Angel. Whose wings legends claimed burned as bright as fire.

I had to be here, Lucidius had written.

"This absolutely sounds like Firebird's Field," Esmond said, closing the journal. "And given what you've said about sites significant to the Angels, that's the strongest I'd recommend for the Bodymelders."

Barrett was already on his feet, striding for Lyria's table. "I'll write to Ophelia."

Esmond's throat bobbed on a swallow as he continued reading the rambling passages. This didn't help us if Kakias was after Thorn's emblem, but at least it was another lead. And it kept the queen off Ophelia's trail for a bit longer.

"What exactly *is* Firebird's Field, Esmond?"

His brows pulled together, scrutinizing Lucidius's words. The hair on the back of my neck stood up as I waited for his answer.

"It's the location where the Angels' ascension ritual was created."

CHAPTER TWENTY-ONE
OPHELIA

THE SEAWATCHERS' CAPITAL WAS LIKE NOTHING I'D ever seen. I'd been here once before, but we were younger then, and I didn't think any of us had truly appreciated the beauty of the city built of canals and bridges. The palms stretching to the sky and shadowing sandy corners.

Salt-water streams cut in from the Neptitian Sea, between city blocks made up of wide expanses of cobblestone. The buildings throughout all looked like they rose out of the ocean, painted in corals and yellows and peaches, light green and blue and brown sea glass adorning windows and illustrating mosaics along the facades. Blown into spires atop domes and some even forged into statues.

Though it was late by the time Sapphire carried me through the winding city streets to the chancellor's manor, it would have been difficult to miss the unique beauty of this city that looked like it had been crafted from the spirits of its warriors. By night it was beautiful, but I imagined the true glory was by day. Like sunlight reflecting off a pristine ocean, I bet it made every crevice iridescent.

It was a shame we wouldn't be staying long enough to enjoy it.

We'd accompanied Ezalia and Seron south, not comfortable leaving them with his injury, and would spend a night here before heading to the war camp. It wasn't much of a detour, just a less direct route than traveling straight through Mystique Territory.

Seron was recovering nicely, considering the severity of what he suffered. Santorina had been doing everything she could, but you couldn't regrow limbs. The Seawatcher was forced to ride in a cart the entire trek to the capital.

He was determined, though. Seron had looked me in the eye more than once and swore he would ride again. That strength was inspiring. If he maintained that attitude after what had happened to him, I could persevere, too. When we left, I'd carry a piece of Seron's bravery with me.

"Ezalia, this is beautiful," I gasped as we crossed onto the grounds of her manor, though the word did not quite do it justice.

Light gray cobblestones continued in from the street, aqua sea glass speckling the spaces between, reflecting the moon and starlight. We dismounted our horses and handed the reins to her staff, more attendees rushing forward to take our packs and assist Seron. Ever the thorough healer, Santorina followed them inside.

"Thank you," Ezalia said proudly. "My family has owned the manor as long as we've held power, but it continues to grow with each new ruler." She waved a hand. "We enjoy expanding."

The rest of us followed Ezalia into a courtyard in the center of her sprawling home, tall palm trees surrounding the space, the greenery dotted with tall flowers now closed for the evening. Sandstone columns and endless corridors with wide windows and breezy airways composed the building, the babbling of slow streams orchestrating a soothing melody.

"Mother!" Two small voices rang out, footsteps rushing down one of the corridors. A young girl with dark hair to her waist threw herself at Ezalia, a boy who appeared the same age nearly tripping himself as he stumbled to a stop.

"Why are you two still awake?" Ezalia quirked a reproachful brow, but squeezed the children tighter. Her eyes closed for a moment, and it was like a weight fell off her shoulders.

"I wasn't aware you had children," Cypherion said once their rushed excuses died off, and they distracted themselves playfighting in their nightclothes. Somehow, they'd dragged Tolek into their games. The girl was currently atop his shoulders, the boy jumping to attempt to reach her.

"It's why Seron usually doesn't travel with me." Ezalia smiled softly for a moment, almost pained. "They're known by Seawatchers here, but it wasn't something we made public knowledge to other clans."

"Why's that?" Jezebel asked.

"They were born a year before the war, and the unrest was already palpable. Word of it reached even our territory."

"Ours, too," Vale added quietly, watching the children mournfully.

Ezalia gazed wistfully at her son and daughter. "Seron and I hadn't planned to start a family for decades, but..." A shrug and a sly grin. "Things happen. The best accident I could have ever dreamed of. And we knew, with tensions growing, that it opened them up to be pawns."

I understood that feeling too well. Malakai had lived it, and we'd all been hurt by extension.

"Auggie, Seli, come say hello to the rest of the Revered's friends and give poor Tolek a break," Ezalia called.

"I don't mind," Tolek answered, walking over without even a limp, one hand across Seli's ankles so she didn't fall from his shoulders and his other hand gripped tightly by her brother.

"Mother, can we go to the tide pools tomorrow?" Seli blurted.

Ezalia's smile wavered. "I think I'll be with your father tomorrow." Tending to his injuries, something she would have to explain to the children.

"I can take them before we leave if you'd like," Tolek offered, catching the tension in the chancellor's words.

"Yes!" Seli cheered. Auggie remained silent, uncertain, but Ezalia's gratefulness was abundant.

"They'll never leave you alone, now," she muttered to Tol, and he only shrugged. Picking up her son, Ezalia propped him on a hip. "This is Auggie—August." Bashfully, he hid his smile.

"I'm Selina!" The girl cheered loudly, arms crossed atop Tolek's head. Carefully, he reached up and removed her, placing her on the ground in front of him.

"It's very nice to meet both of you," I said. "Do you mind if we stay here with you?"

"Like a sleepover?" Selina asked.

"If that's okay with you," I said.

Selina propped her hands on her hips, pretending to consider. "I suppose so." She whirled toward her mother. "They can sleep in my room!"

"Oh, I don't think you want that," Jezebel said. She squatted down and crooked her finger to call Selina over, cupping her hand around the girl's ear as if telling her a secret, but raising her voice. "My sister hogs all the blankets."

Seli looked like she regretted the offer.

"What about you, Auggie?" Cyph asked. "Is it all right with you?"

Face partially hidden in his mom's shoulder, August nodded.

"All right you two, you should have been asleep long ago." Looking to us, Ezalia asked, "Do you mind? Someone can show you to your rooms."

"Of course not," I said. "Go on."

The twins bid us all goodbye, Seli taking time to learn all of our names and hug us each while her brother mumbled a quiet good night.

Once they were gone, a staff member led us to a wide hallway with bedchambers on each side. They weren't grand suites like we were used to, and a part of me was relieved by that. To be closer to everyone.

The rooms were all similar, adorned with various shades of light blues and greens that gave a soothing oceanic effect. Chandeliers dangled with ornate bronze fixtures, swirling like waves. Our packs had been placed within.

After finding mine and taking a few minutes to freshen up in the bathing chamber sink that appeared to be constructed of a large shell, I knocked on Santorina's door.

"How's Seron?" I asked, perching on the polished wooden frame at the foot of the grand bed.

"Settled and recovering." Rina strode to the dressing table and took down her ponytail, combing her straight hair thoughtfully. "He's lucky. It could have been so much worse. Whatever seaweed wrap Ezalia made on the platform probably saved his life."

Her knuckles whitened around the brush.

"What is it?" I asked, rising and taking it from her gently, setting it on the table.

Rina sighed. "It could have been any of you. All of you—" Her voice cracked. "I hadn't been there. Hadn't even said goodbye."

It was a fear I'd been trying to untangle since the platforms. Since the Battle of Damenal, really. So many had suffered—died—because of this mission.

But Rina's apprehension ran deeper, memories of her parents flashing behind her vacant stare.

"I know." I swallowed. "I'm so grateful we're all okay." I almost told her how scared I was, but her round eyes were already glassy. Rina rarely showed this kind of emotion, so instead of giving her more cause to fear, I took her hand and led her to the end of the bed. "We have to keep fighting, but we're going to be smarter about this. The challenge is that we don't know what we're facing or why, but I won't lose any of you. And next time, you'll be with us if you wish. It was mere coincidence that you weren't."

"I'll be there. I won't be left behind to worry again."

"Excellent." We shared twin vengefully-determined smiles. "Now, tell me how it's been with the training."

She brightened, eyes clearing. "Leo has contacts throughout the territory who are willing to help." Reaching over the side of the bed, Rina rummaged in her pack. "He gave me this." She opened her palm.

"A shell?" It was off-white and ordinary, with pink streaks accenting the divots and an oblong shape almost resembling a wing.

"They're supposedly blessed by the God of Nature and can be used to communicate. So we can use them to discuss progress between different cities." Carefully, she tucked it back into her pack and curled her legs beneath her.

God of Nature, I wondered. We rarely spoke of the gods.

"How is that possible? That you can communicate with a shell?"

"It's more of a calling than anything. The shells heat in a pattern. Burning, unceasing is asking for help. Pulsing is code.

Long and short beats to spell the messages. I'm still learning how the system works, but Leo said Seawatchers have been using it for centuries—since they started discovering the shells in coves off the black sand shores—and they believe them to be a gift from Gerrenth himself."

"That's incredible, Rina." The concept of communicating via god-blessed shells almost seemed hard to believe. It wasn't anything I'd ever imagined, but I supposed none of what we were facing was. "Will you show me how it works one day?"

The smile she gave me in answer was so effortless, so full of hopeful radiance, it made me smile, too. Gone was the girl who'd taken over her parents' tavern after their untimely deaths because of duty. Before me was a woman pursuing change. Pursuing a fairer world. And I was honored to be a fraction of her story.

"How are you doing, though?" she asked, her smile vanishing. She'd spent much of the journey from Brontain studying my scar from Kakias. Between her and Tolek, I hadn't been alone for a moment as they worked to figure out why it was getting worse.

"I'm fine, Rina. I promise," I answered too quickly. The scar had been agonizing over the journey, getting worse with each day. It was the same pulsing pain, but more intense.

And I'd started to wonder what exactly Kakias's blade had been infused with. If it somehow was tied to her power itself. Because this essence beating against my Angelblood was familiar in a way I couldn't quite name.

It was clear from the purse of her lips that Rina didn't believe me. "Ophelia, you saying you're fine is the equivalent of someone saying they're warm during a blizzard."

I rolled my eyes. "So dramatic."

"Now you're being hypocritical." I glared at her for a moment before we both smiled softly. "I've been wondering if there might be a way to rework the ritual the queen did that night. If gathering the ingredients and bringing the magic back to life could help us connect with it and siphon it from you, but I'm not sure how it would work. I wrote briefly to Esmond to see if he had any ideas, though it's difficult without being able to put much in writing."

I nodded. "I'll try whatever you advise, but in the meantime, I promise I'm telling you the truth." I wasn't entirely fine, but there was nothing to be done about it, so why bother her with it?

As if on cue, a bolt of pain speared through the scar. I bit my lips, nearly drawing blood as a soft knock echoed on the door. Santorina called that it was open, and Tolek and Cypherion entered. The former caught my expression before I could wipe it away. He came to stand beside the bed, eyes sweeping over me, landing on my arm and immediately understanding.

"Just because that scar isn't the largest threat over us, doesn't mean you need to say it's okay." And I swore in that sentence, Rina sounded more defeated than anything. She was a healer—a damn good one—and this was her greatest challenge yet.

"Don't push the pain away on account of everything else," Cypherion said. "Or Santorina won't know what she's working with."

"We'll find an answer, though," Tolek promised. Whether it was to us or himself, I couldn't be sure.

Unease twisted its way through my gut, but I gave them a genuine smile. "Thank you all. For being here. For fighting this fight with me." Tolek's words from Brontain echoed through my mind. This was all of our battle, but they were not required to be here. They were choosing me. This. And no words could express my gratitude for that.

"I've actually had some thoughts about the emblems. A theory I want to try tonight." Giving Tolek a look with raised brows, I added, "If you're up for it."

"Oh, Gods be damned," Santorina muttered.

"This can't be good." Cyph dragged a hand over his face.

Tolek met my stare with my favorite smirk. "I'm up for anything you've got, Alabath."

CHAPTER TWENTY-TWO
OPHELIA

⋇⋇⋇⋇⋇

"OPHELIA, THIS FEELS LIKE A HORRIBLE IDEA."

I ignored Rina's warning, continuing to pull velvet curtains across wide windows.

"Santorina, by now you know that won't stop any of us," Tolek chided from the wicker chair before the fire, journal in hand to record what we were about to do.

At my request, we'd been given a wide, nearly empty room typically used for formal dinners. Cypherion and Tolek had pushed the table and chairs up against the peach stucco walls. Jezebel and I were drawing the thick teal curtains across clouded glass.

Privacy. What we needed if I was truly going to attempt this.

"Why am I the only one who tries to dissuade the reckless decisions?" Rina muttered, only half-joking, and fell into one of the chairs beside Tolek.

"Because," Cyph began with a huff, shoving a side table in front of the double doors at one end of the room, "the rest of us know by now we have no other option."

Cypherion was striding across the room, boots echoing on worn tile, when a knock sounded at the door he'd just blocked. Immediately, his accusing blue eyes turned to mine. I shrugged a not-so-convincing apology.

He grumbled something unintelligible under his breath, but it sounded like, "Always testing me." Then, he opened the door and came face-to-face with Vale.

The Starsearcher's eyes widened, spine straightening. "Hi," she breathed.

Silently, he stepped aside. Vale walked forward with a furtive look over her shoulder as Cypherion blocked the doors again. When she looked at me, I shook my head softly, telling her to give him time. He'd come around.

I still didn't know what had happened between them, but Cypherion was the most level-headed warrior I knew, and if he was allowing himself to be fueled by emotions right now, it likely meant he didn't know how to process them. Once he figured it out, he'd be better.

At least I hoped so, for the sake of the Starsearcher before me with the downturned eyes, and for Cypherion. Bottling up this rage wouldn't do him any good—I would know. Vale may have tricked us, but she'd been trying. Trying to read, trying to help, trying to apologize.

Besides, I may not totally trust her, but we needed her.

"Okay, Alabath," Tolek said, springing up from his chair and jogging to my side. He placed a hand on my lower back. "Now that we're all here, walk us through the plan."

"Right," I said, eyes flitting to Cyph one last time. "I'm going to try to summon Damien."

The air in the room stilled.

"You're *what*?" Vale gaped.

"Damien hasn't appeared to me since the days after the Battle of Damenal, and it's starting to feel odd. I saw him four times in a matter of months and now...nothing. It feels...wrong." I wrapped my hand around the Angelborn shard on my necklace and our pulses synchronized.

"What can you learn from speaking with him?" Santorina was skeptical. Crossing her arms, she came to stand in our circle, her soft gown swishing below the wide leather belt cinching her waist. A hint of warrior gear.

"Answers," I stated. "We have three emblems now, and we're

no closer to figuring out why or what they're for. *If I can talk to Damien, maybe he can reveal* something.*

It was an idea I'd had since Malakai mentioned he thought Lucidius had been trying to contact Damien. It wasn't technically advised, but we were working beyond the bounds of known magic. Based on the restraint Damien showed last time we spoke, it might be a futile effort, but I had to try. Judging by my friends' expressions and the aimlessness we'd all been feeling, they understood.

"Why am I here, then?" Vale asked. She wasn't arguing with my plan, though. Her head tilted, arms crossing as she considered the possibilities.

"Did you bring what I requested?" I asked. Nodding, she pulled a pouch from her side. "I want you to conduct a session while I try to contact the Angel and see if anything can be found within the overlapping forces."

"To challenge the block I've been getting by siphoning off some of your power." A devious smile split her lips, light returning to her eyes. "I'm in."

"You're going to help us?" Cyph asked, not unkindly.

Vale leveled him a stare. "Some of you may not believe it, but I only want to assist in this mission. You're all the only reason I'm still alive."

"Set up wherever you need to," I said before Cyph could respond.

Vale dropped to the floor, skirt pooling around her, and pulled incense and matches from her pouch.

"Do you have the ingredients Malakai said Lucidius used?" Rina asked.

I shook my head. "I'm going to bleed on the emblems and pray Damien answers."

Tolek stepped closer to me. "Wait a second—"

"Don't start being all overprotective now, Tolek," Jezebel teased.

"I've always been protective of her." He glared at my sister, then flashed me kinder eyes. "I support you doing what you have to, but I don't want you to have to draw your own blood for this damn Angel."

"Blood activates the emblems, Tol." I spoke softly, as if this was some intimate moment between us. I didn't know why it felt as such, but there was a fear in his eyes I couldn't ignore. "I have to try."

He searched my gaze, finally sighing. "Fine, but only a small cut." He cupped my cheek. "You've got to stay in one piece, Alabath."

"You always hold me together," I whispered. If there hadn't been others in the room, I may have said more. Told him how much it saved me when he cared for those pieces I tore apart. That he was the mortar between the bricks of myself.

Spirits, I had so much more I wanted to tell him. But now wasn't the time.

Instead, I closed my eyes when he pressed a kiss to my forehead —allowed his touch to flow through my body and root me to the floor, to this moment. When I turned back to the group, Jezebel was watching me with a knowing smirk. I rolled my eyes at her.

"Let's get to the ill-advised ritual, then, shall we?" Rina drawled.

Tolek brushed my hair around my shoulder and removed my emblem necklace. His fingers trailed down my spine, and I shivered, drawing a quiet chuckle from him. No time for games now.

I removed the fae bargain charm from the necklace and tucked it in the pocket of my leathers, ignoring Rina's narrowed eyes on it. Then, I took out Barrett's ring and the Seawatcher pearl we'd retrieved, placing all three tokens in the center of the room. Vale was already encased in a dove blue fog. Cyph watched her, jaw ticking, probably thinking of the last time he'd seen her do this—when he'd crawled across a cold temple floor, through his own blood, begging her to stop.

"Pull her out if something goes wrong," I told him.

"I will," he swore without looking away from where Vale had her hands palm up on her thighs, head tilted back, muttering.

Pulling the dagger Cypherion had gifted me for my last birthday from my thigh, I kneeled before the emblems. Tolek crouched beside me with his journal, Jezebel and Santorina standing across from us.

A chill worked down my spine as I watched those three tokens, nerves worming through my stomach.

Carefully, I pricked my thumb; red blood bubbled along the slice.

Angelblood.

The word clanged through me with the force of Damien's wings. And it all echoed—every prophecy he'd given me, the Angellight at my induction ceremony. Everything hung in that first drop of crimson sliding down my hand.

"Ophelia..." Tolek's hand was on my shoulder. "You don't have to."

But I did. I'd sworn to protect the Mystiques as Revered. I couldn't do that without answers. I needed to at least try.

Paint the shards with vengeance, Damien said.

I slammed my hand across the first token—the pearl.

Light burst forth. Blinding and all-consuming, streaked with ocean hues. It flooded the corners of the room, bounced off the turquoise sea glass dangling from the chandeliers, sending them clattering against each other like wind chimes. The room became an array of aquas and ceruleans, like sunlight through crashing waves.

Quickly, I pressed my blood to the dark gem in Barrett's ring. A channel of light shot upward, but it was different from the other. Still white and heated, but it gusted like a tunnel of trapped wind, dark and curling at the edges.

And the scar along my arm *burned.* I bit back on the cry clawing its way up my throat.

If I let it out, Tolek would pull me back. His hand was already tightening on my shoulder. But holy fucking Spirits the scar felt like it was going to rip open. Pour out whatever darkness lurked inside. It crawled along my bones searching for release.

Finally, gritting my teeth against tainted power and blinding light, I pressed my thumb to the final token. *My* emblem.

And the light exploded. Scorching.

Pain lanced through the cut on my thumb, but I clenched my eyes tightly against it and called out to Damien.

Help, I begged. *Send a sign, anything. Use that damn eternal power of yours, please.*

As the words flowed through my head, I saw my friends battling the alpheous. I saw Barrett and myself facing down Kakias. I saw every moment we'd almost lost so far.

Something warm crawled through me as the tokens blazed together. A tingle along my spine and a radiating pulse of heat *everywhere*.

"Vale!" Cypherion shouted, but I couldn't open my eyes.

Calamity rose around us, all of their voices mingling together in shouts for both of us.

I wrenched my eyes open, and for a brief moment I thought Vale was sprawled on the ground, seizing through the fog. Then, light burst overhead, and I swore—for a fraction of a second—three outlines of golden figures hovered at the top of the room. Large and domineering, but only a shadow of true power.

Heat tunneled through me and out of my skin, thickening the air around me.

They reached out—and I stretched up, up, up.

To grab them. To touch them.

A hand tightened around my arm. The opposing power roared through my body like dark fire, Angelblood fighting it.

My crimson fingers clawed at burning air. A deafening pop echoed through the room.

And they were gone.

A syrupy thick silence wrapped around us, a dull hum piercing it.

I collapsed to the ground, panting harder than I'd realized. Vision swimming and ears ringing.

Tolek knelt before me, callused hands on my cheeks, tilting my head up. He spoke, but I couldn't hear him. Just watched those lips move and tried to steady myself through the brush of his thumbs across my cheekbones.

She's okay, I realized he was repeating, nerves igniting the amber specks in his eyes.

And because I felt so untethered, I threw myself at him, lips crashing together in a frantic release of all the pressure mounting around me.

My arms tangled around his neck, his wrapping around my waist. He melded me to him like he wouldn't let an Angel rip me away.

Falling back, Tolek pulled me onto his lap and kissed me harder. All the fear tensing his body channeled into each stroke of his tongue against mine. Gripping the back of my neck, he tilted my head back further and devoured me, grounding me there in the silence after the Angels.

When we finally broke apart, the ringing in my ears had dulled, and I could hear his words again, rough and labored. "If that's what I get every time you do something stupid, I'll come up with a lot more reckless ideas."

I laughed into his neck. Gently, he leaned back to search my eyes. "Are you okay?"

"I'm fine," I said, taking a deep breath. "It was a stupid idea. I didn't learn anything." Never mind the fact that something inexplicable had happened.

Tolek frowned. "But—"

"It almost looked like you were glowing," Jezebel burst. In my lust for Tol, I'd forgotten about everyone else.

"I was—what?" That couldn't be possible. At the Battle of Damenal and at the induction ceremony, light came from my shard necklace. That had to have been what Jezebel saw.

"And I wouldn't say we learned nothing." Vale's voice floated to us. Keeping my arms around Tol, I turned to see the Starsearcher propped on one elbow on the tile.

"Are you okay?" I asked.

"Fine." Her voice was weak, but her stare was determined. Rina handed Vale a glass and Jez helped her sit up. Cyph watched —eyes barely containing a murderous calm.

"I think..." Vale sipped the water at Rina's insistence. "I think I found something."

The haze from her session was crowding the room now, making my senses feel lighter, but I focused on her words.

"What did you see?"

My heart quickened as she asked, "How much do any of you know of the gods?"

CHAPTER TWENTY-THREE
OPHELIA

"*THE GODS?*" I REPEATED, SCRAMBLING TO FACE forward in Tolek's lap.

"Essentially nothing," Tolek answered. His arms came around my waist, like he wasn't ready for me to let go after watching me be consumed by Angellight. His entire frame was tense. "We know the legends, but they're only stories, not religious beliefs. More for entertainment than for honor."

"Warriors don't keep gods." Jezebel shook her head.

"I do, though," Santorina offered.

"Mystiques don't keep gods." Vale's correction wasn't harsh. "Starsearchers do maintain a certain level of study, though we don't worship them. Our Angel's power works with the Goddess of Fate and Celestial Movement."

"And the twelve fates, correct?" Rina asked, clarifying warrior lore. "Each Starsearcher is aligned with one fate—that's how you're able to read—and they convene with both higher powers?"

Vale avoided our eyes as she nodded.

"Why do the gods matter, though?" Cypherion asked, arms crossed.

"Two reasons," the Starsearcher began. "First—I think I saw them in my session. The seven Angels were there, six beings behind them." Vale's brow creased, and she exhaled roughly. "Everything appeared to be separated from whatever I was seeing by a veil. It was all blurry."

"But the gods can't be involved in a matter of Angels." Jezebel turned hesitant eyes on me. "Right?"

I shrugged.

"There was someone else I could see more clearly," Vale said, sitting up straighter. "I didn't entirely recognize him, but based on the depictions I saw back in Damenal, I think it was your ancestor." She nodded to me and Jezebel.

"Annellius?" my sister asked, perking up.

His gold-tinged form during the Undertaking fluttered through my mind, the wild inclinations bare in his appearance. And his eyes—

"Were they magenta?" I inquired. "Annellius's eyes?" I pointed at my own.

Vale shook her head, brows creasing. "Brown eyes." That didn't align with the being I'd spoken with during the Undertaking. "He was on his knees. Pleading. It was..." Her face screwed up again, pained at the memory. I'd never considered how seeing the paths of fate might damage one's own present. "Horrible. He was distraught. Bleeding, but trapped in a vortex of wind. Even if allowed, I don't think I would have been able to reach him."

"How does he connect to the gods, though?" Jezebel asked.

"That's the second reason the gods matter." Vale chewed her words as if trying to recall the reading. Her fingers curled tighter around her water glass, tarnished silver ring digging into her skin. "There were seven orbs of light surrounding Annellius, like fireflies in a halo over his head. And it seemed like the gods were feeding them. They grew and grew, almost taking on winged-forms, then one at a time, they evaporated. Became mist above him, then collected, each compacting into a small golden speck, like a far-off star."

"Seven orbs of light?" Cypherion asked.

"One for each Angel?" I suggested.

"Fed by the gods..." Tolek echoed.

I didn't know what to make of that. Of the mere idea that the gods were somehow involved in a game of warriors and Angels. It undid lessons I'd been taught since birth. But I supposed that was common nowadays.

"We're learning more about each Angel every day," I said. "But perhaps we also need to learn of the gods. And maybe we even need to question Annellius's motives."

That was what Missyneth had said to me at the induction party, after all. *Motivations tell a variant story from one's actions. They often complete the picture.*

"We don't know why he wanted the emblems, what he did, or how he failed." I looked around at my friends. "It's clear after what we saw on the islands, this is bigger than any of us imagined. We need to expand our theories to match. We need to figure out what Annellius knew and the meaning of what Vale saw in her vision."

And as I made such drastic claims, worry curled in my stomach. Was this the fate we were condemned to? Had I angered the Angels somehow and they'd left us this abstract task beginning to feel like a fool's errand?

Or was it a god's hand pulling these strings?

It didn't matter, I supposed. If I had to do it, I would. I'd do whatever it took to ensure the safety of not only those in this room, but those across the Mystique Territory and alliance clans. Innocent people had been wronged beyond belief. After taking my vow as Revered, I would do everything in my power to stop it from happening again.

"Thank you," Vale said, pulling me from my reverie, "for letting me help you."

Before I could answer, a note flared to life on the ground beside me, the slight glow of mystlight setting my second pulse pounding.

Quickly, I unfolded it, and recognized Barrett's hand immediately.

"What is it?" Tolek said, looking over my shoulder.

I couldn't help my grin. "We have our next emblem." I looked Cypherion in the eye. "Get those maps of yours. We're heading to Bodymelder Territory."

"Where?" Jezebel asked, an eager spark in her voice.

I extended the note bearing coordinates and a few words. "Have any of you heard of Firebird's Field?"

The group sprang into action, discussing theories as I recovered my emblems from the ground. Holding the bloody shard of Angelborn, a plan unfolding of our next steps, the remnants of Angellight burned beneath my skin.

And the poison trapped in my scar writhed against it, feeling alive.

CHAPTER TWENTY-FOUR
DAMIEN

><×><×><×><

BANT'S WINGS DRAPED AGAINST THE FLOOR CREATING A limp tent around him. Blood streaked his feathers, staining their speckled gray surface a deep crimson. As I tried to force my stare away, the steady drip of blood to the floor became a rhythm my heart might beat to, should it dare to do such a thing.

It was cruel to keep him bleeding this way when magic would usually heal him in seconds, but he deserved cruelty for his recklessness. Something akin to a long-dead shadow of hatred coiled in my gut, but it was dulled. Still trapped.

Gaveny's light fell across the chamber, a myriad of turquoise and deep blues and sea greens rippling with golden rays like sun streaming through the surf. It painted the bloodied scene, clashing and cleansing and immortalizing it.

"How does it feel, brother?" Valyrie asked the Seawatcher. Her eyes widened, silver hair streaming to her waist. Her wings were dim behind her.

Hesitantly, Gaveny rose higher. He flexed those massive wings, the edges tipped in luminescent blue. "It is...sublime." A grin broke across the Angel's face, his brown ringlets fluttering in his wind.

My own light pulsed against my skin, power stirring. It slithered through my veins as naturally as the breath I once drew. I smiled internally at the foreign beast, purring in time with it. Relished the mists within me.

And as the two of us basked in it, the chamber forgot about the one crumpled beneath us, power too consuming. It was what he deserved for the sins he wrought, for the power internally attacking our current chosen because of him.

Finally, as my wonder settled, I found our master once again silent, milky eyes locked on the cracked Angelglass. He did not feel the thrill of what occurred as we did. Power did not simmer for them in the same way.

It was likely rocking his foundation, combined with...that glow.

I thought of the last chosen who had failed. Then, I thought of the woman still prowling the living world, containing unnatural mights. And finally, I thought of the girl, and the radiance she'd emitted that seemed so different.

First, at her induction, as she swore my vow. Then, again just now, as she reached out to me.

I could not place what it was.

"Sir..." My wings slackened at my back, their light sweeping the scene like a fallen tale. I wished his name would roll off my tongue as it once had.

Bant's blood dripped from his hands, angelic and almighty, but dulled. It lacked what he had stupidly sacrificed centuries ago, playing rashly with fate.

"The star warrior," our master said, words melodious.

Despite Gaveny's and my elation, the energy in the chamber dimmed. We had been blind in here for so long, the Angelglass cleaving gaps in our information, but fallen tales of legends still spiraled across the realms.

"We will watch her," Valyrie swore, Xenique and Ptholenix on either side of her as they'd always been, the three sharing a history rife with secrets.

"Good. Fate cannot bend again."

Chapter Twenty-Five
Ophelia

✳✳✳

"I THOUGHT I MIGHT FIND YOU OUT HERE." EZALIA'S voice wrapped around the terrace off the room she'd given me in her home, lacing the dawn air with a peace that opposed my warring thoughts.

"How did you know?" I asked.

"Because when I'm feeling overwhelmed by the pressure we're under as leaders, I find the silence, too."

We were leaving her manor this morning after receiving Barrett's note last night, heading toward the Bodymelder capital, Pthole, and Firebird's Field north of it.

But I hadn't slept. Restless worry combined with the deepening pain in my arm kept me up. I'd readied the horses and packed my belongings while my friends stole what last minutes of sleep they could—all but Tol, who had been with me. Now he was finalizing the route with Cypherion.

"It's beautiful out here," I said, leaning against the east-facing railing. Sunlight bounced off the ocean far in the distance, white caps glistening.

Even as I said it, a bolt of pain lashed through my scar. A reminder that the world may be serene, but I was not meant to enjoy it. I was meant for a curse, a sacrifice for a queen's immortality.

Ezalia folded her hands on the ledge, breathing in the fresh air and stillness. Closing my eyes, I mimicked her. Let the stone beneath my palms ground me and the subtle roar of waves lull my thoughts. Tendrils of sentient power curled against my scar, but I focused on the earth's magic.

"It is okay if this is overwhelming, Ophelia."

My spine straightened. Was it? There were so many lives dependent on my own and so many questions I did not have answers to, yet.

"Sometimes..." I took a breath. "I worry if I let myself become overwhelmed, I would be giving up. I would not be able to keep going once the tidal wave crashed over me." As I admitted it, a bit of the tension in my shoulders melted.

"There is a difference between being overwhelmed and giving up," Ezalia said, turning to face me. Her words echoed through my head, caught in the back of my throat like they were a truth I had not known I'd needed. "Even those of us who are not facing half of what you are feel it. Every warrior who has ever led a clan doubted themselves or wanted to succumb to the pressure. It is necessary to feel all of those fears, but once the wave crashes and you're submerged in the darkest depths of yourself, that is where you will find the strength to keep going. Do not run from it."

Embrace the pressure. Allow myself to sink into what scared me—to really know the hollows and quirks and threats—rather than try to blindly scale them. But what if what I found within was too much?

"And if I'm not truly fit for this? What if the doubts are right?" It was easier to confess these things to Ezalia than the others, despite not knowing her as well. My family's undying belief in me lifted my confidence on the worst days, but Ezalia spoke from experience.

"The fact that you worry about this shows how much you care. I've seen a lot of rulers across clans in my lifetime—and a lot of council members who *aspired* to rule. The difference between those who led successfully and those who didn't was their intention. Anyone can strategize and enforce laws. What matters is how you prioritize those you lead because they are our purpose." Ezalia placed a hand on my shoulder, her sea-glass eyes as soothing as a gentle tide. "Trust your instincts, Ophelia. The Spirits will guide you."

Her words settled over me, my eyes stinging. It was something my father would have said.

As Ezalia left, and I stood alone on the terrace for those last few minutes, I envisioned him beside me. Us staring out over that distant sea together. His strong arm around my shoulder and encouraging words carried on the breeze.

Be with me, I sent the thought out to his spirit, wherever it may be. *Guide us.*

Always, I thought his voice promised back. It stuck with me as I left the suite and met my friends at the front of the manor.

Tolek disentangled himself from Seli and Auggie, who were still under the impression he was spending the day with them. I looked at him with a pointed stare that asked *Are you okay?* And he returned a grim one that said *Let's go*, slinging a new bow and quiver of arrows across his back.

Through it all, my father's promise echoed he was with me, I was on the right path, and it was okay to feel overwhelmed by it all.

And while I may be meant for a dark and bloodied future, as we left Gaveral, I tried to hold on to the beauty of the dawn, the comfort of my father's spirit, and the reminder from Ezalia that it was okay to feel pressure in the face of the unknown.

CHAPTER TWENTY-SIX
MALAKAI

>==><==><

MILA AND I HAD BEEN CONDUCTING PRIVATE TRAINING for three weeks when she pulled a sword from her back and pointed it at me.

She flipped it around in her hand and gave me a sly grin. "Do you think you're ready?"

She may have been smirking, but the question was genuine. Was I ready to hold a real weapon? To challenge the beliefs drilled into my head through blades against my skin?

Removing my sword from its sheath, the blade whistled. I twisted it before me, adjusting my hand on the cold leather grip. It fit me perfectly—made for me. I was beginning to grow an affinity for the weapon that I hadn't felt in years. I may not have used it much, but it was a constant.

As it rotated, a beam of sunlight poked through the clouds and the dusty window high in the rafters. For a moment, my heart stuttered, the cage I'd firmly sealed rattling in anticipation. But as light reflected off metal, I made myself watch. Made myself remember the long nights of moonlight bouncing off axes in my cell and what that triggered in my memory.

Then, I focused on the way the grip curved to my fingers. The weight of the weapon in my hand. I concentrated every fiber of my attention on dancing with the sword forged for me, perfecting each sweep of my arm.

I didn't know how long I glided solo around the stables, Mila waiting patiently. But when I finally turned to her, it was with a confident nod. "I'm ready."

Creeping forward as she had the day we'd fought Engrossians together at the temple, Mila transformed before my eyes. A predator stalking her prey. Except this time, I was the target.

Her leathers hugged her body from neck to ankles, every one of those scars hidden, thank the Spirits. It was hard enough to fight my own scars; hers would ruin me.

We circled, each cataloging every move the other made. Every flinch. Every twitch of a brow.

I waited for her to strike. I hadn't fought her before—didn't know what her style would be other than the few tells I'd picked up. She was smooth and controlled. Quiet and observant.

But when she finally feinted to my left, it was more than that. She moved like a mountain cat, graceful yet elegant. That alone was nearly enough to distract me.

I focused on my own body, though, as she taught me. On the contraction of each muscle as I dodged her strikes, on the places that burned and strained.

"What are you waiting for?" She quirked a brow when I didn't immediately react.

"Learning," I ground out.

"Tell me what you're seeing." Those damn blue eyes lit with the thrill of the match, and it sent a jolt through me.

"You stepped forward with your right foot, so I know your dominant side." A smug smile. "You roll your shoulder after each harsh impact—probably an old injury." Her eyes widened minutely. "And right now"—I adjusted my grip on my sword—"you think having me talk is distracting me."

I swung, but she was ready.

Our blades collided repeatedly, clashes ringing out. And as we danced together around the stables, nothing else existed. She moved too quickly for me, demanded all of my attention so I could only anticipate where she'd attack next and where my sword needed to be to meet it.

"So you're more than just a pretty face, then?" Mila murmured, spinning around my back.

As if tracking where she'd be by instinct alone, I whirled to meet her.

"You think I'm pretty?" I growled. "I'm honored, General."

Her lips quirked into that feline smile again.

My body burned from the intense workout routines Mila had given me these past weeks, but it made me more aware of each placement. My ears were clear of their ringing, the rushing pressure gone.

And I did not want this match to end. A competitive spark ignited within me, feeble but trying to burn.

This was different from usual sparring. I didn't know if it was because Mila was such a fluid opponent or because she was so easy to focus on, but I was figuring out her plan. Those workout techniques had helped me repair a disjointed connection within myself. My physical and mental states had been severed, but we were stitching them back together.

"I finally get it," I panted. Sweat trailed down my spine, a light sheen along Mila's forehead, too.

"What's that?" she breathed. Our faces were close now, swords crossed between our chests. Arms shaking, straining. Pieces of her braid had come loose again, framing her high cheekbones.

I leaned forward, speaking low. "Those workouts. Starting me from the beginning." She smiled. "It wasn't only to get me back in shape. It was to make me aware of my physical skill."

It was to reintroduce myself to positioning and tactics that had been drilled into the younger version of me, as she'd said.

But that boy had died in a dark, dirty cell. Perhaps he'd died atop the Spirit Volcano when his father revealed the twist in his game, or maybe even long before that, when he scratched a pen across a treaty, sealing his fate.

Spirits, it didn't matter when. He was gone.

And he'd left a void I hadn't bothered to fill. I'd refused to properly train, refused to look for a future where I might *need* to. I'd refused everything, really. Became a reclusive excuse for what I was once supposed to be, because it was easier to lock it all away.

Did I want to open that cage, though? Could I let this spark within me consume the past?

"And why would I do that?" Mila ground out, stepping back before attacking again.

She wasn't letting me run away. She was taking the person I'd become and aligning him with a new future. Showing me how to get in touch with this physical routine again and realize I may be different now, but I wasn't broken.

A piece of me relished being broken, though. It was easier than unpacking the heavy truths weighing down my mind.

"You want me to address what's going on up here." I tilted my head, using those words she'd offered when we made our deal. Success gleamed in her eyes.

"You're meant for more than this bottled-up torment, Malakai." Mila's whisper clawed at my caged thoughts, too heartfelt for my warped mind to comprehend. Too good and striking such a deep nerve.

It sent me careening back into my cage, bars slamming shut.

"I'm not." My voice cracked. My arms strained, our blades between us, and under the pressure, I admitted, "Half of me is him. Half of me is rotten."

"Malakai—"

But I shook my head, pushing away from her. Surrendering the match. Letting the spark within me fade.

"I don't want to fix it, Mila."

I may have agreed to this—to hold a sword and learn how to fight again. I may have wanted to be helpful on a battlefield, but there were some battles I wasn't ready to face.

"Giving up, Warrior Prince?" Mila called as I stalked toward the door, both of us breathing heavily.

I froze on the threshold, that familiar roaring back in my ears. It had been such a nice reprieve to fight without it for a few minutes.

"For today."

~

THE THUNDER in my head echoed as I stalked away from the stables and nearly collided with Lyria. She looked as frantic as she had every night since my arrival, purple circles shadowing her eyes and hair falling from her braid, voice shooting up an octave.

"Okay, Malakai?" she asked. Despite her state, she checked on her warrior, like it was her job to hold everything together.

"Fine," I grumbled.

Her eyes swept across my set jaw and clenched fists. Flicked over my shoulder to the stables. I heard the clinking of vambraces being removed and soft steps pass us, but didn't look.

"Walk with me," Lyria said.

Because she seemed so agitated lately, I did.

Lyria didn't speak as she led me away from the heart of camp, to a small outcrop ringed with trees already stripped by the coming winter. She looked at them, lips twisting.

"When we first arrived here, this spot was my favorite. The leaves were turning, a perfect array of oranges and golds, and they were crisp beneath your boots."

I stayed silent as she strolled the circumference of the space.

"Sometimes I came here to cry, to mourn Danya. Sometimes I came here to scream and hoped the foliage would absorb the sound. Would take away every worry, every battle I didn't think I was strong enough for." She ran a hand down a frost-bitten trunk, chipping off a dead piece with her nail. "Sometimes I came here to be quiet."

I cleared my throat. "And why did you bring me here?"

"Because I want you to understand what I'm about to tell you is private, but I also want you to know I'm not telling you to hurt you. I'm showing you this piece of me so you can better understand the pressure we're all under here."

"I—" I cut myself off at the bob of her throat.

I was about to say I understood pressure, but this was fucking warfare. The second war Lyria had fought in twenty-three years of life, and it all sat on her shoulders. Or so she thought.

"You have a team with you, Lyria. It's not all on you."

She huffed a laugh. "And believe me, I know it. I'd be dead without them, I promise you that."

I scratched my hand along the scar on my jaw. "What did you want to tell me, then?"

Lyria, the commander of our armies and Master of Weapons and Warfare, worried the hem of her cloak, considering her words with such gentle care.

"What she's doing for you…it's hard for her."

My stomach hollowed out. "What do you mean?"

"We all faced our own horrors during the last war. We've all been plagued by nightmares every day since it ended. This is bringing those memories into the light."

I leaned against the trunk of a tree, crossing my arms. "I'm not asking you to tell me what she experienced, nor am I asking her. That's her business." Dammit I wanted to fucking know.

"I wouldn't share it even if you did," Lyria said. "But I can share mine. And you can know hers was so much worse."

She looked me directly in the eye as she spoke, and her pain was so thick in the air I thought I'd choke on it.

"I was dragged off the battlefield once," she recounted, and my body chilled. "I was always taught how to be a soldier growing up. Perfect was the standard, accolades were praised. So when we were in one of the most gruesome battles of the war—spirits, the smells, the sounds…" She shivered. "I remember it all so vividly.

"But warriors on our side were falling and I thought I could handle more than I was capable of. Charged through the forest surrounding the field to try to reach their camp myself and secure the general. A stupid plan, but I was foolish and fueled by adrenaline that made me feel unstoppable."

She swallowed, and the next words came out stiff, like she *had* to say them. "I didn't make it thirty feet before an Engrossian pulled me from my horse. He and a friend…held me down. Ripped off my leathers and armor. They were going to…well, they were going to take something no one has a right to take. Mila found me before they could and drove both of her swords through one of their backs, then we continued to dismember him together. The other got away."

Her face didn't expose a bead of emotion as she finished, but if that was her response to what she experienced, I wouldn't comment. She needed to process it her own way.

The story she told had a knot forming in my gut and bile stinging my throat. It was so fucking vile—a side of war many pretended didn't exist. The pillaging, the assault, soldiers high on power, taking a number of things that didn't belong to them.

"I'm sorry, Lyria," I said. "I'm sorry they did that to you, and I know nothing can replace what they tried to take, but I'm glad you got a modicum of revenge." One corner of her lips lifted. "And the fact that you returned here, that you continue to face those troops every day, is really fucking admirable. Damien, I don't know many who could. I can't imagine how strong you have to be to face it every day."

Her shoulders straightened. "I want to end this so it doesn't happen to anyone else."

In a different sense, I understood what she meant. I wanted this war over so Lucidius's actions stopped hurting others.

"Can I ask why you shared this with me?"

"Because, as you said, I'm really fucking strong to be here. Mila went through more than I did during the war, Malakai. The fact that she's here at all is incredible. I don't know if she would be if I wasn't, to be honest. We've stuck together ever since the treaty. When one of us wakes screaming in the night, the other is always there to remind her where we are.

"I told her she didn't have to come. I told her she didn't have to fight. She wanted to be a damn general." Lyria shook her head with a small smile. "And the fact that she's helping you individually? I never thought I'd see it. So be patient with her. She has her reasons for everything she's doing."

Mila's scars flashed through my mind unbidden, imprinted themselves on the back of my eyelids.

"I'll remember," I swore to Lyria. I'd been an ass to walk out of training.

"Good." And quickly, she slipped back into her usual countenance. Still frazzled, but no longer blocking her emotions. "Now let's get back. Breakfast smelled divine and those heathens always eat so quickly."

I followed, but my mind remained in that secret space, wrestling with everything I'd learned.

Chapter Twenty-Seven
Malakai

I was standing on the porch to the main cabin trying to work up the courage to go inside when a horn cleaved the night, quickly followed by a second.

Mila came charging out not a minute later, leathers in place, buckling on her weapon belt and sliding her swords across her back. It was the first time I saw her since storming out of training a few days prior, but she flew down the steps without acknowledging me, a predator homed in on her prey.

"What's happening?" I asked, chasing her down the front steps. All throughout the town, warriors were stirring. Some ran from tents already outfitted, others helped comrades buckle on armor.

"There's an attack," she answered, not slowing her pace.

"What part of the line?" My blood pounded in my ears.

Around us, warriors rushed to attention. Orders were shouted. Horses saddled. This was only one of many battles they'd faced, but it was the first with this level of surprise since I'd arrived at camp.

"That horn came from the west and blew twice." She spoke clinically. I recalled what Lyria had implied about how Mila had suffered during the last war. Maybe grounding herself with the facts was how she charged forward. "It means they're rushing the western border and the battalion stationed there needs rein-forcements."

Mila finished tying off her braid with a leather band, flicking it over her shoulder where it nearly slapped me. "A new fucking tactic, I'll give them that," she added with a growl.

Outside the stables, Mila turned to me. "Find the prince and Dax. We need the general with us now."

Before I could answer, she marched into the stables and began commanding her troops. "First charge—Mystiques, Soulguiders, and Starsearchers, with me. Archers to the ridges to relieve the lookouts." The authority in her voice stole every warrior's atten-tion, despite their clan. Sharp nods responded, movements hurrying to fall into line.

"Searchers, do you have people in the temples?"

"Patrol turned over an hour ago," Cyren confirmed. I hadn't seen the Starsearcher General arrive, but they sat atop a lithe gold mare with an intricately braided mane. The horse was thinner than Mystique horses, but with sure footing, agile yet stable enough for their winding jungle roads. Damn, even the minor clans' animals were accustomed to their magic.

Amara and Quilian were mounted on their horses beside Cyren, conferring with Mila, each of the generals bearing armor of their clans. The only one missing was—

"Wait, what?" *Find the prince and Dax.* Mila's earlier command finally caught up with me.

By the damned Spirits. I'd been evaluating myself and my behavior these past few days. While I didn't have answers, I knew I needed to be a part of this army, on that battlefield, not turning pages in journals every night and wondering who would be here in the morning, even if I was still tormented by my memory.

I charged into the stables and stopped at Ombratta's stall. She exhaled roughly, as if asking what had taken me so long. "Ready, my shadow horse?" It was a nickname I'd given her years before I'd left. One I hadn't used since.

She nudged me at the familiar term.

"I'll be right back," I promised.

Tightening my gloves, I borrowed vambraces and a sword from

the storage shed beside the stables. I hadn't brought mine to see Mila tonight, assuming I'd return to my tent immediately after. Lesson learned—when in the war camp, always be prepared for battle.

"What are you doing?" Mila asked as I finished saddling Ombratta.

"I'm preparing," I retorted without looking. I took the reins, and Ombratta set a determined march from the stables toward the warriors already set out.

"I gave you an order." As she said it, Dax and Barrett passed behind her, and we both knew that order was irrelevant. "You're not coming." It was her general's voice following us, stepping in front of me and pinning me with a hardened stare. Commanding me.

"I can't keep sitting here night after night and not doing anything." My fingers tightened on the leather. "I can't keep hiding."

She searched my expression, but kept up her guard. "You haven't completed the Undertaking."

"Spirits, Mila, you know as well as I do you can wave that rule." A week ago, I wouldn't have pushed, but Lyria's words had stirred in my mind for days. I wanted to display even a modicum of the strength she and Mila had. But I didn't have the time or the desire to complete the ritual. "Right here, right now, our general can declare I fight with the army regardless."

"Malakai, you..." For the first time since the horn sounded, Mila softened. It was clear she didn't want to say it. "Do you think it is wise?"

No, I didn't fucking think it was wise. It was an awful idea for me to be on a battlefield with my...state. But waiting here would be even worse. I'd be driven crazy not knowing the outcome and feel like a damn coward while I was at it. Even now, the roaring rushed my ears.

"It's the only option." I skirted the question. Gripping the pommel, I swung myself into the saddle and looked down at Mila.

She chewed her lip, clearly warring with herself. "You need to train more, Malakai. You're putting yourself in danger."

"That's my reckless decision to make, then." It was growing quieter around us as most of the legion had marched off. Camp still buzzed with activity, a second line preparing to fight if the first couldn't hold off the Engrossians, but here it was only us.

"Why?" Mila asked.

"Because...I need to see it." Needed to reinforce the atrocities Lucidius had been responsible for after everything I'd learned recently. Needed to be fucking useful when I had no clue how to do so. If I got myself hurt, that was my problem, but I'd be damned to the Spirit Realm before I stayed here.

Locked up.

Cowardly.

Alone.

Mila swallowed, shaking her head, and locked up the wall to her fortress. "You stay at the back. Remember what we told you of the power Kakias has over them; they're efficient but messy when too focused on a target. Use that to your advantage. If you can get to the ridge where the archers are stationed, stay there. If not, I hope you're ready."

Without another word, she mounted her own horse and flew off into the night.

Warmth gathered in the cage in my chest. She was not going to hold me back, despite our fight. Didn't tell me I was incapable of this. Instead, she gave me advice and went on her way.

Nudging Ombratta, we followed the path Mila's mare cut through the mountains, my breath gathering before me, and I prayed to Damien that I wasn't making the worst fucking mistake of my life.

As we approached the western border, I heard it.

The familiar roar of warriors bearing down on one another. Sharp clashes of weapons that only came with brutal, desperate warfare. An abrupt drop off of a gargled scream as it was silenced by an enemy's blade. Metallic death coated the air.

Mila had pulled ahead of me before we arrived, disappearing down the incline leading into the melee. At least being stationed in the mountains, we had the higher ground. Lyria and the generals had established the camp's borders at the highest points, so we'd always see them coming should they breach or evade the troops stationed at points along the base of the mountains.

We didn't have enough soldiers to keep the entire perimeter surrounded. Probably how they got here tonight.

Looking around above the fray, I found the highest points of the border: two peaks opposite each other, now lined by dozens of Seawatchers. Amara stood with her people, distinguished by the coral and aquamarine crest on her breastplate. I couldn't hear the orders she shouted, but as one, the Seawatchers nocked their arrows, aimed, and let them fly. I didn't have to hear the squelches of arrowheads through eyes and throats and skulls to know each landed.

Angels, they were incredible.

And they may have been the best asset we had in this war. From the mountainside, a team of archers was an unparalleled advantage.

My eyes bounced between their perches and the fray below. With only the moonlight to see by, it was difficult to count how many Engrossians or Mindshapers had launched the attack. But I was certain there were less of them than in our defense, as Lyria had explained.

As I watched, an Engrossian raised an ax. He swung it down with fine precision, right into the shoulder of a Mystique. I released a deep growl as the warrior fell.

Ombratta pranced beneath me.

"I know, Shadow. I know."

I looked at the Seawatchers' lookouts, then back to the battle below. Moonlight caught on the flick of a long white braid, and my stomach turned over. Mila, no longer on her mare, cut a path through warriors with a sword in each hand and blood streaked across her face. Despite them being larger than her, despite some of them still being seated, she took out one after the other as if fueled by an unholy rage. Those ivy cuffs—not usual vambraces—glinted in the moonlight.

You stay at the back.

As I warred with indecisiveness, Mila pierced one sword beneath a warrior's ribs. She withdrew it, but not quickly enough.

Her opponent kicked a boot into her stomach, right in the center of the steel cuirass that hugged her frame tighter than any armor I'd seen before.

She stumbled backward, but stayed upright.

"No fucking way," I seethed. I wasn't going to sit here and watch like a helpless child while everyone fought down there.

"Come on." I squeezed my calves against Ombratta's ribs, and she tore down the incline, a Mystique mare finally entering her fight. She towered above most of the other horses, leaving me stretching down for some blows but giving me an advantage for others.

Spirits, I'd forgotten how freeing it was to fight from horseback. I'd only ever done it in training, and not often then, but the leverage I gained from up here and the connection with my mare —not much matched it.

Ombratta fell in line with the other horses of various clans as if the spot had been saved for us. Few of their warriors had pushed this far through our front line.

That—

"*Fuck*," I screamed, focus shattering as searing pain shot through my leg.

A dagger was lodged in my calf, a tiny thing, no more than three inches, wedged above my boot.

A few Engrossians *had* made it past unnoticed. They'd snuck below sightline, dispersing quickly after landing their blows.

I left the weapon in as Ombratta turned around, not wanting to remove it when I couldn't be sure what was punctured. She pursued the Engrossians up the hill, and the center point of pain called to me, stealing my attention.

My vision blurred. Warped and twisted, leaching all color from the night until everything was a mess of shades of gray.

They were right before me, but I couldn't be sure who was whom. Ombratta kept up the chase, but I was useless. I tried to lift my borrowed sword but was afraid to swing it. What if I hit a Mystique?

My chest tightened, the relief from being on horseback once again replaced by crushing irrelevance.

"Not again," I muttered under my breath, defeated. Fuck, I'd been so close. I could almost feel my mind shutting down now. Like orbs of mystlight popping out one by one.

Get your act together. This was the risk I took running down here. I knew it—I swore I was ready.

You lied.

Anger bubbled within me, and I swayed atop my horse. My mind was too addled from my torture.

Maybe it always would be.

Maybe training would never help.

Maybe I was meant to be on the side lines forever.

Fine. If the Spirits wanted me there, that's where I'd stay.

"Let's go back, Ombratta." I barely mumbled it, but she was up the hill and back in the stables before I could finish reprimanding myself.

"WHERE IN THE Spirits did you go?"

I didn't even have time to react before hands were gripping the front of my tunic. I'd changed out of my leathers after returning to my tent and dunking cold water over myself to calm my racing thoughts, every intention of going back out to help after I collected myself.

"What are you doing here?" I asked, looking down at Mila's eyes burning with fury.

"I should ask you that!" she roared, her fists beating my chest with each word.

"What do you mean?" I gripped her wrists, stilling her.

"You don't disappear from a battle without checking in with your superiors!" She shoved away from me, but I held on to her, stumbling back into my bed, my sore calf barking at the contact with the post. My glass of drug-laced water spilled over on the nightstand, the fresh herbs I'd gotten from the infirmary soaked.

"When you didn't come back, Barrett and I crawled through the field looking for your *corpse*, Malakai!" I froze. Mila's chest heaved. "When you're on that field, whatever happens, you can't leave! You're a part of a team, and no matter what happens, you stay there for them. You check in with your *fucking general* before coming back to your tent to lick your wounds."

I was dragged off the battlefield once...Mila found me...

Angels, I was an idiot. Everything Mila said was standard protocol, but I was certain she was also experiencing flashbacks of what had happened to Lyria.

What kind of inexperienced, amateur, sham of a warrior flees a battlefield assuming no one will notice their absence? There are systems in place to track these things.

"I—I'm sorry." I released her hands. "I should never have left. I had...an episode."

Mila crossed her arms, inhaling and releasing the breath slowly at my confession. When she spoke again, her voice was level. "I figured as much when we didn't find you dying out there."

The bluntness of her words sliced through my chest.

"We won this one?"

"We did." Mila brushed a loose strand of hair from her face, and I noticed a freshly bandaged slice to her forehead. Something hot spiraled through me, but I forced myself to focus on her words. "Lost a few good warriors in the process but fewer than in the last attacks. Our force is getting stronger."

"Good." I didn't know how else to respond. We were still standing toe-to-toe, so close I could count her lashes and see where they got lighter at the ends. Mystlight flickered against the canvas tent, each of Mila's expressions more pronounced in the light, and for a moment we stood like that, the adrenaline fading. Something else sizzling in the air.

With an inhale and a step back, she looked around us. Her eyes landed on the upturned glass on the table, clouded liquid staining the surface. "What's that?"

I sighed, figuring I owed her a bit of honesty after the shit I pulled tonight. "Most nights I take herbs to help me sleep. To... numb me."

"Drugs," she deadpanned.

I shrugged.

"Malakai," Mila groaned. "I'm trying so hard to help you but this shit"—she flung an arm out—"this is only helping you *run away*." She rubbed her eyes with the heels of her palms. "I shouldn't have allowed you out there tonight."

"It's not your decision to make."

"It is," she said. "I'm a general. Behind Lyria, I'm the highest rank. I make the calls, and I keep an extremely organized process in doing so. I'm sorry I allowed it, and you won't be seeing another battlefield until you're ready." She leaned against the table, avoiding the spill. "And for the sake of the Spirits, cut out the damn drugs. I can't help you if you don't want to help yourself."

I was a child playing games. Mila had seen war. She'd survived its atrocities. She understood how these things worked because she'd lived it—had probably seen warriors struggle with mental blocks the way I did. And I hadn't listened to her.

"I'm sorry I didn't do as I was instructed. I..." I took a huge breath, not wanting to agree to the next bit. "I'll stop with the drugs. And next time I'll follow orders." And I *would*. Then, as a peace offering, I offered a bit of the truth. "An Engrossian got past the line. He sliced a dagger right into my calf, and the pain combined with the fact that I hadn't seen him was..." I trailed off, but she nodded as if she understood what I meant.

"Can I see?" she asked, gesturing to my leg.

Sitting on the edge of the bed, I rolled up my pants for her. The slice wasn't deep, and the mountains had already begun healing it. The makeshift wrap I'd fashioned around it did enough to keep it covered. It barely even hurt physically; it was only the shameful reminder of how I'd fled.

Mila kneeled before me and gently took my calf between her hands. "It looks like it's healing well, and it doesn't feel hot, so I think you should be safe from infection." Her fingers trailed up my leg as she inspected the wound. I wasn't even sure she realized she was doing it, but, fuck, did it feel good to have someone touching me like that. Somewhere between a mix of care and exploration and control. I wanted her hands to keep going up, to reach the waistband of my pants and pull them down until—

"Next time," she interrupted that train of thought, eyes lifting to mine, "go straight to a healer in case you're not as lucky." Her tone was softer now, both hands bracing herself against my legs.

A vision of her in white lace flashed through my mind. Mystlight fell across her features, picking up the slight blush to her cheeks as she swallowed, and I wondered if she was thinking of it, too.

"Right." My voice was rough. "*Next time* I'm stabbed, I'll find a professional."

With a smile, Mila rose to her feet and turned toward the tent entrance. "We're back to training in two days. Give that time to heal and us time to recover from tonight."

"You're still going to train me after I blatantly ignored orders?"

"Yes." She stopped in the entrance, turning back to face me. "Because I'm certain you'll make a stupid decision again."

Chapter Twenty-Eight
Tolek

"Sapphire seems unsettled," Cypherion said, glancing over his shoulder at the blue-maned mare.

She had been riled as we left her in the stable in this small Bodymelder town I didn't even know the name of, but the rest of our horses were with her. With how late it already was, we were only leaving them for a few hours.

"She gets that way when separated from Ophelia sometimes." I gripped the strap of my pack tighter. "But the inn is next door. She'll be okay."

The sun had set a while ago, taking the last of the day's warmth with it. Night wrapped around the narrow cobblestone streets and ivy-draped buildings. Dirt paths forked out behind the stables, leading into the cyphers, and somewhere nearby, a calm stream babbled lazily.

As Cypherion and I entered the inn's dining room and I got us two seats beside the fire, warmth wrapped around me. The girls had all gone upstairs to bathe given that it was our first night in a true inn after a few long days of travel. Firebird's Field was still nearly a week off, but last Lyria's spies reported, Kakias was in Mindshaper territory, so at least one threat to Ptholenix's emblem was out of our way.

And one to Ophelia.

Cypherion ordered drinks from the barkeep, and as he waited, a woman with long dark hair approached him. I couldn't hear what she said, but I watched with a satisfied smirk, leaning back in my chair.

And when Cyph said, "Sorry, I'm unavailable," my eyes widened.

He dropped down in the seat opposite me, sighing heavily as he passed me a glass of liquor, and I raised my brows at him. "Are you going to tell me what that was?"

"What *what* was?"

"*I'm not available.*" I impersonated his gruff tone.

Not that now was an opportune time for any of us to be entertaining random warriors, but I'd never heard him clearly state he was *not available* no matter how many women he'd been with.

Cypherion dragged his palm across the splintered wood. "I don't want to discuss it."

"And is the *it* in question a secretive woman with an affinity for the stars and fates?"

I tipped my glass to my lips, watching for his reaction. You didn't know someone for over a decade, become their other half the way Cypherion and I had, without being able to predict their responses. He would shake his head, mumble something about me that was meant to be insulting but he'd say it so softly it only made me laugh, and cross his arms, looking around the room.

And he did exactly that, but then—

Cypherion sighed, and it weighed down the air like an unburdening. Dropping his hands to his lap, he fiddled with the cuff of his leathers. There was more he wanted to say; it balanced on the tip of his tongue, trying to break from his strictly ordered mind.

Planting both of my boots on the floor, I leaned my elbows on the table. "What happened in Damenal, CK?"

A shrug. "A lot of things I regret."

Fuck. Cypherion did not open himself up easily. While I'd known something was unfolding between Vale and him before her arrangement with Titus was exposed, it was clear whatever they'd shared went deeper than any of us had assumed. To regret was one of the worst sorrows, because it was irreversible. You could reach a place where the remorse did not sting so severely, where it was soothed with a balm of understanding, but you could never rewrite history.

And Cypherion was careful. He rarely put himself in a position where *regret* was a possibility. My fingers curled around my glass. The instinct to march upstairs to Vale and demand she make this right or let Cypherion go and return to Titus, roared inside of me.

But I swallowed it down. Because whatever had happened was clearly hurting Cypherion, which meant he cared. And maybe there was a chance it didn't have to be this way.

"And you're certain it's too far gone to repair?"

"Yes," he said, but he cracked his neck and avoided my gaze.

The door swung open with a squeak and closed softly as two patrons took a table nearby. I lowered my voice and kept my attention on my friend.

"I'm not going to pretend to know precisely what you're going through. That would be presumptuous of me. But I've seen how you regard her. How you cared for her after the platforms and during the Angellight fiasco the other night." My hand clenched atop my knee, but I fought off the scars that memory tore at. "I will always be on your side, but it's clear you care for her despite what has unveiled itself."

"I would have been concerned for any of you." He brushed me off, lifting his mug.

"You agree she's one of us, then?"

He froze on his sip, and a victorious grin split my lips. I hadn't been sure I wanted Vale to be one of us, but she seemed to be genuinely trying. And I thought, maybe she could be good for Cypherion.

Satisfied, I leaned back against my chair. Cyph's gaze flicked to me from the corner of his eye, and he shook his head.

"I hate being on this end of the interrogation," he grumbled.

A barking laugh burst from me. How often had Cypherion sat with Malakai or me, forcing us to discuss things we'd rather leave untouched? Spirits, he'd prodded me for years over my feelings for Ophelia. He'd been the one to help me navigate her relationship with Malakai, ensuring I did nothing to interfere with them or with the nature of our closely-tied group.

Not that I would have intentionally, but there were countless nights when he kicked me beneath the table for staring at her too long or offered to walk home with the two of us after a few too many drinks so we wouldn't be alone in the quiet night. Who knows what my desperately-in-love, alcohol-ridden brain would have decided it had been an opportune moment to share.

"It was only a matter of time until you needed my sage advice," I chirped.

"What do you have for me, Master?" he joked, but I tilted my head, liking the sound of that title.

Not now, Vincienzo, I corrected myself. Twisting my mug between my palms, I mulled over his predicament.

"We know Vale lied to us. She hid secrets that could have aided in saving Damenal, preventing the attack that killed hundreds and devastated a city that was only beginning to come back to life."

"Not helping." His fingers tightened on his mug.

"That anger," I said, pointing at his white-knuckles. "What if *that* is misdirected?"

"I know she didn't cause the attack, Tolek. That's not why I'm angry."

"But have you considered she may not have had a choice in the role she played?"

"I have." He relaxed his grip, but tension held the rest of his body on a sword's edge. "And I don't know what's worse."

There it is. A part of Cypherion cared undeniably for Vale. If he didn't, her confession wouldn't have held such a sting. He'd be angry, but it wouldn't have mattered whether her hand had been forced or if she was operating on her own motives.

Now if only we could figure out how to untangle the mess Titus had made.

"We also know Vale was enslaved to a temple." I didn't know the details of that history, other than its repugnant, illegal existence. From the way Cypherion mumbled beneath his breath and avoided my eye, I wondered if he knew more than we thought. "So it's possible she's still tied to some oaths."

"And if she is," Cypherion sighed, like this was painful to admit, "it's forced."

"It is." I nodded.

"Lyria has not spoken directly with Titus," Cyph said. "I wrote to her to ask after we arrived in Brontain."

I considered. "He's hiding from the alliance."

"He's hiding from *something*, clearly. He sent a general and soldiers, though. Your sister believes them to be well-intentioned and claims their readings have been beneficial to the war effort."

I could not make sense of that. Sabotage us with one ally only to provide a true one. "He isn't against the Mystique alliance," I thought out loud. "He's clearly got an agenda hidden somewhere, but it's not that."

"Unless he wants to topple our army from the inside."

"That general would have to be an extremely talented liar to get past my sister." Even as I said it, though, nerves twisted my gut. "And any idea why Vale's readings aren't working?"

The mention of it had CK curling his hands into fists. "No, but she can't keep reading if it's going to end in her seizing."

I'd barely been aware of what was happening during the Angel-light test, too focused on Ophelia, but the glimpses I'd caught of Vale within the fog had chilled me.

I scrubbed my hand down my face, dragging it across the stubble of my jaw. "I wish I could return to centuries ago and ask Annellius Alabath what this is all about."

"Me, too." With a sigh, Cypherion drained the rest of his ale.

"You know, you're good at this," I said. "The information. Balancing it all."

Cyph grumbled, "Not you, too."

"All I'm wondering is why? Why don't you want to be Second?" He opened his mouth, but I cut him off. "And don't give me the line about only being half Mystique. I'm the only full-blooded one of us, and Spirits know I couldn't do it."

"You could," Cyph said, spinning his empty glass in his hands. "For the record." When I continued to stare at him expectantly, he groaned, leaning back in his chair. "I don't—my mother. You know how she is." His mother had been reclusive as long as we'd known him, but despite his reluctance to talk about it, it was clear it went much deeper. Cypherion had written to her every day since we left Palerman.

As far as I knew, no letters were returned.

"That happened out of nowhere when I was younger," he continued, watching the fire. The flames cast shadows across his face. "One day she was there. The next—gone. Mentally, at least. And it was right when I thought she might start talking about who my father is. Ever since then, I've felt like it happened because I was never supposed to know.

"And if I'm not supposed to know that one basic fact about myself, how can I help lead an entire population? You have to be confident in yourself for these things. I don't know who I am."

"You know who you are," I answered without needing to think. "You're intelligent, dependable, compassionate, and strong. So you don't know your father? Who cares? In some cases, that's better." Perhaps a bit of disdain for my own father was bleeding into my words, but I leaned on the table, invigorated now. "You don't need to know who he is in order for you to be someone great. He has no say in who you become."

"But what if it's all fate giving me a sign?"

"Think of it this way," I said, twirling my liquor glass. "You would still be the same man you are even if he showed up. You would still carry the same ideals. Who you are is a result of everything you've survived and achieved. An amalgamation of everything you've learned. And you've earned a good life for yourself, CK, fate be damned."

He was silent for a long moment, watching his fingers brush dust from the cuffs of his leathers.

"Just consider it," I pleaded.

Finally, eyes still averted, he said, "I have been. Don't tell Ophelia yet."

"I won't," I promised. And though I hated keeping things from her, this was not my story to tell.

"We're leaving at first light," he said, pushing to his feet, effectively ending the conversation. "We should get some sleep."

"I'm going to stay down here for a bit," I said, ignoring his narrowed stare.

Digging in my pack, I pulled out two of the books Ezalia allowed me to borrow from her archives. We needed information on the Angels and gods. The fact that we were traveling didn't change that.

I was spending most of my nights with these books, avoiding sleep. Ever since Ophelia tested those Angel emblems, my nightmares had been worse. I could still smell the cursed Angellight if I thought about it, like windswept seas mixed with musty secrets and a tinge of cleansing. Was that what everyone else experienced when they saw Damien in the council chamber following the Battle of Damenal?

I grimaced at the reminder that I was the only one yet to meet the Angel. That summoning ritual was the closest I'd been, and that wasn't even his full appearance. Only light.

Damien's unholy cock, few things had scared me as much as the moment when I thought I wouldn't be able to pull Ophelia back. The way she'd been consumed by that Angellight, as if her mind and spirit were on another plane, was terrifying enough. I'd been shaking when she finally came back to herself. These Angels could be damned to the Spirit Realm if they ever tried to take her from me.

I knew she had to do it, but dammit did I hate it. Hated the way I couldn't do a damn thing to help. It intensified the darkest parts of my nightmares where she was taken from me again and again—the ones I didn't know how to explain to her, that ended blood-drenched and horror-stricken.

I shoved away the concern now and held up the tomes for Cypherion to see.

"That one is a fairytale, Tolek," Cypherion scolded, pointing to the thicker of the two, *Tales of Seraphs and Steeds* stamped into the cover.

"Well, sometimes we need a break. And look at this." I flipped to a random page and turned the volume toward Cyph. "The stories are written in Endasi on the left, and transcribed to the common tongue on the right."

"That *is* interesting," Cypherion mused, not being able to interpret the language of the Angels.

"But for now, I'll focus on this." I waved my other book at him: *Manipulative Magic: Meditative Practices of Mindshapers Dating Back to the Prime Warrior (Volume I)*.

Cyph's brows flicked up at my choice, but I tucked away the story book and opened the other, not commenting on why I was so invested in unraveling Mindshaper magic in particular. He'd probably guessed, anyway.

The spine cracked with age. The scent of worn parchment wafted around me as Cyph retreated upstairs and I settled in with my journal.

This, I could do. I wasn't as strategically inclined as Cypherion or a battle expert like my sister. I could hold my own in a meeting and would never turn down a fight, but those weren't my strengths. While I preferred a different type of literature to the one currently in my hands, researching and constructing thorough reports of the findings, interpreting the past and what it might mean was a role I could play. Somewhere I wasn't second place.

And if it could help Ophelia, I would never say no.

As my pen scratched against the paper, and I studied Thorn's magic, voices drifted over from the only other occupied table in the room, low and melodic.

"A prince long gone from this earth," one woman told another. Her tale became the tune to which I read and wrote. "The gods waged war, one that would ensure the death of his kingdom. As the battles raged, this prince knew there was no end in sight. Not without a field strewn with death."

Her words were so pointed, it almost sounded as if she was directly beside me. I struggled to focus on what I was reading of Thorn's studies and how he'd tried to use different natural forces to enrich his magic.

In his later decades, the Prime Warrior became fascinated by how gods bled across the land, claiming winged conductors of Angel power feared the potency of this expelling force. Though the efforts were futile; he committed endless years to the legends that were nothing more than folklore.

Thorn was intrigued by the gods? Interesting. Vale suspected she'd seen them in her session, though she wasn't certain. Still, I made a note and continued on, more curious about the Mindshaper himself.

That melodic voice sliced through my thoughts, though. "Because that prince feared what would happen if he lost the war, he made a drastic call."

"What was it?" her companion asked.

"Sacrifice." The word had my pen slipping across the page, a line sharply cutting across my notes. "The prince gave up his mortal life for his kingdom. But in doing so, he set up for the faults of future generations. He was misremembered as greedy, but when his soul was taken, it ripped a gap in the ether. Something wicked stirred for the first time in millennia. Something deep as the darkest tar beneath the soil of the earth and hot as her core."

Frowning down at the smear of ink now marring my notes, I closed my journal and threw back the rest of my drink. With my pack slung over my shoulder, I stalked past the woman's table. Her curious gaze drew goosebumps along my arms, but I kept walking. Until I was in my room with the door closed where the attention-demanding, airy tone of her voice could no longer be heard.

Leaning over the sink, I took in my sleep-deprived face in the mirror. The room's mystlight made me appear gaunt, but it was that echo in my head truly plaguing me.

Sacrifice.

I hated that damn word. Hated the pain it caused those I loved and the threats it still hung over our heads. I swore it would not touch us. It would not touch Ophelia.

As I extinguished the mystlight and tried to force myself to sleep, I promised us both if she was so set on getting everyone else to safety—on making decisions that would ensure the innocents of Gallantia survived and the Angel emblems were found—then I'd be focused on her.

Whatever it took.

I'd keep every one of my nightmares from coming true.

And when I tried to sleep, I dreamt of battling princes and sacrificial blood, a beautiful death at the end of my blade that ripped out my own soul and magenta eyes fading lifelessly.

CHAPTER TWENTY-NINE
OPHELIA

><><><><

I WOKE TO TOLEK SCREAMING.

I tore from my room, threw the door to his open, and climbed onto the bed, talking to him until he realized he was awake. He was safe.

I ignored Cypherion, who followed me in—ignored everything else.

Once our heart rates both calmed, I pulled Tolek out into the crisp night air and down a winding path away from the inn. Away from our friends and the shadows of his fears.

Only us, the draping branches of cypher trees, and constellations winking in a star-speckled sky.

When we reached a small wooden bridge stretching across a narrow stream, we stopped. I leaned my hip against the railing, and Tolek braced his elbows on it. He looked out over the gentle dips of the water, the paths it carved around stone, and I looked at him. At the shadows beneath his eyes and the disarray of his hair. His uncanny silence bit into my heart.

I knew of the false beliefs his father had planted in his head and how the Undertaking weaponized them, but what was Tolek so afraid of that the Mindshaper torture he underwent last summer continued to feed it into his subconscious night after night?

As if reading my thoughts, he finally said, "I think I'm ready to talk about some of it."

My heart pounded.

"I let it get to me," Tol began, staring out over the water. "The things my father used to say and do." He stroked the back of my hand with his thumb, the touch raising goosebumps along my arms.

"You don't have to tell me," I whispered.

He nodded as if he knew. "I want to. I want you to know the parts of me I'm too scared to face. But I'm afraid of how they'll sound."

His voice was unsteady. A slight waver over the last few words gave me an inkling of how hard this was for him. It was the same way he'd reassured himself I was okay after I'd attempted to contact Damien. I wasn't sure how those paired together, but I knew no matter what he told me, my mind would not change about *him*.

I squeezed his hand, silently letting him know, but giving him room to speak.

"He used to tell me life would be better if I didn't exist." My blood chilled. Not only at the words but at the defeated acceptance in Tolek's voice as if it was a message branded into his brain. "And I thought one time he was going to make it happen."

"*What?*"

"It was an accident—I think. I was fifteen. You know those stairs in our entry way? The marble ones?" I nodded, cold horror in my chest. "He got a little too forceful, and I went down them. I don't think he even realized what he was doing. But he...left after. Never said a thing. And it was all because I stayed out too late one night getting into Angels knew what, and he thought I was putting a stain on the family name. It didn't matter if Lyria stayed out to all hours; she was the perfect heiress who could do no wrong. She wasn't *me*." A distaste I hadn't realized he retained for his sister twisted his words.

"That's part of my nightmares. Night after night, down those stairs, and stumbling into things even more awful, all stemming from the failure he made me out to be in those moments."

I shivered at the way his voice darkened over the last words. At the consideration of what he couldn't find it in himself to voice.

He cleared his throat. "The cuts healed over quickly, and the bruises were easy enough to hide from our friends as long as I kept my leathers on during training. In other activities, it didn't matter if they showed. As long as you all didn't see." Though impossible for anyone who wasn't Tolek, one corner of his lips curled up. The way he smiled through his pain twisted my gut. He shouldn't have to mask it. "I came to your manor afterward, though. Slept on that large couch in the sitting room for three nights."

"I remember that," I said, thinking back to the mornings we'd shared over tea, bare feet and untidy hair. "You kept feigning exhaustion when the others left and asked if you could stay." I'd never hesitated to tell him yes. If I'd known the reason, though, he likely would have had to tie me down to keep my wrath from his father. "You could have gone to Malakai's. Why didn't you?"

"You always made me feel safest." He said it so simply, so boldly, and his words rang through my body in recognition. "I knew you loved me—not in the way I did, or you didn't know you did in the way I did." He shook his head. "I knew you'd protect me. Unwaveringly and unquestioningly. It was the only place I wanted to be."

"I'll protect you until the day I die, Tolek. I'm sorry for what he did, for the thoughts it left you with, but thank you for trusting me enough to share it with me." Wrapping my arms around his waist, I added, "You make me feel safe, too."

"I always will," he whispered against my hair.

I contemplated what he'd said. He knew then I loved him, though he wasn't sure how.

I loved Tolek in a lot of small ways. It was the soft drifting of fingertips across skin that raised goosebumps in their wake, and the gentle ruffle of pages of a book turning on a beach at midnight. It was the low, husky laugh when I said something particularly challenging, and the spicy citrus scent that meant home and comfort and fulfilled promises. In the sparkling childhood memories, each morning over tea or races on our mares after long school days.

All those small ways added up to the big ones, too. To the feeling of throwing yourself over the edge of a cliff and praying the other person was there to catch you. To something as powerful as stars bursting and Angels falling. It burned the darkest parts of my life and forged the dawn.

Resting my chin against his chest, I looked up to find him already watching me.

"Yes?" he asked.

I loved him in every language, but I chose one only he would understand.

"You're my best friend," I told him.

I'm in love with you, is what it meant.

And from the way he grinned, proudly and almost in disbelief, I knew he understood.

"You're my best friend, too, Alabath."

For a few minutes, we stood like that. A pair of hurting and healing warriors beneath a moonlit night, entrusting their hopes and fears unto the other, fingers wrapping tightly around secrets poured into palms as battle worn as our souls. Burdens exchanged to lighten our hearts because two were stronger than one, the two of us the strongest of all.

Tolek saw his past as his flaws. As things making him imperfect and damaged and not worthy. And I had a feeling if this was the first piece he'd chosen to share, it was only the tip of the iceberg of how deeply his pain bled.

"You've always made my life better, Tol. You know that?" I tilted my head back to look at him, at the awe seeping into his stare. "You make *me* want to be a better person. The kind of person who deserves someone as good as you and works to make you feel appreciated every day."

"You think much too highly of me, Alabath." He tried to laugh—to lighten the truth of what he'd admitted.

No more, I decided. No longer would he mask his emotions with humor because he was afraid of handing them over or telling me something I didn't like.

"I don't." I shook my head. "I only see you truly. Your mind, your soul, your bravery. I see it all as if drawn out like a map of my own heart."

He kissed my forehead. "I don't deserve you. And you deserve better."

"No," I said. "I haven't always been good. I've been awful to a lot of people and done many things that are arguably not *good*. But you make me want to be a better person."

And slowly, like an unraveling of a tightly wound spool of thread, tension seeped from his muscles. It was incremental at first, nerves over what he'd told me still clinging to every facet of him, but his heart calmed beneath my palm and his shoulders fell.

"You make me want to fight my demons," Tol whispered, kissing me softly.

Twining my fingers through his, I led him back to the inn. Across the paths lined with cyphers, bantering easily about the day. No thought of haunted nightmares or torturous parents or cursed emblems even crossing our lips. Just my best friend—my infinite tether to all things good and true—and me.

"Will you come in?" I asked at the door to my room.

"I can for a while, yeah," he said, holding the door wide for me.

"No," I corrected, walking through and tugging him after me into the circle of moonlight through deep burgundy curtains. "I'd like you to stay."

He eyed me. "Are you sure?" Hope lifted his voice.

"Yes, Tol. I want you to stay. I want you to close your eyes and go to sleep and if those cursed nightmares wake you in the middle of the night, I'll be here. Because I'm going to keep you safe."

A different kind of intimacy, that's what I was offering.

Something flourished within his eyes as I spoke. *Desire.* In revealing these pieces of himself tonight, he'd also pulled back a bit of the restraint we'd both been clinging to.

Heat gathered between my legs, needy and wanton. But I wouldn't turn his admission into that, wouldn't take this new bond between us and make it an impetus for something physical. Every touch already fanned the flame within me, but I wanted to nurture the other half of a relationship first.

Tolek smiled, wide and uninhibited, cheeks tinting pink. "Keep me safe, Alabath."

CHAPTER THIRTY
MALAKAI

THE LIGHTS IN LYRIA AND MILA'S CABIN GLOWED against the snow-flecked night. Winter was moving in earlier this year, even in the frigid southern mountains. They didn't typically receive snow quite this early. Foreboding swirled in my gut at the consideration of how that would affect our armies.

It would give the Mindshapers another advantage for sure.

Knocking the powder from my boots, I hurried up the steps and through the door, into the haven of mystlight warmth. Everyone on Lyria's council was already here.

"There he is." Barrett sighed when I entered, rolling his eyes. He was laying across one of the worn leather couches, legs kicked over the arm, and Rebel surprisingly not at his side.

Once I approached the table, Barrett joined us. Under the dim lantern light from above, he completed our circle. Lyria, Mila, Dax, Cyren, Quilian, and Amara. The commander, the generals of the alliance army, Barrett, and me.

Standing among them, some unfamiliar weight settled on my shoulders.

"Sorry I'm late," I said. "I was helping Ronders and Gustal straighten the training arena." Two of the Mystiques who hadn't shunned me upon my arrival. Though, it had been less icy lately.

Most didn't look up, but Mila gave me a nod of approval. A little relief loosened my chest, but I wasn't sure why. All I'd done was polish swords, a task I've known to do since I was a child. I gave her a tight-lipped smile in return.

"That's fine." Lyria's voice was all Master of Weapons and Warfare. "We're going to have a long night regardless."

My stomach twisted. "What happened?" I tried to catch anyone's eye, but none of the generals seemed to know what she was talking about. Quil gave me a bemused shake of his head. Amara narrowed her eyes on the figures on the table, deciphering.

Lyria leaned forward, propping her weight on her fists atop the table. Her eyes locked on the map and the clan sigils marking it.

"They're moving," she clipped. "My spies through the territories have reported that an Engrossian legion has been spotted."

"Where?" Barrett asked.

"Along the base of the Mystique mountains. First, it was only in Mindshaper territory. We were preparing for them to push through the passes to reach us here." Lyria dragged a finger along the eastern edge of the range. "They're in Bodymelder land now."

"What?" Esmond growled, and every head in the room whipped toward the kitchen. He never spoke in these meetings except to provide reports. "We're neutral." He gripped the vial he'd been filling with a deep purple liquid so tightly, I thought it might shatter.

"I don't think Kakias much cares for technicalities," Amara seethed, her arms crossed as she studied the new map.

"Brigiet won't take well to this." Esmond's stare was distant, as if calculating how the Engrossian movements could progress and how his chancellor would react.

"Do you think it will be enough to force her hand into joining the efforts?" Mila asked.

Esmond contemplated, balancing the odds of various possible outcomes and the forces on each side. The number of warriors his clan may be able to offer while keeping infirmaries staffed.

"It might be. She'll need to be sent every detail we're aware of to be persuaded."

"Mila, will you help him write the report?" Lyria asked.

"Of course." Immediately, she and Esmond pulled out chairs

at the small kitchen table, discussing in low voices. The Bodymelder scrawled a quick note—probably notifying his chancellor of what was to come—and the two set to work on the larger correspondence.

"How far have they gotten?" Cyren asked from the background.

"They'd barely passed the Pthole city limits." Lyria pointed to the metal ax in Bodymelder territory marking the Engrossian troops. "That's the last we heard, but they're likely further north now."

I thought of Darrell and his family who had hosted us on the journey here, and a lump formed in my throat. Their serene, hard-working way of life didn't deserve to be upheaved by any kind of raid of their village. Most of the towns we'd stopped at weren't fit to defend against an Engrossian host. They were spread too thin between the fields and infirmaries.

"How many were there?" I asked.

"A host of two dozen." As Lyria said it, Rebel trotted over. Where he'd come from, I didn't know, but he carried a scrap of parchment in his mouth. Lyria took it from him, seeming unsurprised.

When she read it, her face paled. "Kakias travels with them," she muttered.

Tension congealed in the air.

"My mother is in Mindshaper Territory," Barrett said, but disbelief lifted the edges of his words. "Your spy said so."

"Apparently the information was bad." Lyria tore from the table, crumpling the note and tossing it in the fire. When she spun back toward us, she was trying to cover her delicately frenzied state. Hands on her hips, eyes scanning the board. "It was wrong or planted, but Kakias is definitely in Bodymelder Territory."

Cyren immediately left to conduct a session in the town's temple. A growl rumbled through my chest as I watched them go, scars from the last Starsearcher who had offered to help us threatening to open.

That had only been Vale and Titus, I reminded myself. Some agreement between the two of them which Ophelia seemed much more eager to untangle than I was. When I saw the numbers on Lyria's statistics sheet, it was hard to come up with an excuse as to why we shouldn't accept the troops. Overall, and when it came to this war against the queen, we could trust the Starsearchers. Titus's army was our army.

"But Kakias isn't making a claim for land," Dax considered. "Her strategy has never been about conquering territories. Not even in the last war." His voice was firm, much different than the Engrossian I'd traveled with for weeks. When it was only Barrett and us, he was affable. Now, though, surrounded by people who once thought him an enemy, he proved himself a strong ally, wrought of experience and insight.

"But this path would make sense to move into Mystique territory," Quilian added. "She'd either have to cut through Bodymelder or Seawatcher land. Which is more direct and less of a threat?"

It clicked into place with the reminder, and dread rattled my chest.

"That's not what she's after, though." My eyes flicked over the map again, tracing the red lines marking Kakias's path. "We know she isn't after land or power—not solely. She's after Ophelia."

And then, it was like those routes jumped off the page, each one tugging against the lifeless tattoo on my chest.

No.

Those arrows pointed to one clear destination, and Lyria saw it, too.

"She's after *Ophelia*," she muttered, eyes wide. "That scar—the one from Kakias's knife..." Her head snapped up, looking between me and Barrett.

"It's been bothering her since the summer," Barrett gasped, racing to the table where Mila and Esmond had fallen silent.

"I don't follow," Amara said.

In as little detail as possible, I explained the confrontation between Ophelia and Kakias at the Battle of Damenal. How the queen had left our Revered with a poisoned wound, and she nearly didn't survive—how it had plagued Ophelia ever since. Left out the bit about Kakias's immortality ritual—they didn't need to know that.

"So you all think the power left behind in this wound is somehow...summoning the queen to Ophelia?" Quilian asked, uncertain. "I've never heard of magic of that kind. Not even in Artale's legends."

"Ophelia and the others left Damenal and headed straight east to Brontain precisely when Lyria said her spies caught the first party heading north." I drew it for them. "And now they're heading toward Firebird's Field and Kakias cut back south.

"Barrett!" I shouted, whirling to find him already bent over a piece of parchment.

"On it."

The scratch of the pen against paper roared through my ears as I fought off the panic gripping me. My friends were out there, and sure, they were some of the best fighters I knew, but they would also be greatly outnumbered by any troop Kakias sent after them.

And if she went herself, with that untamed power, they might not survive it.

"We don't even know where they are now." I frantically looked between the others.

"The letter will find them, Malakai." Lyria attempted to soothe me, but fear for her brother burned in her stare.

My breath was coming in short gasps now. "They're traveling," I roared. "It could take time to locate them if they're moving quickly." And that power Kakias exerted over Ophelia could be stronger. We didn't know its full extent.

I rubbed the heel of my hand against the knot forming in my chest. "Dammit if this fucking tattoo worked properly I could reach her!" The Bind had never been a bigger disappointment. My hands raked through my hair as panic closed my throat. My hearing muddled, like I was beneath water.

I spun away from the table. And across the room, Mila's eyes caught mine.

Breathe, she mouthed.

I couldn't fucking breathe, not when the people I loved—my

family—were outrunning a queen they didn't even know had a direct link to them and we may not be able to reach them in time.

Breathe, Mila mouthed again, taking a deep inhale. The voices in the room swam together.

Forcing myself to mimic her, I counted as air inflated my lungs. Held it. Counted. Released it. Counted that, too.

Kept repeating that method until my heart had returned to a normal rhythm and clarity focused my vision and mind.

We would write to them, and they'd be safe.

"What can we do from here?" I asked, once my hearing had returned to normal.

"Kakias is going after our own." Mila's lips curled into a vicious smile that only belonged on a battlefield. "We'll find her first."

CHAPTER THIRTY-ONE
TOLEK

COULD I WAKE UP WITH HER EVERY DAY? FUCKING Spirits, what did I have to do to make that a possibility, because I'd do it. Whatever it was, whatever I needed to sacrifice, I'd give it over right this moment to make waking up with Ophelia's head on my bare chest, her breath tickling my skin, and her arms wrapped around me a reality.

I was obsessed after being denied the one thing I wanted more than life itself for so long. She'd given me a small taste. The addiction was full-fledged now. Bars down, my heart in her hands, no going back.

I'd woken long before her, and the first thing I did was grab my journal from my room and come back. My thoughts never made sense in my head. I had to turn my feelings into written words to understand them. Didn't know why; I'd always been that way.

Despite every damn flaw I'd exposed last night, she didn't run. I didn't understand how. I shouldn't have shared any of it truly. Block those faults in their own compartments and bury them deep beneath the smiles and humor and try to be better than the man who sired me, that's what I'd always trained myself to do. No one knew the truly dark side within me. The selfishness, the anguish, the helplessness.

Maybe I shouldn't have shared any of it, but she'd been so

happy to protect me. So perhaps I could tell her the rest? Spirits, my head was a damn mess.

Exactly as it was last night when she straddled me and used that mouth to make me forget all of my issues. She'd tried to make me talk, but I wasn't having it. Not when all she wore was a thin silk nightgown and I could feel her heat through my undershorts.

When things had gotten a little too carried away for her comfort, and she rolled to the side disappearing into that mind of hers, I'd pulled her tighter against me to remind her I wasn't going anywhere. Her thoughts had been so loud, nerves over whatever she still struggled to say bouncing around her head, so I gave her silence and time.

Nothing we did or didn't do would make me love her less, no matter how long she needed. Probably the opposite, but I didn't say that out loud.

I didn't give a damn that all we'd done was talk and kiss. Beneath the sheets, hands trailing up her spine as she arched into me, laughing as I teased her and she playfully threatened me...it was a side of her she rarely dared to show. Carefree and relaxed.

Damn, I needed all of it. As she slept beside me, I poured a poem onto the page about the weightless look in her eyes and the way it tied a string around my heart and tugged.

The world was calm, the distant sea a lullaby in the dawn, and I was so fucking in love with the girl sleeping beside me.

When she shifted against me and stretched one arm up, that North Star tattoo caught the light and my stomach fucking plummeted. Ophelia's eyes fluttered open, and I tucked away the uncertainty her Bind dragged up in me every time I saw it. Like claws scraping against my gut, piercing and utterly bloodthirsty.

"Good morning," Ophelia breathed, nuzzling into my shoulder.

"Morning, beautiful." I pressed a kiss to her forehead, and she sighed into it.

"You slept?" She sounded so hopeful, voice lilting up at the end, I didn't have the heart to tell her barely. We'd stayed up late, and once she'd drifted off, I'd tried to also. Hung on the edge of the sheer curtain between waking and sleeping for hours. Each time I fell a little more toward the latter, I'd jolted awake with thoughts of blood and magenta eyes and—

Sighing, I kissed her again. "Enough." It wasn't exactly a lie. I'd gotten used to functioning on barely any sleep since the Undertaking. I was more energized by her presence than anything.

"Tol," she scolded, the sleepy haze clearing from her stare.

"Alabath," I mimicked her tone. Rolling so her back was to the bed and I hovered over her, I ran my hand down her arm and interlocked our fingers. Brought hers to my lips. "I'm okay."

War played out behind her eyes, but if you didn't know her as I did, you wouldn't have seen it, she was that good at hiding. It couldn't escape me, though. The clashes of wanting to solve my problems versus waiting for me to be ready. Patience had never been her strong suit.

"Do you ever think keeping it locked up could be doing more harm than good?" She posed the question I'd been really fucking hoping she wouldn't, but of course she plucked that query right out of my mind. Ophelia knew me better than the Spirits.

I toyed with her fingers. "Every day." But not enough to know how to face it.

She nodded with an understanding exhale. "No lies."

"I will never lie to you, Alabath." Though so much had changed since we swore that to each other at the Sunquist Ball, that had not.

Her eyes heated with the promise, and I was a damn goner. Angellight could have flared around us, the Spirits rising from their realm themselves, and I wouldn't have noticed. All that existed for me was the woman in my arms and ensuring she was all right despite my past haunting me.

She stretched, and her hand landed on my journal. "What's this?" Picking it up, she looked at it with a sly smirk.

"No, you don't!" I plucked it out of her hand and tossed it across the room. I certainly couldn't have her looking in there.

Her gaze ignited in challenge, but before she could move, I had her hips pinned beneath mine and a gasp escaping her lips. I caught it with my own, kissing her until she forgot that damn notebook.

When we broke apart, she said, a little breathless, "One day, I'm going to know what you write about."

You already do. "Some dreams may never come true."

She rolled her eyes, turning contemplative. "Is there anything else bothering you?"

My eyes dropped to her body, trailing down that silk nightgown hugging her so perfectly. The lace at the neckline outlining the swell of her breasts.

"Tol?" she prodded, a laugh in her voice when she caught where my eyes had fallen. Damn, that sound. How had I gone so long without hearing it?

Shaking my head, my eyes fell to the Bind again. *Tell her,* a voice prodded. And with how well she responded last night, perhaps I could.

The door burst open, slamming back against the wall.

"Told you they'd both be in here," Jez bragged to Cyph as they entered uninvited.

"Jezebel!" Ophelia shot up, shoving me off of her.

I flopped back against the pillows, squeezing the bridge of my nose. "Do you even consider knocking, Jezzie?"

"No." She made herself comfortable at the foot of the bed. "I knew you'd be somewhat decent."

Wasn't sure what that meant given the last time we'd been in a similar situation, she'd left a contraceptive tonic. The sisters exchanged a glance, some kind of silent communication.

"I said it was a bad idea," Cyph offered, crossing his arms and leaning against the wall.

"Thank you!" I burst.

"Enough, you two," Ophelia said, rising from the bed and swinging on her tiny silk robe, though I tried to pull her back. "I'm assuming there's a reason you're here?"

Santorina and Vale appeared, both looking like they'd just woken up. Cyph shut the door behind them, and everyone turned to Jezebel.

"This arrived for you," she told her sister, holding up a hastily folded piece of yellowed parchment with Ophelia's name on the front. "I didn't read it."

"Why did it come to you?" Ophelia took the letter and unfolded it, eyes on her sister.

Jez shrugged, but it was Cyph who answered. "We've been traveling a lot. The ink probably miscalculated."

It was possible, but a bit unsettling. The reason we were always so careful about what we put in letters. Ophelia's lips pursed, eyes dropping to the paper in her hands.

Instantly, her fingers curled into it, tightening, nearly tearing. Her face paled, icy rage narrowing her eyes.

"What is it?" I scrambled to her side. Wrapping an arm around her waist, I gently uncurled her fingers from the paper one by one and smoothed out her hands to ease the tension.

But when I read what had been written to her, unease shot through my own body.

That scar is calling her, Revered. Through the fields and leaves.

- B

"What in the ever-damned Angels?" I growled. My hand latched around Ophelia's arm, right below the scar. Gently, I turned it toward the window, watching the dark lines branching out from it. They seemed to breathe in the daylight, ebbing under her skin.

"What does it say?" Jezebel rushed to us now, taking the letter and reading it aloud.

Calling her? *Calling her?*

This fucking wound was telling the queen exactly where Ophelia was? My eyes found Ophelia's, and for the briefest moment, she didn't mask the terror this missive had wrought. She let it show to me only, then snapped up her wall of fury.

My heart twisted because she thought she needed to do that. The damn thing pounded faster than a horse's hooves against my ribs. She didn't need to hide when she was afraid in order to protect us, but that would always be Ophelia's tendency. She was a protector to her core. Of us, of the Mystiques, but putting herself last.

And...*fuck.*

Ophelia was quiet, as if putting pieces together.

"Listen to me, Alabath." I carefully turned her chin to me.

Nothing but burning anger looked back. "We're going to figure out a way around this."

We locked eyes and communicated in our silent way. Mentally, she was weighing the pros and cons of running to the queen to end this once and for all before any of us got in harm's way. She wouldn't see the danger in that—not if it was only her life at risk. She believed in herself and that Angellight enough to tackle whatever power Kakias wielded but *I* wasn't willing to risk her. I'd tie us together before she got away without me.

"It's been feeling...different," she said, eyes on her scar. The others quieted. "It's been feeling sentient."

I gripped the back of her neck and dropped my forehead to hers. "She won't get to you."

"She's already in me." Her eyes rested on that scar, then turned up to me with a stare that could incinerate Angels. "But I'll have her blood on my hands before she has mine again."

"That's my girl." She was beautiful when basking in vengeance.

"We need to leave," she rushed. "If she's already heading toward us, we need to get to Firebird's Field as soon as possible and secure the emblem."

"What if that's not where it is?" Jezebel asked.

"It's the best lead we have," Ophelia said. "Cyph?"

"The trench," he answered her unspoken question.

"The Fytar Trench?" Vale gasped.

"It'll be the quickest way," Ophelia explained. The trench stretched along the east side of the Bodymelder capital city and was dangerous to cross, putting it simply. We'd been planning to head north and around it. "Kakias will expect us to take another route. It'll save days."

As we finalized our plan and everyone rushed out to pack, Rina remained. She hadn't spoken since the note was read.

"I thought I'd gotten out the worst of it." Her eyes narrowed. "I was so certain nothing this vicious was left. I thought maybe lingering tendrils of her poison were causing you discomfort but I didn't ever think it was something so...threatening. I—"

Ophelia wrapped her arms around her friend. "You couldn't have known."

"I'm not giving up. I'm going to figure out what's doing it." Santorina hugged her tighter, then pulled back. "I'm going to write to Esmond and check if he's found anything that could qualify as elements of sacred land."

Even hearing them speak about the ingredients of Kakias's immortality ritual had a growl rumbling in my chest. Though I'd bite it back if somehow reconstructing the potion could heal the scar.

Ophelia didn't answer Santorina, but something in her silence told me she was still gathering those pieces of theories about this invasive power.

As Rina left, I imagined very terrifying promises were being forged about the queen's life in her mind. When she prided herself on something—like her healing capabilities—you were a fool to challenge them. She wasn't like Ophelia, taking a knife to you, but Santorina Cordelian was brutal and determined in her own way.

Kakias was wronging each of us, personally, one by one. And dammit if she wasn't writing her own death into the fates as well.

Chapter Thirty-Two
Malakai

"Who exactly are Lyria's spies?" I asked as Mila sat down opposite me, handing a serving of dried meat and cheese across the mystlight. Cypher trees ringed our camp for the night, breeze whistling through the branches and stars speckling the sky.

"I don't know." Mila cleared her throat, avoiding my gaze.

"They've saved our asses a number of times, though," Esmond said, dropping his voice low enough that none of the others in our party would hear.

They were our cover, traveling to Pthole to retrieve supplies to cart back to the infirmary at camp.

"Yeah and gotten us into worse trouble now," I grumbled and took a long sip of ale. Whoever had brought it was doing us a favor. It always tasted better after a day of travel.

"They've given clear information now, though. The queen is moving and heading toward Firebird's Field, as is Ophelia," Mila said, mesmerized with the mystlight between us. "And Engrossian-Mindshaper troops continue to hammer ours."

Mila twirled her bottle absently between her hands.

"Do you regret leaving?" I asked.

But she shook her head. Was that relief in her sigh? "They're in good hands with Lyria and the others. Dax has told us a lot about what to expect from the Engrossian strategy."

Thankfully, most of our warriors had grown to trust Dax and

Barrett in our ranks after the good intel they provided. It was odd to be away from them all.

"But?" I prompted, sensing she felt the same. Things had been stiff between us lately; we'd barely communicated outside of training, but I could tell there was something more.

She shook her head.

"You want to fight alongside them," I finished for her. Behind us, the warriors laughed around their mystlight lantern, playing a word game.

"Something like that." Mila twisted her gold cuffs, watching the others.

"Those are beautiful, by the way," I said, gesturing at the intricately carved metal around her wrists. I'd noticed them when we first met and every day we'd trained since. They were unique, clearly hand-crafted and not typically a part of Mystique leathers. "Where are they from?"

Mila's eyes snapped to mine, then fleeted quickly away. "I got them at a market in Turren," she explained, hands clutching the gold tightly.

Esmond and I exchanged a look when she offered no more explanation. The Bodymelder shrugged, turning back to the letter in his hands.

"Santorina?" I asked.

"She's looking for some ingredients, though she didn't give much detail why." He folded it up, tossing it over the mystlight. "I have someone working on it for her."

At least someone was making progress in one task, then.

"Come on," I said, standing and extending a hand to Mila. "Let's all rest so we can move early and arrive at Firebird's Field before midday."

She slid her hand into mine to pull herself up. As I went to release her, she tugged me a step closer, the hesitancy of a moment ago gone. "Don't think I've forgotten about your training, Warrior Prince." Her eyes searched mine before stepping back and sauntering away toward the group.

I waited for the frustration to rattle the bars in my chest at the name, but it never came.

～

"I DON'T UNDERSTAND why we're stopping here," I complained as Esmond led Mila and me through Pthole the next day.

The Bodymelder capital was much like the villages sprinkled throughout their territory, but with grander buildings instead of small cottages. They towered above us, ivy and wisteria crawling over the facades. The foundation of every building was a slate gray but the flora and burnished orange trees overflowing the nearby Gennium Forest brought the city to life.

"We can't just walk into Firebird's Field," Esmond explained. "It's a historic site, and there's a level of clearance needed. Besides, I need to meet with Brigiet while we're here about the missive we sent her before leaving camp."

"What do you mean clearance?" I paused. "How is Ophelia going to get in there?"

Esmond gestured for me to keep following, and we emerged into the city center, marked by a two-story-tall golden statue in a bubbling fountain where children tossed coins. Ptholenix, I guessed, but without his wings.

I was studying the statue as Esmond explained, "*She* is going to give us approval, and then I'm going to find the person who happens to have direct access to the site."

Following his voice, I turned. Brigiet, the Bodymelder Chancellor, came charging down the stairs of a building that reminded me of a reverent mausoleum more than anything, with its plain pillared architecture and flat rectangular shape. Most of the structures were simple in the city, I realized. All plain, aside from the plants crawling over them.

I didn't get to respond to Esmond, barely got to greet the chancellor. She wasted no time, leading us into an office within the building that held little more than packed bookshelves, an orderly desk, and an abundance of plants.

"Where was the queen last spotted?" she asked.

"First north past the capital, then they looped southeast again," Mila answered. "We have a team of spies trailing them."

Brigiet nodded, the braids in the front of her wine-red hair swaying. She directed her next words at Esmond. "She is kept out of the capital at all costs."

"Yes, Chancellor," he responded. His hands were folded behind his back, spine and shoulders straight.

"We pull from the infirmaries and station guards around the borders."

"Yes, ma'am."

"I've already written to the village heads and instructed them to do the same. Harvest will be slower until the threat is resolved. We may be neutral, but she shouldn't have been here without my knowledge." Brigiet sat in the chair behind her desk, but she did not relax. Her hands folded atop the surface, fingers absently brushing over the *K L P* tattoo on her knuckles the only sign of discomfort. "And what will you two do?"

I glanced at Mila, deferring to my superior, and she raised her brows at Esmond. He cleared his throat. "They need access to Firebird's Field."

Briefly, he explained the updates to the emblem hunt and why he believed that site to be important. He told her Ophelia would be arriving there and would hopefully find the token quickly so we could return to the mountains.

"It should guarantee Kakias vacates Bodymelder Territory, too," Mila added when Esmond was done.

I couldn't make out Brigiet's opinion. Whether she cared about the Angel emblems at all or simply wanted to safeguard her land.

It didn't matter, though. As long as we all got what we needed from this arrangement. A queen one step closer to death and another piece of this Angelcurse in our hands.

"Whatever you need is yours," Brigiet said. She turned to Esmond. "Gatrielle is on your assignment but will be back this evening. He can escort you all to Firebird's Field as soon as Ophelia arrives."

I assumed that was the contact Esmond had mentioned based on the fact that the information didn't faze him.

Outside, sun broke through the clouds, streaming through the windows. It ignited the shades of pine, sage, and jade of the plants dotting the room, their leaves suddenly seeming to breathe in. Brigiet did with them.

"Now, if you two don't mind," she said to Mila and me, "I'd like an update from my apprentice."

"Of course," Mila said, with a small nod. Esmond remained at attention until we closed the door behind us.

Before we descended the staircase back into the atrium, I pulled Mila into an empty room. She looked at me, brows raised.

"Isn't there something we can do now?" There was a restlessness in my chest, one that was familiar and new all at once. I thought it resembled how I'd felt when I'd first uncovered Lucidius's plan, back before signing the treaty—resembled the desire to act I'd had then, the one that had been returning to me the longer I spent at the war camp. It ran down my spine and extended through my limbs.

Mila gently pulled her arm from my grip. I hadn't realized I'd still been holding it, that my hand slid down to rest above her ivy cuffs. "Everyone needs to be aligned on this plan—on all plans if we're going to make it out of this war in one piece." Her eyes searched my face, like she was trying to unpack something within me. "We wait. No more questioning orders. That's a command from your general."

"Understood." I'd told her after I fled that battle I would heed instructions from now on. Placing my hand on the pommel of my sword, I tried to stifle my nervous energy.

Mila tracked the movement. "There is something you can do, though." She grinned, and the rattled feeling in my chest soothed at the sight. "Training."

MILA LED me away from the center of the capital, to the very edge of the Gennium Forest, where ash white cyphers trees grew, but—

"These don't look like they normally do," I observed. The sweeping branches still lined the path in places, but they also stretched up and over, forming grand arches.

"They call this the arteries," Mila explained. "It's tied up in

Bodymelder lore, but Esmond told me about it weeks ago. I've wanted to see it since."

The tunnel of trees had a collection of offshoots like little burrows through the gnarled branches, and I understood the comparison to veins. Surrounded by foliage in oranges and reds and golds, it was a stark contrast to traveling across the Wild Plains in Mystique Territory with lush plants and wildflowers. Different from the rocky, grass-covered peaks of the mountains I'd grown used to or the snowy southern region of the camp.

Mila led me into one of these tunnels, surrounded by tall interwoven branches forming an arch overhead.

"Sword out, Warrior Prince."

I shook my head at the title, but it didn't bring that grating feeling in my chest it used to. Not when she said it like it had become a joke between us.

After warming up, Mila stood before me with her own weapon. The trees around us seemed to buzz with the land's energy, and it called to the power I'd shunned for so long.

In a dance of metal, Mila struck first. I met her, forcing her back. Then, I swung for my own attack, surprising her with the forward offense.

"That's new," she commented, blocking a tactic I hadn't tried before.

"Learned it back at camp," I said, trying not to break my focus. Again and again our swords flashed between us, nothing but silver blurs. Grunts and screeches of metal flooded the forest, the trees absorbing every sound and granting us privacy.

"You've been practicing?" Mila asked. This was the first time we trained since I stormed away from her. Since before the attack on the western edge of camp when I fled.

But I hadn't been entirely stagnant in that time.

"I asked Ronders to work with me."

With my revelation, Mila's eyes lit up, her grin from earlier returning even as I ducked her next blow. Spirits, I liked that smile more than I'd realized. It shot through me, a better balm than those drugs I was trying to quit. My next movements were more precise, control back in my hands as I fought to get my blade on her.

She was damn skilled, though, and moved like water through the tunneled trees, just out of reach of my blade. She seemed impressed that I'd taken the initiative to keep training. Truthfully, I was impressed with myself.

"Is he your new teacher, then?" Mila teased.

"Are you giving up your post?" I clicked my tongue. "Not very professional of you."

"If you're making better progress with him," she growled, not liking my response, "then perhaps it's for the best."

"Are you jealous, General?" I goaded, sidestepping her.

"Of course not." She mirrored the move.

With the added space, I pulled the Engrossian ax from my belt and charged. Before she could counter, I used the thick blade to knock aside her own. Catching her wrist in my grip, I swung her arm behind her back. Her chest was forced toward mine with the motion, but the sharpened edge of my ax was between us, beneath her chin.

"Don't worry, Mila. You're still my favorite teacher." The buzzing of the forest seemed to magnify around us as we caught our breath. It matched the restlessness within me, fed it and soothed it in some unnatural way.

"Next lesson," she muttered. I had to lean in to hear her. But the hand I didn't have locked behind her flicked out faster than I could react and snatched my father's dagger from my waist, pressing the tip into my ribcage. "Your own weapons can be your greatest downfall."

Shaking my head at my own mistake, I couldn't help myself from laughing. What she said was true in more ways than one, I realized as a lightness I hadn't felt in a while pushed against the guard I usually kept up.

As I dropped my weapon, my head swam back to the present. The air between us was charged like a lightning strike. That was sort of how training with Mila felt. A bolt of searing illumination that tore through the clouds I'd been shrouded beneath.

Mila's chest rose and fell as she watched me for a long moment.

Her tongue flicked out across her lips, and if I didn't turn away soon I didn't know what I'd do. My cock was already paying way too much attention to the way her leathers hugged her figure.

She tilted her head to the side, the silky strands of her braid sliding over her shoulder.

"What?" I panted.

"You don't smile very often," she said, a small crease forming between her brows. "Did you realize that?"

I shook my head.

"You should." She grinned, and if it meant I got that in return, I'd try to smile more.

~

THE ROOMS we'd been given were set above a tavern. When I descended the stairs that evening after bathing, Mila and Esmond were already around a table with another Bodymelder. They pulled out a chair between them for me.

"Thanks," I said, sinking into it. "You wrote to Lyria?"

"No update," Mila offered.

"I don't like that." I took a sip of the ale set before me. "We should have word of what Kakias is doing now." She couldn't be in Bodymelder Territory undetected and silent. My nerves prickled at the possibility.

"Malakai," Esmond said. "Meet Gatrielle. We grew up together."

I extended my hand to the Bodymelder. When he leaned across the table, his brown curls shifted across his shoulders, pale skin illuminated by the mystlight overhead to highlight the soft lines of his face and amicable grin. He looked about Esmond's age—thirty or so.

"Nice to meet you," I said.

"And you." He gripped his drink with the hand I'd shook, and I noticed he did not have the *KLP* tattoos on his knuckles like other Bodymelders. "Esmond has been catching me up on his time with you all."

I cast a glance at Esmond. With one ankle crossed over his

knee, he seemed more at ease here than I'd ever seen of him before. "Gatrielle returned today from a special task for Brigiet and me," he explained. "Collecting those ingredients Santorina wrote about. He's the friend I told you about earlier."

I sat up straighter, the noise in the tavern muting to a din. Gatrielle was not just any Bodymelder then—he was the one who had access to Firebird's Field.

"I hear you can help us." I dropped my voice, running a hand over the scar on my jaw.

"That I can."

Though the hum in my veins had been stifled a bit during training, it kicked back up again. Lucidius's ramblings of Firebird's Field spurred through my mind. "Could we go tomorrow?"

"Don't we need Ophelia?" Mila asked, but she watched my fingers tapping the table and seemed to understand.

"No reason we can't take a look around," I said, turning back to Esmond and Gatrielle. "If that's allowed?"

The energy at the table shifted as Gatrielle grinned, hungry for an Angel's adventure. "Absolutely."

CHAPTER THIRTY-THREE
OPHELIA

THE SMALL VILLAGES THE BODYMELDERS STRUCTURED their territory in made it immensely harder to travel unnoticed. Now that we knew Kakias was coming, we needed to get to Firebird's Field as quickly and covertly as possible.

We didn't want to go through fields out of respect for the produce and flora they worked so hard to grow. Given that the towns and their crops formed a checkerboard across the territory, it was hard to avoid. They used every inch of the land besides the forests, a few vacant stretches of plains, and the trench near the capital.

We were left skirting the perimeters of fields on the outskirts of village borders. We pulled up our hoods when we couldn't duck into the forests for coverage, avoiding any warriors, humans, or animals we saw. It was a stark contrast to the welcome we'd received from Ezalia and her Seawatchers, first at Brontain and then in her own home.

We could have written to Brigiet or Esmond and asked for assistance in securing passage, but with Kakias tracking me, it was too risky. It was a hazard to be anywhere near the innocent villages, truly.

The forests, though—those were safest. The Gennium Forest in particular stretched between fields of flowers, produce, and herbs, forming a network of gnarled branches and natural shelters.

That was the route we'd been on for days now, barely resting.

It was the cyphers' ash-white trunks I was observing when a needle of pain stabbed through my arm. It twisted, and I bit back on a cry.

"All right, Alabath?" Tolek asked from atop Astania.

"Fine." My brows pulled together as I looked at my scar. Those warring forces tugged within me.

A presence hovered over my right shoulder, though. Whipping my head around, I searched the trees.

Nothing.

A breeze rifled my hair on the other side. I spun.

Still, nothing.

My stomach knotted as I tried to wade through the haunting sensation and focus on the lulling sway of Sapphire's trot. She continued through the curtain of autumn leaves blanketing the forest, pine needles crunching beneath her hooves, right on Elektra's tail, but that phantom feeling kept its grip around my gut.

"You sure?" Tolek asked, and it was clear he knew I was lying. "You have a theory."

"I have a...I'm unsure what I have." An instinct, maybe, but I wasn't even sure how to put it into words, yet. "I'm trying to work it out."

We stopped and dismounted, the pressure in my arm mounting again, pulling at the strings of my thoughts.

Tolek studied me for a moment, putting my pieces together, then tugged me into the trees, away from our friends. "Give me a thought," he said. "Something you're afraid of right now."

He brushed a stray lock of hair off his forehead. It fell right back down, and my gaze followed it, drinking him in for a moment. Scruff growing out, leathers open at his chest, hair more disarrayed than its usual intentional mess. Disheveled. That's what Tolek had become. The first strands of it, at least, like the full control hadn't snapped yet but the limits were being tested.

Because of me. Because of this Angelcurse and the threats of a queen desperate for my life. It was ruining him, utterly and painfully. And to watch that happen to him ruined me, too.

"I don't know what to think of any of this." Truthfully, I was scrambling and lost. Overwhelmed, but not succumbing. "We're walking unmapped territory on this journey, the words of the story not yet written. That scares me. Your turn." I crossed my arms, trying to stifle the pain in my scar.

His gaze tracked down my body, cataloging every mark, and stopped on my necklace. Tolek sighed, the sound heavy with defeat. "I'm afraid of what's going through your mind when you won't speak. What decisions you're making because you think you *need* to, not because you *want* to." His eyes flared as he let out the frustrations piling up like bricks inside of him, his voice rough with irritation. "I'm worried about you, Ophelia. I can't—nothing can happen to you. Every time that scar pains you it rips through my chest, like I feel it, too. The queen? She'll die before she ever touches you again, I'll be sure of that. But I'm concerned, because I can hear your mind working out a way for you to be the only one in her path, and I can't let that happen. I need to keep you safe." He dropped his forehead to mine. "Please. I want to help."

So much pain weighed those words; I could see their edges fracturing. Felt it like it was my own ribs cracking and pouring my heart out between us. I was doing this to him.

My Angelcurse. My destiny. Me.

"I will ask for help, Tol," I promised, voice rising in desperation to take away anything hurting him. "I don't know what I need yet, but I swear I'll tell you."

Something played out behind his eyes. A decision being made maybe, but I wasn't sure what.

He pulled me to him, cradling my head against his chest with one hand and rubbing his other down my back. I wound my arms around his waist and breathed him in.

"Honestly, Alabath, I'm fucking terrified. I know you are, too, and all I want is to take those fears away, not take it out on you." He kissed the top of my head, the heat of that small action spreading all the way to my toes.

"I don't want us to fight, Tol." Flashes of my past's heated arguments and the pain that always followed danced in the shadows of my words. "We're fighting everyone else. Can't *we* just be?"

He laughed gently, his hand slipping beneath my hair to rub the back of my neck. I leaned my cheek on his chest as his fingers toyed absently with my necklace. "We will fight with each other, sweetheart. Spirits, I know you'll be angry with me at times for the idiotic things I do. But we'll always make up."

"Sometimes the dumb things you do end up being my favorite."

"I'll remember that," he promised.

My heart thudded in realization of how subtle these feelings had been. Promises woven between us for years to create an inherent foundation, like we had never truly existed without the rope tethering us together. It ran bone deep, his breath and blood my own, a thing that always called us back despite how far the walls may push us.

And each time it did, it changed a bit. Became something new and exciting and rich with possibility.

That was another thing to be scared of, though. Where there was the possibility for good, there were infinite chances for mistakes. We were living through war and prophesied secrets, and it was unraveling him. From the shaking tenor of his voice to the way his hands gripped me, it was clear.

And it twisted my gut.

At times it felt like there was an iron chain around me, pulling me further and further toward a fate desperate to crush me, and I could do nothing about it but reach out to him and hope that together we were strong enough to withstand the Angels.

But Tolek would allow himself to break for me. If that happened, I'd curse every being in the heavens until their blood coated the land, flooded the rivers, and scorched the stars. As he and I looked at each other, I sealed the promise within my warrior heart, anointed it with the Angelblood running through my veins and whatever other power I may have held.

There was a lingering sadness in Tolek's eyes that said he saw every fear on my soul. Did he agree with them? Were these threats coming between us or would they drive us closer?

Angels, I couldn't lose him. Not like this. Not to something already taking such control of my life. My lungs constricted at the thought.

But before I could ask about it, Tol kissed me and said he'd take the horses to get settled for the evening.

He walked away, but all I heard as his footfalls faded was the possibility of me breaking his heart.

≈

"WHERE WERE YOU?" I looked up at Tolek from my spot sprawled on the ground in the network of tunneled trees in the Gennium forest. I hadn't seen him since he took the horses. The rest of us had already settled in for the evening, Jezebel laying out a small meal and Cypherion polishing all of our weapons.

"Caring for Astania," Tolek said. He didn't meet my eyes when he came over, removed the pack I was propped against, and tugged me into his lap instead. Instantly, though, his casual affection eased my concerns. "She seemed unsettled, but I left her near Sapphire, and she calmed down."

"I'm glad," I sighed. My friends' voices washed over me as I observed the branches woven above us.

The shelter was barely tall enough for Cypherion to stand without his head scraping the canopy of leaves and wide enough for the six of us to set up sleeping mats around a dim mystlight. The horses had to be left in another pocket, but it was nice that while we couldn't stay in a village, we were able to find this natural haven, like Gallantia itself was providing for us.

That thought alone lifted my spirit, twining with the wild threads of my soul that belonged to our land. No matter what else existed within me, at least I had that. Threats from a dark queen, the blood of the Angels, and the agent to activate their curse aside, I knew my heart beat with the truth of a warrior. It was the mantra I reminded myself of—prided myself on—as I forged forward each day of this hunt.

Jezebel was meditating on a recommendation from Vale, trying to tame the power within her so it no longer overwhelmed her. The Starsearcher sat beside her, organizing her reading materials.

As I watched her fingers pick over the dried leaves and flowers, I considered the ingredients Rina was searching for, and I blurted a question that had been pestering me. "Do you think there's a way to use my scar to find Kakias as she finds me?"

Everyone froze, stares ranging from suspicious to curious.

"I imagine," Rina began, mind whirling with antidotes and theories, "if we knew how it worked, that tracking could be used two ways."

"Yes, but it hurts Ophelia whereas it doesn't seem to do damage to the queen," Tolek said. Mystlight flickered over his features, hardening the slope of his brows and darkening the scruff around his ticking jaw.

"We don't know that." Cypherion shook his head.

I pushed myself upright. "It could be just as detrimental to her."

"Not willing to risk it, *Revered*."

I narrowed my eyes at his specific use of my title. The reminder that it wasn't only me at stake, but everyone I was responsible for. Dammit, he knew how to work me. He knew exactly what my motives were and what I wasn't willing to risk. Absently, thinking of a retort that might sway him, I dragged a hand up the scar.

"Still, it feels alive sometimes. There must be more to it." It reminded me of the false Curse. Looked similar to that ailment, too, but I hadn't quite figured out why or how when one was a trick of the Angelcurse and one was derived from the queen's poisoned blade.

Before anyone could respond, a shooting pain went through my arm. I cried out, doubling over and clutching it to my chest.

Santorina and Tolek were by me immediately, the former gently taking my arm while the latter brushed my hair back from my sweat-pebbled brow. Cypherion, Jezebel, and Vale stood behind them, concern lacing their stares.

"It's—something's moving in there." I gritted my teeth.

Santorina prodded the wound. "It's hardened. Like there's something beneath the skin. Can you feel that?"

"Yes, I can fucking feel it," I hissed. It was like something gathered, embedded in me, not quite firmed but molten. A separation of the power from the queen's dagger and my own Angelblood. "It's been getting worse—but not—" I gasped. "Damien's fucking Spirit, not like this!"

Rina gave me a reproachful glare, but she didn't reprimand me for the tone. Thank the Spirits, because I wouldn't have taken it.

"Sorry," I panted regardless. "It's been happening more since the Angellight the other night."

"You didn't say anything?" Jezebel asked.

"It hasn't been this bad," I bit out. It twisted through me again, eerie fingers wringing my veins and picking apart the two substances to turn that poison into something *else*.

"I'm afraid..." Rina started, observing the spot where there did in fact seem to be something budding beneath my skin. Then, her eyes lifted to mine. "We could be running out of time to try my theory."

Fear gathered in my stomach, but I was too busy squirming under the sensation of the battle in my blood to indulge it.

"What can—we do?" I asked through gritted teeth.

"What can we do *now*?" Cypherion corrected, recognizing the need for a quick remedy. Tolek watched Rina intently, eyes begging for a way to ease my pain.

"If it's...firm enough"—Rina swallowed—"I could try to remove—"

"No," Tolek cut her off, panic raising his voice.

"It's still eating at me," I said as a wave of nausea rolled through my gut. There would be no removing the poison while its claws were in this deep.

"I can give you a sleeping tonic," Rina offered. I opened my mouth to argue, but she cut me off. "A small dose to allow you a few hours, but you'll be fully lucid before we have to head out."

I gritted my teeth at another burst of pain.

"We can afford to sleep an extra hour or so," Cypherion added with a sincere nod.

"Take it, Ophelia," Jezebel pleaded.

"Okay," I relented. And when I met Tol's eyes, the words

burning and begging in those amber specks were clear: *don't search for Kakias.*

Everyone was somber as Rina brewed the tonic. Cyph asked Vale to distract us with a story of some Starsearcher legend about fated lovers destroying one another only to wake an evil spirit instead, but all I heard was the clinking of vials in Santorina's hands and the soft threats of a queen against my cheek months ago.

"Only a few hours," I clarified to Rina with a raised brow, biting back a hiss as another wave of pain shot through my arm.

She handed me the tonic. "You'll be up before the sun."

I threw it back, its syrupy taste fruity and thick as it coated my throat. As I rolled out my sleeping mat and ensured Starfire and Angelborn were beside me, my limbs grew heavy, but the pain in my arm was already dulling. My vision blurred at the edges as the tonic kicked in. Curling up beneath my cloak, I settled against Tolek's side.

"Is this yours, Ophelia?" Vale's voice cut through the haze.

Forcing an eye to crack open, I found the Starsearcher across the mystlight. She held something between her thumb and finger. A small, gold charm—

I shot upright, wobbling. "That's from Lancaster." The symbol he'd given me to string on my necklace when we'd made our bargain. "I can't lose that."

"It was on the floor over there." Vale motioned to where she'd found the bargain charm, then returned to her bedroll. I thought I felt a glare from Rina on the trinket but was too dazed to be sure.

"How odd," I said, already yawning again. "Help me?" I asked Tolek.

Silently, he returned the symbol to my necklace, hanging beside Angelborn's emblem. "Back where it belongs," he said, pulling me down beside him while he kept watch.

"Wish you'd sleep," I slurred. My eyes drooped again, and I cuddled into my safest place.

"I'll try," he promised.

"Good," I murmured. "And I'm glad Vale saw this." Another

large yawn as I grasped the charm. "I would've hated losing that bargain."

And as I slept painlessly with the aid of Rina's tonic, dreams of burning fields of flowers and shattering heavens played out in my mind.

CHAPTER THIRTY-FOUR
MALAKAI

~※◈※~

"WEAPONS AT THE PERIMETER," GATRIELLE SAID, unhooking his sword belt from his waist and hanging it on a rack at the edge of Firebird's Field.

"What?" Instinctually, my hand went to my sword. Mila hesitated, too. We were entering near the capital, shrouded on all sides by the Gennium Forest, and though the sky was blue and the air crisp, his instruction sent a writhing beast of uncertainty through my chest.

"It's a sacred site," Gatrielle explained. "We can't bring weapons into the field or we're viewed as untrusting by the Spirits who rest here and the Angel they guard."

"I've brought weapons into temples before," I argued. "The Angels carried fucking weapons when they were mortal."

"There's not a chance you're getting Ophelia in there without a weapon when she arrives," Mila added.

"She has a point," Esmond told his friend. "And you won't want to fight with Ophelia. Trust me."

Gatrielle groaned, eyes fleeting between us and the field. "You all are challenging every vow of my designation," he grumbled.

"Gatrielle," Esmond chastised, leveling him a harsh stare. The two communicated quietly for a moment, Esmond seeming to relay precisely how imperative this task was to all of our futures.

"Fine," Gatrielle finally conceded. "One weapon each. But

don't pull them, and for the love of Ptholenix, do *not* tell anyone I allowed this."

As he turned away, he murmured something about disrupting resting Spirits and it being on our heads.

Mila, Esmond, and I silently hung up our weapons and followed him toward the field. I kept my sword at my waist, but at the last moment, I turned back. The Engrossian ax glinted in the light, taunting me. And I wasn't sure if it was that memory or the desire to challenge the damn thing that had me swapping my weapons out at the last moment, leaving my newly-forged sword behind.

Stomping toward the field, I ignored Mila's raised brows and took in the sacred site instead.

The fiery flora spread as far as we could see, hills rolling and dipping like flames flickering in the breeze. About a hundred yards away, a pyre was stacked to the sky, wooden frame singed and ashy but bold against the orange hues.

Gatrielle entered first, brushing his hand across a wooden post that flashed with something resembling mystlight and indicating for the rest of us to pass. The flowers at the edge of the field were an array of bright yellows and brushed my ankles as I waded a few feet in. Their scents mingled in the air, that thing in my chest still stirring.

"What was that?" I asked Gatrielle when he took the lead again, gesturing to the marker he'd touched.

"Only allures can grant access to ritualistic sites in our territory. Since most are outdoors, it ensures some level of control over the boundaries."

I knew a bit about allures—a designation of rank within the Bodymelder clan—though I didn't know the specifics of their work or magic.

"How does that work?"

"Through this." Holding up his palm, Gatrielle angled it until the light illuminated an outline of white ink. A tattoo formed jagged lines across his palm, a lightning bolt entwined with a length of softly draping ivy. "Allures are considered Angelblessed. We find our calling around eighteen like you Mystiques. Whether it's to be an active warrior, an infirmary-contained healer, harvester, allure, or something else. The ink is imbued and solidifies any position. The posts around the perimeter ensure no one enters without an allure to guide them."

"And if they try to?"

Gatrielle smirked. "Let's just say the *firebird* got his name for a reason."

I froze. As he kept walking, I could almost smell the dregs of smoke wafting on the air, of charred flesh and the vengeful fire of Angels.

"Why so many inquiries?" Mila asked, voice low as she caught up to me.

"I don't like this." The back of my neck prickled. My hand went to where the pommel of my sword should have been, finding only empty air.

I'd been nervous about this all night, even going as far as to pull out the pouch of herbs I'd brought with me. But as I watched them dissolve in a glass, turning the water murky, I only heard Mila's voice asking me to stop.

I'd dumped them out the window instead.

"This field is sacred to them," Mila said, and I focused on the tone that calmed me. "Even if it has a bit of a gruesome history. They're sharing something of their clan with us. Let them."

Releasing a reluctant growl, I hurried toward Esmond and Gatrielle and barked, "Let's get to the pyre."

"Not what I meant." Mila's voice carried on the air as she caught up to me, the mixed scents of florals and her own aura replacing the imagined smoke. "Cranky today?"

Wheeling around to face her, I dropped my voice. "Just because you're my superior doesn't mean I won't throw you over my shoulder and carry you away from this damn field if you fight me today, General."

Mila's cheeks flushed. Something swooped through my stomach at the sight.

Fuck. I didn't have time for that right now.

Instead of waiting for her to reply, I continued wading through the flowers. They stretched higher as we got closer to the center of the field. Every so often, a scorched ring cut through the plants, scarring the dusty ground, and my skin tingled.

The earth seemed to inhale as we walked, a pulsing sensation stirring beneath my feet. It timed itself with the beat of my own blood, and settled against my chest, angering that writhing creature within.

"Are the burn marks from others attempting to enter?" Mila asked, pointing to one of the rings.

"Those are from a worship ceremony," Gatrielle explained.

I rolled my neck and shoulders to try to relieve the pressure subtly mounting against my bones. My jaw ticked.

"What kind?" I asked Esmond, working to make my tone more friendly, but my eyes flickered across the scene. Impossibly thick clouds gathered in the distance above the eastern stretch of Gennium Forest, toward the Fytar Trench.

Gatrielle did not seem to notice and continued, "The nearest village is responsible for the chamomile harvest and processing before it's transported to the infirmaries to be manipulated for tonics. I assumed that's who was here."

The melody of his voice rolled like the hills before us. Was that where the Bodymelder accent had stemmed from, a trait absorbed straight from the land itself?

"What are the other nearest villages responsible for?" I didn't truly need to know, but I wanted to keep him talking. To distract me from the prickling of my skin.

Spirits, we shouldn't stay here much longer. It felt wrong, the land teeming with a pulsing power. The others did not seem bothered by it, though.

"There's ginger root and lavender both north of here," Esmond explained. "There's not much of a rhyme or reason to the pattern of fields."

"The town south of the trench is in charge of textile production for stitching thread and linen wraps," Gatrielle added. "It's where I grew up until I moved to the capital to study and became an allure. Sutures are my specialty."

"Have they all been having difficult growing seasons?" I

remembered what Darell had said about their aloe fields luckily not being affected.

"Most have," Gatrielle said, lips drawn tight. "Crops are dying inexplicably quickly."

With interjections from Mila clarifying what she'd learned during the first war, the three kept up a steady conversation of healing practices. I tried to absorb what I could, but my focus was stolen by thoughts of Lucidius being here. Kneeling in the grass. Searching the weeds.

Was this insistent pull I felt toward this field nothing more than his mad ramblings? Was the pulsing presence a lingering remnant of the man who tried to ruin me, returning to claim me?

Please, Damien, I began, *don't make me like him.*

As the concern wedged itself into my mind, we approached the pyre in the center of the field, and I took it in.

"Is that Ptholenix?"

It was not simply a pyre. There was an intricate frame of branches built around a stone statue, a nest for its bird, but those wings arcing out from either side were more legend than anything.

This was an Angel monument.

"Some swear they've seen him move," Gatrielle said, looking admirably at the rendition of their Prime Warrior.

Esmond scoffed. "I don't believe it."

Mila crept around the statue, observing. "I don't see how it could. It's solid stone."

"Some swear on Ascension Day, they've seen Ptholenix blink or flutter his wings," Gatrielle said. No one knew what day the Angels truly ascended from warriors to their immortal form, but the holiday was remembered about a week before the end of the year.

"Because the minds of the drunk are always to be trusted," Esmond drawled. I had to agree with him.

The air around the statue was thick with the remnants of smoke and whatever herbs the Bodymelders had offered at the last service. I got as close as the pyre would allow, blinking up at the almighty being depicted. The stone was worn after centuries, but I could almost make out the hair dropping to his shoulders and the long, pointed nose. His hands were open, tilted down toward the land as if calling it to him, and his stance and build were stronger than the most formidable warriors I'd seen alive. Even within his wooden cage, he commanded power.

I wanted to set him free.

Reaching forward, I rested a hand against the wood. It was no longer hot from the flame it had conducted, somehow not turning to ash during the ritual, but it still warmed beneath my palm.

Carefully, avoiding any weak spots that might send the structure tumbling to the ground, I reached through the crossed pieces of wood and brushed my fingers against the statue. A beat of recognition flooded from the stone into me. Something hummed in my chest. My breath stuttered, my other hand pressing against my sternum.

It crawled around my ribs, unnatural and burning. A beast seemed to raise its head within me, evaluating me. Expanding and testing and pulsing.

The earth trembled, the statue with it.

And a shriek split the air.

Mila.

Chapter Thirty-Five

Ophelia

It was barely midday when we reached the trench, but that ghostly presence had breathed over my shoulder the entire journey. The yawning mouth cracked the land, six warriors and their mares set against a force threatening to pull us within. I was sweating in the saddle despite the autumn breezes whipping through Bodymelder territory.

"The bridges are ancient," Jezebel observed. I followed her stare down the cliff-face. Cracked brown rock stretched across the gap, chunks missing sporadically. At our backs loomed the orange and red tangles of the Gennium forest. They sprouted up from the land across from us, too, like this crack in the earth was a severance of the forest, never meant to be here.

There were legends about how the trench had formed, torrential storms to cataclysmic quakes. Each dated back many millennia, and there were too many to even call to memory now.

"They're wide enough that the horses can cross, though." Cypherion dismounted Erini and stood before one of the many paths across the trench. "We can walk, they can follow."

"Are you certain it wouldn't be better to go around?" Santorina offered.

"It would take much longer," Vale said. She joined Cypherion at the cliff edge and leaned forward, searching for another path. His jaw ticked as he watched her.

Going around the trench—while the safer option—meant extra days of travel. More time for Kakias to realize where I was and put my friends in danger. Perhaps I should have separated from them. Taken different routes and reconvened in the mountains where the queen was less likely to reach me.

As I opened my mouth to suggest it, though, Tolek hopped off Astania and approached me. "Don't even think about it."

"What?" I tilted my head and swung one leg over the saddle so I was facing him, a picture of sweet innocence.

"We stay together." He placed his hands on my thighs, fingers curling into my skin. "You can't run off. *Please.*"

It was the pure hint of begging underscoring that final word that reminded me how unfair it would be to him if I left. How I was already hurting him each time my scar ached. How he felt safest when I was within arm's reach, flesh against flesh.

I slid off Sapphire, landing perfectly in the cave of his arms. Those chocolate eyes stared down at me, a mixture of heat and vulnerability and need that scorched through my body.

"Never," I promised.

Wind whipped around us again as I pushed onto my toes and kissed him. Blatantly and openly, not caring where we were or what we faced next. Only Tolek and me, centering each other for a moment of lips against lips, his tongue caressing mine.

"I will never leave you," I swore as we caught our breath. A relief I wasn't sure I understood swept through him, so fierce it seeped into the air between us.

Before I could question it, though, another blast of wind battered us with the force of a stampeding army. All six of our mares stomped their hooves, whinnying. Sapphire and Astania pranced circles around us.

"What in the fucking Angels?" Tolek muttered, his arms wrapping around me. Jezebel and Santorina attempted to soothe their horses.

Vale shrieked. I spun to see Cypherion pulling her back from the cliff edge.

"Damien's cursed Spirit." He stumbled back, picking Vale up. Cyph turned to us, eyes wide. "We have company."

Shoving out of Tol's arms, I rushed to the edge of the cliff. He gripped my wrist to keep me from leaning too far, but it was unnecessary. Looking down into that trench even the slightest revealed a swarming black cloud gathered at the northern end.

Power like inky tar speared outward, speeding toward us. They twisted above the forest across the way, like a dusty burst of an Angel's power, but dark and twisted.

As I had the thought, the ground rumbled beneath our feet, leaves shaking from their branches.

A bolt of agony shot through my scar, fighting against my Angelblood as it had at the induction ceremony but so much worse.

And I shrieked as a war broke out within my body, and Engrossians poured over the edge of the trench.

Chapter Thirty-Six
Malakai

꒷꒦꒷꒦꒷꒦

A GROANING ROAR FOLLOWED MILA'S SCREAM, AND THE ground erupted, vines shooting into the air.

The pounding in my chest intensified until it was all I could focus on, a wild animal trying to break out.

"Malakai, move!" Esmond shoved me, and my back hit the dirt, flowers crushed around me. A moment later, the pyre came crumbling down. Chunks of stone from Ptholenix's statue rained with it, striking the earth with booming echoes.

I laid among the rubble, trying to think through my pounding heart and focus.

"Mila!" I finally shouted, shoving myself to my feet. Esmond and Gatrielle stood shakily on the rocking ground.

"I'm fine!" she answered, her voice nearly drowned out, but I needed to see her to believe it. Another roar brought a chunk of the Angel's hand within an inch of my foot. Carving a wide arc among the flowers and trying to keep my balance, I tore through the field toward Mila's voice.

"What in the damned Spirits is that?" Mila gaped at the Angel statue. She stood back from it, the pyre having completely collapsed before her.

I took stock of her first. Of the platinum hair swirling around her shoulders and the determined—albeit alarmed—glint to her eye. An unfamiliar relief swarmed through me, drowning out the panic.

"That wasn't there before," Esmond said, shock bursting through his words as he joined us.

Following their gazes, I saw it. A golden image unfurling between the Angel's wings like a freshly inked tattoo. An orchid, petals blooming and lively. Vines danced away from the flower to curl down and around the stone wings, climbing his broad shoulders and spine.

"That's not portrayed on any artwork," Gatrielle gasped. Wind rustled his hair, his jaw dropping open.

I had an idea of what it reminded me of—what the entire phenomenon reeked of—but as the earth's shaking leveled out to rolling tremors, vines ripped from the ground again and caught around my wrists.

They pulled at me, but I wrenched myself free. The greenery grabbed Mila by the waist, yanking her back. As more erupted, a rumble coated the air.

One slippery appendage tangled around Esmond's ankles and tugged his legs out from beneath him. The Bodymelder crashed to the ground, his head snapping back.

"No!" I roared.

Gatrielle was already there, fighting his own vines. "He's breathing! He's okay."

Thank the Angels.

"What the fuck is happening?" Mila growled, unsheathing her lone sword to cut off her captors at the root. I mimicked her with my ax as best I could with the shackles grabbing at my wrists again.

Fucking Angels, if only we had all of our weapons. These things were too quick for a single blade.

"I'm not sure," I answered.

"We need to get out of here." Mila's eyes were wild, alternating between Esmond on the ground and me, still slicing my way through. "Malakai, look out!"

A vine shot toward my throat, but I swiveled. It locked around my bicep instead.

"Gatrielle." I tugged against it. "Is there anything else we need to know about this location?"

Over the forest to the east, darkness continued to gather. Distantly, I thought I felt a chill creep through the air but I couldn't stop to focus on it. Only kept hacking at the vines now working their way up my legs.

"I've never heard of anything like this happening." Gatrielle circled Esmond, slicing through vines to defend both of them. I tried to make my way toward the pair.

I'd only gone a few feet when a gust of wind wrapped around the statue, and Ptholenix's wings ignited. The heat of the flame scorched across us, near-burning.

Around the base of the Angel, flowers wilted in three spots, wide circles browning at the edges.

"By the Spirits." Gatrielle's eyes roved across the field. "I think it's recreating it."

"Recreating *what*?" Mila gasped as the vines around her waist tightened. Her strained voice twisted something primal in my chest.

Pulling with every ounce of force I had, I ripped away from my captors and ran to her, battling off the magic with pure desperation. I swung my ax through the taut, slithering plants holding her and watched them wither.

"The Ascension ceremony!" Gatrielle screamed over the eruption of more searching, tentacle-like limbs. "It wants us to reenact it."

"Why?" I asked, but I knew.

This field was not only an altar.

This was a memorial ground touched by the highest of Angel magic.

"We're being forced to ascend as damn Angels because Malakai touched the pyre?" Mila growled.

"It was when I touched the statue itself," I corrected, though I wasn't sure why I would have that impetus on the Angels.

"Not ascend," Gatrielle corrected, calling our attention back. His words grew hoarse as a vine tightened around his throat. "I think it wants—us to pretend. Warriors can't—become Angels."

He was right. No one could simply choose to become an

Angel, and I doubted a loosely guarded ceremony in a field would change that.

"Three warriors here." The vine loosened the pressure on Gatrielle's windpipe as he put the pieces together. "Three Angels who created the ceremony." A bit more lax. He panted, "We have to use knowledge and logic to prove ourselves."

Of course. Use the Bodymelder's pillars and values to win this task against the Angels, and likely find more in the process if my hunch was correct.

"Tell us what to do," I demanded.

"Each of us needs to stand in one of those rings of fallen flowers," Gatrielle directed. Mila and I hurried to our spots, the vines seeming to give way now that we'd deduced what they wanted. They trailed us along the ground, their leashes slack, but still watching. "How much do you know of the ascension?"

"Every clan's account is different." I watched the statue warily, ready to shove the others out of the way should pieces begin to crumble again. "I know Damien's tale, but I think we need yours."

"It's said that Ptholenix had a close relationship with Valyrie and Xenique." The Starsearcher and Soulguider Prime Warriors. That aligned with what I knew of the Angels. "When the seven split to maintain their own domains, those were the only three who remained in contact, though very rarely. They are the three who discovered how they could ascend and birthed the ritual for their peers."

"What did they do?" *What do we need to do?*

"All of our magic comes from the land." Gatrielle swallowed. "So they each sacrificed something to the earth."

My stomach turned over.

I was so damn tired of sacrificing. I had nothing left to offer—was simply trying to repair the husk I'd turned into—and now the world wanted *more*.

"What did they give?" Mila asked, voice soft but gaze studying me.

Jaw grinding, I kept my eyes on Ptholenix. Fuck the Angels for this. Fuck the Angels for all of this.

"We don't know exactly," Gatrielle said, fists clenched at his sides, a distrust in his narrowed stare at his Angel. "One gave a sign of life. One released the fears and mistakes that tethered them to this world. One, a promise of service."

What in the Spirits did any of that mean? I had a lifetime of mistakes weighing me down, but how was I to release them to a statue in this stupid field?

"I'll take the second one," Mila asserted. My head whipped toward her, finding nothing but resolve and maybe a hint of understanding.

"I can give a sign of life," Gatrielle offered.

"Then I'll give the promise." I had an inkling of what it wanted, but I was reluctant to offer it. I supposed that was the point of a sacrifice, though.

Confidently, Gatrielle held his rapier high. "What are you—"

He sliced it down across his palm, right across his allure tattoo. Red sprinkled the field like warm rain drops.

A sign of life.

His blood that made him a Bodymelder, drawn from the tattoo that proved he was blessed by the Angels.

Gatrielle did not even cry out as he watched his life sink into the earth. In response, the ground around us hummed. It wasn't the unsteadying rocking from before that tried to undo us. It was a warm beckoning that seeped into my own bones.

Mila crouched next, bending low behind the bushels of poppies and lilies.

Her hands trembled as she braced them on the ground. I sank down to a crouch in my own scorched ring. I couldn't get any closer, but I tracked that slight quaking, the most rattled I'd seen her. Other than when she chastised me for fleeing the battle, I supposed. She'd been unsettled then. This was deeper. It almost felt like something personal that I shouldn't watch.

But I couldn't look away.

Not as her head hung forward and she took a breath.

Not as her lips moved slowly, whispering something to the land. Some confession meant only for the Angels. Something she'd held within her for Damien knew how long.

When she was done, she didn't rise immediately. She took a long silent moment to collect herself. The only sound was the mounting hum of the earth. Finally, eyes shining, she stood and faced me.

I didn't know what she said, but it was clear it had taken a toll on her. I hated that. But I hated more that I could do nothing about her being trapped there with that pain.

The ground's buzzing intensified, warmth melting into the air like lava. It called me. This final sacrifice.

"When you're ready, Malakai," Gatrielle encouraged.

A promise of service. My hand curved around my ax.

For a moment, I wished I'd brought Lucidius's dagger. The one I'd carried unexpectedly since he'd died. Polished it, wielded it. But a piece of me was hesitant at even the consideration of letting it go.

Those twisted parts inside me needed that one thing until I had all of my answers regarding that man's lies. I was glad I'd left it behind.

I tugged the Engrossian ax from my belt.

This...this would be a sacrifice. I'd hated the weapons, couldn't face them after my imprisonment, and had now claimed one as my own. I'd conquered the fear of it against my skin.

Giving it up now would be a loss, but okay.

Still, even with that peaceful acceptance, I wanted one last swing at the Angels who caused this.

So, I pulled my arm back behind my head and let it fly.

The ax soared toward the stone statue, end-over-blade. The sharpened corner shouldn't have stuck, but it found a crevice in the deteriorating rock and lodged itself there with a ring of metal against stone, handle swinging.

"A weapon," I panted. "A symbol of the service we commit to as warriors."

A weight lifted from my shoulders, a release of my self-imposed punishment.

Ptholenix's flaming wings burned brighter. The buzzing swarmed through the ground.

Then, in one breath, the fire was extinguished.

The tattoo on the Angel's back glowed. Inked gold vines inflated, protruding from the surface. Crawling across his stone skin, they descended his body until they formed a tangled nest in the dirt like writhing, shimmering snakes.

The scorched rings in the ground disappeared, and we crept forward.

"What happens now?" Mila asked.

Those vines unwound their mess, something nestled in the center catching the light.

"I don't know," Gatrielle hedged. "The sacrifices are all we're sure of."

Peeling back one by one, the serpentine vines retreated to their stone house, like ligaments of a sentient beast. Where they'd been, a small gold item winked up at us.

I crouched and brushed my fingers across it. We waited for the earth to riot or the statue to crumble, but nothing happened.

When I picked the warm metal up, my chest pounded again.

It was almost a teardrop shape but elongated with small details carved into the curved surface. Turning it over, the underside had veins running through it.

My head snapped up, taking in the flowers around us.

Then, I looked at the Angel statue.

At the orchid tattoo on his back that now had one petal missing.

The one resting in my palm, having been fairly earned by the warriors who deciphered what it wanted, initiated the test somehow, and sacrificed to prove their worth.

A living piece of an Angel.

"What is it?" Mila asked. Behind us, Esmond was stirring. Gatrielle ran to care for him.

It was...how the fuck was this happening? I didn't know, but there was one thing I was sure of—

I looked at Mila. "This is one of Ophelia's emblems."

This was a piece of a Prime Warrior's power. Solidified, hidden among a field of fire flowers, and guarded by the Angel and earth itself.

Why was I able to find it? Why had me touching the statue set off this reaction? Ophelia was the cursed one.

"How do you know?" Mila asked.

"I can..." I wasn't sure how I knew. But like when Ophelia's spear had first broken and I'd held that emblem in my hand, a presence slumbered in this gilded case. "I just know."

"Why, though?" Mila asked, gently lifting the petal from my palm and holding it to the sun. "And does it do anything?"

"I don't know those either." I straightened up. "But we should get it to—"

In the distance, beyond Firebird's Field and through the burning expanse of Gennium's gnarled tree branches, from the direction of the Fytar Trench, a scream I recognized cut through the air.

Chapter Thirty-Seven
Ophelia

The poison from Kakias's dagger dug its claws in deeper, that point in my arm centralizing. The Angellight from my necklace speared back against it—two living entities of magic battling.

It made my head ring—my bones shake—but I tried to focus over it.

We retreated from the cliff, drawing weapons as Santorina screamed. Whirling, I found her in the grip of a dark-armored soldier. More ran from the trees.

Engrossians.

Cypherion dove for the one holding Santorina. "Forward, Rina!"

She leaned as far as the warrior's grip would allow, and Cypherion's scythe sliced through his arm. He screamed, and Rina tumbled away.

The limb dangled at his side, connected only by thin fibers of skin and tissue, leather armor gleaming red.

Santorina pulled her own knife and jammed it into the Engrossian's neck. Blood sprayed across her.

We exchanged a vengeful smile as I raced past. Another warrior raised her ax, but I slid across the grass, an inch below the scarred blade, and swiped Starfire across the back of her calf.

She crumpled to her knees. Popping to my feet behind her, I raised my short sword and swung down.

The booming of Damenal as it exploded echoed through my ears with the motion, followed by the memory of rocks slicing against my bare feet as I ran to find my father's body. The pride in his eyes when I'd last seen him. The empty, lost feeling upon realizing I'd never see him again.

And as my sword that had been a gift from my father sliced across the woman's neck, her head rolling from her body, the hungry thing inside of me, the one surviving on grief and promises of revenge, sang.

But still, those two powers battling within my body raged, flashes of light stealing my vision. Two bright forces, one dark and curling at the edges, the other shining and intrinsic.

The back of my neck prickled, and I forced myself to focus on the battle. I shoved aside the warring sensations and spun on the balls of my feet, raising Starfire on instinct, and came blade to blade with a masked warrior.

He bore down on me, forcing me back.

I jumped over the woman's body I'd slain and put more space between me and this new opponent. Enough to rip Angelborn from my back and thrust her forward.

The gleaming gold tip went through the man's eye before it even had a moment to widen. I wrenched it from his head, and the way the blood spilled across his face and into his gaping mouth stirred a deranged satisfaction within me.

"Vale, guard me!" Jezebel shouted.

As I whirled toward her, my sister fell into her power.

She reached out, and the warrior I killed rose, swinging around toward his own men. It was a ghastly sight: blood pouring through the air, limbs stumbling as Jez seized hold through his spirit. She used his weight to slam into another Engrossian and drew the man's ax sloppily across his fellow's neck.

Then, she was manipulating the two of them like an army of dead warriors.

"Two is all I can handle!" she shouted.

But two was better than one, and she used her deathly

puppets' spirits to control their bodies and add numbers and strength to our side.

Cypherion and Tolek battled back-to-back, operating like a scale in perfect balance. Where one swung, the other dodged, a bond guiding their movements as Cyph sliced his scythe across one warrior's stomach, guts pouring out, and Tol fired off an arrow. It shot through the neck of an Engrossian charging Jez, the man's body going limp with the impact.

I threw Angelborn across my back and ran to join Vale guarding my sister, meeting the cruel, lifeless eyes of an Engrossian.

And Starfire met her ax.

A pang of sorrow clanged through me in time with our weapons. Kakias did this. She'd stolen these warriors' lives. She'd fed them with her power and turned them into her destructive tools.

Never mind the anomaly of her being able to manipulate anyone, let alone another clan. Did they want this? *Perhaps they did*, I thought as the woman's blade came within an inch of my stomach. If that was the case, they were our enemies. I couldn't tell myself otherwise. Not if I wanted to get my friends out of this alive.

The wind gusted, ghostly tendrils skating down my skin. In my periphery, curling, whip-like black tendrils crawled over the cliff edge and seeped across the ground like fresh ink, toward me and my friends.

And I knew in my bones what that power was.

Was certain as I ducked my opponent's next swing and rammed Starfire into her side, clean through her leather armor, it belonged to the queen.

The Engrossian's ax tumbled from her hand, skinning my shoulder as it fell. I cried out, pressing my hand to the wound.

My blood trickled over the Engrossian emblem ring, and a beam of Angellight shot forward.

It pushed against the soldier, forcing her back. I sucked in a gasp, and in response the Angellight recoiled to the ring in time with my breath. Warmth seeped through my hand, spreading over the scrape to my shoulder and healing it quicker than even our mountains could.

Before I could question that unusual connection with the Angellight, that wild wind howled around us again. Tendrils oozed like tar along the ground.

Something tugged behind my navel, jerking me backward.

And the pain radiating from my scar shot through my arm, like bones cracking. That poisonous power solidified beneath the skin, responding to the coils as they got closer. Reaching for them.

A scream wrenched up my throat, and I fell to my knees, Starfire tumbling from my grasp.

Crimson bled around the Engrossian warrior's hands as they pressed to her side. She sneered down at me, pure hatred tinted with victory in her snarl. Her skin paled by the second, but she ripped a dagger from her side and stumbled toward me.

All I could do was writhe with the pain beneath my scar and scramble back, uninjured arm flailing across the ground. My fingers locked around a rock, and I threw it.

The impact was harsh—leaving an instant slice to her forehead —but she kept coming.

And I kept crawling through dirt and leaves. Tried to see through the blinding pain in my arm and light-flecked vision. It was all growing more distorted—the growls of battle echoing and forms melting into shapeless masses.

Kakias was here. She had to be with the way her magic swarmed around us.

But the warrior bore down on me, blocking my view of the field. And two opposing forces of light continued to war through my body. The poison tried to stretch out.

Her ax was raised before me, my body shrieking in pain. All I could think was that I needed Kakias's power gone from my body if I was going to stand a chance in this fight.

But then, the Engrossian stopped approaching.

And she tumbled to the ground.

A shadow loomed in her spot, sword dripping the woman's blood. Warm arms wrapped around me, pulling me away from the battle and into the shallows of the tree line.

"What's happening?" It was Tolek. I'd know his voice even from the Spirit Realm.

I tried to steady my vision, count how many Engrossians were left. Jezebel still wielded another, Cypherion fighting one.

And in the distance, a swirling form emerged from a veil of dark Angelic power.

Pain radiated in my skull. She was blurry, but I remembered that display of flowing, whip-like magic from the Battle of Damenal. Would never forget the cruel smile and scar dragging across her face. Blood-red lips and sharp teeth.

Even with my blurred vision, I thought our eyes locked.

And my vengeful stare matched Kakias's.

Agony writhed beneath my skin, two forces as real and potent as each of our powers fighting. I could *feel* her within my scar. With each step closer, the poison reached for her.

"She's—" I gasped, pressing down on the angry mark. The solidified magic within pressed back. "She's here."

I could barely make out the hands trying to soothe me, the voices shouting around me. My friends stormed toward Kakias, but her power reacted erratically, lashing out in those tendrils of tar.

Sapphire stormed a circle around Tolek and me. Pain vibrated along my veins, bones drowning it all out until the only thing I had room for was *her*.

The chill of the queen's magic pressed through every available space in my body, melting into my nerves. It was familiar, like it was saying hello to an old friend.

It poured and poured and poured.

It took and took and took.

It siphoned ether from my cursed blood into that point of my arm.

I needed to get up. Kakias was here. I needed to fight, but—

Memories of her voice in my ear and blade against my arm. And fucking Angels, did it *burn*. A searing, blinding black fire centralized in the solidified poison beneath my skin.

A scream I couldn't control ripped its way out of my throat.

"GET IT OUT!" I demanded. Another shock of pain had me curling over my knees on a bed of crumbling leaves and needles.

Rina had said she could try to cut it out. I needed it out.

The thing within my arm felt like those whips. Each rope of dark power beading beneath the skin, tying into me. My Angel-blood clawed at it, pulled from it.

"What?" Tolek fell to his knees with me, forcing my back up.

"Get it out!" I repeated. Salty tears flooded my mouth. I hadn't realized I was crying but heaving sobs ripped through my chest. "The power. Her power. GET IT OUT OF ME."

My words sounded like the edges of jagged knives.

"I don't know how I can do that." He kept his voice calm for me, but even through my blurred vision the panic in his eyes was jarring.

"Cut it out! Cut it out, cut it out, please. Now." I shoved my arm toward him, screaming over another burst of pain, and I was certain he understood when he saw how it was pushing against the scar.

I writhed, falling to the side.

It was sharp. Piercing. Claiming.

I couldn't tell if the others were still fighting. I thought I heard the singing of blades and saw their shadows circling us, but there were too many people.

All blurred forms.

Too much of Kakias's power. We couldn't match it.

Sapphire continued to whinny, a high and torturous sound and holy fucking Angels if Kakias touched my horse I'd cut out her unfeeling heart while she still lived.

"I—I can't do that." Tol's voice sounded far away, but when I pried my eyes open, his fingers shook around the Vincienzo dagger.

"I need—I need you—ah—" My voice scraped up my vocal cords as if they were shredding, too. Every piece of me was disintegrating under these two warring powers. Bolts of Angellight against dark fire, too much for my mortal flesh to contain. "Get it out of me. *Please*. Tol, I need you to do this for me."

Anguish twisted his features, tears rolling down his cheeks, too —the reluctance morphing to acceptance at what I was asking him to do. There was something tortured in his stare that broke both of our hearts. Something that said we both understood we were going to have to do horrific things before this ended, but it was a deeply-rooted nightmare to have to do them to the other.

I almost relented. Almost grabbed the blade myself so he didn't have to do it because Tolek had suffered too much already, but nothing about my body was under my control.

Tolek gripped my wrist, his hands sure.

"Okay." It was a low reassurance. "Okay, love, I've got you." With the hand holding the dagger, he lifted my chin. Made this horrendous moment surrounded by bloodshed feel as if it was only us two. "Give me those beautiful eyes." His voice shook, and I didn't know why he sounded like he was carving out his own heart, but if this was what he needed, I would do it. "Don't look away. Please."

And he cut.

And I held my scream, bit my lip until I tasted blood, but I did as he asked. Eyes locked to his, the rest of the world gone. Blood poured over my arm, across the searing slices he left as that poisoned tar left my body in unspooling coils, solid and seemingly alive.

And the whole time, Tolek whispered shaking, soothing words to the both of us.

When it was done, purged, and the only pain left was from the new incision he'd had to give me, darkness edged around my vision.

But my body was lighter than it had been since Daminius.

A high scream pierced the fog. I thought I knew who it was but couldn't remember.

"Close your eyes," Tolek whispered. "I'll get you out of here."

I collapsed, Tol's solid arms catching me. He scooped me up, cradling me, kissing the side of my head as he started to run.

"I'm sorry. I'm so sorry," he repeated in my ear, voice thick.

I didn't know why. This wasn't his fault. He'd been the one to take away the pain, not cause it. Tolek Vincienzo had saved my life again.

Bodies moved around us. It sounded like more than our horses and friends, but we were shadowed by the forest, and I couldn't make out more than shapes.

I thought I heard a familiar deep voice saying my name. Thought something thudded against the crease beneath my elbow. Thought Tolek answered over his shoulder.

But I couldn't be sure of any of it.

"*Wherearewegoing?*" My words were slurred.

"Somewhere safe," Tolek answered.

Safe.

For every day I lived, I'd ensure he was safe from his own thoughts, his own past, as he did what I needed today to guarantee I was safe from the queen's wrath. He was my safety as I was his.

With that unbreakable promise softening the edges of unconsciousness and tethering me to him, I let darkness take me.

PART THREE
ZELOS

CHAPTER THIRTY-EIGHT
DAMIEN

THE ANGELGLASS FLASHED AN ARRAY OF DARK CLOUDS and the girl's tear-streaked face, frozen in an anguished scream.

Bant's torture had ceased days before, but as the image faded, our master lashed out one final time. A roar of power struck the Angelglass, and shards rained to the floor, chiming against rock.

Then, it whipped directly between Bant's wings, the most sensitive place on an Angel, next to the extremities themselves.

Our master raised a large slice of glass and dragged it down Bant's wing. Crimson erupted from the wound. It once would have been gold, I realized. Another reminder of the vital pieces of himself he sacrificed centuries ago on a foolish whim.

Bant would not scream.

He knew better.

The others averted their stares, but I watched. Perhaps it was for my own selfish vendetta, perhaps a piece of solidarity as someone who had once failed. I could not be sure until I was restored.

Everyone else lingered before the Angelglass, debating what we had seen, but I could not look away from Bant. History was pouring through my mind, worries of the past beginning to surface.

Of a man on his knees cursing our kind.

Of a spirit ripped from eternal existence.

Of hope tunneling from our grasp.

The Angel tensed, jaw clenching. His dark hair was sopping with sweat, sticking to the back of his neck and forehead. Pieces curled at the ends, reaching out like fingers needy for saving.

None of us could, though.

We had all been there at one time or another. You did not bow to our master for eternity without stepping out of his bounds at least once. And when you did, you felt the force of his wrath on feathers and flesh. Those strikes seared my own memories as the jagged pieces of glass ripped through his other wing, slow and torturous.

Bant's eyes met mine. Silently, I forced myself to look back.

Brother, what have you done? A distant voice echoed.

I was not sure.

I watched in jaw-grinding silence as a feather fell from the Angel's wings. Only one at first, drifting slowly to the ground. It landed in a pool of blood, weighed down and sodden.

This was what happened when Angels shed their power. It was a rare phenomenon. Magic was so scarcely given up and even harder to take. But a second feather fell, and there was only one other time I had seen it done. One other time Bant had, too.

Then, the room gave an almighty shiver. Ptholenix cried out, alarmed, not pained, and fire burst along his wings.

Beastly roars made of creatures long sleeping echoed against the walls of our chamber.

"Ptholenix?" our master asked, milky eyes wide. He spun the bloody shard between his fingers.

Ptholenix looked in wonder at the fiery wings surrounding him, a light in his gaze I had not seen in millennia. The Bodymelder's eyes fell shut, and he breathed in for a moment. The flames along the tips of his burnished feathers flickered.

"Partially," he confirmed. His skin remained the same tawny hue, no light emitted.

"Why only partially?" I wondered.

Ptholenix's wings set the room alight as he tested them. Beside him, Gaveny's ocean light spilled around the chamber floor. Together, they took the form of a glowing sunset against the waves.

My own golden light burned along with it, Bant's consumed by working to heal him.

Though questions continued to bloom, those sleeping sparks of our power emerged. As I watched Bant shiver in his pain and felt my own light flare, I longed to restore this ether, despite my doubts.

Fate had clipped our wings before. I hoped she did not treat hers in the same way.

CHAPTER THIRTY-NINE
OPHELIA

✶✶✶✶✶

"SHE'S BEEN OUT FOR A WHOLE DAY." THAT VOICE...I recognized it. But it sounded far away.

Tremors wracked my body. I tried to curl my knees to my chest but wasn't sure I actually moved. Every part of me was heavy.

"I know." The second voice soothed the fear rioting in my gut.

"Santorina said her arm is healing." Santorina...Rina...she was here? Why did worry slice through me at the reminder of my friends? *"She should be awake."* Concern turned the first voice guttural.

"She will be." The second voice sounded uncertain. I wanted to appease it, but it was all blurry.

"The wound needs to be rewrapped."

"I know!" the second voice snapped.

For a moment, one of my leaden limbs got lighter. A gentle pressure on my arm.

"It looks better." The second voice again, a note near pleading, like it was trying to convince itself.

"It does." The first voice sighed.

Something fluttered across my forehead, a gentle touch. *"This is my fault."*

My fault...

The self-deprecating tone called to me, and I fought through the muddled, sticky tar of unconsciousness to reach it. Sense tumbled back into my body in slow spurts as I blinked my eyes open.

Tolek was leaning over me, head bowed against my shoulder, hand holding my own. Rock walls curved around us, orbs of mystlight providing streaky illumination that frayed the edges of the room.

Wherever we were, it was freezing. Despite the heavy fur blankets draped across me, I shivered.

"My fault..." Tolek mumbled again. His voice was so broken and mournful, so etched with hatred, it helped me find my own.

"It's not," I croaked.

His head snapped up, eyes red as they bore into mine as if unable to believe I'd spoken.

"Thank the fucking Angels." Tolek brushed matted and sweaty hair from my forehead.

"How do you feel?" The second voice was back, and I placed it now.

"Malakai?" He stepped out of the shadows in the small chamber, frame blocking the mystlight. I blinked as my eyes adjusted to the relief from the brightness, and his harrowed expression came into view. "What are you doing here?"

My voice was hoarse. Tolek uncapped a canteen and helped me sit up so I could drink, my head spinning. I squeezed my eyes tight, and when I opened them again, I could make out more of the room. A small fire crackled in a wood stove in the corner, but it must have been mystlight because there was no smoke in the room. A pile of thick fur throws sat at the foot of my cot, and a table held medicinal supplies I assumed Santorina used on me.

"How are you, Ophelia?" Though Malakai hadn't answered my question, his sounded so sincere, inquiring about everything we'd been through, not only how I was physically after waking.

"I...confused."

The events leading to my unconsciousness came back to me in flashes. The queen ambushing us at the trench. Jezebel using her power to command fallen soldiers. Asking Tolek to cut the poison from my arm.

At the last one, my eyes shot to the old scar. It was larger now —a jagged cross of lines where before it had been one clean swipe. But the black veins stretching out from it were entirely gone. Only healing pink skin remained.

"We got it all out," Tolek assured me, watching with worried eyes as I processed. "Everyone is safe."

It was gone. And all of my friends survived the attack.

The queen's power no longer tainted my blood. As if to test it, I called on my Angelblood—the power that had warred with the queen's within me—and prodded the wound internally.

It was silent in response. No hint of Kakias or her claim on me existed in my blood any longer.

I am free of the queen.

A sigh slipped from my lips, so heavy I thought it would crack my chest wide open. And for the first time, I let the tears fall.

I'd been so scared and powerless against the queen at the trench, I wasn't sure I'd ever be free again. I thought the only future was to succumb. To give myself over in order to build a safer world for those relying on me.

But Tolek saved me.

As I cried, I curled into him, letting his arm band around my shoulders and his soothing assurances steady me.

I didn't know how long I sat there with these two men I loved so fiercely watching me break beneath fears and relief, but eventually I righted myself. Taking in big gulps of air, I calmed my breathing, wiped my cheeks, and tugged the fur tighter around me.

"She was there," I stated.

"She was," Tolek confirmed. His fingers drifted over my shoulder, as if he was unable to calm the nerves rioting through him. "Hope was not on our side for a moment there. But something happened when I—" He flinched. "When we got the poison out of you, Kakias collapsed."

The scream that had wrenched the air, so pained it could crumble realms—it had been her.

"It seems whatever she was doing to you was taking a toll on her own power so when she no longer had you to siphon from, she fell," Malakai added.

"Or whatever the power was rebounded," Tolek suggested and Malakai nodded. "We can't be sure, but we didn't stay to find out."

"What happened to it?" I asked nervously. "The power." It had been a sharp, physical presence in my arm. The ghost of it lingered.

"When it came free, it was a mirror of those tendrils Kakias wielded, inching across the ground. Santorina took it." My eyes widened, but Tolek continued, "She has it contained with some of her other supplies and has been studying it. It seems to be losing its solid form and now exists as a syrupy substance."

"It's unlike anything we've seen," Malakai warned. "It almost seems...aware."

I mulled over those details, creeping coils of Kakias's power curling around the edges of my memory. Blood and searing pain and the grass gripped in my palms as I writhed against it. A physical source of power melting and gaining sentience.

"It doesn't make sense that not having me would weaken Kakias," I mused, watching the fire, not really addressing either of them. "She needs me dead to fulfill her immortality ritual. You'd think a disconnect would make her stronger."

"I have a feeling none of this is what we assume," Malakai said. Tolek and I both nodded in agreement. Every day we were walking uncharted paths, trying to make sense of routes that crossed and dipped and peaked without warning.

The mystlight fire crackled, pulling my attention back into the room. Sighing, I asked, "Where are we now?"

Malakai looked at Tolek. A swallow worked the latter's throat, but he answered without breaking my stare. "We're in an underground system of tunnels in Mindshaper Territory."

Panic seized my chest. "We can't be here." My head pounded as I shot to my feet and stumbled. Enemy territory. And they'd said I'd been unconscious for a day already. Where were my weapons?

But Tolek's arm wrapped around my waist, tugging me back to the cot beside him and securing the blanket I'd shucked. Mindshaper Territory explained the chill in the air.

"We *can* be here," he said.

"No, we can't." I looked between him and Malakai who nodded, standing against the wall with his arms crossed.

"Relax, Alabath." Tolek rubbed a hand down my arm. "We're safe."

"*Safe?*"

"We *are* safe here." Malakai swallowed, lips pulled into a line.

"They call it the Labyrinth," Tolek added, as if a name made this all make any more sense.

"Oh, lovely. Glad I know what it's called." I pursed my lips, jutting my chin out. "Now, what are we *doing* here?"

"She's feeling better, I see," Santorina entered, pulling a fur cloak around her shoulders. Cypherion and Jezebel followed her.

"Quite a bit," Tolek answered without looking away from me.

"Not good at recovering quietly? How shocking." Jezebel strode through the cavern and stood beside the stove, warming her hands. She and the others were all wearing fresh leathers, but they weren't Mystique. These were layered over thick tunics we didn't typically need in our territory.

Cypherion joined my sister beside the fire, claiming one of the room's shoddy wooden chairs.

Though my aching head was only growing worse with the lack of explanation, I looked over my friends. Tears threatened to fall again. "I'm glad you're all okay."

"We all made it out," Tolek reminded me, rising from the cot to allow Santorina to redress the wound on my arm. She gently applied an ointment, and the heat from the healing scar was instantly dulled.

Relaxing at her touch, my gaze swept the room, putting together the pieces now. I pressed a palm flat against the wall. We were underground. The surroundings I'd thought were rock were actually tightly-packed earth. They insulated the chamber, holding in the mystlight's warmth and providing the slightest protection from the snowy terrain above.

"Sapphire?" I blurted, my mare's panicked whinny echoing in my head.

"All the horses are accounted for," Cypherion said.

"Where are they?" There was no chance they'd fit in here.

Tolek explained, "There's an adjacent tunnel that pours into a wide cavern that's being used as stables."

"Sapphire wasn't happy to not be with you," Jez added. "She was skittish when we first got her down here."

I tried to push to my feet, but Rina put a hand on my shoulder. "She's okay. Let us take care of you first."

I groaned and sat back down. "But *how* are we here?" Though I was consumed by pain during most of the battle, I'd heard it. The screams and clashes. It hadn't seemed like we were winning. "And where did you come from?" I gestured at Malakai. He didn't stand near the fire, as if the chill did not bother him at all.

"Esmond, Mila, and I had already made it to Firebird's Field to meet you all. We heard the attack and made it through the Gennium forest in time to see Kakias fall and take out a few of her soldiers. Her power was ricocheting from her, though, and a few survived along with the queen."

My brows shot up.

"There's more," Cypherion added, nodding at Malakai.

"There's this." He removed something small and gold from his pocket, stepping forward to close the space between us.

Before I even touched it, I knew. It called to me like a voice on the wind, an instinctive tug in my gut, and my second pulse pounded.

When Malakai tipped the emblem into my hand, it seared, but I curled my fingers around it and sank into the pain. Vengeful thoughts against the Angels compiled in my memory, and a vicious grin broke across my face.

"The Bodymelder one?" I clarified. Though, who else would the gilded petal belong to? Malakai's nod of confirmation sent my entire body buzzing. "How?"

He told me a wild tale of the endeavor they'd faced to retrieve this emblem. How it didn't burn for him the way they did for me, yet he knew what it was.

"Everyone with you made it out, too?" I had to know before getting distracted by the emblem. Nerves clenched my stomach.

"Mila, Esmond, and Gatrielle are all in the Labyrinth."

I nodded, looking back to the shard of Angel power in my palm. "Why do you think it would do that?" I tossed theories around in my head. "Your bloodline does not have Angelblood, does it?"

"I don't think so, but as we've learned in recent years, there's a lot we don't know about my family history." His jaw ground.

Biting my lip, I considered the possibility. For Malakai's sake, I hoped there was no Angelblood in his line. We still didn't know what activated it, and the thought of him being sucked into this curse with me turned my stomach. "You don't react to it at all?"

He shook his head.

"Not Angelblood, then," Jezebel said, rubbing her hands together over the fire.

"Or not active Angelblood," Cypherion corrected. "You said the earth erupted when you touched the statue?"

Malakai nodded, and Cyph and I exchanged a grim nod. It sounded similar to how the one platform in Seawatcher Territory had exploded when I set foot on the top expanse of the island.

"Why, though?" I asked, turning the emblem over in my hand. "Why was this hidden in the first place? The nature of the test makes sense with what we've hypothesized after Gaveny's. Each is tailored to its Angel. But *why*?"

The gilded petal winked in the mystlight as an uncertain silence thickened.

Spirits, my head was spinning again. Tugging the blanket tighter around me and clutching the new emblem, I leaned back against the wall. Letting my eyes fall closed, I breathed in deeply. Listened to the crackling fire and massaged the rough fur beneath my fingers.

Four. We had four emblems now and still were no closer to figuring out why we needed them or what they did.

"If we're safe in Mindshaper Territory," I finally said, cracking my eyes open, "who does the Labyrinth belong to?"

"The rebel Mindshaper group who is not under Kakias's influence," Tolek responded immediately.

"What?" I blinked at him.

"I'll let them explain the intricacies of their power," Tol continued, a guarded edge to his voice, "but there is a faction of Mindshapers who are not affected by the power the queen is manipulating over her army."

"A rather large faction," Cyph added. His eyes brightened, and

I could see his mind whirling with curiosity. That was the brain of my Second at work—once he grew into the idea of accepting the role. But there were more important things than pushing him right now.

"They have this network of tunnels beneath the land that they use to travel and communicate." Jezebel tilted her head. "It's rather impressive."

I tried to brush off the shock, but I couldn't ignore the fact that if not all the Mindshapers were loyal to the queen, if some would fight on our side, this could turn the tide of the war.

"And how did we find them?"

The cavern fell quiet at my question, everyone shifting, not looking at me. Malakai's and Cypherion's eyes flitted to Tolek, who sighed. "Leave," he clipped, and the four of them filed out, Santorina shooting him a narrowed glare on her way.

"Tol?" I hedged, my pulse pounding faster as he came to sit beside me. For the first time in a while, he didn't reach out to touch me in some way.

"Let me explain myself before you get angry, okay?"

My stomach bottomed out. "I don't like how this is beginning."

He breathed a sad laugh. "You remember the deal you made with that fae when you came to rescue me during the summer?"

I nodded. Of course I remembered it, but—"You didn't."

"I made my own bargain," he confirmed, reaching into his pocket. He removed a thick silver ring and slid it onto the middle finger of his right hand. Engravings around the metal caught the light.

A symbol of a fae bargain. My hand went to my own around my neck.

"When the charm fell from your necklace while traveling through Bodymelder Territory last week, it was because I took it. I summoned Lancaster—who was furious to learn it was not you invoking his help—and convinced him to make a bargain with me in order to ensure we safely survived the confrontation with the queen. I dropped the token on the ground in our camp afterwards, intending to *find* it in the morning, but Vale beat me to that."

The more he spoke, the tighter my chest got, but I let him continue. "Lancaster is still gathering information on fae magic, and in the process he discovered the rebel faction. He told me how to find them if we needed an escape and arranged for them to aid us. I had this contingency plan in case something went wrong."

He retained that calm demeanor and forced my gaze to hold his, but his fingers drummed against his knee as he awaited my response.

Tolek made a deal with a fae in order to save me.

The exact thing I'd done last summer without a second thought. I couldn't be angry about that, and I didn't want to be.

"You didn't tell me," I finally forced out.

"He made me swear I wouldn't until it came to light naturally. One of his parameters."

That was out of his control, then. I took a deep breath. Surprisingly, it wasn't the bargain that had anger bubbling within me. Truthfully, I understood why he did it. I'd come to learn that sometimes secrets did not intend to burn you, but that didn't mean there wasn't a small sting.

What flamed my anger was that Tolek already dealt with enough, shoving aside his own pain to shoulder more of mine each day. Here he was again, putting me before himself.

The confessions he'd shared about his father tore through me, the hurt he'd lived with for so long, it became a part of him. Tolek should be able to focus on healing his pain and seeing his own value, not pushing himself to the side or carrying more for my sake.

"I don't want you to take on my burdens, Tol," I whispered. "You shouldn't have done that."

"You shouldn't have done it either," he challenged. "Now we're both tied to the fae."

"I did that to save you," I argued, giving in to the bait.

"And so did I." He brushed a strand of hair behind my ear and cupped my cheek; though our tones were harsh and demanding, the subtle touch comforted me. Reminded me he was still my tether in the storm brewing between us. "You're so busy trying to save everyone else, it's going to get you killed. I couldn't sit by and watch that happen. Not when I had an idea of something that might help you."

"I could have called on Lancaster and invoked my own bargain. You didn't need to commit yourself to him, too." The fae were dangerous, their deals more so. What if he tricked Tolek? No, Tol was smarter than that, especially when it came to words. He would have sealed his debts without loopholes.

"I don't have the weight of a clan on my shoulders or an ancient prophecy chasing me. Let me do these things, Alabath." His breathing turned raspy, eyes harried. "Let me care for you and protect you so you live to see the end of this mess."

Spirits, I wanted to. I wanted to fall into Tolek and allow him to shelter me from all of this damn chaos, but I didn't want to harm him in the process.

"I—" I swallowed. "This entire mess we're in is made of so many sharp edges." *I am made of sharp edges.* "What if I put those in your hands and you bleed out because of it?"

"Then I gladly will because I love you!" His words rang through the cavern, along my bones in recognition. *I love you.* It wasn't new information, but with the distress peaking his voice and the frantic grip of his hands on my shoulders, it felt raw and vulnerable all the same. "And you don't have to say it back. I know I've felt it longer and you're still healing. But I will happily slice myself up for you, Alabath. Don't hide those pieces from me."

With the way my head continued to spin, I wasn't sure I would win this argument. It was one we'd continue to have, I assumed. Me trying to save him. Him trying to save me. It was a sweet sort of love, in a twisted way. Wanting to die for the other if you must.

But I did not want that for us. I longed for the peace Tolek made me believe in. The dawn on the horizon of this darkness we'd sunk into. We'd get there one day. We had to.

And once I was certain I wasn't doing so out of distress or fear, I'd give those words back to him.

"What did you give him?" I asked, unsure if I truly wanted the answer.

"Well, I had to kiss him, which he was not thrilled about."

Tolek tilted his head, a smirk curling his lips and slicing through the tension. "Bit insulting, really. I didn't mind, though."

"I mind," I snapped.

"Jealousy looks beautiful on you," he joked, stroking the flush in my cheek. But I felt the blow before he delivered it, like it sucked all the air from the room. "He made me confess the task from the Angels."

"You what?" I gasped, shoving up from the cot. The blanket fell to my feet. "We can't trust them, Tolek! How could you hand over that information?"

"He's sworn to secrecy, Alabath. He might be able to help us, but he is not allowed to share what I revealed. That was my stipulation."

That was a small comfort. I reined in my anger, taking a breath. Of course Tol sealed the bargain. He wasn't foolish.

"His queen is a master of trickery," I said, scratching at my Curse scar. "What if she pulls it from his head somehow?"

"Then, so be it!" Tolek towered over me, his control snapping. "If I'm being quite honest, I could not care less about the Angels if it means you're safe. I'm being entirely selfish, but I don't give a fuck anymore. You're focused on saving the damn continent and delivering the Angels what they asked? Fine. Let me be selfish and ensure you survive it because when the sun sets and the moon slips into its place night after night, *you* are the only thing that truly matters to me. It's selfish of me, and I can admit that. I've never once claimed to be a perfect man, never once believed myself worthy of you, and if guarding your life is what sends me to the Spirit Realm, then so be it. I'll be selfish for us both, and you'll be okay."

I was never going to believe my life was worth more than his. These disparities sliced a wound between us, and I needed to figure out how to repair it fully if we were going to survive this together.

Cupping his cheeks, I rose up onto my toes and pressed my mouth lightly to his. His hands wrapped around my back, hungry to get closer, but the kiss was soft and slow.

Then, I gave him the words I could offer when I couldn't

promise I wouldn't put myself in danger. "Thank you, Tolek. Thank you for always taking care of me. For being selfish for me."

"Ophelia." He breathed my name like a prayer. One he'd been saying his entire life and only just realized someone was listening. That someone had answered. "I will always protect you."

His hand tightened in my hair, and it was clear there was more plaguing him, but instead of sharing, he stepped back and grabbed my hand. "Come on. Let's get you prepared to meet our new allies."

The tension still vibrated between us, not all the walls down yet. I thought there were fears we were both keeping from the other, reasons for not being able to heal the wound, but I took his hand.

We would repair it.

Chapter Forty
Malakai

Perhaps alliances weren't as bad as I once thought.

Did I *want* to be in Mindshaper Territory when the majority of their clan were our enemies in this war? No.

Originally, when we'd found our friends fighting Kakias's host, and I saw the queen's power pouring from the trench, I'd said we needed to get far away from there as quickly as possible. When her magic was snapping from her like uncontrollable whips and she was screaming, I'd wanted to run. When Tolek told me where we were going to hide, I'd nearly ripped Ophelia from his arms and tackled him to the ground, convinced he was corrupted, too.

He'd explained quickly, and Mila, Cyph, and the others had followed him without a second thought. I didn't have a choice.

Now, as we all waited in a large cavern serving as a meeting room with its brick walls and reinforcement beams stretching across the ceiling, I believed we could trust the rebels. Though my skin itched being trapped here, and I found myself counting my breaths frequently, my prejudices did not apply to the entire clan.

Searching for a way to distract myself from where we were, I took out Lucidius's journal on Firebird's Field and leaned back in my chair at the large meeting table. He had pointed us toward one emblem successfully. It only reasoned that if we could decode more of his ramblings, we might find more clues.

I'd been in the middle of the next entry while waiting for Ophelia to wake today.

magic is alive here and i both fear and worship it

Would be helpful if he said where "here" was.

it lives in the winds and skies her wings gracing my every breath but when magic takes life from another what happens? is it terminable for the host? can magic be killed? i believe magic can be killed by an extinguishing of that which it relies on or reversing that which spawned its poor life and if living magic is killed the world may be a duller place or the host may be a lifeless husk but perhaps taking that which is unnatural will be better for us all

that is what i will tell myself when i do it

extract the source i must learn to extract the source

Again, he could have been more helpful.

Spirits, this was becoming insufferable. I was a bit concerned with how easily my brain was learning to translate the nonsense. It made sense given how much time I'd spent dissecting these words over the past months, but my skin prickled. Groaning, I shut the notebook and tossed it aside.

"How is she?" Mila asked, taking the seat next to me. The agitation in my chest calmed.

I dragged my hand through my hair, sighing. "She's confused and worried, but I think relieved." I paused, then with a laugh added, "I'm glad I'm not Tolek, though."

Ophelia was always frightening when she was angry, and I doubted him making a fae bargain would go over smoothly.

Mila assessed me for a moment. "Is it weird for you?"

"Is what weird?"

"Them," she said.

Them. The girl I'd loved and thought I would spend my life with, had received the Bind with, and one of my best friends, practically my brother.

"No," I said, honestly. "It once would have been, but so much has...changed." I thought of the way Ophelia had clung to Tolek when she woke, how a piece of him had been untamable when he waited for her. How both of them relaxed in the other's presence. "It makes sense, really."

They had always been that way. They fit together—were pulled toward each other. I'd always known it, even before I signed the treaty. I hadn't been jealous or threatened back then. I was aware of where we'd all stood.

Ophelia and I used to belong to each other even more than they did, but where they still fit, we did not. After everything I went through, seeing them together now didn't hurt. It was okay.

Mila nodded. "Being down here is hard for you, isn't it?"

"You noticed?" I asked, but of course she had. I'd been on alert, waiting for a threat, since I realized we were venturing into tunnels and caves.

"At first I thought maybe it was because of Ophelia, but you've been quiet. Your eyes catalog everything, and..." She gestured to where my fingers drummed a nervous beat on the table. I hadn't even noticed I'd been doing it. "It's because of your imprisonment."

She always spoke of what I went through so blandly. Not minimizing it—there was always a deep understanding beneath her words—but she did not shy away from it the way others did. It made it easier for me to speak about, too.

"I believe we're safe," I said. "But the halls look similar. It's easy to be pushed back there."

"I understand," Mila said quietly. "It's hard for me, too."

For a minute I watched her. How her fingers traced patterns around her knee as she thought. How she chewed her lip in a way I was envious of. She was watching something across the room, but dammit I didn't care what. I couldn't look away.

"Why's that?" I asked.

Those blue eyes blinked up at me, and I realized it was the first time I'd really asked her. Though I'd been wondering for weeks, I hadn't pulled myself out of my own damn head enough to figure out what was going on in hers.

Right as I thought she might answer, Cypherion took the chair on her other side, asking about the alliance army. I kept my attention on Mila as she answered. How easily she fell into the routine of statistics and strategies. How being in control relaxed a bit of the unease she clearly suffered from these caves—for whatever reason.

When there was a lull in the conversation, and Cypherion turned to tell Santorina something, I leaned toward Mila, whispering low in her ear, "It may be hard for us both, but you're not alone, Mila."

I wasn't sure if her answering shiver was from the proximity or the chord my words struck.

Chapter Forty-One

Ophelia

I washed and changed into warmer clothing provided by these *allies* I had yet to meet. A pair of leather pants lined with soft fur, a thick tunic that was somewhat stiff, and a leather corset strapped over it. With my dagger at my thigh, Angelborn across my back, and my sword belt around my waist, I was ready to present the Mystique Revered to those we hoped to sway to our side.

Tol stood in the corner mumbling suggestively the entire time it took me to prepare, but swearing he averted his eyes. Though I didn't really mind either way, the strain his fae revelation strung between us made me want him to suffer a bit. Vindictive? Perhaps, but it was another of our games. Having to look away while I changed my clothes seemed like his personal form of torture.

Once I was ready, he laced our fingers and pulled me through the tunnels, stopping first to check on Sapphire. She eased at my presence, and I wished I could have stood there all day muttering soothing words to her and brushing her coat.

Tol didn't rush me, but with one last lingering look and a kiss on her nose, we left the horses to rest.

The ground in the tunnels was soft beneath the boots I'd been loaned—shorter than my usual pair and lined, as well. My breath gathered before me on each exhale, visible by the flickering yellow orbs of mystlight ingrained in the dirt walls. They bathed the Labyrinth in their warm glow, making it cozy despite the circumstances that landed us here and the threats over our heads.

Strolling through with Tol, I tried to take everything in. The wooden beams stretched across the ceilings and reinforcing the walls. The brick arches appeared to have been crafted to the doorways with such care.

We passed rooms that looked much like those I'd woken up in —impersonal and bare but comfortable enough. Then, he took me through a path of twists and turns I tried to memorize. No doors lined these walls, clearly more for passage than anything.

One thing was clear from the tunnels: The Labyrinth was more elaborate than I could have imagined. There were secrets here that made my fingers dance, itching to uncover them.

I stopped in my tracks when we reached a large open space where six tunnels converged, circling around with my head tilted back.

"This is incredible," I said. More than any of the others, this space seemed tended to. Along the walls, square gaps were carved into the dirt looking on to winding staircases. The bulbs of mystlight didn't flicker; they shone.

"It spans almost the entirety of their territory." My gaze snapped down to Tolek's. "In some places it's merely a thin tunnel. There are pockets like this where it's vast."

"Wow," I breathed, unsure what else to say.

Tolek laughed. "It's not often I see you speechless." His voice was wistful as he squeezed my hand. "Come on, they're waiting."

As we turned down one of the six offshoots, I noticed crumbling rock filling another. Foreboding twisted through my stomach at the possibility of a cave in, but I pushed the concern aside.

Despite the chilled air, my skin was beginning to feel sticky beneath my leathers. "I may be impressed by their excavation skills," I said, fidgeting with the sleeves of my tunic, "but I cannot say I'm a fan of their fashion choices."

"Why's that?" Tolek quirked a brow.

"There're so many layers." I preferred leathers crafted specifically for me, and the temperate climates meaning I could display whatever I wanted. I liked looking down and seeing the scars across my arms and torso, symbols of the battles I survived.

"Mm-hmm, I'd prefer fewer layers, too," Tolek teased with a wink, quickly pulling me into a room. "We're here."

That devilish smirk remained on his lips as I took in this new cavern. With the mystlight stove in the corner warming the space and the long wooden table and chairs in the center, I almost could have believed we were aboveground in any common meeting chamber.

Everyone was waiting for us. Cypherion and Malakai were sprawled in chairs, and my heart jumped to see them together again and at ease. Santorina, Mila, and Esmond sat with them; a man I assumed was Esmond's friend, Gatrielle, entertained their group with a story. His thick brown curls bounced as he spoke animatedly, hands waving.

At the head of the table, Jezebel and Vale spoke to a boy with shockingly bright red hair. He flashed a goofy grin at something my sister said.

"General." I nodded to Mila as Tolek and I took seats at the table, his hand sliding around the back of my chair. "I'm glad you guys made it here safely. Thank you for coming to our aid."

"Always, Revered," she answered. I didn't know her well, but I respected Mila for her dedication, history in the first war, and kindness to us all. The smile she gave me in return felt personal. Friendly.

"Have there been any updates from camp?" My fingers tightened around the hem of my tunic.

"Nothing since we left Pthole." Mila looked between Tolek and me, adding, "I believe it's good we have not heard. It means there's more time to prepare our troops."

Thanking her, I addressed the group at large. "Our army is under expert guidance with Lyria and the team of generals she's recruited from the minor clans. I firmly believe we have nothing to worry over, but"—I squeezed Tol's hand—"I'll feel better once we arrive."

He squeezed back.

"We should move as soon as possible," Cyph agreed.

I nodded and exchanged quick hellos with Esmond and Gatrielle, then shifted my attention to the red-headed boy and smiled at him. "I suppose you'll be able to explain a bit more about this?" I waved my hand around the room, then rose and leaned across the table, extending it to him. "I'm Ophelia, by the way."

"I know." He grinned back, cheeks turning pink. He must've been so young, his face retaining the roundness of childhood. He was perhaps only five years younger than myself, but I felt as though I'd aged twenty years in the past six months. "I'm Trevaneth."

Despite his youth, he had a firm grip on my hand.

"Pleasure to meet you, and thank you for the...accommodations." *Thank you for allowing my friends to bring my unconscious body here when we fled the queen and they waited for me to heal.*

"Of course," Trevaneth said. "It's really my father who is responsible, though. He left to gather supplies when the fae told us you might be seeking haven here. He should be back tomorrow." I wondered why they trusted Lancaster so easily, but brushed it off.

Trevaneth straightened to his full height, as if remembering responsibility fell on his shoulders until his father returned. I couldn't help but be curious about this boy, about how he ended up here and what he had seen at his young age. I hoped he held on to the innocence we'd all been robbed of.

"Can you tell me more about the Labyrinth?" I asked, leaning back in my seat.

Trevaneth's eyes gleamed. "What do you want to know?" He pulled his own seat back and sank into it, leaning his elbows on the table.

"I assume you've explained some of it to my friends, but I truly don't know much. They said there's a faction of your clan who aren't...under Kakias's control?" I chose my words carefully, not wanting to strike any sensitive topics.

"Only about thirty percent of us." His tone shifted, the blush fading quickly from his cheeks. "The rest are susceptible to her power. We don't know much beyond that because those of us who aren't corrupted segmented ourselves off."

"Did that create a rift?" I asked softly.

Trevaneth shook his head, eyes downcast. "They hardly noticed."

An ache went through my chest at his expression. The rest of the room was quiet. Discreetly, I turned my eyes to Tolek, but he shook his head. They didn't know Trevaneth's story either.

Giving the boy my full attention again, I cleared my throat. "I'm very sorry about that. I'm not sure how much my friends have told you, but you're probably aware of the war and the two alliances." He nodded, looking at me from beneath his lashes. "We're going to do everything we can to free the Mindshapers from the queen's clutches. I promise you."

I promise you'll get back whomever you think you've lost.

When the thought went through my mind, I turned and found Malakai already watching me. My father's eyes flashed through my memory. The wicked queen had taken plenty from me. I'd do everything in my power to ensure she didn't harm Trevaneth further.

"Thank you," he said, round cheeks flushing again as Jezebel took the seat next to him and slung an arm around his shoulders.

"Tell her how this place works, Trev," Tolek encouraged, and the boy lifted his chin, eyes a little brighter. Though they'd barely known him over a day, warmth spread behind my ribs to see them comfort him.

"The Labyrinth has been here since the days of Angels," Trev began. I perked up, but let him continue. "It was always known tunnels existed but never the extent of them. Not until a few years ago when...well, many members of our clan were no longer acting like themselves. Small groups started hosting meetings down here, and eventually word spread among those of us not infected and our rebel faction was born."

"How many of you are there?"

"Only a few thousand. The rest are afraid to act against the queen. Many were terrified of Aird before he died." I avoided my friends' eyes at the reminder. As far as we knew, no new ruler had been appointed to replace the chancellor I'd killed.

"No one stays in one place too long. It's safer that way,"

Trevaneth elaborated. That explained the nearly identical, impersonal rooms I'd seen. "But we all essentially live down here now. We travel between the pockets of housing, sharing news others bring from above. We hope to—" He cut himself off, eyes widening.

"If there's sensitive information, you don't have to share it." Though we were on the same side, I didn't want him to get in trouble. Pushing his boundaries would not earn trust.

He considered, thumbs twitching on the table where his hands were folded. "Our goal has been to figure out how to train our powers to unravel what the queen is doing to our clan. We haven't had much progress, though, given how risky it is to take...test subjects."

Warriors from her army. Not only would they be unpredictable and likely violent, but if the rebels didn't understand the control Kakias held on her warriors, we couldn't be sure what damage she could inflict if they were taken. If she could somehow find the Labyrinth.

"Perhaps when your father returns we can all work together on a plan," I offered.

Trevaneth's face lit up, green eyes sparkling and brows raised. "We'd be honored to have your assistance." He looked around the room. "All of you, truly. Stories of the border fights and the Battle of Damenal have reached us, even down here. It's a privilege to host you."

Now my cheeks were warming. "It's our honor."

My eyes swept over my friends—those I'd known my entire life and those who I'd barely met. They were a devastatingly incredible group, and though I grew frustrated with the Angels, I supposed they'd done right by me in some ways. Trev had given me plenty to consider regarding this Labyrinth's formation and the way his clan's power worked, but for right now, I'd relax and consider how fortunate I was to have the people around me.

"Now that we're all honored," Jezebel said. "How about dinner?"

CHAPTER FORTY-TWO
TOLEK

"YOU'RE CARRYING THAT THING AROUND?" I ASKED Ophelia as I settled down beside her in the cavern where Jezebel and Trevaneth were preparing dinner for us all. There were no dining tables in here, but there was plenty of space for all of us and a make-shift kitchen setup Trevaneth and Jezebel used to heat up rice and beans over mystlight. They stored mainly dry foods down here, he'd explained.

Ophelia held out her hand, the Bodymelder emblem shining in her palm. "I'm trying to get an understanding of it," she explained.

"How does it feel?" I asked. She tipped it into my hand, but the metal was cool, sucking the chill from the Mindshaper air.

I tried to ignore the prickles the environment drew along my spine. The clothing, the snowy terrain above us, even Trevaneth's slightly flat accent clawed at my mind, trying to dig up memories of my torture at the hands of the Mindshapers. Instead of letting it get to me, though, I watched Ophelia. Focused on those magenta eyes and the crease between her brows as she studied the newest emblem.

"They each feel different," she said, plucking it back from my hand and clenching her fingers around it. "This one feels like...fire personified." There was a mystical tone to her voice, and she closed her eyes, focusing harder on that shard of metal in her hand. "It feels like—"

A clattering sound echoed across the cavern.

"Vale?" Cypherion shouted, jumping up from where he sat with Malakai and rushing to the Starsearcher. "Vale!"

But she didn't answer.

Vale lay on the ground, thrashing, eyes rolled back. Cyph threw off his cloak and folded it beneath her head, turning her onto her side. Rina was beside him, clearing the shards of the metal cup Vale had knocked over. It split on the rock, but she hadn't cut herself.

Cyph didn't hold her down or attempt to wake her, only watched and counted beneath his breath as if timing how long it lasted. As we all stood around, I watched Cypherion. Noted the concern he tried to hide, the way his hands fluttered around, assisting Santorina, like he knew precisely what he should be doing.

And as Ophelia gripped my hand, I felt Cypherion's panic like a knife through my own gut.

"Had she been reading?" I asked quietly.

"I think so," Malakai answered, appearing at my shoulder. "Has this happened before?"

"I've seen it once," Ophelia said, biting her lip, remembering the Angellight test. "We tried...well she was attempting a powerful reading."

"It's happened more, from what I understand," I added. Cyph hadn't wanted to talk about Vale at all, but the way his voice had nearly crumpled as he told me had said enough. "He's told me of one other time."

I didn't add that I thought there were more he had not told me of.

"It's connected to her sessions?" Malakai asked, and Ophelia and I both nodded.

We all remained quiet until Vale fully woke, then gave her space for Santorina and the Bodymelders to assess her. Cyph remained on the edge of the conversation.

"I'm going to see if he needs anything," I finally said when Cypherion showed no sign of moving.

He said nothing when I approached. Didn't comment as I

remained by his side, absorbing every word of the healers' inspection and Vale's answers. He only watched the Starsearcher with a resolved stare.

"Are *you* okay?" I asked him.

"Fine," he gritted out. When he looked at me, it was with that same vulnerable stare he had when he discussed the position of Second. The lost one that communicated he didn't know who he was. "She needs to find a solution to this."

He needed to, I thought he meant.

When Vale's eyes finally lifted and found Cyph's, searing to the point of pain, I thought she wanted answers, too.

OPHELIA and I shared a cavern that night, but I didn't sleep. I watched her rest soundly in my arms as I tried to time my breaths to her own. Every time I closed my eyes, I saw it again and again. Heard her screaming for me to get that poison out of her. Felt the drag of my dagger slicing through her skin and tasted the bile in the back of my throat.

I wouldn't apologize for making a deal with Lancaster. He was the only reason she was alive right now. It was a risk I was willing to take for her, despite the wall now between us.

Dammit, I'd risk anything for her, throw myself on that damn dagger instead.

"You okay?" Ophelia asked as we walked through the tunnels the next morning. She scratched at the old Curse scar on her wrist. Spirits, I needed to tell her what was going through my head.

"I'm fine." I kissed her forehead instead of looking in her eyes because I wasn't fucking fine. Being locked in Mindshaper Territory was stifling, memories of the last time I was here sharp and piercing. It was all piling up, colliding, ready to burst. It pulled each breath from my lungs with a little more force, feeding me my worst nightmares instead.

Ones I'd seen come true recently.

"Come on. We'll be late." Wrapping an arm around Ophelia's

waist, I guided her forward. I'd figure out how to explain it to her later.

Cypherion waited for us in the large open space in the center of this pocket of the Labyrinth. He leaned against the wall, spinning a knife around his hand.

"How are you?" I asked, watching him closely. The sunken, dark circles beneath his eyes told me he hadn't slept much either.

"I'm fine." It appeared we were all lying today.

Ophelia gripped my hand. "Cypherion, you can go be with—"

"I said I would be here, so I am," Cyph interrupted. He rolled his wrists, an old injury from when we were young cracking in the left one. "Let's go."

"CK is becoming the most stubborn of us all," I whispered to Ophelia as we followed him across the open cavern and down one of the offshoots.

"I know he's going through a lot with Vale, and I want to allow him time to heal on his own, but..." She trailed off, lips pursing.

"But at some point we'll need to start pushing."

Ophelia nodded, chewing her lip against the instinct to address him right now.

"I can speak with him again," I offered, but she shook her head.

"Thank you." She pulled me to a stop, placing one hand on my shoulder as she stretched onto her toes to kiss me. "I appreciate how willing you are to help, but this is between him and me."

She had a point. I hated staying out of her business, though. Had never been good at it when it came to her.

"He'll come around," I promised, pulling her down the hall.

Trev's father's door was propped ajar, but we knocked when we arrived. "Come in," his deep voice rumbled. "Ah." He looked over his shoulder as we filed into the room. "My son said you'd be stopping by. Forgive the mess."

He waved his arm around the cavern, an open pack spilling onto the desk, leathers and furs and empty canteens decorating the surface. The man straightened up, turning toward us fully, and we were greeted by the same warm eyes as Trev. His skin was a shade darker, his hair sandy and streaked with gray. He probably was an older father, then. Most warriors did not have children until they were well past their first century. He might be past his second.

"We're the ones imposing," Ophelia said. "I'm sure you're tired from your journey, but thank you for giving us the immediate attention."

Spirits, I loved seeing her like this. The way Ophelia handled adversaries was one of the most attractive things about her. Not backing down, not showing an ounce of fear or regret when it came to protecting those she was responsible for. She'd been a glorious sight before she fell to Kakias's power in that battle, drawing her enemies' blood without remorse.

But when she met with allies, she was entirely different. A balance of commanding yet amiable. Watching her learn it was okay to drop her mask a little and show softer sides to the world was something I would never tire of. Maybe I was depraved, but it made me hard just to witness.

It was a challenge to not sate that need now, but I stifled it. I knew the face she wanted to present to the Mindshapers and wouldn't interfere.

"We're honored to help your cause. My name is Ricordan, by the way. Ric to my friends." He held his hand out to her.

"I'm Ophelia Alabath. This is Cypherion Kastroff and Tolek Vincienzo." She pointed to each of us in turn, and we greeted him.

"Yes, my son has filled me in on everything that happened since you've arrived." Ric perched on the edge of his cot. "Please, make yourselves comfortable. I know you've had a rough few days, Revered."

So had he, if the worn lines in his face and bags beneath his eyes were anything to go by. Ophelia took the chair at his desk, and I perched on the edge. Cyph leaned against the wall beside me.

"First of all," Ophelia began. "Thank you. There's a good chance all of my friends would have died without your help back there."

"As I said, we're happy to, but I assume there's more of a reason you wanted to speak so urgently?" Ric didn't say it unkindly, but he didn't waste time.

"Your son mentioned the Labyrinth was excavated during the

time of the Angels." Ophelia scratched at her scar again. "We were wondering, how exactly is it tied to Thorn?"

She'd been buzzing with anticipation since Trev mentioned the Mindshaper Prime Warrior last night. The name of the Angel had tension bubbling beneath my skin, though. I rolled my neck to alleviate the pressure, pulling out my ledger and pen, focusing on recording whatever Ric shared. Cyph's focused stare told me he was ready, too.

"How much have you studied Thorn?" Ric asked.

"Mainly his powers and how they work for your clan presently," Ophelia answered.

"I've looked into his life a bit," Cypherion added, "but all I've found aligns with the rest of the Angels' lore. About how they split off from one another when their powers began creating rifts."

"I've studied the corrupted side a bit," I confessed, ignoring Ophelia's and Cyph's fleeting glances.

Ricordan nodded, releasing a heavy breath. He propped a hand on one knee, extending the other with a crack. "Most do not dig too deeply into Angels other than their own. It's typical of our ways, to research the ability rather than the being." That thought nagged at my mind as he continued. "It's why our clan has been able to keep secrets for millennia."

"Secrets?" Ophelia leaned forward.

"The truth about our Angel is that Thorn was mad. When the power created a divide, each Angel was driven to bouts of delirium in their isolation, but most were temporary. Hallucinations or dreams."

"Thorn's wasn't?" Cypherion guessed.

"Given the nature of our magic, Thorn's turned on him, eating away his sanity from the inside out. He took many lovers during the slow progression, and from what our scholars have deduced, the mental ailment has been passed down through his offspring. Nowadays, with how many years have passed and how intertwined family lines have become, it's spread far across the clan.

"Our Angel was sick." He said it so sadly my pen stilled. I looked up, meeting his sullen expression. "And those who have it strongest in them are those whom the queen is able to use her power against."

"But how does that make sense?" Ophelia's voice was low. "Why is Kakias able to manipulate the minds of warriors outside her own clan? Her power should be linked to the Engrossians."

"Her power is unlike anything we've seen," Cypherion said. "She's gone to lengths we didn't imagine. Perhaps it extends farther because of that."

"Perhaps," Ric echoed, considering Cyph. Mystlight flickered behind him, deepening the shadows on his face. "Or perhaps there's more to it. To her crimes. Either way, she's taking advantage of our innocent."

"And that can't continue," Ophelia confirmed.

"It did not even begin until recent years when our chancellor partnered with that woman."

My hand tightened around my pen, remembering all Aird did to me. Screams echoed through my mind, and blood splattered my vision. Those memories...a knife...her...marble stairs.

Not real, I reminded myself.

Taking a breath, I closed my journal. "That man is dead, and soon Kakias will be, too." My voice was harsher than usual. Ophelia and Cypherion shot me wary looks.

"Yes," Ric confirmed. "She will be."

"The tunnels were created by Thorn, then?" Ophelia tried to redirect the conversation, but her stare kept inquiring if I was okay.

Ricordan nodded. "He dug each one himself, if the stories are to be believed. Cared for them and crafted them to his perfection, fused the land with his magic. When it came time to ascend, the other Prime Warriors dragged him from beneath the ground kicking and screaming. At that point, he was lost."

"Is that why the Angels ascended?" Cypherion asked. "Because their power was turning them mad?"

"Could be." Ric shrugged. "There's no way to be certain."

I could feel the questions running through Ophelia's and Cyph's heads as we sat here, and while I had many of my own, the main thought plaguing me was the tragedy of the Angels. These figments were revered as long as warriors had existed, absolute and ever-lasting, and yet they'd carved their own battles during their mortal lives. It was devastating to consider, despite the situation they'd put us in now.

I wondered how those losses bled into the rest of history, staining the pages crimson in the wake of tragedy.

Had the battles ceased when they ascended? Or were they still fighting?

"Is there anything of Thorn's remaining in these tunnels?" My eyes locked on Ophelia when she asked, quickly latching on to her motive. This beautiful, brilliant woman.

"Very few items remain. What we do have has been split between factions. A few books. Jewels. Daggers. Pieces of his crown."

"Crown?" she asked. I tilted my head, reopening my ledger. Warriors did not honor crowns, aside from the Engrossians.

"Thorn fashioned one of obsidian metal mined from the deepest stretches of the Labyrinth. He wore it down here until the day he was dragged away."

Ophelia scratched at her wrist, fingers twitching, suppressing excitement I bet. "Would it be possible for us to see the pieces?"

"It's not in this pocket," Ric explained. "But it's a few days' journey toward your mountains. We could see it on the way to your camp."

"You'll show us?" I asked.

The man's large shoulders fell with a heavy exhale. "I assume if you're asking, it's tied into this war we find ourselves in. I want it over as much as you do."

It was the genuineness in his voice that knocked the last of my nightmares from my mind, at least for now. The Mindshapers were not all Aird. Here, I would not be tormented beyond my own thoughts.

"If you don't mind me asking," Ophelia hedged, "why? Why help us when you have the Labyrinth to protect?"

"Selfishly?" Ric sighed. "If this war ends, I hope to see my wife returned to our family and make sure Trevaneth does not fall to the queen's control." *His wife.* Though not all warriors chose to marry when we had other rituals, it made sense. Ric's wife was in the other faction, maybe fighting on the frontlines. And that meant Trevaneth contained some of a bloodline that could be manipulated. "In the greater scheme, I want to see everyone in my son's generation thrive in a better world. One I'll be proud to leave to them. Will showing you this bring about that peace?"

Ophelia's voice cracked when she said, "I hope it will."

"Then of course I am going to help you. We can leave tomorrow, if you're rested."

A wicked gleam entered her eye, lips curling into a smirk. "I'm always ready, sir."

Fucking Angels, I loved her.

We left Ricordan to unpack his things and prepare. Cypherion dismissed himself quickly after we exited, leaving Ophelia and me to stroll through the tunnels on our own. I lost track of where we walked, mulling over everything Ric had exposed.

The silence thickened with each moment, though. The back of my neck itched like I was being watched. Looking over my shoulder, I found no one.

"What's wrong?" Ophelia broke our silence.

"Nothing," I answered, searching the dark one more time. "Let's turn this way." I pulled her tighter against my side and kept walking, listening for any sounds of pebbles beneath boots.

"You were following my theories back there?" Ophelia asked.

"Yes, you're brilliant." A shuffle sounded down the tunnel. I kept from turning over my shoulder this time, but she noticed me stiffen.

"What is it? And don't say nothing; you've been oddly silent since yesterday." Her voice was rimmed with hurt that sliced through me.

I sighed, gently drawing circles on her shoulder as we walked. "There's a lot on my mind right now."

"Share it with me," she encouraged, lacing her fingers through my own. "Let me help."

I chewed over that inquiry, not sure how to say it.

"Is it about Lancaster?" she asked quietly.

"No, it's not about the damn fae." I sighed. It came out harsher than I intended, and Ophelia stiffened beneath my arm.

"I'm sorry I am concerned by it, Tolek. I know you sealed the bargain, but I can't help but worry over what will happen now that he knows."

"I told you I made sure he won't tell his queen." My temper was rising. Dammit I never let it get the best of me. I was not an angry person by nature, but fear was quickly morphing within me. All of the things I'd hidden because I didn't know how to say them were rising up my throat.

As we passed an empty cavern, I pulled Ophelia inside. There wasn't even a cot, but there was a mystlight and a pile of abandoned supplies in the corner.

"I don't want to talk about the faerie or any bargains either of us have made," I began.

"But if they're causing strife, then we must talk about them!" Ophelia cried. "I don't want to avoid this, Tol."

Not like she had with Malakai. It had become a twisted game between them, who could hide more to spite the other. It broke my heart that she thought we could ever become that. I wasn't him, and she was no longer that version of herself. She was aware of those mistakes and working to avoid them. To heal the bad habits. As long as we kept fighting, we'd get through it.

"We aren't avoiding them, but that's not where our problems lie, Alabath." Spirits, why did we feel so off-kilter?

Because you're not being honest, you fool.

"Which problems are you referencing?" She stepped away from me. "I'm trying, Tol. I'm trying to support you. Please, help me."

As she said the last words, a groaning roar echoed from the tunnel outside our chamber, and the walls came crashing down.

CHAPTER FORTY-THREE
MALAKAI

"What in the Spirits was that?" Esmond's eyes widened as the walls stopped shaking. A roar had echoed in the distance, too loud to be above ground.

We tore down the passage, hastening to the meeting space Trev had pointed out on his tour. "For emergencies," he'd explained. The walls quaking seemed like a damn emergency.

Skidding to stop in the open cavern, I wrapped my hand around the pommel of my sword. Cypherion emerged from one of the other five brick arches, panting. Vale, Santorina, and Gatrielle were on his heels. Jezebel flew through another arch, Trev and the man I assumed was his father from a third.

"Is everyone okay?" the older Mindshaper asked. His eyes traveled over the group, taking stock.

"What was that?" I asked, fingers still tight around my weapon. I scanned the depths of the tunnels around us, waiting for someone to emerge.

"Cave in," Trevaneth answered, his usual enthusiasm stifled.

"*What?*" We shouldn't have trusted these damn tunnels. We were Spirits knew how far underground, and the walls were literally crumbling around us. My chest tightened, and I rubbed my palm across it, my jaw grinding. Trying to steady my blurring vision, I swept my gaze over the gathered group, counting.

It wasn't enough.

"How?" Cyph asked.

"These tunnels are old," Ric answered, circling to investigate the support beams. "It can happen."

I paced around the cavern, glancing down each offshoot.

"Does it happen often?" Cypherion continued, voice hard.

Nerves sent my muscles twitching as I listened for hurried footsteps down the passages. I thought I saw shadows moving, but it could have been my harried mind.

"No, and normally some sort of accident or natural shift of the earth causes it when it does." Ric didn't look at us as he spoke, continuing his routine checks.

My heart rate sped as nothing but silence drifted down the corridors.

"Where's Ophelia?" Jezebel's voice rose with panic.

"And Tolek," Cyph added.

Action exploded around us as Cyph barked orders of pairs to split into and Ric added advice of how to tell if a stretch of tunnel was structurally sound. *Should have given us that advice earlier.*

Everyone took off down different pathways, but I remained where I stood, watching them disappear into shadows and hoping I was wrong. Hoping she'd still emerge.

"Malakai?" Esmond asked when the others were gone and I didn't move.

I touched each of my fingertips to my thumb, counting the fluttering movements as I tried to breathe. In and out. In and out.

"Mila isn't here."

I DIDN'T KNOW how long had passed until Esmond and I found the source of the cave in. Every minute blurred into the next, and there was no sun or moon to judge by in the Labyrinth. It was disorienting on a normal day, but paired with the jittering nerves through my gut, it had me crawling out of my skin and snapping at the others.

There was a long stretch of tunnel deep within the Labyrinth that held a number of abandoned rooms to host travelers. From one end to the other, it likely spanned fifty feet. Now, a wall of rubble stood at the entrance.

Ricordan couldn't say how a wreck of this magnitude would have happened. "It's usually a small rockslide," he'd said, stunned.

I didn't truly care *how* it happened, though. Esmond, Gatrielle, Santorina, and I went to work digging out one end, but progress was slow. We had to be diligent with each rock moved, careful not to worsen the collapse.

Impatience made me frantic. My hands shook, sending a stone clattering to the ground.

"Malakai." Santorina grabbed my shoulders, turning me toward her. "You need to calm down."

I looked right over her head and counted the rocks stacked floor to ceiling—or what I could. The larger ones were easier to catalog. The small pebbles more volatile. Miss one tiny, seemingly-harmless enemy and watch them crumble your empire.

"How the fuck can I?" I threw back at her. "She's in there!"

Four large chunks of rock formed the ridge of the cave in, a thin sliver of mystlight outlining them. How could I get up there? Could I climb and make a hole along the top?

"I know, Malakai, and we're going to find her." The sincerity in Rina's voice convinced me to meet her eyes. "You're throwing rocks around wildly, though, and that could make it worse. Worse for *her*."

"I'm sorry," I panted, "but I—what if she's not okay?"

"Ophelia is going to be okay," Rina comforted.

I stilled. "Not Ophelia! She's with Tolek. He'll take care of her. What about Mila?"

Santorina's hands fell from my shoulders, head tilting to the side. "I thought...was she not with us?" Her eyes flicked side to side as she ran through the group at the meeting point and realized I was right.

Had truly no one noticed she hadn't joined us earlier? I knew they had been traveling with their small group and were used to accounting for the six of them, but Mila was our general, and she looked out for *every* soldier in her army.

She searched for me when I fled that battlefield. She searched for Lyria when she was taken during the first war. Now, I would search for her.

"Mila is alone, and she's likely trapped somewhere in this cave-in." I only hoped she was not beneath the rubble. "She is the priority of this team." I gestured to Esmond and Gatrielle, who nodded.

"I'm sorry. You're right." Santorina looked at me with some level of clarity I didn't have the patience to dissect. "Let's find her."

I shoved aside the fear and turned back to the rocks, doing my best to move more slowly. I counted each pile of dirt and rubble I carted away, using the monotony to steady myself. Tried not to imagine finding bloodstained hair poking out between each rock.

She'd be fine.

But fuck, when did I begin to care so much?

It was hours later when we had enough of the rock excavated to form a hole through. Or I assumed hours had passed based on the exhaustion weighing my bones. Adrenaline kept me upright, though. Kept every movement alert and focused.

The others were likely still on the opposite end of the cave-in, continuing their search. We hadn't ventured over there often, the only path being long and convoluted. Aside from Gatrielle leaving to get us food and refill our canteens, we'd avoided stopping at all costs.

"You have to be careful," Santorina instructed for the hundredth time. "You shouldn't be going through there at all."

"There's a pathway." We'd carved a tunnel through the rubble. It was narrow, but we'd supported it by breaking a wooden chair and using the slats to brace the sides. Mystlight flickered around the cracks between stones not too far ahead, leading us to believe there were pockets within the collapse that were reinforced enough to stand. "I'll crawl through and see what can be found."

"If you can't safely continue, you come back," Esmond commanded. "Once you get to the end of the tunnel, we'll continue digging." They'd be able to see the end from here, so they'd know when I was safely out of the way in case proceeding to dig caused another collapse.

"Good luck," Gatrielle said.

Nodding in thanks, I swung a canteen over my shoulder and grabbed the remaining wooden legs of the chair in case I needed more support. Then, I dropped to my elbows and pulled myself through the opening on my stomach.

It was tight. My shoulders nearly brushed the walls if I moved too quickly. I had to wiggle my way through with small movements rather than rushing along like instinct said to. Counting my breaths, I ignored the panic tickling the back of my neck. Shut down every scarred memory trying to push through.

I almost shouted back to the others to let them know it was okay so far, but the vibrations of my voice could cause some sort of collapse. So, I kept on ahead, following the flickering yellow light in the distance.

With slow, precise movements, I moved rocks aside to lengthen the tunnel. After each chunk, I paused, ensuring it was safe to continue forward. The pace was agonizing, but I kept track of my breathing both to keep myself focused and keep my muscles from locking up beneath the strain.

The mystlight grew brighter.

My arms ached. The tunnel was slightly uphill, I realized, and I'd been dragging myself on an incline.

Light trickled across the ground beyond my fingertips.

Three more large pieces. It took every shred of my control not to shove them away, but I remembered Santorina's warning. I could make it worse for Mila.

When I finally widened the gap enough to slip through and mystlight rained down the tunnel, I released a relieved breath. I pulled myself free, set down the chair legs, and shook my limbs out, taking a long sip from my canteen and splashing a little over my face.

Once my eyes adjusted to the new light, I observed the pocket. The walls here *had* been stronger, fortified by brick along one side, arching over two doorways.

"Mila?" I called quietly.

No response.

Fuck, my heart rate quickened. She wasn't here. Of course the Angels would not make it that easy. Still, trying to summon a shred of hope, I approached the arches. Neither had actual doors on them, simply dim chambers.

I looked past the rounded edge of the first. Empty.

Quickly, I turned away, reminded too much of my own cell with its bare cot and stone walls.

I guess that's why these rooms were sound, though. The walls were solid rock.

As I crept to the second one, a steady plunk of water met my ears. Something dripping. Bile crept up my throat at the possibilities, every heinous thing that could sound like that, but when I rounded the corner, I saw—

"Mila?" I burst, running forward and falling to my knees beside her.

I tried to wrap an arm around her, but she jerked away, stuttering, "D-don't t-touch."

My heart sank to my stomach, but I leaned back on my heels, giving her air. The dripping filled the silence as she shook, a stream of water trailing from a crack in the ceiling and pooling on the floor a few feet away. And beside that—

My stomach turned over.

A body lay clad in black leathers, a jagged piece of metal sticking out of his neck. I smelled the blood then—I'd been too preoccupied before to make sense of it. It clung to the air like only death could, mixing with the musty scent of wet stone and dirt.

A combination I knew really fucking well.

I looked between Mila and the intruder. His alliance wasn't obvious, but I'd bet he wasn't affiliated with ours.

"Who is that, Mila?" I tried a question with a specific answer, not about her. Mila worked best with organization.

"N-no one. A soldier. Kakias's. He caused the cave in. I saw him do it."

She was answering. That was good. "Did you kill him?"

"I rammed the first thing I found in his throat when I realized we were trapped together." Her voice was impersonal, lacking the passion this usually would have caused in her. "Didn't interrogate him. Couldn't. He didn't even realize I was there. He'd been following Ophelia."

I tucked away that bit of information to give to the group later.

From the way Mila was recounting the fight so clinically, I didn't think that was what had caused her to crawl into herself and fortify her own borders.

"And what happened next?"

But she didn't answer. She couldn't.

Her hands clutched her wrist cuffs, and she rocked right there on the stone floor.

I shifted so I blocked the corpse from view. "Why didn't you answer when I called?"

Silence. Muttering under her breath. I ran my hands through my hair, refraining from reaching out to her.

"Mila?" Worry cracked my voice.

She didn't look at me. Just watched the floor with vacant eyes as water dripped from the ceiling, her hands wrapped around her wrist braces.

Mila was here. She was safe.

But she was not all right.

I tried to follow her line of sight but there was nothing in here besides the water, the body, and a dull mystlight orb overheard. Not even a cot or desk.

Had he hurt her? Death was kind if he had. Didn't matter right now, though. We'd figure that out later.

"Can I pick you up? I'll get us out of this room, and then I'll put you down." She might be able to walk herself, but with the way she was shaking it wasn't likely. Still, I wouldn't move her without her consent.

After a long moment of shallow breaths, her chin bobbed once. My arms nearly fell slack with relief.

There was no way I would get her out through the tunnel like this. Instead, I cradled her in my arms, careful to only touch her leathers in case it was skin on skin contact she didn't want. Her shocked wide eyes clenched tightly as we passed the body, not opening again until we were settled in the room with the rickety cot.

I didn't think about how much it reminded me of my cell. Didn't remember my fears at all as I laid her down on the cot and lowered beside it with my back pressed against the wall.

I felt so fucking useless, sitting at the foot of her bed as she curled into a ball. I stayed where she could see me, in case she didn't want to be alone, but I tried not to stare at her. Instead, I counted her breaths until they fell into a steady rhythm and waited for someone to find us.

Despite the fact that I didn't know what happened, I'd promised her earlier she wouldn't be alone in these tunnels. I wasn't leaving now.

Chapter Forty-Four
Ophelia

Tolek pulled me flush against him the moment the walls caved in. I clenched his tunic, flashbacks of another collapse when he'd been buried making my knees weak. Visions of my father's last moments tightened my chest.

I whimpered as all the memories of that day slammed into me. It should have been me in that temple, not my father, not Danya, or any of the innocents who died. Tolek should not have broken half the bones in his body pushing me out of the way. I was the one the queen wanted; I should have seen the brunt of her destruction.

"You're okay. You're okay," Tol soothed us both as the roaring stopped.

Only half of the room we were in suffered, the back half of the ceiling being sturdier rock, but the door to the tunnel was gone.

We started digging but took a break after what felt like hours. Now, we sat in silence, the conversation we'd been having before the collapse creeping through the cracks of our facade.

My throat was scratchy and dry, my muscles stiff, but the tension layered between Tolek and me in this small caved-in alcove was more painful than the rest of it. Fighting with him was unnatural, like thorns driving between my ribs and wrapping around my heart. Constricting, piercing, and *wrong*.

"Can we talk?" I forced out.

Hearing my croaking voice, he tossed me the last of the water we'd found in the corner. We sat on opposite sides of what remained of the room, backs pressed to the walls. If we stretched our legs out fully, our toes could barely touch.

I kept mine hugged to my chest. He had one folded up, an elbow resting on it.

Tolek sighed, and it was layered with such a heavy pain, I almost wanted to take back the request. It sounded like he balanced on a precipice, though. So, I waited.

"Every time I fall asleep at night," he finally began, "I have nightmares of myself being responsible for your death."

I blinked at him, trying to process his confession and figure out how it made sense with his current behavior. "Tol, you didn't—I'm fine. You protected me at the trench." I curved my fingers around the fresh scar beneath my tunic. "You always have."

Not only at the trench, but during the Battle of Damenal, on the journey to the Undertaking when he jumped in front of that ax.

"No, Alabath. You don't get it." He shoved himself to his feet, and in shock, I stood, too. It only took him two steps to be looming over me, my back against the cold stone, spine arching at the contact. "Every night, long before the fight at the trench, when I close my eyes, I see myself holding the knife that ends your life." He placed one hand to the wall above my head, the other pressing over my wildly beating heart. "It goes right here, and in every one of those nightmares, I am terrified and fighting it, but there's nothing I can do."

"I—" It came out a rasp. I swallowed over my dry throat. "I don't understand." He dreamed of killing me? No, Tolek couldn't. He'd never hurt me.

"It's my greatest failure." He hung his head, hair flopping into his eyes.

And I understood it, then. This truth he'd hid rained down between us, drops sharp and icy like a fresh winter storm. How his father had treated him as a child, and the guilt Tolek carried his entire life because of it. How he'd grown up thinking he was not good enough for anyone's love because he'd nearly been the cause of his mother's death. How the Undertaking and the torture he suffered with Aird had latched on to those beliefs and twisted them until they haunted him.

Until they found the thing he loved most and made him believe he was the reason he would lose it. Lose *me*.

And, Spirits, I'd asked him to take a dagger to me at the trench. He'd seemed so distraught and frenzied. I'd brought those nightmares to life.

My bones chilled, skin prickling. I tried to gather my thoughts around the freezing, murderous rage and swarms of sorrow building inside of me.

His greatest failure.

"There is nothing about you that's a failure." Cupping Tol's cheek, I forced his gaze to mine. "I know you can't easily rid yourself of these thoughts, but Tolek Vincienzo, you are anything but a failure. You're *my* saving grace, and no matter what nightmares the Spirits show you, you are so worthy of love. You're worthy of being seen and cherished." A resigned shadow dimmed his eyes, almost like he didn't see the point in my words. And that—

That wasn't Tolek. It wasn't the cheerful, exuberant warrior he showed to the world, eager for adventure and thrills, but it was the *true* him. The one he hid because he was afraid he didn't deserve love. Didn't deserve to be chosen.

It was the pieces of him that needed someone, not the pieces that wanted someone. Perhaps those sides were two different beings within us all, fighting for attention. Or they were interwoven threads forming the tapestry of our souls. Whatever his soul was—no matter the shades of strands comprising that piece of art —it belonged with mine, to be treasured and tended.

"There is nothing you could do to make me view you as a failure," I continued. "And *I choose you*. I did in Damenal, I do now, and I will every day forward." I brushed my thumb across the scruff on his jaw. He leaned into my palm as these fears finally unspooled between us, unknotting the tension we'd brewed.

"It's fucking terrifying, Alabath. Thinking of losing you. Even worse when I imagine it's my fault." He sighed, and my heart thudded a desperate beat with the sound. "That's what the Mind-shapers did when they had me. They dragged up that guilt and fear. For those days I was their prisoner, all I saw was myself being responsible for your—"

His sentence cut off at the last word. *Death.*

Fury heated my chest. This was the final piece he'd been keeping from me, too scared that if he spoke it, I would somehow agree.

"Swear it to me on the Angels right now, Vincienzo: Do you believe there is a world in which you would be capable of hurting me?"

He shook his head. "Not in this life or the next. But what if it's unintentional?"

"Accidents happen, Tol. I may be thrown from my horse while we race one day or you may slip up while we spar and leave a scratch on me, but you would never do something as severe as what haunts you."

"You don't understand." His hand dropped from my heart to my hip, gripping it bruisingly, like he had to solidify my presence. "If anything happens to you, and I fail to protect you, I may as well be twisting the blade or casting the Angelcurse myself."

Using both hands to turn his face to me, I searched his gaze and found the boy who'd been convinced his entire life that he was a killer. The one who thought he had to hide these tormented pieces of himself, that he deserved beatings and disdain.

"You're not another curse in my life, Tolek. And if you were, you'd be the one I'd gladly carry."

He met my eyes. "If I am a curse, then you're my remedy, *apeagna.*"

I was what kept him present when the fears were too great, as he did for me. Tolek Vincienzo was the cure to all my curses, his unyielding love the healing to each broken piece of myself.

"What nearly happened to your mother was not your fault, and Angels forbid, if something does happen to me one day—an act of nature or the Spirits or someone else's blade—that will not be your fault either. You'd spend your last breath protecting me."

"And then I'd protect you from the darkness," he swore.

"I know you would," I whispered. "We need to convince *you* that it's enough, though." *That you are enough.*

His forehead fell to mine, heavy, as if that connection held him upright. "When I had to cut Kakias's power out of you...it was every fear I'd ever had crashing to fruition. A blade in my hand angled at your skin. I thought—I thought something was going to possess me and those nightmares would come true."

A tide of guilt poured over me for asking him to do something that dredged up his deepest fears. Sharing the weight of the waves was better than drowning, though. We could find the surface together.

"I'm sorry. I'm so sorry you had to do that."

Slowly, Tolek leaned forward until his lips brushed mine. It was tender, a flutter really, but the heat that had coiled within me for weeks raged like it had been waiting for this one confession to unleash itself. My arms locked around his neck, hands exploring his hair as my tongue did his mouth.

He kept one hand beside my head, but the other took its time dragging up my body. Every movement was timed perfectly to the sweep of his lips.

I allowed myself to get lost in him for a moment. To pull a curtain over my own fears and indulge in what he needed right now, but even that could only last so long. As his words played through my head, his fears so potent in this small cavern, my own panic winked back to life like stars in a dark sky.

Sighing, I pulled back. My lips rolled between my teeth as I caught my breath, eyes dropping to the floor.

"Hey," Tolek said with nothing but patience. I lifted my gaze. "Talk to me. What's happening in your head?"

The vulnerabilities he'd shared sat between us, and I was wary to brush them away with my own issues.

Tolek would. The moment I opened my mouth, he'd make his fears vanish to wherever he stored them within himself. But then they'd be left to fester, and I did not want to steal this healing from him.

"It's nothing."

Tolek exhaled and stepped back. I swore the air between us

chilled. "After everything I told you, you're truly going to say that?"

"What?" My eyes went wide.

"I ripped open my wounds for you—things I've spent years burying—and you're not willing to give even a thought?" There was something in his voice I'd never heard. Anger directed toward me. We'd fought before, but this was something deeper. Something hurt.

"I—that's not it, Tolek. I tell you *everything*."

"Not this," he snapped. "Not whatever it is making you keep a wall between us."

Tolek deserved more than I offered him, but how was I supposed to get past a fear of hurting him when he was already hurting so deeply?

"You need to meet me halfway here," Tol continued. His voice didn't rise, but it grew more impassioned. "I know you've been scarred. I know you've dragged yourself back from heartbreaks you didn't think you'd survive. But dammit, Alabath, I need to know what's going on inside that head of yours."

"But we're talking about you!"

"This *is* about me. Tell me why you always stop if it isn't a regret you have about being with me."

A regret? Those words rang like a slap to my cheek. And when he phrased it like that, when it tangled with this doubt he couldn't shake, I finally understood how he saw my actions. That he thought I was not committed to him as deeply as I was. Infinitely.

There was no more running from it.

"Because I'm scared!" I finally shouted, the words exploding like shrapnel between us. "I'm scared once we go there, there's no going back."

"Going back?" The shadows of his childhood fell on him, like the vow I'd sworn to *choose him* was a lie. "You do have doubts, then?"

"No!" I rushed out. "Not about you. I'm so sure you're what I want. You're what I *need*, but it's more than that. More than clinging to someone out of comfort or familiarity." Damn Angels, if that's what I'd wanted I would have stayed with Malakai. "I need you, yes, but I *want* you, too. I want the life you've helped me see is possible. The way you make every day feel easier by simply being there. I want every teasing smile, but I also want the dark fears you hide away. All of it and all at once, give me every piece of you in every way you can think to offer it, Tolek Vincienzo."

I was panting, the words unable to get out fast enough. "I'm more sure of you than I am about my damn title or the emblems or anything, but I'm scared I'll mess it up and hurt you. I'm scared because I used physical intimacy as an escape from the real problems in my last relationship, and I refuse to let that happen to us. If I keep this wall up and don't take that final step, I can pretend I'm not scared."

"Be scared," he begged, eyes wild and hair on end. "Be scared but brave and wonderfully daring and all the things I love most about you, because if you take that wall down I'll prove to you we're different. That you never needed it in the first place. Spirits, I'll demolish the damn thing if you let me. Be scared, but dive right in, head first and eyes open. Dammit, *destroy me* if you must, Alabath—I don't give a damn. Rip my heart from my chest and trample it. Leave me wrecked and ruined, but don't hold back because you're afraid."

He crossed to me, and when his spicy citrus scent overwhelmed me, my heart rioted in my chest. "I'm fucking terrified you'll change your mind about this." His hands cupped my cheeks. "Every time I see that tattoo on your arm, I think this is all a beautiful dream that I get to have you. That we'll all wake up one day and the world will snap back onto its axis and you'll be his again. And I'd take it if you truly tried and decided you didn't want me, but don't put up a wall. Be mine. Fully, uninhibited, and recklessly loving. Be mine, Alabath. *Mine.* Destroy me."

When he was already fighting battles no one should have to? It would be selfish of me. But dammit, I wanted him. Destroying Tolek—loving Tolek as I truly wanted to—could be my destruction, as well.

And I'd gladly send us both to ashes if it meant we burned together.

"Kiss me, Vincienzo." It was a plea. "Kiss me and show me

what reckless, uninhibited love really feels like. Let's destroy each other."

There, in that caved in alcove that had no room for curses and queens and spiteful fathers, he *did*.

Tolek's lips crashed to mine with the kiss we'd both been suppressing and yearning for. Every inch of my body burned with his touch as he devoured me like he never had before, tongues and lips moving in a synchronized dance of wanton need and fated promises, both desiring and reverent.

I dug my hands into his hair. Tolek groaned against my mouth, the rumble radiating into me. Bending but not breaking the kiss, he gripped the back of my thighs and lifted me. My legs locked around his waist, his hard length pressing perfectly against my center. I gasped, nails dragging over everywhere they could reach, scoring the back of his neck.

"A little rough there, Alabath?" He panted, smirking against my lips.

"You like it."

He huffed a laugh. "You have no idea."

But based on the way he strained against his leathers, I was certain I did.

Tol drove me back against the wall, one hand gripping my backside, the other tangled in my hair. I gasped as he tugged my head to the side and dragged his teeth down the column of my throat, biting to mark me as his.

Heat gathered between my thighs as I rocked against him, using the wall as leverage for friction. "I want you," I begged as he met my frantic movements.

"Thank the fucking Angels." He turned us away from the wall and sank to the ground. Gently, he laid me on my back, making sure my hair wasn't caught on anything and no sharp rocks remained.

Of course we'd end up in a room with no bed.

We were frantic, our lips each consuming the other. My core ached, and I wrapped my leg around him again, seeking relief. He tried to pull back, but I only pressed tighter to him and gripped his shoulders.

But Tolek grabbed my wrists, pinning them to the earth above my head.

"Are you going to fight for control here, too?" He pulled my bottom lip between his teeth, squeezing my wrists. "You own every aspect of our lives, and you have no idea how much I love watching you do it." His words were husky as he kissed down my neck and collarbone. "How hard I get watching you commanding a room and arguing with Angels. Makes me want to drop to my knees and worship you there in front of everyone."

That needy spot at the apex of my thighs pulsed with the praise. A moan slipped up my throat, and Tol kissed me bruisingly to catch it.

"I'll spend every day standing beside you in front of our allies and every night kneeling before you behind closed doors. But now..." My whole body burned as his lips skimmed my jaw, stopping at my ear. "Can I show you pleasure now, Alabath?"

"Yes," I breathed. If he didn't, I'd combust. I wanted him to bring all those promises to life, to sate this need that had been mounting between us for months.

"Good girl."

He flipped me over, pulling me to my knees so he could carefully untie the bindings of my leathers. His fingers swept across my back expertly, and I tried not to think of why he was so deft at removing women's clothing. *He is mine*, the possessive mantra echoed in my head.

When the vest fell open, he gently tugged it off, then spun me around to pull the thick tunic over my head. His eyes dropped to that last layer of silk and lace, the only thing still covering my breasts.

"I really hate Mindshaper clothing," Tolek repeated my sentiment from yesterday, chasing me as I lowered back to the ground.

"Why's that?" I gasped. He kneeled between my legs and swept light fingers up my ribs, circling my peaked nipples.

Then, Tol's hands curled around the lace trim on my chest. "There's too much of it." With barely any effort, he shredded the thin fabric so my breasts were bare before him, and he groaned. "Perfect isn't enough of a word for you."

He ducked his head to kiss me first, then worked his way down my neck, across my collarbones, leaving no part of me untouched.

"Those sonnets the Angels could write would never be enough to describe you."

One hand cupped my breast, thumb dragging across my nipple. I arched into him at the sensation fluttering through my body, my hips grinding against him.

"Needy girl," he laughed, sucking my nipple into his mouth.

"You're a tease," I breathed.

He flashed a crooked smile, kissing his way down my stomach. As he did, one hand swept up the inside of my thigh, dragging over my core. Even through my leathers, I could feel every stroke of pressure his long fingers taunted me with.

I watched as his lips continued south, meeting the ties at my waist. Couldn't look away as he used his teeth to undo them—as each touch undid me. He slid his hands between my skin and the tight fabric to shimmy my pants and undergarments down my thighs so I was naked beneath him.

"I told you once that I wanted to take my time with you, Ophelia." Tol pressed his lips to the inside of my knee, tongue and teeth dragging a slow rhythm back up my thigh, then looked up at me with a devilish smirk. "I intend to honor my word."

And when he finally pressed his mouth to me, I knew he meant it. His tongue dragged up my center, flattening against me with a pressure that had stars popping into my vision before sucking gently. He started up a pattern of biting and licking that had my release coiling within minutes.

Right as I toed that edge and was about to tip over it, he pulled back.

"What?" I gasped, lifting my head. He grinned. "Fucking tease," I growled, reaching for him.

Tol shot up, gripping my hands in one of his and pressing his other against my throat as he kissed me. I tasted myself on his lips and groaned into his mouth because it was so fucking *right*.

"Do I need to tie these hands down, or will you let me devour you as I wish?"

Kissing him once more, I exhaled against his lips and answered, "I'll behave."

With one lingering—disbelieving—look, Tol traveled back down my body. This time, he slid two fingers inside of me as his mouth returned to my clit. Two more times he brought me right to that breaking point before edging me back, working me until my legs were shaking. Every movement was controlled, though. Like that trembling need within us both would wait until *he* said it was okay to let go.

By the time I was panting, he pushed another finger into me and moved slowly. My climax was building through my spine and hips, every part of my body loosening. Gradually, he increased the pace of his fingers and added more pressure with his tongue in perfect tandem.

I moaned, and when his name slipped from my lips, he curled his fingers inside of me, like it was what he'd been waiting for, and hit that perfect spot. I crashed over the edge he'd held me on harder than ever before.

Every part of my body undulated beneath his hands and tongue, completely at his mercy as he continued to stroke me through it. When I finally stopped fluttering around his fingers, he crawled back up my body.

"That," he said, as breathless as I was, "is how I want you to say my name from now on."

I rolled my eyes but pushed up to kiss him. I already needed more. Needed him fully.

As the kisses turned hurried and he read my desire, we worked together to pull his clothes from his body.

"So many fucking layers," I growled.

He laughed, making quick work of his tunic and pants, until he remained in only his undershorts, kneeling before me. I rose to my knees, too, dragging a hand down his chest and abs, admiring every perfectly defined muscle on his beautiful body and all the scars he'd been left with after the Battle of Damenal. They littered his skin, tiny white crescents and barbed lines. One scored the length of his ribs, harsh and unforgiving.

I kissed each, letting my tongue press against them, and worshiped those scars. He hissed when I reached the lowest one, disappearing around his hip and beneath his undershorts. My eyes flicked up to his, and those amber flecks burned with lust.

Not dropping Tolek's gaze, I worked my way back up his body, taking my time. Wanting him to see how much I appreciated every inch of him—how beautiful I found the things he deemed flaws. I palmed his length through his undershorts, teasing him.

Once I'd reached the last scar along his shoulder and was fully upright, I gripped his waistband.

"You're certain, right?" His eyes searched mine, his vulnerability gathering between us. "Because you should know that once you're mine, I can never let you go."

"I've been yours, Tolek." Pressing my hands against his shoulders, I eased him back and gave him a reassuring kiss. "And I started taking a contraceptive tonic a week ago."

His eyes widened with the understanding that this wasn't only a moment nor was it a distraction. I wanted him and had made that choice before we got trapped in this cave.

"Now if you'll stop arguing," I teased. He lifted his hips so I could pull his shorts down and discard them. When I saw him for the first time, my thighs nearly pressed together to absolve the ache already building there.

I gripped him at the base, working my hand up, and moved to straddle him. I was ready after the attention he'd showered me with and didn't want to wait another second to feel him inside of me.

Positioning him at my entrance and bracing my hands on his chest, I slowly sank down onto him, one inch at a time.

"Fuck," he exhaled once I was fully seated. "You're straight from my dreams."

He was right; he fit me like we were made for this, like we were two halves of a whole and every day had been spent waiting for us to join together. I rolled my hips, hands gliding over his body because I couldn't decide what part of him I wanted to touch the most.

"You dream of me?" I gasped as he hit a deeper spot.

"I dream of little else," he said. And he didn't mean the plaguing nightmares. It was the pieces of light that slid between them, the promises of good that kept us both going in the darkness.

I lifted myself up and lowered back down, pace increasing as I stretched around him. Tol held my hips, meeting me with each stroke. Heat built as the base of my spine, and my head dropped back, but Tol stopped moving.

"I have control here, Alabath. Remember?" He banded an arm around my waist and flipped us so my back fell gently to the ground, our clothes beneath us. "I want you to look at me when you come."

He gripped the back of my thigh, bending my knee toward my chest, and slowly pushed inside of me once again. Just an inch, then he moved his hips back and sank forward further. He kept repeating that torturous rhythm, wringing out my pleasure.

"I need more," I begged. Finally, with one punishing thrust, he slammed forward to the hilt.

"Fucking, Angels," I moaned as he filled me.

Tolek rolled his hips against me so that he hit every spot I needed. When I cried out, he did it again and again. Long, languid strokes that were also hard and precise. Like he knew my body and what it craved better than anyone.

"I love you like this," he said, kissing my neck, nipping my collarbone. "I love you unraveling for me. *Only me.*"

"Only you." There was no one else—would never be anyone else. This was all I needed or wanted in my life. Him saying he loved me was a drug I'd take again and again. His praise and adoration something I could survive on.

"Faster," I breathed. "Please, Tolek."

He listened, snapping his hips forward in an impossibly quick rhythm as he chased both of our releases.

"Spirits, I'm close," I told him, reaching to pull him down so I could kiss him. His stare seared, and I wanted to burn this moment into my memory, to remember the way he was looking at me right now like everything in the world began and ended with this connection between us and as long as we had that nothing else would matter.

"Come with me, Alabath." His forehead pressed against mine, sweat beading between us. "Fall apart with me."

Those words tore the last strings holding me together until we were spiraling through the universe, two stars set on colliding and sending the galaxy aflame around us.

CHAPTER FORTY-FIVE
TOLEK

HOLY FUCKING ANGELS.

Finishing with Ophelia was cataclysmic. That off-kilter sensation we'd been fighting to balance? Blown away, the walls torn down, everything spinning back on its axis, in the correct direction, right where we were supposed to be.

She was made for me, a perfect fit, like I always knew we were in every other way. To find it in this sense, too, was more than I ever thought I'd experience. Because I never dared think I'd be lucky enough to experience her.

I wished for it. Every shooting star or wildflower had been for her, but not once did I dare to believe I would actually have her. I knew I wasn't worthy of her, but I'd somehow convinced her otherwise. And now that I had her, I was never letting her go.

I kept my forehead against hers until my heart stopped pounding. I waited for the haze to clear around my thoughts, watching as her own chest stopped heaving. Then, I bent to brush my lips across hers. Her features were blissful when I pulled back, magenta eyes clouded with lust and pleasure, the lines of tension set in her brow *finally* fucking gone.

She wrapped her arms around my neck, pulling me back down. Our tongues lashed against each other, and already my cock was getting hard again.

Laughing, I did the last thing I wanted to and gave her one

more soft kiss before standing up and rummaging through the pile of supplies in the corner.

"Perhaps I don't hate being caved in as much as I thought I did," Ophelia murmured.

Flashing her a smirk over my shoulder and catching her eyes exploring my body, I agreed. "It certainly has its perks."

She stretched her arms over her head, more relaxed than I'd ever seen her. For a moment I watched her. The rise and fall of her breasts. The legs that stretched on for fucking ever that I wanted wrapped around my waist, head, wherever she'd let me. The gentle curve of her waist and the pale scars the *lupine daimons* left in the skin there—I'd hated that she'd been hurt, but her scars were damn attractive. Symbols of everything she'd fought for and survived. The way she proudly refused to cover them, how she'd kissed each of mine...

Yeah, I'd be okay never leaving this damn cave again. It was one of my new favorite places in the world. That bathing chamber off the palace ballroom had been in its place until now but was quickly surpassed.

Shaking my head to snap back to the present, I finally found a rag in the supplies—or an old tunic I ripped so the stretch of fabric resembled a rag. Whoever left it here wouldn't mind.

I cleaned us both up then pulled Ophelia against me. Skin to skin, nothing more between us. All the secrets were on the table from both of us now. All the fears and nightmares and torment. Nothing left to hide.

And she was still here, gazing up at me with that stunning smile as she tangled her legs with mine and nestled against me.

We stayed like that for a while, talking about nothing and everything. The room was no longer cold, air heavy with steam. We should have been trying to dig ourselves out of here, but something between us shifted while trapped, and we'd been forced to unveil our demons. I wasn't ready to face the real world yet. For what could have been hours, we laid there. I twirled strands of her silky hair around my fingers, happiest I'd been in memory.

Eventually, we fell into a comfortable silence, and I went over everything we'd poured out to each other.

Her confession about how she'd viewed sex with Malakai hadn't shocked me. I'd known for a while they were using it to avoid their problems. What had surprised me was that she'd feared that was even a possibility for us. I understood it was all she knew and why she was afraid of the past repeating itself, but I would never allow that to happen.

I'd always been the one to push her, and that didn't stop now. If she fell back on those bad habits, I'd challenge her to heal them, not feed them.

I thought she might have been sleeping until she turned so she was on her stomach, chin on my chest. "I've never considered how the Bind would affect you, Tolek. I'm sorry for that."

"I didn't tell you that to make you feel guilty. I only said it so you would know I'm scared, too. That all of this still feels a little too good to be true."

"What do you mean?" She pushed onto her elbows, head tilting.

I propped myself up, too, running fingers lightly down her spine. "I mean that I've loved you since I was young and had accepted you would never be mine. That I was second place." I shrugged one shoulder. "Sometimes it's not believable that I get you to myself."

She frowned at her tattoo. "And this makes that worse? Because you think since I'm still technically tied to him I may wake up one day and feel that pull back." She didn't sound hurt—she was only trying to understand how I felt.

I nodded.

Ophelia brushed her thumb back and forth over the North Star. "I once thought these traditions were the pillars of my life. The Undertaking, the Bind...I'd framed my entire existence around them, letting them be my only purpose. Milestones." Those magenta eyes lifted to mine, seeming to glow. "A lot has changed since then. Not only Malakai and me, but in all of our lives. So many secrets have been exposed; so many things have been tarnished.

"The Undertaking is not as infallible as we thought," she continued, and I nodded in agreement, not quite sure where she was going with this. The ritual had tortured me, yes, and allowed Lucidius to succeed despite his motives, but it still had been transformative for her and our friends. "The Angels are not only reverent beings, but they're pulling strings in our lives. Ever since the Curse first appeared on me, I've felt like everything I know is being turned on its head."

She had a point.

"I don't regret receiving the Bind with Malakai, because I did love him. I wish I'd known the whole truth before making that decision, but I refuse to regret what I once wanted." She swallowed, fingers tightening over her tattoo for a moment before she released it. "I've felt so out of control of my future for years now, but you've always made me feel steadier. You are the one thing I've been able to freely choose, Tol. I don't need a tattoo to know I'm tied to you for life. I'd be honored to receive the Bind with you one day, but it doesn't change anything if we never do. I am infinitely yours, Tolek Vincienzo, as you are mine."

My heart lit up like damn Angellight igniting in my chest. "Infinitely," I echoed, leaning forward to kiss her.

When I took her this time it was slow and reverent, expressing every desire we'd hidden and fought for so long, and when we came together one thing echoed through my mind: perhaps I could be enough for her.

~

WE DIDN'T ALLOW ourselves to continue wasting time after that one, quickly dressing.

I'd protested we could stay in this cave.

"What if someone finds us while we're still naked?" Ophelia had taunted, and the idea of another man seeing her had me throwing her tunic back over her head and strapping those leathers tight enough she was slapping my hands away.

"So, you think Thorn's crown is his emblem?" I asked as we hauled rocks and dirt to try to reach the doorway. Progress was slow.

"I think either the crown itself or something hidden within it.

A jewel maybe?" She stretched out her back after moving a particularly heavy rock. "The other emblems have all either been something forged or mined. The shard from Angelborn, the pearl, and the gilded petal were all created while the stone in Barrett's ring was likely from Engrossian territory somewhere."

"He never said where that's from, has he?" I asked.

"I've never asked about the gem. Only where the ring was found." She stopped, brows scrunching.

"What is it?" I asked, smoothing out the crease and accidentally brushing dirt across her face. I laughed and wiped it away with my sleeve.

"Nothing. It's a good question. How were the emblems created? How did the Angels select their items?"

"And why?" I tacked on, groaning as I got back to work. "That's the most important one."

"And who, I suppose." I raised my brows at her, assuming that was one question we knew the answer to. She continued. "Not who they're for or who they're connected to, but who hid them. I don't think the Angels themselves did it. If they want me to find these tokens, why would they make it so difficult?"

"To prove your worth?" I offered.

"I don't think they'd give the task to someone they found to be of questionable worth." She shook her head. "That seems proven in the fact that I'm the only one who can feel them. There's some reason they need these emblems and some reason they can't get them themselves that requires the Angelcurse." She said the words as if she was realizing them for the first time.

"You think Annellius was unworthy?" Though it didn't always feel that way, we were raised to believe the Angels visiting you was an unheard-of honor.

"Annellius was greedy, remember. He may have been worthy, but his focus shifted along the way." She waved a hand. "The trials of power and what not."

Magic was so volatile, seemingly more so the greater you had. The stronger the power, the larger the possibility for destruction.

"We need to learn more about Annellius's motives," she continued. "And figure out the meaning behind whatever it is Vale saw when she read and I bled on the emblems." Ophelia stopped piling up debris and looked at me, eyes concerned. "Have you found anything in those books from Ezalia?"

Though the research I'd been doing was important to this hunt, it wasn't the Angels she was truly asking about now. Her nerves were evident in the way she worried her lip.

"It helps me come to terms with what I experienced the more I learn about Thorn and his magic," I answered her unspoken question. How was I faring, especially being down in these tunnels?

The gravity of everything I'd confessed to her weighed down the air.

But when I thought back to the books I'd been studying, I remembered something else.

"There were a few passages that caught my eye in the Mindshaper volume," I said, continuing to move rocks. Ophelia followed, anxious energy rolling off of her. "It spoke of Thorn being fascinated by the gods. It was only a mention, but the first I can remember from books about Angels."

Ophelia considered, but in my mind I only heard that lulling voice that had interrupted my studying. The one speaking of sacrificial princes and tragic battlefields amid a war of the gods.

And I hoped we were not being dragged into something as drastic.

Ophelia's pensive voice pulled me from those thoughts. "Truly, I feel lost in this talk about gods."

"Hey," I said, tilting her chin up, "we're going to decipher it all. And no matter who the enemy is—you're going to defeat them."

My words seemed to relax her. "If it was Annellius who Vale saw, what was he doing?"

"She said he was surrounded by seven orbs of light in her reading," I said. "That they took on winged forms."

Ophelia quietly shuffled around the cavern. "He seemed so considerate when I met him, like he was warning me. It's hard to reconcile that spirit with the greedy legacy he claimed."

I had a feeling it was less about connecting the two sides of

Annellius and more so concern over whether the same divide existed within herself, since she was also Angelcursed.

"Suppose you found out Annellius had good reason for whatever he did that was deemed greedy. Would you do the same?"

Ophelia paused, bracing her hands on her hips. "I don't think I know enough about it either way." Her teeth gnawed her lip.

"You would do what is right, Ophelia," I countered, tugging her lip from between her teeth and kissing her once. "It's in the marrow of your bones."

"You got dirt on my face," she mumbled.

I brushed more across her nose. "Oops."

"Vincienzo!" she burst, but she couldn't contain a small laugh.

"I fucked you on the floor of this cave, Alabath. I don't think a little dirt will hurt you." I raised my brows, waiting for her to challenge me.

All she did was grumble, "We were on top of our tunics, at least," and continue carefully hauling away rubble.

"I think," I said, returning to our earlier conversation, "we need to continue to ask questions. I agree there must be more to the motives here."

"Annellius did *die* trying to fulfill this task," Ophelia said. "How can that have been greedy?"

"You won't follow his path. I'll be sure of it." I ignored the thrill of fear spreading along my bones at the thought. "But maybe he knew more than we do. There are a lot of possible explanations. We can't speak with him, though, so I'm not certain we'll ever know."

She was quiet for a moment, eyes flying back and forth as she thought. "He said things during the Undertaking...I'll have to try to recall it all."

"You work on that." I brushed a hand down her back and gestured to the rubble before us with the other. "And let's turn this into a game."

"A game?" she echoed, cocking her head.

"Let's race to see who can clear more rocks. Carefully." I tacked on that last condition, not wanting to worsen the situation or risk her safety.

Ophelia huffed a laugh, but her eyes gleamed. "Is everything a competition with you?"

A lot of things were even though I was okay with falling to second in the important things. Should I offer up the explanation, though?

Yes. She proved she wouldn't run when I unveiled my flaws so far.

"With my father, everything was a competition," I deadpanned. At this point, it was nothing more than a blatant fact of how I was raised. Her eyes softened, hand reaching for my own. "He pitted me against Lyria in every way he could imagine, always knowing she'd be the winner no matter the outcome. I resented her for a while because of it, but eventually I learned to make my own games. I taught myself not to care about coming in second in his and how to win mine instead."

"It's why you like to gamble so much," she whispered, understanding.

"It's why I like to win. I couldn't with him, so I spent every day of my childhood trying to prove myself elsewhere. Until I stopped. When Lyria left for the war, I realized that even with her gone, I'd never be enough for him because of how I came into the world. I tried to let go of a lot of my feelings toward her then, especially when I didn't know if I'd ever see her again.

"Lyria and I hadn't been close before she came to Damenal. I only told her I was leaving Palerman because I felt obligated." A shrug. "I wanted someone to know so I could tell myself perhaps someone cared, even if it was a lie."

"For what it's worth," Ophelia said, "I don't think it was a lie."

I turned that over in my head. I never thought Lyria would come after me when I was captured. Now, with her on Ophelia's council, maybe I could heal that relationship.

Ophelia squeezed my hand once, and that connection soothed every unworthy feeling within me. Then, she turned toward the rubble before us. "I'll play any game you want, Vincienzo." She flashed a wicked smile over her shoulder. "But I won't let you win."

The time passed quickly after that, lost in laughs and a

competitiveness we shared. Angels help any children we may have in the future. I lost count of how many times I cheated, picking her up by the waist or throwing her over my shoulder to move her away from the mess so I could get extra points.

Eventually, though, we found the door. And then, we met our friends' relieved faces digging us out from the other side.

As we reunited, I felt like I was leaving something behind in that cavern, but I'd gained so much more walking out of it.

CHAPTER FORTY-SIX
OPHELIA

EVER SINCE KAKIAS'S POISON LEFT MY BODY, I WAS lighter. Enough so that the days journeying from the tunnels we'd been staying in to a pocket nearer the Mystique Mountains was easy, filled with jokes and chatter among my friends and stolen moments of Tolek dragging me down offshoots to kiss me senseless.

I'd known that once we unleashed this fire I'd become ravenous for him. Unfortunately, we couldn't spare more than a few minutes at a time. Stolen kisses and whispered promises against dirt-packed walls with rocks digging into my spine. Rare touches under orbs of mystlight casting shadows across features I'd memorized years ago, but was seeing entirely differently now.

I wouldn't trade it for all the Angel emblems, though.

When Ricordan eventually stopped us on the third evening in a wide rectangular cavern that faded into shadow at the end, desire heated my core immediately, thinking we'd be given rooms for the night and continue in the morning.

That was not the case.

"We're here," Ric said. He leaned his pack against the wall and rolled out his shoulders. We'd walked most of the way, horses following in a train behind us given the low height of the ceilings through most of the Labyrinth, and we were all stiff.

I exchanged confused glances with my friends. Everyone except

Mila, who continued the silence she'd kept since Malakai found her during the cave in. They'd been freed before Tolek and me, and Malakai told us of the intruder Mila had killed.

Knowing someone had been following us planted hot roots of fury in my gut.

Were there more of them? We needed to get Thorn's crown and get out of here.

Since the cave in, Mila had slipped into a catatonic state, not speaking, and flinching if touched. We'd been watching her carefully, making sure she was never truly alone, but even the healers did not know how to help her. Malakai had diligently cared for her, somehow getting her to move without laying a hand on her and ensuring she ate and drank.

As the rest of us looked between our surroundings and the Mindshapers, he kept one eye on her. I took a breath, reminding myself she wouldn't get help if we did not find the crown and get out of here.

"Where is here?" I asked Ric.

This cavern had higher ceilings than any of the tunnels or caves we'd seen so far. Aside from the stalagmites and stalactites fittingly mirroring the icicles tapering across Mindshaper land above, there was nothing.

Trevaneth was digging through his pack, throwing clothing and books aside in his search.

"The heart of the Labyrinth," Ricordan stated. "Don't you feel the life here?"

When he said it, when I closed my eyes and tuned out the shuffles and whispers of my friends around me for the first time, when I truly focused—I did. The steady hum of land blessed with magic and the stirring of a pulse within me. The tickling sensation at the back of my neck—of the Bond finding itself closer to its purpose.

My eyes shot open, meeting Tol's. Based on the grin he returned, I was certain I looked wild with excitement.

"Is this where the crown is?" I tried not to appear too eager to Ric. Warriors were so defensive about their Angel, and I didn't want him to think I was a threat.

"It is," he confirmed. The rest of my friends fell silent, buzzing with the same anticipation as Tolek and me, those who had the Bond likely digging into the effects of the connective magic.

"Can we see it?" My fingers twitched at my sides, and I scratched at my Curse scar to soothe the energy riling within me.

"First we have some work to do, but I promise you will see it," Ricordan assured me. Though vague, his warm smile was comforting.

Trev straightened up, pulling what looked like long cords from his pack. On and on they went, unraveling on the floor at his feet. I imagined they would have had to be coiled tightly to have fit in there in the first place.

"I'll get the others," Trevaneth said, looking at his immense pile of ropes with displeasure. "They'll have more." Without another word, he turned and disappeared down a corridor.

"More?" I asked.

"Others?" Malakai said at the same time.

"While this hall is empty, there's a pocket nearby with supplies. Trev will get a few of the rebels to help."

"What exactly are they helping with?" Jezebel asked.

"Preparing for the descent," Ricordan said.

The subtle hum of power in the walls itched against my skin, my second pulse quickening more than the first.

"What does that mean?" I nearly snapped. Frustration bubbled within me despite the fact that I was relying on Ric for this.

"Can you clarify how we're to prepare?" Cypherion adjusted my original question, tempering it a bit. I nodded my appreciation to him.

"Let me show you something." Ricordan turned, walking toward the shadowed end of the chamber. We all shuffled along behind him silently.

When he reached the end, he held out an arm to stop us. "One moment," he said. "Sometimes the mystlight takes a second to register when someone has arrived." This place was not visited often, then, if the magic was idle.

Finally, orbs flickered to light, half a dozen of them forming a circle along the ceiling before us. And at our feet—

"What's this?" I toed the edge of the cliff descending into nowhere.

"The pit," Ricordan answered.

"It's where the crown is," Trev said behind us, returning with a handful of Mindshapers in tow. A tall woman with pale skin and dark hair shaved close to her head went directly to Ricordan, pulling him to the side.

"Down there?" Vale gasped, stepping closer to the edge to peer over it. She'd been quiet since her latest episode. I wasn't sure if she'd attempted any sessions. Right now, though, she seemed alert and steady.

I swept the perimeter of the circular hole carved into the ground, plunging Spirits knew how far down. There were no stairs, no divots in the rock to form hand and foot holds.

"How do I get to it?" I asked. My second pulse rioted, ready to dive in.

"That's what these are for." Trev held up the cords he'd dragged behind him. They were sturdy, but not as thick as I'd like.

"You have to repel down?" Cypherion looked between the boy and me.

"Using these?" Tolek held a cord between both hands and tugged. It did not snap, surprisingly strong, but a frown twisted his lips.

"This does not seem safe," Santorina chastised. Beside her, Esmond and Gatrielle muttered to each other quickly.

"How do we know the crown is even down there? So... unprotected." Jezebel squared her hands on her hips, but I followed her thought. How could an Angel emblem be so defenseless that all the warrior had to do was drop into the pit and grab it?

Esmond cleared his throat. "I think there's more to it." Stepping forward, he held a hand out to Trev. "May I?"

The boy looked to his father who was still deep in conversation, then decided he could trust the Bodymelder. Esmond took the bundle of outstretched cords and weighed them in his hands, running long fingers along the material. He snapped and folded and twisted them.

"Thoughts?" Esmond held it to Gatrielle, who repeated the tests.

"I think you're right," the latter agreed, bobbing his head, brown curls bouncing around his face.

"Will the two of you explain?" Malakai demanded, exasperated, as if the Bodymelders had this secret level of communication often.

Esmond looked to Trevaneth, searching the boy's expression as he said, "We have to create the materials used to repel, don't we?"

"Braid the rope, craft the hooks," Gatrielle added.

Ric barked a laugh, rejoining the conversation. "We won't be welding anything down here, but you're correct. In order to descend into the pit, the warrior seeking entrance must braid the rope."

"Why?" Jezebel asked, head quirking to the side.

"It's a meditative practice, isn't it?" Cypherion asked, and then I understood.

The Seawatcher task had been a physical challenge, an adventure crafted for the Prime Warrior who traveled the oceans. The Bodymelder was about logical puzzle solving and sacrifice.

When used properly, Mindshaper magic was intended to relax and unravel the mind. There were a number of techniques they employed. The repetitive action of something like braiding rope would soothe, similar to my own knot tying habit.

Looking down into the pit again—realizing how deeply it stretched—I guessed the point of this task. "It's meant to prove you can calm yourself and be patient enough to be worthy of seeing the crown."

"Correct, Revered," Ric said, nodding, and I thought there was a beat of pride in his voice.

"Good thing you're so patient," Tolek teased, wrapping his arm around my waist and squeezing my hip.

"I can be patient," I argued, and everyone around us laughed.

"Patient is certainly not a word anyone would use to describe you." Jezebel shook her head as she helped Trev gather the rope he'd unraveled. "Passionate and determined, yes, but patient? I'm sorry, no."

Even Cypherion chuckled. "She has a point."

"Well, I will be tonight." I'd have to be. I told that second pulse in my veins to calm, assured it we would find what it sought. "But let's hurry and get started."

"Actually," Ricordan interrupted, lips pressing together grimly, "before you can do that, we have a guest you may want to meet."

~

"HE'S CHAINED, but he's...unpredictable," Zaina, the Mindshaper who'd approached Ricordan, explained as she led us down a narrow corridor of the Labyrinth.

"How so?" I asked.

"He hasn't fought back with anything other than words since we disarmed him. But he's becoming volatile. We don't know when he'll try..."

"His magic," Cypherion finished from over my shoulder.

Zaina nodded, one sharp bob of her head. The stony corridor she led us down was more constructed than some parts of the Labyrinth. The brick arches we'd seen throughout extended to form solid walls and ceilings, doors with barred windows locked firmly—

"Cells," Malakai breathed.

I hadn't realized he'd come. Most of the others stayed back with Trevaneth, setting up for the ropes we needed to weave. My sister, Rina, Cypherion, and Tolek had also followed.

"You don't have to stay here," I offered to Malakai. My chest hurt for the boy who'd been imprisoned, like a rip going right down the center. It was an effort to throw my mask over my face, not letting that emotion crack through. Not now.

Stepping forward, Malakai scanned the door, lifting a hand to inspect the lock. "It's funny," he said. "You have stronger locks down here than they ever did on my cage. The bars on mine weren't even this sturdy."

We were all silent for a moment. He never spoke about his imprisonment. We hadn't pushed him to, and though it might seem like an inconsequential fact to offer now, it wasn't.

Tolek clapped a hand to Malakai's shoulder. "They knew your sword work had gotten sloppy."

"I can put you on your ass." Malakai elbowed Tolek in the ribs, smiling, and the atmosphere in the room lifted as if all six of us exhaled at once.

"With the way he's been training," Cyph said, "I think he might be able to, Tol."

Tol's jaw dropped. "No way—"

"Boys!" Santorina said as Jezebel and I opened our mouths to join. "We have something important to do."

I turned to Ricordan and Zaina who had been silently observing the whole exchange, amused smirks on their faces. "Sorry. Where did you find the prisoner?"

"He was near one of the tunnel entrances to the Labyrinth, at the convergence of the Mindshaper, Bodymelder, and Mystique borders."

"That's not far from where we entered," Tolek said.

"Close enough that he could be tied to the one Mila killed," Malakai continued, crossing his arms. Tension wormed between us all, a bubble expanding in my chest. My fingers twitched at my sides with the need to grab my weapons. To search the Labyrinth. To do *something* to alleviate the threat.

"Was he alone?" Cyph asked.

"Yes," Zaina said, her lips twisting to the side. "Which is more worrisome than if he wasn't."

"Why?" Jez crossed her arms.

"You think he may have been bait," I answered for the Mindshapers, forcing my nerves to focus on the challenge before me.

Zaina nodded. "We've reinforced patrols on nearby entrances, but there aren't enough of us to man all of them."

Lack of warriors. It was a problem we were facing on all sides of the war. I couldn't promise them assistance—didn't know if Lyria had the soldiers to spare to guard the Labyrinth.

"Once we end this war it won't matter," I swore. "Let's get one step closer." I threw my hair behind my shoulders and stepped forward.

"Wait!" Vale's voice drifted down the tunnel. She skidded to a stop before us, her Mindshaper boots and thick layers looking out of place on her usually chiffon-clad frame. "I think I should come with you."

There was more color in her cheeks than there had been in days, a determined brightness to her eyes.

"Why?" Cypherion asked, eyes narrowed.

She lifted her chin. "Because real life experience with this magic might make my readings stronger."

"Or give you information—"

Tolek hit Cyph in the back of the head to stop that sentence from forming, but not before hurt bloomed in Vale's eyes. Regret darkened Cyph's expression, but he said nothing.

The Starsearcher turned to me. "I promise, Ophelia. I won't sabotage your effort."

I looked between Cypherion and Vale. Despite his words, he cast a heavy glance at her, and it didn't feel angry. It felt like a stare that wanted to speak a thousand words—with a touch of hatred for that wanting.

Vale's readings had been endangering her lately—perhaps that was where Cyph's uncertainty was rooted—but I trusted her with whatever information we heard in there. And she deserved to make her own decisions regarding her sessions.

"How many can we have?" I asked Zaina and Ric.

"Four would be best." Zaina placed a hand to her chest. "Five counting me. The cell isn't large."

I pursed my lips, looking back to my friends.

"Jezebel should go," Tolek said, and all eyes swung to him. "I've been studying Mindshaper magic, and I think she should try hers around this twisted source. To see if there are any connections."

He had been digging through those books at every possible chance. I worried about how it would affect his own nightmares, but he was too curious to be convinced otherwise.

"And Rina," I added. She may not be a Bodymelder, but she was the healer I wanted by my side.

"You four go." Malakai waved a hand at us. "You're the ones with the most reason."

"Mali's right," Tolek said. "We don't need to be there."

Cypherion said nothing, but he nodded, and they left. These three men had been through death and torture and war together, and a piece of me warmed to see them walking down the corridor peacefully. The weight of the future gave them a brief reprieve. With so much uncertainty in our lives, I'd never take those small moments for granted again.

"All right." I brought myself back to the moment, checking that Starfire, Angelborn, and my dagger were all secure. Met my sister's, Rina's, and finally Vale's eyes. "Let's go, then."

Chapter Forty-Seven
Ophelia

The prisoner's head hung between his shoulders, dark hair slicking to sweaty skin as he muttered to himself. His fingers flexed over the iron arms of the chair in time with his feet fluttering where they were chained.

Dried blood splattered across his face. Drops speckled his lips and chin. His boots were gone, replaced with thick, lined slippers, and he retained no weapons belt or bandoliers. If I didn't know better, he looked as plain as a baker in Palerman, dressed in a thick tunic and leathers.

Zaina circled around him, leading our small train. Rina stationed herself nearest, quick eyes assessing his physical state. Beside her, Vale pulled out a small wrapped cylinder of crushed herbs like she'd once given us all at Renaiss. How long ago those days felt.

"Easier to prepare for spontaneous readings," she explained. The match she struck was a loud hiss in the cell, the prisoner's head cocking at the sound. Soon, the hazy lavender smoke surrounded Vale, a much thinner layer than her recent readings.

Jezebel lingered in the shadowed corner, eyes intent and power bubbling within her frame, as I stepped up to the prisoner.

His eyes stuck to my boots first, slowly dragging up my body— not leering, simply taking me all in.

And when they landed on my face, a manic smile split his own.

"It's you," he gasped. Then, he was shouting. "Call the queen! Call the queen!"

It reminded me of Aird. Of the hinges in his mind slowly coming loose, the power swirling within him when I'd rescued Tolek.

But this was far worse.

The way this warrior cracked his neck and flexed his hands almost seemed like he had no control over himself. Like his power was pushing at the edges of his skin, fighting to pop bones and tear flesh.

I hardened my voice against the nausea that image drew.

"Pleased you recognize me. But your queen will not hear any calls you make."

Those wild eyes widened. I thought Vale was muttering something. Santorina circled around, eyes on the man's twitching fingers.

"You nearly took her last time, but oh, how the queen waits. Her anger stews and wounds run deep, but she'll win her prize."

"What does he mean?" Jezebel snapped.

"The blood of the girl across her hands. We are not allowed to touch. We must only deliver. And I found you." He thrashed, not seeming to remember he was in chains. The clanking echoed in the small cell.

"You can't touch me," I said. "None of you can. I will die by my own blade before I fall to your queen's." I brushed my fingers across the handle of my dagger.

Vale's muttering grew louder. "*Breath of lungs and threads of heart.*" Santorina and I exchanged a nod, and Rina moved closer to the Starsearcher.

"Little angel child, is that what you think?" The prisoner cackled. "She will destroy what she wishes, or did you not learn with your father?"

My fist cracked into the side of his face before I realized what I was doing. Again and again until my knuckles split open and our blood mingled.

"You are not worth the dirt beneath my father's boots," I said through gritted teeth. Anger was a molten thing, souring in my stomach, and grief swept up with it. "Your queen is not worthy to speak his name."

Crimson dripped down his cheek, one eye swelling shut. "He died screaming like they all do."

I whipped my dagger to his throat, gripping his hair to expose his neck. He laughed again, the vibration angling him against the blade so a bead of blood appeared.

"What do you know?" I growled, leaning over him. I tried to shut out every thought of my father, every ache his death wrought within me, and focus on what this warrior implied between his words.

His taunts felt aimless, rambling but pointed. Had she told them of my blood? I doubted there was a warrior alive she trusted enough to share that information with. But how much did the queen herself know?

He continued to cackle, spit gathering in the corners of his mouth, dripping across the blood.

My grip tightened on the dagger handle. Flipping it around, I pointed the end directly at the corner of his mouth and dragged slowly outward, a shallow line that had maroon rolling like raindrops.

"If you don't want me to slice true, I suggest you talk."

He barely flinched.

"Tell us what your mission was, or I get a sliver of revenge for the lives taken in my city."

His fingers drummed the arms of the chair. The incessant beat drilled into my mind and became the cataclysmic *booms* of buildings toppling in Damenal. I gripped his jaw, tugging it down.

"If you're not going to speak, you won't need your tongue."

But he was too far gone. There was nothing left behind his eyes for me to interrogate. Exactly as Lyria had said happened with her prisoners, this Mindshaper's magic had turned internal, eating away at him.

My hand shook, straining to carve him up for his taunts—for the lives he may have taken.

But I thought of my father.

Not of the way he'd died. But of how he'd *lived*.

Of how he'd raised me to handle leadership—to retain a level of both fairness and firmness. I tried to picture what he would tell me to do now. If this was a different prisoner beneath me, one not lost to a power he did not ask for, my father's advice might be different. Now, though, I knew what he'd say. What instincts he'd tell me to taper.

My heart ached for the warriors across the continent enthralled by Kakias's power. For the families who lost them. Behind him, Zaina's face was unreadable, but her hands clenched into fists at her side, within reach of a jagged-edged dagger.

"You won't win," the prisoner sang. "Her power is eternal. The winged gods flourish within her."

I gritted my teeth, my dagger shaking at his jaw.

"Magic *lives*," he drawled. "It sings and dances."

"*Breath of lungs and threads of heart*," Vale echoed again, and at her voice something snapped within the prisoner.

"The sp—" His words cut off, eyes widening. He searched my face, seeming more alert for a brief moment, then looked wildly around the room.

Jezebel stepped from the shadows, a harsh, narrowed stare on the prisoner. They locked eyes, silently communicating, and Jez softened.

Then, my sister nodded at me, remorse swirling behind her gaze.

And I dragged my dagger across his throat, stepping aside quickly so as not to get his blood on me.

Vale snapped from the shallow depths of her reading. She swayed for a moment, but waved off Santorina's assistance. She took in the dagger in my hand and blood pooling on the floor but shook her head. A frustrated sigh deflated her frame as she left the room—nothing concrete in her session.

"He asked for it," Jezebel said to Rina and me as we walked back down the tunnel. Zaina said her team would clean up. Jez kept her voice low and slowed our steps enough that Ricordan wouldn't hear. "At the end. When Vale said...whatever she said, and I tried to wrangle his spirit at the same time, he returned to himself, and he did not want to live."

That leash had somehow snapped within him, and the warrior reclaimed his mind.

"That does not mean he deserved to die," I said. No one forced into this war deserved to meet their end. Spirits, my hands still shook over the anger from his taunts about Daminius, but I wasn't sure those had truly been him.

"No." Jezzie's lips pulled into a tight line. "It doesn't."

~

DESPITE MY FRIENDS' jokes at my lack of patience and the confusion from the interrogation, I enjoyed the mindlessness of the braiding. My muscles loosened as we worked, fingers absently taking control.

Apparently, this style of rope braiding was something the Mindshapers practiced often with cords produced by Bodymelders —it was how Esmond and Gatrielle guessed their purpose. Trevaneth set up an assembly line to guarantee we wouldn't hinder each other's progress and could finish the task as quickly as possible.

Though I was the only one who would be dropping into the pit—a fact none of my family was fond of, but one Ric insisted must be—they were all allowed to assist with the construction of the materials. Which was good, considering how deep the descent would be.

Well into the session, our lengths of completed rope growing longer, I found myself sitting with Tolek, Jezebel, Cypherion, Santorina, and Malakai.

My heart clenched to think about the many times we'd sat around tables like this before life had turned ruinous. Though my sister had not normally joined us, it was right that she was here now. She was always meant to be a part of us.

Though we'd seen more death and destruction than I'd imagined possible, we could still sit here. Be here. Maybe not whole as we once were, but together. Each with our own wounds buried beneath our skin, but our paths still converging, our shoulders still holding the others up.

"Malakai?" I waited for him to look at me, then I jerked my chin toward someone behind him. "How is she?"

Though I was sure he knew who I meant, he followed my gaze. Mila sat on her own, a length of rope sliding through her fingers. She didn't follow the pattern as the rest of us had; instead, she let the rough material twist around itself and back out again. Vale sat nearby keeping an eye on her without turning too much attention on the general.

"She's f—" Malakai paused, releasing a breath that deflated his body. "I don't know." He tugged at the rope more aggressively. "She hasn't spoken since she told me of the intruder. Not even to me."

Under the dim reach of the mystlight, I could barely make out his expression. Brows furrowed and jaw grinding.

"I believe all we can offer her is time," Santorina said. "Something happened to trigger her while she was stuck in there. We can't force her to speak about it."

"She's strong, Mali," Cypherion encouraged. "She's clearly been through something traumatic, but it will not be the end."

"I know." Malakai flicked a distressed look over his shoulder again, and I recognized something in it. A melding of defensive and soft each time he found her.

Protectiveness.

It was deeply rooted, beyond a warrior and his general. Likely beyond friendship, if I knew his tells as well as I thought I did. I'd once been on the receiving end of them, after all. His inner struggle between shielding and soothing was something I'd experienced all our lives.

It had become a wedge between us, that conflicting attitude. But now, as he restrained himself from running to her and demanding answers or closing himself away to hide, as he sat here where she may need him but not infringing on her space, he was balancing those instincts whether he realized it or not. Someone was making him want to.

Malakai cared for Mila, and I wondered if he even realized how deeply the extent of those feelings stretched.

As my fingers continued to work the rope mindlessly, I looked up at Tolek beside me and nudged him with my elbow. One corner of his lips lifted, a brow quirking.

Yes? it said.

I flicked my gaze back to Malakai and over his shoulder as if to say, *Do you see what I'm seeing?*

Tol shook his head with a laugh. If we were alone, I knew the answer would be: *You're just catching on?*

I rolled my eyes and turned back to my work. Tolek leaned down to kiss my temple, letting our silent exchange melt between us.

Cypherion and Santorina were updating Malakai on Rina's progress with her human training program. Her last correspondence was before we went below ground but Ezalia's brother, Leo, had been recruiting widely. He'd used their shell communication to inform her when he needed to write, which the boys found fascinating. Between Mystique and Seawatcher territories, there were a number of human cities, and residents were eager.

"Were you able to speak to anyone in Bodymelder territory before..." Malakai trailed off.

Santorina shook her head, her long ponytail swaying. "We didn't stop in any villages on our way."

"We didn't want Kakias to target them if she found out I was there," I added. Again, exhilaration buzzed through me at the reminder that I was free of the queen's poison.

Malakai nodded, understanding the weight of lives on my shoulders better than anyone. "Esmond and Gatrielle would help, I bet. If you haven't already spoken to them about it."

"I have a bit," Santorina confirmed. "Before Daminius, I told Esmond of my dream to see humans as prepared against threats as warriors are. So we do not have to rely on others to fight our battles. We may not be a match for fae, still," Rina muttered, hand absently coming to her neck. Was she remembering our first encounter with Lancaster? She'd sworn she was not upset Tolek and I now had bargains with the fae because she knew we needed them, but a piece of me thought that wasn't the whole truth.

"Humans can help, though. This war is greater than the clans."

Rina's eyes lifted to my neck, landing on the shard of Angelborn. "That one likely is, too."

Dressed in her Mindshaper tunic and leathers and maneuvering the rope between her skilled fingers, Santorina looked as much a warrior as any of us. She was, if not in the literal sense.

"You're right," I said, gripping her hand so she stilled. "We don't know what waits, but everyone must be prepared."

That seemed to remind Malakai of something else. "Brigiet was furious when Kakias crossed into their land."

"Is she offering troops now?" Cypherion asked.

"Not to the camp, but she's fortifying their borders. Slowing their harvest to do it." A frown twisted Malakai's lips. "I don't like that they're sacrificing time in the fields."

"Me neither," I agreed. This was the first I'd heard of it. "Once we're out of here, we'll discuss with Lyria and the generals and see what can be rearranged. Maybe we can direct some of our own troops that way." Or to the Labyrinth. Spirits, we needed numbers everywhere.

"Yeah." Malakai nodded, enthused. "Let's see what Lyria thinks." Again, his eyes flicked to Mila.

For a moment, Malakai seemed like he was becoming his old self again.

No, not his old self exactly. A hardened version of that person. One who had seen and experienced tragedies and injustices, but instead of the hopeless void he'd fallen into, he was working to right them.

Cypherion and Tolek exchanged a glance, having remained quiet for most of the conversation. The relief in their eyes said they shared my thoughts.

"Jezebel," Malakai said. Tearing his eyes away from Mila, he found my sister with a hesitant glance. "Tell me more about this power."

Jez had been keeping to herself since we sat down. I had yet to see her engage with Malakai. It was odd. Before he'd left, they'd been as close as siblings. My sister had always had her own relationships with my friends. She bickered uncontrollably with Tolek while sharing a respect for warrior training and traditions with Cyph.

With Malakai, though, she'd had someone to admire. She'd talked to him about things she was not comfortable talking to others about and loved him deeply.

When he left, she'd been hurt—more so when she found out he knew he wouldn't return.

Now though, as he asked her about the power we'd told him little of, she visibly relaxed, something between them softening.

"I've been trying to figure out how it works myself." The hum of our task and chatter of the other companions filled the cavern as we considered.

"Whatever power I have that communicates with spirits can pull threads," Jezebel said. "I was able to separate the Mindshaper from his born spirit to reach it since he was so far gone. It's almost like the release of death. Or it feels like it from my end of the manipulation. I don't think I'm actually communicating with the dead; I need a spirit on the brink of freedom from life, not from a body." She shrugged. "It doesn't work on a healthy Mindshaper. Trev and I tried."

"Do you think it's an effect of your dormant Angelblood?" Tolek offered. Curiosity spun questions of Mindshaper magic through his active mind.

Cypherion shook his head, though. "Can't be, can it? All Alabaths have to have Angelblood if these two do. None of them have been able to communicate with spirits."

"That we know of," Rina said, shrugging.

"I'm starting to wonder if perhaps it's from elsewhere," Jez admitted, looking at her hands.

"What do you mean?" I asked gently.

She was quiet for a moment. Then, she said, "Ricordan told you all of Thorn. Of how his life progressed and how his power ate away at him." Her shining eyes lifted to mine, so raw and vulnerable. "What if that's happening to me? His life became a tragedy. What if I'm the next installment?"

I set down my rope, crawling around Tolek to sit beside my sister. "What happened to Thorn was devastating, but his life was still great beyond his illness. I don't think it sounds like the same thing as your powers, but even if something like that were beginning, it would not be the end of you, Jezzie. It would only be a new hurdle for us to understand."

"Thorn's life was tragic because of his isolation," Tolek added. "Because no one was here to help understand what was happening to his mind, and as a result, he suffered. It is sad, yes, but that's not you."

Jezebel took a deep breath and exhaled it slowly, nodding. "I know you're right. I think I'm just...defeated." Her head tilted to the side. "That's not something I'm used to."

"I think we're all adjusting to things we've never experienced before," Cypherion said.

My hand went to my necklace on instinct. While this connection I'd grown with the Angels certainly applied to what he said, it was so much more than that.

Our world had been torn open at the seams, a tapestry unraveling the moment the Curse appeared on my arm. I had not known it then—Spirits, I still did not know what it all meant—but we were leaning into that discomfort and learning to navigate the challenges it brought.

Looking around at our group, I thought we all were. Whether it was acknowledging truths long buried or forging new paths, we were discovering and growing and conquering—and Angels, sometimes failing—together.

"You're very wise, Cypherion," I said. "Has anyone ever told you that?"

He rolled his eyes, understanding my implication of how that wisdom should be used, and brushed me off. But I saw the small smile he tried to hide.

"He's right." Jezebel squared her shoulders, and Tolek moved over so I could remain between him and my sister as we continued our progress on the rope. "Sorry, Malakai, you had questions? I'll do my best to answer." She flashed him a soft smile.

He fidgeted with the rope. "I only wondered how it works. Can you reach any spirit?"

"Only those who are passing."

Malakai mulled that over. "And are they lucid?"

"In a sense. They are aware they're no longer here, but most are so close to being gone, they're more focused on that loss than communicating."

Our father hadn't been, though. He'd hung on to pass us a last message, a light in the dark.

He said he loves us and he's proud of us. Reminded us to protect each other.

I wrapped an arm around my sister and squeezed, determined to adhere to my father's last wishes with my dying breath.

"That's...interesting." Malakai strung out the last word, considering whatever theory was brewing in his mind.

When he did not ask any more questions, Jezebel continued. "The only thing that had a...different reaction than dying was that beast in the forest on our original journey to the Undertaking." Everyone in our circle stilled. I supposed she hadn't told them of this piece after she told me.

"What did that one say?" Cyph asked, voice guarded. We were likely all remembering that first encounter with the threats beyond our haven of Palerman.

I thought back to what Jezebel had revealed about that experience.

"It screamed. It sounded confused."

"I wake," I murmured, the memory coming back. "That's what it said to you, right?"

Jezebel nodded. "It repeated it over and over again."

My second pulse sped, and I knew it well enough now to recognize the sign. Whatever instincts the Angelblood birthed within me reacted to this story.

There was no way to say for certain, but it seemed like a thread of this larger tapestry.

I wake.

CHAPTER FORTY-EIGHT
OPHELIA

"YOU'RE CERTAIN THESE THINGS ARE STABLE?" TOLEK nudged one of the hooks screwed into the rock at the edge of the pit with his boot. Anchors, Ric told us they were called. They were installed throughout the descent for me to clip the ropes into as I went, too.

"That's the tenth time you've asked, Tolek," I chastised as Ricordan circled me, tightening the buckles on my harness and checking every clip.

"And I'll ask ten more," Tol responded, kicking the metal a little harder this time. When it did not move—again—he sighed in acceptance.

Cypherion clapped a hand to his shoulder. "We've been looking at them all night, Tol. They're secure." Cyph had been personally checking each and every anchor around the rim of the pit with Ricordan, deciding which were the most secure. A few other Mindshapers had offered to help, but Ricordan allowed us privacy, telling them we had it under control. Only one anchor had cracked from the ledge when weight was applied.

We would not use any near it.

The hooks we'd slid the ropes through and knotted them around were safe. It was the only possibility I would consider.

Tolek was before me, then, hands traveling over the harness.

"Hey," I said, gripping his wrists and pulling his attention to me. "I'll be okay. I can do this."

The concern in his eyes melted. "It's not your ability I'm worried about, Alabath." But he removed his hands from the equipment and cupped my cheeks. "Just ensuring you come back up from that descent for my own selfish sake."

Though he smirked as he said it, it was the truth. Tolek believed I could pull the moon to earth if I tried hard enough. That the stars would turn to ice if I said it was so. And he was comfortable enough in my skill to sit back while I fought or debated or discovered.

But he'd always been protective of me and was only beginning to allow those fears to show overtly. I wouldn't discourage his vulnerability by making him feel wrong for it.

"Thank you, Vincienzo." I turned my head to kiss his hand softly. "I rather like living, and I hope to not careen to the floor of that hole today."

He attempted a laugh. "Let's not joke about that."

"You?" I gasped. "Dismissing a joke? I never thought the day would come."

"I have something I'm not willing to gamble over." He brushed his thumb across my cheekbone, his demeanor shifting easily from playful to serious as his eyes heated.

"We're ready!" Trev called from across the chamber where he, Malakai, Vale, and Jezebel had been feeding the rope through a series of hooks, setting up the pulley system in case I couldn't climb back up myself. We weren't sure what the bottom of the pit would be like, how sound the walls were or what sort of hand-and-foot holds existed. Santorina, Esmond, and Gatrielle had tied a pouch of ointments around my belt—just in case. Now, they all gathered to the side, voices low.

"Me, too," I answered, looking around at everyone assembled, reporting to their stations as planned.

Tol's eyes hadn't left my face. When I looked back at him, heat still burned in his gaze. He ducked his head, capturing my lips in a warm, desperate kiss that flipped my stomach over. I opened to him, because—and I would not say this aloud—if there was a chance this next emblem trial took my life, I wanted to go with the taste of him on my tongue.

"Go, love," he breathed when he pulled away. "I'll be here if you need anything. And when you're back with that emblem in hand, I'll get on my knees and worship you better than any Angel."

Heat was still flaring through me from the kiss and his words as he stepped back, a knowing smirk on his lips, and he let me go. I approached the edge of the pit and faced the darkness below.

Ric wandered over again, hooking the ropes to the back of my harness and tugging aggressively. "Remember," he whispered, the edge in his voice straightening my spine, "do not wear the crown."

"Why?" I asked, moving my lips minutely so no one would notice.

"It holds power we don't understand, Ophelia." He tightened the strap around my right shoulder. "The thing our Angel created was always strong, but since it broke, it's been unstable."

"How so?" I fought the instinct to scratch at my wrist.

"The heart of the labyrinth is where Thorn forged his crown," Ric reminded me. "It's where he bore it, where he was pulled from the earth to ascend, and where we found the relic thousands of years later. But the pit was not always this deep."

My stomach turned leaden. "The crown's power hollowed out the ground here?" That magic swarmed in the pit below, a swirling mass of darkness and shadows calling to me.

"Legends are only legends. But on the off chance they're true..." Ric stepped back, and it was clear his quiet warning was over. "Be smart, Revered." He clapped a hand to my shoulder. My chest tightened at the comforting, fatherly gesture, but I wouldn't allow the hole in my heart to bloom right now. My father would want me to be focused. He'd want me to do as I'd practiced.

I flicked a glance to my friends, clearing my throat. "Why are you only telling me?"

"Best not to worry them."

I nodded, turning my attention back to the pit's captivating power. With Ric's words in my head, there was one more person I had to speak with.

"Cypherion," I called over my shoulder.

He was at my side in a second. "Yes?"

"In case..." I looked away from the pit, up to Cyph. "If something happens when I'm down there, I need you to promise me you'll be here."

"Ophelia—"

"Not as a Second," I continued. "Not in a formal capacity or a ruler. But be there for them." For Tolek and Jezebel and Rina. And then, because the longer I watched the pit, the more I was reminded how dangerous those first two trials had been, I added, "It doesn't matter what position you hold, Cypherion. You hold us all together regardless. You may not think you're capable of being my Second, but it's those little things that show that you are."

He was quiet for a long moment, watching the tempting pull into the pit, too. "It's not that I fear I'm incapable. It's that I fear I don't know myself enough to stay true when it's demanded of me."

Because of his father, no doubt. I hadn't realized how deep those fears had rooted themselves.

"I think being open to discovering more about who you are deep down and the potential that person can reach is one of the biggest favors you can do for yourself, Cyph." Each day I felt myself sliding further along that journey. Learning more about what I could withstand, what I wasn't willing to lose. "Perhaps the best parts of us are forged under the harshest of circumstances."

Cypherion gave me a smile, tucking me into his side with a quick hug. "You're going to do just fine down there, Revered."

"But in case—"

"I promise, Ophelia," he said, bending down to meet my eyes better. "But it won't be necessary."

He returned to the others, then, and I faced the arresting power. With the distractions gone, it became a siphon. Dropping down, I swung my legs over the edge, tugged on my rope twice to give the signal that I was moving, and lowered into the pit.

My arms shook as I turned, bracing myself against the rock and securing my grip.

"No," I told my body. "There will be no nerves today."

The Mindshapers were creatures of mental strength and

emotional complexities. Manipulation, while possible for evil, could also be a skill. My emotions today were mine to regulate. I was Ophelia Alabath, Revered of the Mystique Warriors, Chosen of the Angels, and I was stronger than fear.

Closing my eyes and inhaling, I practiced the meditative breathing Ric had advised me in. I'd asked him if he would be able to use his magic to calm my nerves while I was in the pit, but he said no. It didn't surprise me. This task was about independent control and emotional balance.

Instead, I summoned serene memories. Riding Sapphire, exploring Damenal at night, quiet moments with my friends around a splintered tavern table, Tol's breath tickling my neck as we laid together in comfortable silence or vibrant laughter.

I forced those thoughts to the surface as I slowly lowered one foot down and made sure each movement was strong. Certain. Muscles in my thighs, glutes, and abdominals all braced. Tension in my arms. Hands wrapped tightly around the rope we'd all taken care to create, love and sweat and the strength of those waiting poured into it.

The lower I got in the descent, the smaller the mystlights were above. I was careful to attach myself to each anchor with the clips Ric had provided, tugging to make sure they were secure before I moved. I couldn't hear anyone's voice—didn't know if they were talking or standing in nervous silence.

That chilled presence wrapped around me again.

Fingers whispered across my skin beneath my leathers, feeling alive and cognizant of me, and I shivered.

Then, one of the straps around my shoulder slipped. And I was falling, holding in a scream.

My palms slid down the rope, boots skidding on rock.

I grappled for that lifeline with my heart careening through my chest. As I locked my fingers around it, the force of my fall spun my body out and swung me back toward the wall. I slammed into rock, and pain radiated through my right shoulder.

"Fucking Spirits," I swore, teeth clenching at the impact.

The rope tugged from above, but I pulled back twice to signal

I was okay. Not three times—I did not want them to hoist me up yet.

Shoulder throbbing, I waited for my heart rate to return to normal, though my second pulse refused to calm. A hot, vicious ache pounded through my body. I hesitated a moment longer to see if the chilled presence continued to investigate me, but no more tendrils caressed my skin.

It was there, though.

Its eyes—if it had eyes—burrowed into me. Exhaling, I gathered my peaceful memories again and continued down. I kept as much tension as possible in my uninjured arm, grimacing each time I needed to use my right hand to shuffle downward. It slowed the descent, but it was necessary.

With each foot, the darkness shifted.

It became sweet, a flavor and scent tempting me to its depths. Flashes of salacious images prodded my carefully-curated memories, fingers curling around the edges. Teeth on skin and sweat-flecked flesh moving together. Moans and cries of pleasure floated with the images, bringing them to life.

I fought back with images of my own, calming and grounding. With braiding Sapphire's mane and the slide of her silky hair between my fingers. With the sounds of dawn breaking over the Mystique Mountains and the tickle in my Bond.

As I focused on moving one foot at a time, darkness thickened. That temptation solidified, harder to resist.

Descending into this pit was entering a place of primal lust.

Give in, little seraph child, the darkness cooed in a voice neither male nor female but fluctuating between the two. *Come play, and forget that which frightens you.*

I couldn't answer. It was all I could do to force my memories to the surface, because the purpose of the ghostly voice struck me: by telling me to forget my fears, they hoped I would bring them to the surface. Let them breathe down a gulp of air before shoving them to the depths of my cavernous heart.

If I did, the alluring darkness would latch on to them and feed me my own terror.

Instead, I doubled my efforts. Sweat beaded across the back of my neck where the Bond was inked, and I focused on those mountains. The purpose and peace they instilled in me.

My shoulder ached, but I thought of Tolek's hands exploring my body instead. The joints in my fingers screamed, but I remembered the calluses I worked so hard to form in training and the power in my blood when I wielded Starfire and Angelborn.

Angelborn? The darkness breathed, almost in recognition. It caressed the spear across my back, but I did not let it break my guard.

"One foot at a time," I coached myself. "Brace the other, lower carefully."

I wasn't sure how many steps it took until I met rocky earth. I couldn't see past the rush of images in the pressing darkness. Blindly stretching out a toe, I tested the ground. It appeared solid, if on an incline of staggered rock. With a breath, securing my memories against the Pit's, I placed both feet on the ground.

Mystlight flickered, as if it had not been used in decades. Ric had said that though they knew the crown was here, no one had been permitted to descend the pit in years due to its volatility. The mystlight would need to wake. Buried so far beneath the earth, the starkness of it seemed slightly different than our usual imbued light.

The onslaught of wanton images faded as I steadied myself, giving me a chance to reinforce my defenses. I tested the ground with a small jump. When it did not collapse beneath me, I tugged the rope twice again and unhooked it from my harness.

I cradled my injured arm in the other, relieving a bit of the stress on my shoulder while I could. It was likely only badly bruised and would be healed before I even made it out of here, Angels willing.

Blinking to allow my eyes to adjust to the new light, I surveyed the base of the pit. It was much narrower than the mouth towering above, maybe two dozen feet across and made of sharp, rocky steps and spikes. The chill seeped through my fur-lined Mindshaper boots.

The majority of it, though, was empty. A filter of fog or dust moved about, something prickling the back of my neck, but no one and nothing filled the center of the pit.

And about halfway around the wall, at the lowest point of the pit, a stone case protruded, wooden doors sealed tightly over it.

That is where the power comes from. That is what's been calling to me.

I crept closer, bracing for something to lash back at me.

I thought back to the fight on the Seawatcher platforms and what Malakai had told us of Firebird's Field. Each had been tailored to their Angel's and clan's practices and pillars. As I approached the stone case, wariness bracketing my muscles, I searched history for indications of what would be planted here. To decode what the Angel who had descended into madness would consider a test of valor.

And when I reached the case and stretched a hand out to wrap my fingers around the metal with assured, unflappable movements, pain radiated through my skull.

I collapsed to my knees. It took everything in my power to maintain my hold on the handle. My head was splitting, pain shooting down the center between my eyes and around the back.

Warmth spread along my neck, uncomfortable and burning. My injured shoulder screamed.

And under the mounting pressure, I dropped my mental defenses.

A swarm of images assaulted me, my fears rising to the surface. The Battle of Damenal played on repeat in my mind, each death reoccurring in slow motion. The initial blast that took out the Sacra Temple and the council rumbled my memory again and again and *again*.

I shook with it, my body convulsing on the floor of the pit.

She is playing now, the darkness cooed with glee. *Little seraph, it is so fun feeding me.*

The memories magnified. Each explosion was bigger. Each death bloodier. My feet froze to the cobblestones, and all I could do was watch.

Watch as each of my friends died.

As Jezebel took a blade through the heart, her eyes wide.

As a spear went through Cypherion's skull this time, and he fell, lifeless.

As Tolek was buried beneath rubble, never to be found.

That one—that was the one that nearly broke me. But instead of giving in to the darkness, fury burned a spiral through my chest. It shot up my spine and ignited the rage I'd fallen to so many times before.

The one I'd tried to suppress.

Only now, I allowed it to flare freely. It powered the Angelblood instilled in my veins, ravaged the darkness until it swallowed back the temptations. In its place, I shoved my strongest, formative moments. I embraced the power of my Revered's vow that had scared me. I indulged in the pain I'd suffered with Malakai and flooded my heart with the safety and adoration Tolek ingrained in me—with the dreams he allowed me to consider.

As burning power thrummed through me, I cried out against the pain and forced myself upright, swinging the door open.

The hinges cracked. The wood splintered.

And before me sat a twisted piece of obsidian metal, forged into vines with thorns jutting from the gnarled surface.

Thorn's crown. Not whole, but half of a small circle.

She has found it, the darkness called. I couldn't decipher what was in its tone, but fog swirled around me, obscuring my vision. Swiping the crown from its case, I ran. Dust clouded the air, but I pushed back the way I came.

Then, maniacal laughter echoed against the walls, jarring my bones.

My boot caught on a rock, and I flew to the ground. I kept my hand locked tight on the shard of crown, but my bad arm caught the impact. My tunic tore, elbow scraping across the dirt, the roaring darkness swallowing my hiss of pain.

Blood bloomed quickly in the wound, dripping to the ground, and sprinkling small dots of crimson.

And—those spots shone. They sent beacons of light up through the fog.

Angellight. I knew it from the rioting of my own Angelblood.

"What in the fucking Angels?" Frantically, I looked around me.

It was still only me in this pit, the mouth towering high above, obscured.

Calm, I reminded myself. *I needed to remain in control.*

Watching those small drops of my blood fade into the ground, their light extinguishing slowly, I tried to breathe deeply enough to steady my heart rate. I looked at the broken crown in my hand, and told myself to ignore the icy fingers crawling beneath my leathers. They danced across my spine, around my ribs, assessing my bones, and that nameless voice whispered temptations in my ear.

Let me see your deepest wants.

"No!" I shouted. I needed to force it back. I needed—

As the last of the light from my blood faded, a final hope fluttered to mind.

I lifted my scraped elbow and swiped a fresh line of crimson across the crown's thorny surface.

And Angellight burst forth from the emblem.

It was different from the others I'd bled on. This Angellight was cold and scattered patches, silver clouds gathering. Uncertain and lost, but trying to guide me, perhaps.

The voice shrieked as it was forced back.

In its place, a window opened. I blinked against the harshness of its luminous edges. They faded as it spread out, an image transposed over the pit rather than a physical chamber here itself. A veil was draped across the scene, the contents murky. Figures fluttered behind it. They seemed familiar, but my head spun too much to decipher who it was.

They looked at me, though. Truly *saw* me. Whoever they were, they were aware I was here, looking back at them.

I should go to them, speak to them, but the moment I took a step, the veil thickened. The vision dimmed until it shattered to golden particles of dust mingling with the earth around me.

Shaking my head, I turned. Whatever that was—whoever it was—would wait. I had what I came for, and I needed to get out of this pit before the voice returned.

I fumbled against the rock wall until I found the rope and clipped myself back in. My body was too wrung out to make the entire climb on my own, so I braced my feet against the rock and tugged three times.

I walked upward, helping where I could, but with everyone above, it didn't take long for them to hoist me out. The mouth of the pit grew larger, the lights piercing through the fog, and encroaching safety wrapped its arms around me.

No—those were real, strong arms lifting me from the ledge and holding me tightly. I breathed in Tolek's spicy citrus scent as I caught my breath, and I let myself sink into him. The security which had helped me below was reinforced.

"What happened?" he whispered once I was breathing regularly. I realized how disheveled I must be—torn and bloodstained tunic, dirt smeared on every surface. I met Cyph's eye over Tolek's head, and we exchanged a grim nod of understanding.

"I—" I took a deep breath. "I got it."

Holding my hand open, I presented them the piece of Thorn's crown, a half-circle the size of my palm. "There was only half. The fifth Angel emblem."

"You're certain?" Malakai asked.

I nodded. Now that I wasn't being assaulted by my fears and... whatever else had been down there, the pulsing connection with this item was strong. To prove it, I removed a glove and pinched one of the thorns between my fingers. The instant burn was a welcomed confirmation.

"Spirits," Tolek grumbled as he watched.

As I told them of every moment of the pit I could recall, Santorina crouched beside me and cleaned the dirt from my scrape, setting my shoulder in a makeshift sling. She assured me it was okay, but this would take the strain off. Ric asked a number of questions about the forces against me, and I answered as best as I could remember, unsure what the Mindshaper was making of it all. I'd find out later.

Relaxing back into Tolek's arms when Rina finished, I surveyed my friends and realized only the Mindshapers and my core group were around me.

"Where are the others?" Leaning around them, I spotted Vale a way down the cavern, clutching her head.

"Preparing," Malakai said. My body chilled. "We received a letter while you were down there." He extended a piece of worn parchment. Behind him, Esmond and Gatrielle walked back into view, assisting a vacant Mila with her pack.

Unfolding the note, I recognized our Master of Weapon's handwriting, and my stomach plummeted deeper than the pit with her vague but immediate command.

Get your asses back to camp NOW.

Chapter Forty-Nine
Damien

Thorn's keening wails split the air. They bounced off craggy rock walls, each stalagmite and stalactite amplifying them. His shrieks shattered into a cackling laugh and murky silver light burst around him, wings inflating and diluting.

"She comes to play. She comes to play," Thorn cheered. He released another chilling laugh, and a shining crown flared to life around his head.

On the edge of the chamber, the veil fluttered, ebbing with a life we could not touch. Thorn lunged toward it. Ptholenix and I gripped his arms, and he sank against us without a fight.

"Feed the fears, little child, kissed by Angels," the Mindshaper guffawed. "Frights and horrors and dismays—they are so fun to play."

His wails bit through me.

Vaguely, I remembered a time when his force ran deep and strong. When his frame was sturdy, not wracked by tremors. But my brother was no longer that mortal man. The light rimming his head only reinforced that. It pulsed with sharp, dark thorns, the silver melting into black.

Before my eyes, an inky substance dripped from one spike. Thorn cackled again.

A glance at Bant and the slight shake of his head confirmed

what I already knew. This was not a result of shedding power as I had once seen, nor as Bant had conducted. This was different.

"Compose yourself," our master commanded, as if Thorn could so easily regulate these matters. As if we had not longed to help him since before we had ascended.

Thorn only continued to laugh.

"Kissed by Angels," he repeated.

And the veil continued to ripple through our chamber. Pushing. Stretching. But the shadow wavering behind it was gone.

Kissed by Angels—those words echoed through my mind. Could he mean the ones we mourned?

I read the question across our master's storm-laced stare as well.

"Millennia," he whispered, a softer sound than he usually bore, an unrecognizable tone to it. One of tangled fear and hope. Of star-bound, fate-kissed beings.

Chapter Fifty
Malakai

I breathed a surprising sigh of relief when we returned to the mountains, and I saw my tent. That small, unfurnished haven on the border of camp was comforting as I approached to deposit my pack. It was as untidy and empty as I'd left it, yet as I stepped across the threshold and tucked the tent flaps back to let in the fresh dawn air, the nerves I hadn't realized I was carrying in my shoulders unknotted.

Well, a bit. There was still—

"My long-lost brother returns." Barrett formed a shadow in the open entrance to my living quarters, his lean frame outlined by the rising sun. Rebel bounced around his feet, seeming to triple in size in the weeks I was gone.

"I assume this is your doing?" I gestured to the burning myst-light and the wrapped parcel on the side table that smelled suspiciously of smoked meats. My stomach rumbled as I looked at it. Quickly splashing water on my face and hands, I unwrapped the package and dug in to the first fresh food I'd had in days.

"I wouldn't want our poor former-Mystique heir to suffer a chill." Barrett dragged a ringed hand through his dark curls. I didn't flinch at the reference to my former life. Perhaps because it was Barrett who said it, having given up his own title, or perhaps because I was desensitized to it all. Maybe I was healing? Spirits if I knew.

"Thank you," I said, bending to pull spare leathers from my trunk and kicking off my boots. Though winter whipped through the southern mountains, it was mild compared to the underground Mindshaper weather I was dressed for.

"He's missed you terribly, Malakai," a taunting voice echoed from around the side of the tent. Dax approached, dressed in a fine gray tunic, leather pants, and boots much like Barrett's. I'd thought our meeting with Lyria was urgent, but neither of them were dressed for battle.

Slinging an arm around his partner's shoulder, Dax added, "Hasn't stopped whining. If you weren't related I'd be jealous."

"You don't get jealous." Barrett rolled his eyes, swatting Dax's hand from his shoulder. "I wouldn't mind it every so often."

Dax snorted. "Not that you are aware of."

I shucked the thick tunic over my head and replaced it with a lighter linen shirt, buckling leathers over top. Then, I changed into a clean pair of pants and sat down to pull on the worn boots I preferred, everything molded to me.

Barrett's jaw dropped. "What does that mean? Are you jealous over someone else?"

As I listened to their bickering, I looked over the scar on my calf. The one I'd received for my own cowardice. It had healed nicely, and when I saw it, I didn't remember the pain. Angels, it was likely the only one I didn't feel anguish over.

Instead, delicate hands assessed it in my mind. Wide eyes looked up at me from between my legs, and my pulse sped at every indecent thought whirling through my head—thoughts of other scars and the way I wanted to know their stories, if only to avenge them.

Shaking my head, I pulled my boots up and laced them tightly.

"No, you insufferable ass." Dax sighed, exasperated despite the smile on his lips. He took Barrett's face between his hands. "It means I show the possessive side to other men who look at you but I'm sure to behave myself when you're around. A prince's consort must always be well-trained, mustn't he?"

Barrett fisted a hand in Dax's tunic and forced him a step closer. "I prefer to see the untamed side if I have any—"

"All right," I interrupted, straightening up from my cot and wrapping a cloak around my shoulders. "Before you two start fucking on the floor of my tent, I was under the impression we were in a hurry."

I wouldn't tell them, but I thought a part of me missed them.

Camp was starting to wake as we made our way to the commander's cabin. There were less lively cheers than normal, fewer taunting remarks and booming laughs from our soldiers as they prepared for breakfast, training, or whatever duties they were assigned.

"What's happened?" I finally asked.

"Lyria wants to discuss everything together," Dax answered, slipping into the seriousness of general.

"What happened with you all?" Barrett followed up, stealing a bite of the food he'd given me.

"Ophelia wants the same." She'd requested we all wait to discuss the new emblems we'd found until we were secure in Lyria's cabin. Fine by me, as only a fraction of my attention was on those damn Angels anyway. Truthfully, I'd handed Lucidius's journal to Ophelia, unable to focus on it. My mind was swimming with a blank, blue-eyed stare and echoing with sobs.

Stomach suddenly rocking, I flung the last bites of my food to Rebel as I climbed the porch steps to Lyria's cabin. I knocked the snow off my boots and swung the door open, wary of what awaited us.

The living room turned war council was quiet, though. Only Lyria and Cyren stood off the kitchen, muttering in low voices. The Starsearcher was forcing a mug into the Master of Weapons' hands, expression stern. Lyria scoffed, but accepted.

"Hello, you two." Barrett strolled right in, flopping down on the couch. Dax fell beside him, and the former prince kicked his feet into his consort's lap.

Lyria and Cyren snapped to attention as if they had not even heard us enter. "Hello," Lyria rushed. "You've all finally made it back." She fiddled with her mug.

"We have." I flashed the Engrossians a glance, my brows pulling together at Lyria's stiffness. They both only shrugged.

Boots echoed down one of the hallways, and my heart kicked up hopefully. But it wasn't the person I expected to join us.

"Erista?" Jezebel gasped behind me.

Spinning, I found her gripping the front door handle. A cold breeze shoved her hair into her face as Tolek and Cypherion stepped around her, but Jez didn't even appear to notice.

Her eyes were locked on the figure striding through the living room as if she'd disappear if Jezebel looked away.

Stopping in the center of the wide rug and squaring her hands on her hips, Erista said with a feline smile, "Hi, J."

Jezebel catapulted across the room, then, arms and legs tangling around her partner's body like she'd never let go. "I missed you so much," she breathed, voice catching in her throat with a rawness I'd rarely heard from the girl.

She had been through so much lately, trying to navigate this newfound power while fearing what it meant. And since she and Erista parted ways back in the mountains—on the heels of an argument, from what Ophelia had implied—she'd seemed lonely.

She had her sister—she had all of us—but we weren't Erista.

"This is the reunion I've been waiting for!" Barrett cheered, clapping his hands. Cypherion, Tolek, and I embraced Erista, too, but my eyes kept sweeping over the scene, looking for one person.

Finally, I caught Lyria's gaze. With a subtle downturn of her lips, she inclined her head toward the stairs. Without another word, I slipped up to the second door on the right.

I rapped my knuckles on the wood, the sound as hollow as the hole widening in my chest.

"Mila?" I said quietly enough that no one in the living room would hear. The last time I stood outside this door flashed through my mind. When I'd walked in on her in nothing but white lace and scarred skin. So much had changed since then, and still one thing had not: I wanted to support her. Whether that meant bickering during training, avenging those scars, or sitting quietly beside her while she found her voice again.

Finally, a dull voice floated through the wood. "Come in." And my chest nearly collapsed to hear her speak again.

The room was lit by candles, not a hint of mystlight brightening the warm wooden walls. She stood before the mirror, mind-lessly running a comb through her hair. Leathers and dirt still clung to her and that damn haunting stare met mine in the glass.

"Are you okay?" I asked, hesitating in the doorway. *Stupid question. Of course she's not okay.*

I wasn't sure if I should approach or give her space. Wasn't sure at all what was going through her head or what she needed. All I knew was I wanted to be here.

"Mmhmm," she hummed, but it was flat. Unconvincing.

Taking a deep breath, I stepped fully into the room. When she didn't argue, I closed the door behind me. I waited for her to ask me to open it, to ask me to leave, but she only kept combing her gnarled hair. Her strokes only skimmed the knots, not truly trying to detangle them at the roots but burying them beneath a silken facade.

With hesitant steps, I approached her. I made sure to keep myself fully visible in the mirror. Her pleas to not be touched echoed in my mind.

"May I?" I asked, pointing at the comb in her hands.

Without saying anything, she held the comb over her shoulder. Relief unfolded in my chest.

There was clearly still so much wrong, but this—a slight offer of her hand, a bead of invitation to stay here with her when she was drowning—it was something.

In silence, I parted her hair into small sections and began running the comb through it. I'd spent enough time with Ophelia and Jezebel to understand I needed to work from the bottom up. At the larger tangles, I sprinkled water over the strands to ease the damage.

With the proximity and a physical action to assist her with, my nerves cooled. I thought her frame relaxed a bit, too.

"Sorry," I gasped, when the comb jerked her head.

"It's okay," she said, voice hollow still. "Didn't hurt."

As I worked a particularly stubborn knot through the ends of her hair, the questions pushed up my throat. I suppressed them until I was done. Only once I'd set the comb down on the dresser did I capture her eyes in the mirror again and asked, "What happened in the Labyrinth, Mila?"

Fuck subtlety, I supposed. She wasn't going to be coaxed out of this mood gently after days.

Her spine straightened, fingers curling into fists. "What do you mean?"

"I mean you disappeared on us." I swallowed. "On me. You were there one day and gone the next. When I found you— " She flinched, and I cut off my question. "Why?"

She was quiet.

"You can trust me." I hoped after all the hours we spent together, after the steps we'd been steadily taking to unravel the scarred parts of ourselves, she knew that was true. "Whatever happened, I won't repeat it."

If someone had hurt her, if whoever had been dead beside her had done something to cause this, I might summon an Angel just to resurrect the bastard and kill him again. But I wouldn't have to tell anyone *why*.

Mila was too lively to shrink into herself this way. The effects of that hopeful light had brightened my shadows in the temple in Damenal and every day we'd trained since. It pushed my own boundaries, forcing me to address the pain I buried. It couldn't be snuffed out now. *She* couldn't be.

"Nothing happened," she mumbled. Her eyes stayed on mine, though, and there was a silent question there. A tremor of someone begging for help but unsure of the words. Of someone trapped in her own mind when she'd fought so hard to break free.

"Talk to me," I pleaded. Why did I feel as desperate for this answer as she looked to speak it? "I promise you'll be safe. I'll help you."

That was why.

Because Mila had gotten through to me when no one else could, had challenged me in a way I'd needed while never crossing the blurred lines I didn't even understand. Now I wanted—needed —to help her.

"Nothing happened." Tears rolled down her cheeks, a crack in her armor as those eyes continued to beg. *Help me say it.* "Nothing

—nothing—" *Help me.* Her voice went ragged. And then, a sob racked her body. "Nothing."

Her entire frame shuddered, usually as solid as a fortress before me, now collapsing to her knees.

I fell right beside her, palms pressing into the wooden floor as I resisted the urge to pull her to me. My throat thickened with whatever misery she was going through. It coated the air and made my nerves stand on end.

Mila's hands were tight around her wrists as she rocked, clutching those gold cuffs like they were her last lifeline—like her heart beat within them, and if she let go, it would be giving up. She shook her head violently, muttering words I couldn't hear beneath her breath.

Help me say it, her stare continued to plead.

"One word, Mila. Give me one word, and then we'll get to the next one."

She blinked at me a few times, seeming to realize I was here. I wasn't leaving.

"A crack." She tried to breathe evenly over the sobs, but the words came out choppy.

"A crack?" I repeated quietly.

"A crack." She nodded. Her tears still flowed, but her eyes held mine, and she summoned some kind of unprecedented strength. "Up near the ceiling. Water trickling down from it. *Drip. Drip. Drip.*" Her hands twisted around her wrists with each word. "All the hours I spent in there. *Drip. Drip. Drip.*"

Slowly, gently, I extended a hand, stopping inches away from her. "Can I?" I looked between her wrists and her eyes.

Help me.

A few deep breaths. A nod.

Carefully, I unlatched her fingers from her cuffs and pulled both of her hands between my own. They were cold, palms sweaty. I rubbed them softly to warm her, and fuck, being able to at least touch her smoothed over the hole in my chest, helping me focus.

"Why did that bother you, Mila?"

"Because." She took a huge breath, deciding. Her blue eyes, usually so assessing, but now so vulnerable, explored mine. She searched for something—I didn't know what. Seemed to find it, though. "I was a prisoner of war for three months, Malakai."

My world froze.

Then, it exploded. All I saw was dawning realization bathed in blood as my heart cracked open for the woman before me.

A prisoner.

Three months.

The scars covering her body—

Oh, fucking Spirits, it made so much sense. Her ability to be in my head. To somehow understand what I was feeling when no one else could. Her strength, her recovery expertise, and her sensitivity to touch when she'd been trapped.

When I'd met her, it was obvious she hadn't been training recently based on the lack of calluses on her hands, how smooth they'd been. She probably hadn't fought since the war. Until Daminius, and then she dove headfirst into the new phase. Everything Lyria had said came back to me.

We've stuck together ever since the treaty.

When one of us wakes screaming in the night, the other is always there to remind her where we are.

And it was all Lucidius's fault. She'd suffered worse than I'd ever imagined due to the war that man and his mistress had ignited. That brought bile up my throat—I shouldn't be the one to comfort her—but as she opened her mouth to continue, I forced it aside. This was about her.

"For nearly one hundred days, I lived in a pit in the ground with bars over my head and brush dragged across them. I rarely saw the sun or the sky. They only let me out for..." She gestured to the scars on her legs. "And for this..."

Then, she did something I never thought I'd see. Pulling her hands from mine, she unclasped the ivy-carved cuffs she wore every day. They clattered to the wood. And what was beneath—

Scars, but so much worse than those peppering the rest of her skin or even my own. Ridges from restraints, and twisted flesh so mangled, the magic of our mountains had barely been able to heal it.

I swallowed thickly, forcing the lump in my throat down. "How?"

"Fire. Repeatedly." She didn't elaborate—didn't need to. I could imagine the agony of burning ropes tied around your wrists.

"And how...how did you end up there?" I probably should have shut up. Should have stopped making her talk about it. But that *help me* stare echoed, and I needed to know everything she was willing to share. How she'd endured and how she continued on so I could help her find that strength again.

And I think she needed to say it.

"Raid gone wrong." Her eyes dropped to her wrists. "I wasn't quick enough. They killed most, but kept me. Probably thought I was the easiest because I was the smallest."

"And being in the Labyrinth cave-in brought those memories back?" I held one of her hands in my own again and rubbed circles between her shoulder blades with the other. She didn't recoil from the touch this time, instead relaxing into it.

"Yes, because of that damn *drip, drip, drip.*" The tears had stopped flowing, her glassy, red-rimmed eyes heating. "Water dripped through the roof of the pit every night I was trapped there. From the edges of the ferns they covered it with, to the rocks I had as a bed. For nearly one hundred days, all I saw was a puddle that would dry up each afternoon only to replenish itself overnight. All I heard was *drip, drip, drip.* I'd gone so long, healed so much, and then *that* had to ruin it."

She shrank into herself, reliving her pain.

"Just because you had a setback doesn't mean you haven't still healed, Mila," I said. "It doesn't mean you won't heal again."

Her isolated stare as she dragged a finger over her scars as if they were disgraceful and must be erased wrenched my gut. So I reminded her she wasn't alone anymore and told her something of my own experience.

"I counted," I said. Finally, she turned inquisitive, wet eyes on me. "When I was in my cell. I counted things. The drops of blood on the walls, the days passing, the splinters in my skin. I counted when I thought I was spiraling. Eventually, the repetition numbed my brain enough that I didn't feel anything."

"I couldn't count," she responded softly, sniffing. "The

number would have been too high. It would have driven me crazy even faster, knowing how much that water dripped." There was no judgment in her voice. No indication that either of our experiences were worse than the other. Nothing but a shared understanding of doing whatever it was you had to do in order to survive.

The fact that she still stood each day was astounding. Never mind the fact that she had eagerly rejoined the war force. *I told her she didn't have to come*, Lyria had said. She wanted to be our Angel-damned *general*.

Her breath shuddered again. Moving in front of her, I ducked to catch her eye. "You're not there anymore, Mila. You're out. You're safe."

"Am I?" she asked, and it was the most doubt I'd ever seen her show. "Look at what we're facing. What if it happens again?"

"It won't," I growled, stopping myself from gripping her hands too tightly. "I won't allow it."

"You can't protect me." She shook her head, another tear escaping. "The odds are against us."

"Fuck the odds." I wiped the tears from beneath her eyes, grateful she was allowing me to touch her now. "The odds were against you surviving what you did. The odds were against me ever making it out of my own horrors, and here I am. I'd say we're good at defying them."

She sighed, shoulders slackening, but I couldn't tell if it was relief or exhaustion weighing her down. She turned to watch her reflection in the mirror. "I think I'd take my own life before I ended up there again."

My heart lurched into my throat. "It will never come to that, Mila. I promise. I will protect you."

And somehow, in the span of a sentence, my life switched from my own mere survival to centering around her. To protecting *her*. To bringing back her light and nurturing it. Because Mila...she was a survivor.

She wasn't a fortress as I'd thought her to be, impenetrable walls towering to keep everything out. There was a gate—one she opened sparingly. Cautiously.

She hadn't locked her problems out like I had. Her scars were in the mortar, holding the bricks together. Her past and present, her fears and dreams, formed those bricks. It was obvious based on the anger she expressed at her progress being knocked back. Those scars built her, but they did not control her. She allowed them to retain their strength—enough to melt her down again—because it forged her.

And I didn't want to break those walls down as I once thought I did. I wanted to wait until the day she opened that gate for me. She'd given an inch, but I'd wait for her to throw it wide. Until then, I'd take what she gave and set up guard outside. When she was ready for me and my fucked-up past to venture within those walls and help her secure the foundation, I would.

"We make quite a pair, don't we?" Mila asked with a forced half-smile.

I swallowed. "Yeah, we do."

Her eyes flitted to the door. "Can we stay here for a little longer?"

"As long as you need," I promised.

Then, I scooped her up and pulled her into my lap. I didn't care that there was a war council waiting for us. That death was knocking on our doors. We sat there like that until her small breaths stopped shuddering, her demons easing.

And even then, a piece of me did not want to let go.

CHAPTER FIFTY-ONE
OPHELIA

"OPHELIA!" A VOICE CALLED THROUGH THE STIRRING camp as I left Sapphire in the stables. She'd been slightly skittish, which was unusual, but then, she and the other horses hadn't known why we were underground for days. It had set even my nerves on edge, the Bond soothing now that we were back among our mountains.

"Hello, Vale." I smiled at her easily, picking my stride back up as she fell in beside me. Lyria wanted us at her cabin as soon as possible. "Where have you been?"

Snow dusted the tops of cabins and tents, powdering the ground. The start of a storm. I wrapped my cloak tighter around me, willing the Angels to make it an easy one.

"The temple," she said.

My step nearly faltered. Flicking my gaze to her, I caught her rolling her lips between her teeth. "How was that?"

"It was...not as bad as it has been. Perhaps because I was actually in a temple this time."

"Has that been known to happen? To falter when you're in other locations?"

"Well, no." We walked between two single-occupant cabins belonging to a couple of the generals, I believed. Vale fidgeted with her cloak. "Typically, we can read wherever. The sessions are stronger in temples and strongest in our own territory."

That made sense. The Angels all had boundaries to their power, a scope they and those who wielded it were confined to. Like Thorn's restriction of Ricordan to not manipulate my mind as I dropped into the pit. Still, Vale seemed unsettled.

With a hand on her arm, I stopped her outside of Lyria's cabin. Pools of buttery light poured through the windows and warmed the icy ground beneath our boots. The last blades of the year's grass withered in the encroaching-winter air.

"Have you been feeling okay otherwise?"

She scuffed her boot across the slush of dirty snow lining the stairs. "You noticed."

I nodded. She'd been crouched against a wall as I emerged from the pit, her head in her trembling hands, fighting to stay conscious. I'd caught similar ailments a few times on the remaining journey. "Did you try to read while I was down there?"

"No." She shook her head softly, the light emphasizing the purse of her lips and her wide olive eyes. "I think it has something to do with the emblems and this Angel power."

I twirled the ends of my hair between my fingers, leaning against the banister. "The first time it happened was when we tried to summon Damien, correct?"

She nodded. "It happened again in Gaveral, and there had been other spells, but nothing as drastic until the Labyrinth at breakfast that morning. While you were in the pit, I thought I saw..."

I stood up straighter. "What did you see?"

"I thought I saw them again. Your ancestor. Angels and...and gods shrouded by their own light."

Had that been who I saw behind the veil in the pit? Angels? Gods?

"And during the interrogation, when Jezebel and I used our power at the same time, they seemed to...converge."

I chewed my lip, watching the ground as I considered. I had an obvious, explicit connection to these emblems, but Malakai had found the Bodymelder token—not me—and now Vale's readings seemed to be disturbed by them, too. And Jezebel...none of it was adding up.

"I have an idea, though," Vale interrupted.

Lifting my chin to see a hesitant smile, I nodded. "Whatever you need."

~

VALE and I were some of the last to enter the war council. Barrett and Dax both crashed into me before the door had even shut fully behind us. After releasing me from a crushing hug, the former prince took my arm in his hand, gently turning it over to look at the spot where his mother's poison had once puckered my skin. The creeping black tendrils were gone, a fresh pink scar fading in their place.

"How does it feel?" Dax asked as Barrett gently dragged his thumb over it.

"Like new." I smiled up at them. Though there were still questions hovering around us, I'd take each small win. "And Santorina saved the...whatever came from my arm." I wasn't sure what to call the thing—that poison. "It's dissolved into a tar-like substance, but she's studying it now."

They grinned back. "Thank the Angels," Barrett said, his eyes flicking over my shoulder. "I see you've remained unchained?"

I turned to see Vale's eyes drop to her wrists, rolling and flexing her hands. "Earned my way out, much as you did, Prince."

If possible, Barrett's grin widened, all white teeth on display as a laugh burst from him. "To those who have broken their chains." He offered her a small nod, but I didn't think he noticed when Vale averted her gaze. I thought of the brand marking her shoulder, now tattooed over with silver ink. She had spent too much of her life in chains, and that was another reason I would honor the request she made of me outside—with my own parameters, that is.

"Artale will see that queen rot in the Spirit Realm for what she's done to you," a voice I recognized called from the living room. But how—

Pushing past Barrett and Dax to step into the cabin fully, I found Erista perched on the back of a leather couch, arms firmly around Jezebel's shoulders in front of her.

"Erista!" I rushed over, hugging the two of them and meeting the smile my sister couldn't hide. "What are you doing here?"

Over her shoulder, Tolek smirked at me. At his side, Cypherion talked animatedly with Lyria and three warriors I assumed were the generals. Ricordan stood with them, acting as our official liaison with the Mindshaper rebels.

"Research can only be so helpful," the Soulguider offered. I understood. This war was pressing down on all of us now, and we wanted to act. "Meridat and the other apprentices will handle things on that front. The Spirits have been loud lately; I needed to be here." She rested her chin on my sister's shoulder, and my heart thudded. Not only for them, but for all of us. For this band of warriors stitching itself together to fight this battle. There were armies beyond these walls, yes, but in here—these were the people who led the charge. The ones who made me feel whole. Unstoppable.

Stepping back, I assessed the room for the first time. It was a large open space with stairs leading up on one side and a hallway off the back. A kitchen took up one side of the cabin, Esmond's supplies littering the counters, though he, Gatrielle, and Santorina were in the infirmary tent. A simple light fixture hung from the ceiling, orbs of mystlight undulating within and matching ones fixed to the walls. Walls that had been decorated with plans and maps and lists of troops. Numbers and names and strategies.

The permanence of it all struck me, unsettling something in my gut.

I brushed it aside and circled the large table strewn with information, sigils defining the location of various clans' forces. Not for the first time, the depth of this war settled on my shoulders. And my inexperience pressed down with it.

I had been raised to be a hand in diplomacy, but that was vastly different from actually standing on a front line. I had been handed prophecies and sent to find emblems. That was territory I was comfortable navigating, though it held so many mysteries. As my eyes roved the pages pinned to the walls, I knew the breadth of what we faced went beyond me.

Lyria and her generals, though—they had done this. They had survived this before. Fought for this. Defended this.

We were in capable, victorious hands.

"How has it been?" And with my question, the mood shifted, weighing heavily on all of us. Conversation faded, eyes and smiles dropped, and everyone turned to Lyria.

"There's no point hedging it." Lyria strode to join me at the far wall, the pleats of her leather skirt swinging around her thighs, her boots echoing hollowly against the wood. Vambraces shone with sharpened knives against her wrists as she extended a hand. Always ready for her next fight, the commander embodied every bit the war leader she'd become. "They're planning something. We don't know what. See here." She dragged a finger down a piece of parchment scribbled with dark ink. "These are the accounts of their recent attempts."

"Each has been short," Dax continued, coming up on my other side. "Testing different points in our defenses. They're erratic and unpredictable. Not the organized strategy their infantry took in the Engrossian-Mystique war. All pull back before they become too devastating for us or them."

"*Have* any been devastating for them?" I asked, stepping closer to take in each skirmish.

"Less so than us," Dax confirmed, grimacing. We still stood, though. Hope was not yet lost.

"Tell her of the shocks," said a warrior I didn't know with long dark hair braided in a coronet.

"I take it you're the Starsearcher," I said, noting the sigil printed across their leathers and the blue cloak. "Nice to meet you, despite the circumstances."

"Cyren Marvana," they said, nodding their chin. "And likewise."

"And this is Amara, cousin to Chancellor Ezalia," Lyria said, gesturing to the next general. Her hair was as sandy as their beaches, and she shared Ezalia's sea-glass eyes. "And our Soulguider General, Quilian."

"Brother to your beloved Erista," the man added. They bore the same bright smile and thick eyebrows, though Quilian appeared much older.

"Our parents can never seem to decide when they're finished

having children." Erista answered that unspoken question as if it was one they often received.

"We have a sister nearing her first century," Quilian continued. "But Erista and Temy are the youngest."

"And the most beautiful and wisest," Erista bragged.

Despite the tension in the room, their banter calmed me. It reminded me of the ease and levity we were fighting to restore.

"I suppose we'll see who's the wisest after this meeting," I joked. "Now, you mentioned shocks?" I turned back to Cyren, but it was Barrett who stepped forward.

"Ripples of power have been rocking the mountains. We believe they're coming from my mother."

My stomach squirmed. Natural disasters were not something we could fight. That was a power no one should control.

"But your mother isn't on their line." I tilted my head and walked to the large table in the center of the room, surveying the map of Gallantia. A game board with pieces scattered about. "She was last seen here." I pointed to the Fytar Trench. "When we fought her and..." I met Tol's hardened stare, and sorrow swept through me at what I'd asked him to do.

"When was this, again?" Lyria asked, shuffling sigils about her map.

"About a week and a half ago," Malakai said. I hadn't seen him guide Mila down the stairs. He helped her to the table, pulling a chair out for her to ease into. "Give or take a day." Malakai's eyes did not leave the general for a long moment, but I swore a bit of color had returned to her features.

"That lines up with one of the quakes," Dax confirmed, looking over Barrett's shoulder at their notes. "There was another four days ago."

"And when was the earliest?" Cyph asked. My mind flew down the same path.

"Weeks prior." My stomach swooped at Barrett's words. Cypherion and I locked eyes, his jaw hard as we silently communicated.

"It lines up," I whispered. Cyph nodded, and I addressed the group at large. "It's not the queen doing this."

We explained how the search for the emblems had been progressing. How we'd found three in our time away and how each quake they'd recorded lined up with me bleeding on them.

Erista gasped, looking to her brother. "The rites."

"Xenique's tits," he sighed.

"What're the rites?" I asked.

"The Rites of Dusk. They're sort of sporadic sand storms," Quilian said, "but they occur in the skies. A myriad of purples and reds in a dust cloud hovering above the earth. It's always been believed they're tied to Artale, though the exact purpose is legend. We use them to strengthen our magic."

"There were two lately," Erista added. "The second was the reason I decided to travel here." Her hand locked with Jezebel's. "And Temy—my twin—wrote me that another occurred after I'd left."

"What does that mean?" Amara finally asked. She had fallen into a stunned silence. Ricordan was nodding, finally understanding why we'd been so eager for Thorn's crown.

"It means we're again at a loss for the queen's motives or tactics, but we have a worse opponent in the Angels and potentially Artale, too, if it all connects." Quilian dragged a hand down his face, but something in his words did not sit right with me.

The Rites, the quakes, the trials...Spirits, we'd all been too split. Perhaps if our alliance had been communicating these odd occurrences more frequently, we'd have caught the similarities earlier.

"On the subject of the Angels," Barrett said, casting Malakai a glance.

"You have news?"

Barrett nodded, then addressed the rest of the room. "I've been going through what records I have here, and only one ring can historically be tied to Bant."

"Let me guess," Tolek said, lifting my hand to display the Engrossian sigil ring.

"And you'll never believe how Bant came to own that piece of jewelry," Barrett said. "In a battle with your own Angel."

"Damien," I breathed.

"It seems our rivalry truly stretches back to the age of Angels. Engrossian history is colorful with descriptions of their fights, an infamous one being when Bant himself won a precious gem from his opponent at our Blackfyre and had it embedded in a ring to wear for eternity."

"Why haven't we heard of this?" Cypherion asked.

"History is often written by the victor," Dax said. "Damien likely disguised the loss as something else."

We didn't have time to pick apart Mystique accounts for that, though. "Why does this feud matter?"

"Because," Barrett said as if it was logical, "do you truly believe the Angels stopped feuding when they ascended?" The room absorbed that suggestion. Barrett continued, "I bet it pursued. And if our Angels are still at war, I'd think it safe to presume they're watching ours keenly."

An immortal investment in mortal affairs. It added another layer to everything currently occurring on Ambrisk.

"Perhaps that's what Lucidius knew," Malakai said. He rubbed a hand across his jaw, over that scar. "He was trying to summon Angels, searching for something and traveling the territories, obsessed with this concept of living magic."

"Living magic?" I echoed.

"He kept writing about killing living magic." Malakai shrugged. "Said he had to extract the source."

The room was silent, everyone at a loss for what it meant. I took in all these pieces and continued to sort them in my mind. From how Kakias's power in my arm had felt *alive* against my Angelblood, to how the piece we'd cut out now retained that sentience in its vial. There was an answer here; my shard necklace heated with assurance.

"Regardless of the Angels, there is still a very real threat assaulting our mountains," Lyria said, returning us to the problem we could do something about in this moment. "We need a strategy of how we're going to survive a larger attack." She turned to me. "I want you on the front line with me, Revered."

"Oh, for Damien's sake," Tolek muttered. We both shot him

407

narrowed stares, and he shook his head, knowing it was inevitable. "You two will be my death, I'm sure of it."

He may want to protect me, but when we locked eyes, his nod said he understood there was no way I wouldn't be in the heart of battle. And I knew he loved that determination, even if it scared him. He'd never try to stifle it.

Still, I turned back to Lyria. "With all due respect, Commander, I can't be on the front line."

Her brows shot up. "Why?"

"Because where I am, Kakias will go. It is better for me to lure her away from our troops so she won't endanger anyone else."

"Now to that, I will argue," Tolek blurted. "No way in the Spirit-guarded-Realm are you going after her alone."

I turned to him with a smirk. "Like I'd ever go alone." I tossed him a wink and faced his sister again. "If Kakias dies, her army loses their motivation. *This ends.* We have a much better chance of that if she can't hide behind them."

Lyria's chocolate eyes glimmered with the hope in my voice—with the dream of this war ending before it became as tragic as the last.

"I can offer a small host to accompany you," she said.

"Not warriors whose absence will weaken the line," I argued. "It's going to come down to me and her."

She nodded, her gaze saying a reassured *thank you.* I briefly wondered about the pressure on the young Master's shoulders. She commanded an army of warriors centuries older than her, to the dismay of some of those soldiers. We knew that would be the case, much like my appointment to Revered had been challenged, but Lyria had a mind for battle, and was chosen by Danya herself before her death. She was sharp-witted and well-trained, keen instincts helping her choose which route any given scenario called for.

"My brother will attend you, obviously."

"You can bet Damien's cock I will," Tolek chimed in. A devilish smile lifted his lips, the thought of the adventure heating the air between us.

"I don't think the Angel likes when you say such things," I teased. The back of my neck prickled.

Tolek clasped his hands behind his back. "I don't much like things he says, either."

"Yes, yes, the Angels are frustrating." Lyria waved a hand at her brother, turning back to me. "Who else?"

"I'm going," Barrett asserted. His fingers curled around the arm of his chair. "If you're after my mother, I will be there."

Beside him, Dax looked conflicted. Torn between his position as general and the man he loved. He met Lyria's eyes, a silent question there. She nodded.

"I'm with you, too, Ophelia."

I smiled at the two Engrossians I had never imagined would stand beside us a year ago, now friends I cherished dearly. "I'd be proud to have you both."

"Go to my family's manor in Thorentil," Ricordan offered, arms crossed. "It's abandoned and so far enough on the edge of the city, you should be able to get in without trouble, but the estate will be a good location to lure the queen."

"Thank you." I nodded at the Mindshaper, my heart pounding at the fact that we were truly doing this. Devising a plan. Trapping a queen.

"And Cypherion?" Lyria asked. "He's in your guard, as well?"

"Actually," I said, looking at Cyph. "I have something else I need him to do."

Auburn brows pulled together. "What?" Confusion peaked Cyph's voice.

Vale and I exchanged a quick glance, her head tilted. "Ophelia..."

"Vale needs to return to Starsearcher Territory immediately to reorient her sessions and decipher what has gone wrong with them. Not only are they putting her at risk, but we've determined —based on the timing of her recent episodes—it could be related to the emblems, which means there's a chance something she *needs* to read to help us could be blocked."

Everyone looked to Vale, but her heated gaze remained on me. "And I will be leaving tonight as soon as the sun has set and heading north to avoid the troops, but I will be going alone."

"No, Vale." My voice was firm, bordering on harsh. "You will not be." I turned to Cyph, whose jaw ticked. "You will go with her."

Cypherion pointedly did not look at Vale, though other heads in the room silently swiveled between them.

"No," he finally said. "No, I will not leave when a battle is approaching any day now. I'm needed here."

My chest tightened at the hurt in his voice. Pain from thinking his contribution would be dashed so easily. "You are wanted here." I spoke softly. "Cypherion, you are an asset to every force you're a part of, but we have soldiers trained to be on that line, to see us through that battle. We do not have many that are able to carry out this sensitive mission."

In truth, the only ones I trusted to do so stood in this room.

"I—" He searched for an argument, jaw grinding. "I can't."

"Are you rejecting your orders?" My brows shot up, partially playfully.

"Maybe," he said.

I did not want to pull rank, but if it came to that I would. Still, I had not exhausted my artillery.

"Cyph," I said, not letting his gaze drop but instilling every ounce of vulnerability I could muster into my voice. "I need you to do this for us. I need *my Second* to complete this mission for the good of this entire war, prophecy, and whatever else waits. *Please.*"

Those blue eyes, heavy with uncertainty, bore into mine. We communicated silently, a battle of two stubborn wills. The words we exchanged before I descended into the pit passed between us. Perhaps he needed to get out to truly find himself, to remind him of his promise in the world we all saw so plainly.

"You're unrelenting with this, aren't you?" he finally said.

"Which part?" I asked, not daring to let my hope at that non-denial show.

Cyph leaned forward, bracing his fists against the table, and that analytical mind of his assessed the maps spread before us. He took in every sigil, every border, and calculated how the Angel emblems fit into them.

Briefly, he glanced at Vale.

Then, he said, "All of it." His lip barely quirked at the corner, but I saw it.

Hope flourished, my smile beaming. "Is that a yes? You accept?"

With a sigh, he straightened up. "I accept the position of Second to the Revered of the Mystique Warriors." Tolek cheered, striding around the table to clap Cypherion on the back. "I don't want a formal induction or any sort of celebration. I still think I am a poor choice for this, but you're so damn persistent."

My heart inflated in my chest.

"Thank you." Without a doubt, this was the best decision I had made in my short rule. Likely one of the best I would ever make. "And..."

"And I will accompany Vale to her territory so we may decipher what is causing the faults in her readings and if it connects to the emblems as you suspect." He crossed his arms. "We'll leave tonight. I'll go prepare."

He left without once looking in the Starsearcher's direction. If they were to be traveling together for weeks, that could only last so long.

Vale had been quiet throughout the entire altercation. Meeting her gaze, I asked, "Is that okay with you?"

It was a formality, and she knew that. "Of course. The... company will be well appreciated."

If Cypherion did not pull himself out of whatever grudge he still held against the Starsearcher, I wasn't sure how true that statement would hold. As Vale left to prepare, the timid nod of her head seemed to agree with me.

"The rest of you," Lyria said, calling our attention back. I sank into a chair beside Tolek. "We are directing more attention to the highest lookout points. Amara has secured another unit of Seawatchers, giving us more archery forces."

Longing hung on the sharpened points of those words. It thickened the air around us and bolstered everyone's moods.

"What about the Mindshapers?" Cyren asked. "I've been targeting them in my sessions but the fates are still fogged."

"What about them?" Ricordan echoed.

"Spirits." Lyria rubbed her brow. "I nearly forgot. Kakias's control over her armies and the ability to manipulate Mindshaper magic against us." Tolek tensed, and I placed my hand atop his. "This isn't a normal army we're fighting."

She did not need to explain how that power could drive a whole legion of warriors to madness. How it could torture them with their own thoughts. I heard Tolek's screams every night.

"I might be able to help." I hadn't expected Jezebel to be the one to speak, but realization dawned on me. How she'd communicated with the prisoner and had been working with Trevaneth, using Tolek's research. "My power doesn't work quite the same as theirs, but I have been able to slip through certain things. It may be enough to...assist." There was something in the way her lips pursed that told me she knew more than she let on, but I didn't question it in front of the group.

"You can't be in the battle, then," I said. "Not where you're vulnerable."

I had assumed Jez would be with my team. I hated leaving without her, but if this could help, it was what she was meant to do.

"She can be positioned with the archers on the lookout points," Amara offered. "It is the safest place."

"I'll stay with her as a guard," Erista confirmed, and I thought her brother's shoulders sagged with relief, too.

"Okay." I nodded, deferring to Lyria. "If this is all right with you, I'll support it."

"It's an incredible asset." Lyria's eyes were still slightly wide at Jezebel's revelation. "You Alabaths might save us yet."

"Let's hope." *Or doom us all*, I thought.

We spent the next hours laying a plan against the queen's army with the help of Ricordan, Trev delivering food and lingering on the stairs. Once the sun was high, Lyria adjourned the council, sending us all off with various orders.

There was a storm building across the southern mountains, one that would pose a threat to our troops, but a fiercer one stood around that war table.

"We are securing our defenses," Lyria said from the head of the table as we all stood. Her eyes landed on me. "All except you. You drive as fiercely into their ranks as they've tried to ours. Lure her out, and the rest of us will protect the namesake we were born for. Your group moves tonight."

CHAPTER FIFTY-TWO
OPHELIA

"ARE YOU OKAY WITH THIS?" I ASKED TOLEK AS WE climbed the creaking stairs to our cabin. We'd all agreed to take a few hours to rest before we started preparing.

"Ophelia, when have I ever tried to talk you out of a plan?" One hand guided my lower back as he swung open the front door. Warm mystlight woke with our presence, and I considered. Tolek had always questioned me when necessary, had raised concerns, but never stood against me. That wasn't all that mattered anymore, though.

"I suppose you have a point," I said, removing my cloak. "But as long as we're together, our lives are entwined. I want to be sure you're in agreement with whatever we do."

Gently taking my cloak from my hands, Tolek caught my eyes. "You act as if I wouldn't venture to the Spirit Realm and walk through burning Angellight for you, Alabath. A little trap for a queen is hardly a challenge."

He spoke so casually, but my breath lodged in my throat at the promise. At how my heart fluttered to return it. "Let's focus on the queen for now."

Chuckling, he turned to hang our cloaks by the door. I strode into the room, propping my hip against the leather couch and crossing my arms. Knit blankets hung over the back, their warm tones accenting the thick rug beneath my feet and the dark wood

414

shelves lining one wall. As opposed to Lyria's cabin, which had been converted into a strategy center, this one was quiet and cozy.

It was the second largest next to hers as well. They had saved it for us, which I thought was rather unnecessary given how many warriors had been here much longer than we had. I was fine in a tent. Spirits, as long as we had mystlight or a fire, I was fine outdoors. Angels knew we'd grown used to it. Four bedrooms with a small living space and kitchen was plenty more than we needed. Especially considering how soon we would be leaving.

When I'd asked Malakai why he hadn't taken a room here, he'd mumbled a dismissive excuse. I thought he liked the privacy of his tent. He had never been one for extravagance, now even less so.

Tolek removed his boots, leaving them by the door. The action was so mundane, it made my heart clench. I hoped one day we could lead a life in a home where boots lined the entryway. I hoped cloaks and books and blankets littered the rooms. I hoped lives could be indulged in, not run through as they were now.

My eyes dropped to my Curse scar—the start of all of this—and for a moment I just *hoped*.

A finger touched my chin, tilting it up until I met chocolate eyes. "What's wrong?"

I searched the cabin. "I don't know. This place feels...uncomfortable. Wrong." Like there was so much suffering beyond these walls, how could we hide away in a cabin? It twisted my stomach. "Do you think we'll be fighting like this forever?"

Taking my face in his hands, Tolek pressed one soft kiss to my lips. "We won't be."

"How can you be so certain?" A bit of fear wavered through my words, and I exhaled at finally letting it out.

He sighed, grabbing my hips and placing me on the arm of the couch, then he crouched before me. His hands dragged down my legs, over the Mindshaper leather pants I was still wearing. When he reached my boots, he untied the laces.

"I am certain because I have watched you persevere for years now. I may have been in the background," he said, working one boot off, "but the shadows are a great place to observe. I have seen your strength and the undying love you hold for our people. I have seen how the queen's actions have affected not only us but planted the continent with seeds of reasons to resist. They're growing now, love." Kissing the inside of my ankle, he stood back up and placed his hands on my thighs. "In you, in me. In Malakai and Barrett and every other warrior on the council and beyond. So I feel confident in saying we will fight our way out of this, regardless of how brutal that battle may be, because I have seen it."

Tolek looked around the room, seeming to understand everything I'd seen a moment before. "You want a house like this when we're done? I'll build it myself." He squeezed my thighs, pulling me to the edge of the couch so my legs wrapped around his hips. "I am infinitely yours, *apeagna*, and I will weave new constellations to light the night sky in your honor, if that is what you wish when this is done. A house seems small in comparison."

His nose skimmed my jaw, working a shiver up my spine.

"A life," I said, breathless, "where we aren't running or fighting —that's what I want with you, Tol."

"You can admit you like the thrill of the game, Alabath." His lips ghosted down my neck, pushing aside my tunic to drift across my collarbone. "I see it when you fight. The way you come alive, even if it is to deliver death. Though you want serenity, this is a part of you, too."

Relief unspooled in my chest, warm and inviting, at the reminder that Tolek saw every side of me. He saw the brutal and bloodthirsty, but also the wistful dreamer. Loved them both, too.

"I was born a warrior, and I will always love that," I admitted. "But there is so much more I want to do and become."

I wanted to fall asleep at night and wake to tea in the morning without worrying about who would come for us that day. I wanted to fight, yes, because I'd never be satisfied if I was idle, but not like this.

Two sides of me had been sharpened in this battle thus far. A need for reassurance and a need for revenge. They'd cleaved me after my world was destroyed at the Battle of Damenal, but I was beginning to see how they balanced me instead.

Tolek pulled back to meet my gaze, the amber specks in his eyes completely ignited. "And those constellations?"

"I've had enough of promises built on stars." I needed roots in the ground to steady us, not wishes to the heavens we may never reach. One day, I wanted both. A life of assured safety and endless dreams. For now, though, I just wanted him.

He exhaled a laugh because he certainly had not meant for me to spin the conversation that way, but then his lips dipped to meet me. As his tongue slipped against mine, I melted into him, hands hungrily in his hair and legs wrapping tighter around his hips.

"No way," Cypherion's deep voice boomed through the room causing us to break apart. "Not out here. We are *all* living here!"

"Technically, we're all leaving tonight," I shot back. Tolek's shoulders shook with laughter, his forehead dropping against my temple.

Cyph's eyes narrowed. "I think I might have liked it better when you only bickered with him."

"I prefer this," Tolek said, eyes locked on me.

"I still bicker with him," I corrected. I still enjoyed it, too.

"Yes, but now it ends like this." Cyph waved a hand at us. "And while I love you, Ophelia, I do not want our fights to turn into that."

For the first time since Cypherion entered the room, Tolek looked at his friend, shooting him a murderous glare.

Cyph sighed. "I'm going to take care of some preparations, and when I return, I do not want to find you two naked in the living room, regardless of how long we are calling this place home." Cyph gestured over his shoulder. "You have a room right there."

His stern tone made me laugh, but before I could answer, Tolek grabbed the back of my thighs and lifted me. He kissed me deeply, one hand diving into my hair, the other gripping me to him.

As we passed Cyph, Tol released the hand in my hair and pulled back. "I'll see you later."

"Later?" I asked, as he carried me to our room.

"He and I have things to take care of before we go." Tol kicked the door shut and deposited me on a large bed. The flickering and crackling of a fire filled the room. "But I have more important business here."

I couldn't evaluate the vagueness in his first sentence. Not with his lips warm against mine and his hands deftly untying the binds of my leathers behind my back.

"Before we run again," Tolek breathed against my lips, "I want you properly. In a bed, where your screams can shake the walls." My core ached for him, and I tugged his tunic from his pants, throwing it to the side. When he kissed me again, I moaned against his lips. "That's a start."

He pulled my top over my head, then lifted my hips for my pants to follow. Once we were both only in our undergarments, Tolek slowed down. His tongue stroked lazily against mine, hands roving slowly over my body, not leaving an inch untouched.

Wanting to touch him, too, I dipped my hand beneath the waistband of his undershorts and gripped him. Slowly rotating around his length, I dragged my hand from base to tip.

"Spirits." He shuddered, dropping his head to my shoulder. "I was trying to go slowly with you." His hand ghosted up the inside of my thigh, teasing the thin layer still separating us until I was squirming.

"Not slow," I breathed, watching his fingers skim the trim.

With a devilish smirk, Tolek dragged two fingers over my center, circling over the silk. "Are you sure?" He added pressure, and my legs fell further open around his hips.

"Please," I begged.

At the tremble in my voice, he pushed that layer of silk aside. Two fingers plunged into my center, dragging a moan from my lips.

"Angels, I'm addicted to that sound," he breathed and curled his fingers, making me cry louder. His other hand cupped my breast as he bent down to kiss me. Every sensitive nerve in my body ignited under those skilled hands and tongue. His rough fingers stroking the silk against my nipple were a torturous tease.

I needed more. "I thought you wanted the walls to shake," I breathed.

Tolek looked down at me, that wicked smirk back and his eyes drunk with lust. "If you insist."

Before I realized what was happening, he flipped me onto my

hands and knees and dragged me to the edge of the bed, tearing off my undergarments. His chest pressed against my back, skin warm against mine, as he trailed kisses down my spine. His shorts hit the floor as his fingers continued to slowly coax me toward oblivion.

Then, Tol gripped my hips, lining himself up with my entrance, and pounded into me. From this position, it was so deliciously filling I cried out—his name maybe, or just a cry, I couldn't even be sure as the fire flickering in the room melded with the one between us and everything turned burning.

He alternated between slow, teasing strokes and faster pounding, his hands kneading my backside until I was held right over that edge and begging for release.

"You feel so good like this," Tolek murmured. "On your hands and knees for me, Revered."

"What else?" I asked.

"Hmm?" He hummed, as he slowly pulled back out to the tip and sank forward again.

I glanced over my shoulder, pushing back against him. "What else do you like, Tolek?"

His grip on my hips tightened, eyes darkening. Then, his arm wrapped around my front, pulling my back flush against his chest, and I gasped at the new angle.

Slowly, one hand drifted down my body, stopping on my scars. "I love these," he said. "For so many reasons. But it makes me want to mark you as mine, too."

"I am yours," I breathed as he hit a deeper spot inside of me and his fingers lowered to my clit. "Angels."

With his other hand, Tolek turned my face toward him. His eyes were burning. "Enough of those fucking Angels, love." He kissed me roughly, his tongue timed to the movement of his fingers against my center, his entire body working together to get me where he wanted. My head fell back against his shoulder, and Tolek moved his lips to my neck. When he reached my shoulder, he sunk his teeth in gently. *Marking me as his.*

Spirits, the idea lit up like Angellight within me.

I was barreling toward climax with his hands all over me and him filling me. Right as I thought I would explode, he turned me so my back was against the bed again.

I whined in protest, but Tol brushed my hair from my face. "I want to see you when you come, Ophelia." The sound of his voice nearly undid me. He pushed into me again, and this time he did not take anything slow, driving us both to that edge in a hurry.

And as the spiral of heat built within me, I thought of every promise he'd made to me. Of the safety and the dreams and the home. The home he had become, the one he had always been.

The echo of every vow swam through my mind in a tangle of this lustful oblivion, stars exploding around us and through us. I thought of us planting roots in the ground to tether us together and of wishes upon stars that only we would fulfill together.

I thought of how deeply I loved him and how my world would never be right without him.

My safety, my home. My tether to all that was good. Mine, infinitely.

"Tolek," I cried as I came, and he followed, my name on his lips a sound so heady and lustful and adoring it had me searching for his kiss again.

When we collapsed together on the bed after cleaning ourselves up, sweaty and equally spent, our legs tangled together and my head found the spot above his heart. Tol ran a hand absently through my hair, toying with the ends as we both watched the fire and talked about everything except the looming battles.

This is what it is to be happy, I realized as his laugh rumbled against my ear. Truly happy, despite the circumstances of the world around me or the darkness blooming in my soul. To have someone who shone through it all.

I'd always had it as one or the other. The easy bliss or the crushing pain. This was an all-consuming euphoria in the face of the looming unknown, and I would hold onto that until the Angels forced it from my hands.

"Get some rest," he finally said, kissing my forehead.

"You, too," I demanded.

"I'll try." The promise in his voice was so sincere, even those two words had my heart inflating in my chest.

CHAPTER FIFTY-THREE
TOLEK

I SLEPT.

For the first time in memory, I slept soundly for four hours. For most, that wasn't much. For me, it was everything. Because the woman sleeping beside me who was *my* everything made it happen. She'd listened to my fears over recent weeks, reminded me of the facts stacked against them, and did not turn away or cast judgment.

I was not naive enough to think I had escaped nightmares forever—healing did not happen overnight—but as I strolled through the war camp to meet Cypherion and Malakai, I felt the best I had in a while.

They were huddled around a fire when I found them, smoke coiling into the violet sky. The winter sun had already set, sucking out the bit of warmth we were awarded in the southern mountains.

"Fucking Spirits." I rubbed my hands down my arms. "It's colder than an Angel's heart here. How have you been surviving?" I raised a brow at Mali, his cloak open as if worn for formality, not necessity.

"Don't know." He shrugged. "I got used to it."

"Hopefully we won't have to," I added to Cypherion. Even as I said it, though, I couldn't ignore the way Malakai's cheeks were fuller than before. The lift of his shoulders where they'd once drooped under the weight of his scars.

"I won't have a chance to." Cyph kept his narrowed eyes on the fire.

"Are you upset to be going?" Malakai asked. He swung open the pack at his feet and removed three bottles, uncorking each. I wasn't a fan of ale, but I took it regardless. Something about Mali extending this to us, about the three of us gathered around a fire on a cold night, simply discussing our lives, was soothing.

"Not upset to be going," CK grumbled. He sipped his drink and dragged a hand across his mouth as he framed an answer. "I'm going because it's orders from our Revered."

"Try again," I said.

Cypherion raised an auburn brow, but Malakai and I watched quietly until he started fidgeting from the attention. "All right, I'm curious. Does that make you happy?"

"Curious about what?" I asked with a playful lilt.

"Curious about what the fuck is happening to her," he grumbled.

"And why is that?" Malakai mimicked my tone.

"No," Cyph argued, gesturing to Mali with his ale. "Nope, *you* don't get to question me. At least Tol wears his damn heart on his sleeve." He shifted the bottle to me. "I have to answer *his* questions."

"You've barely answered any of my questions in months," I challenged.

"And if I ignore you, I'm sure as Spirits ignoring him."

"Fair enough." Malakai laughed and ran a hand through his hair, a small smile on his lips. Damn was it good to see.

"How's Mila?" I asked.

That smile fell. "She's...okay." He blew out a breath. "No, she's not. She will be okay, though." *I'll make sure of it*, he left unsaid.

His fingers tightened around the neck of his bottle, eyes squinting at the fire. All mirth of a moment ago was gone. Something had shifted. He'd been protective after the cave in, but the dark gleam in his eye was new.

"Is there anything we can do?" Cypherion offered.

"No." Malakai shook his head. "It's her story to tell and hers to ask for help with. She's survived hell, though." He grimaced, and his hand swept across the scar on his jaw. "She's strong."

"You have a type, then." I smirked around the mouth of my bottle.

Malakai narrowed his eyes. "I'm not sharing this time."

I choked at that. Wiping my arm across my mouth as I coughed, I said, "So there is something to share?"

"Not yet."

"Mali," I began. "I think you learned that keeping things in does nothing for you." Now he and Cypherion both turned skeptical looks on me. "Okay, fine. We've both learned how that can hurt. My point is, don't run from this. We can all see what she's done for you. When we left Damenal, you were still that damn shadow of yourself. You've got a bit of your old spark back since being here."

"Tolek's right," Cyph added when Malakai opened his mouth to argue. "You seem like you have...purpose again."

Malakai straightened his spine, running a hand down his leathers. "I think I might. Or an idea of it, at least." Then he deflated a bit, some realization crossing behind his eyes. "I don't know, though. What she survived...what she faced during the war..." He chose his words carefully. "Lucidius did that."

Ah...his reluctance was not because of Mila, then. It wasn't even because of himself or the ghosts of his past he still battled. This doubt was because of Lucidius's hand in whatever Mila had endured.

"That is not your doing, Mali," Cyph said.

"I don't know if she agrees."

"Have you asked her?" Cypherion prodded.

Malakai averted his eyes, so the answer was clearly no. Because he was scared or did not want to push her or some combination of the two. "Do you still blame Barrett for Kakias's actions?"

"No," Mali said, grimacing. "I know better than that now."

I didn't linger on the fact that Malakai had accepted his half-brother in these last few months, though it warmed my spirit.

"And do you think Mila is smart and compassionate enough to see the same?"

"She is extremely intelligent and understands emotional trauma better than anyone I've ever met."

"And you deserve good things," I said.

"Don't stand in your own way," Cyph finished.

Malakai contemplated that, kicking his boot through the snow. I studied his expression, how it morphed from thoughtful to pained to a sly smirk as he considered our words.

Cyph dropped to one of the stumps surrounding the fire. He rested his arms on his knees, his bottle dangling between his fingers as he chewed over his own dilemmas he *refused* to discuss with us. I wished he would. Wished he'd stop bottling up his pain, but when you grew up the way he did, it was easier I supposed.

Cypherion had been alone for a long time before we took him in. He carried more on his shoulders than any young boy should have. A caretaker—that's what he was. One who took what was thrown at him without complaint and found a way to make it work.

I hoped one day he'd stop only making it work. I hoped he would recognize his worth the same way he tried to show Malakai his.

Standing here between the two stubborn asses that were my chosen brothers, I relaxed a bit. They made me feel at home. The second most at home I'd ever felt. The goodbye we'd be saying soon tore through my chest. There were a lot of those happening lately.

"Have you spoken with your sister much?" Malakai asked.

I furrowed my brow at the abrupt change of topic. "No?"

"You should." Malakai nodded.

Lyria was a sensitive topic. I was still understanding the wedges my father dug between us. But when I'd explained it to Ophelia, she'd had nothing but gentle encouragement.

"Yeah..." My voice trailed off for a long pause. "You know," I said, draining the rest of my ale, "I think I have to go."

Cyph's head snapped up from where he'd been entranced with the fire.

"Yeah," Malakai agreed, suddenly eager. "I do, too."

Cypherion sighed as we both clapped him on the shoulder and left. "Don't mind me," his voice followed us. "I'll be here alone."

Chapter Fifty-Four
Malakai

"Mila?" I called, rushing into the stables. I didn't know how I knew she'd be here. I somehow did. And when I saw that long, silky white braid flip through the air as her head turned to me, saw those crystal eyes widen and the sword in her hand, it was like an answer to a question I didn't know I was asking.

"Malakai?" she asked, a hint of amusement I'd missed in her voice. Her cuffs were back around her wrists, her leathers back in place, but a bit of her was looser than this morning.

"I—" I came to a stop in front of her, suddenly unsure about what I was going to ask. Fuck, was this too soon after what she went through? But she licked her full lips, and I didn't give an Angel's wings about anything else. "Do you think children are inherently dictated by the actions of their parents?"

It was certainly not the question she'd expected. Her eyes widened even further, if it was possible. They flicked around my face, picking me into fucking pieces, like she had been all these months.

After a moment, she set down the sword.

She stepped closer to me and lifted the hand I'd clenched into a fist, uncurling my fingers without taking those eyes off me. My muscles eased.

"No, Malakai. I do not think children bear any responsibility for what their parents do." Had she stepped closer again? She was

426

speaking slowly. Each word pointed. "I do not think the decisions your father made have any say in the man you are, unless you let them."

Unless I let them. As I had been since I was imprisoned. I let that man throw away my life and continue to ruin it after his death.

But maybe, if I really was not beholden to the atrocities he was responsible for, if someone who had suffered the brunt of his monstrous actions really felt this way, maybe I could change that path.

Carefully, I reached for one of the stubborn tendrils of hair that always pulled free of Mila's braid. She watched my fingers as I twirled that strand, her lips parting.

"Mila?" A dormant instinct vibrated beneath my skin, begging to be unlocked.

"Mm-hmm," she hummed, eyes bouncing between my hand and my lips.

"Can I kiss you?" I needed clear permission after how her autonomy had been ripped from her before. Needed to hear her say it was all right.

When her eyes finally met mine, and she whispered, "Yes," that beast beneath my skin thrummed.

Slowly, I tucked that strand of hair behind her ear and lowered my lips to hers. She sighed as we met, needing no insistence to let me in. I dragged my tongue against hers with slow but sure strokes, channeling all those promises of safety I'd made her into this one kiss.

Mila tasted like everything I'd imagined and more, sweet and sinful all at once, as if the ghosts of what we'd both survived comprised *us* and were woven into every move we made. She was a damn dream, our lips in perfect sync. She grabbed at my leathers, one hand wrapping around my neck and tugging me closer.

I was hard in an instant, but I didn't want to force past any boundaries. This needed to move at her pace—whatever that was.

Still, gripping her hips, I backed her up to the wooden wall. She leaned against it, and I dragged my hands down her body, memorizing every curve, even through her leathers, and every sound she made. Fuck, I wanted all of her. Every scarred piece— would fall to my knees and devour her if she'd let me.

Keeping one hand in her hair, I gripped her ass with the other and pulled her closer. She gasped as my cock pressed against her and dragged her hands into my hair hungrily. I leaned further over her, her head tilting back against the wall.

I didn't know how much time had passed before I forced myself to break apart from her. Chests heaving, we stood there for a moment, my forehead dropping to hers.

"I was wondering when you would finally do that," she panted. Her cheeks were flushed, a sight I committed to memory.

I cleared my throat. "I guess I was slow to figure it out."

"Best pick up the pace, Warrior Prince." Before I could ask what she meant, she ducked out of my hold, retrieved her swords, and sheathed them across her back, heading for the door. "Are you coming? We have a war waiting for us."

For a moment, I watched her, shocked. This woman was truly a mystery. Every time I thought I had her figured out, she showed another side of herself. A new piece of the puzzle.

I wanted them all.

Catching up to her at the door, I ducked and whispered in her ear, "Yes, General."

Chapter Fifty-Five
Ophelia

WHEN TOLEK LEFT TO MEET MALAKAI AND CYPHERION, I sat on the couch with a cup of tea for what was likely the last few minutes of quiet I would get before we left. I soaked them in, letting the silence settle across my skin with the warmth from the fire.

I picked up Lucidius's journal. Malakai had given it to me in the Labyrinth after the cave-in, not being able to focus on much other than Mila.

As I dragged my finger around the leather edge, I considered. Lucidius had known there was something in Firebird's Field. Perhaps he didn't know what, but somehow, he'd uncovered a secret. What else had he explored?

Flipping through the pages, the crackle of the flames filling the air, I skimmed his script. It was hard to decipher. How had Malakai and Barrett been doing this for weeks?

I found the entry about what we had figured out was Firebird's Field and skipped to a few pages past it, skimming to see where the mention of burning flowers ended. Eventually, it faded to long-winded musings about light-speckled skies and temple art.

"Starsearchers," I mumbled to myself as I picked apart his words. That was an emblem we did not have yet. My fingers toyed with the corner of the page, restless with possibilities.

I nestled back into the couch, tucking my knees up.

I was a few paragraphs in, my tea already growing cold, when I froze.

Breath of lungs restored it a magic alive like the others and pulling at the threads of heart—

"Alive," I murmured.

Malakai had said Lucidius had become fixated on this concept of living magic. Though we couldn't know what our former Revered meant exactly, the sensation of Kakias's power crawled through my memory. The sentience of it, as if the queen's magic was a breathing thing.

"Breath of lungs..." I traced the words in his looping, slanted script. I'd heard those words before. Where—

Starsearchers.

Vale.

My thoughts were like stampeding horses in the quiet room, galloping toward an idea.

I slammed the journal shut and tore from the cabin.

~

"Ophelia, why in Bant's name are you taking us here?" Barrett asked as I tugged him and Vale after me into the infirmary tent.

"Because we need to find Santorina," I said, searching along the rows of cots, some occupied, some with sheets stained with blood, and some freshly changed, awaiting their next patient. Healers rushed through the space, a rustle of activity that had me walking quicker.

"And what good will finding Santorina do?" Barrett wrenched his arm from my grasp, but kept following.

"Ophelia, we really should be packing," Vale said, untangling herself from my grip much more gently than the prince.

"No, trust me—ah!" I spotted a long dark ponytail and took off running past curtains and warriors toward the back corner, where a workstation and shelves of supplies were tucked away. "Rina!"

She looked up as I skidded to a stop across from her table. "Yes?" she asked, warily eyeing all of us.

Barrett shook his head at her, Vale shrugging with wide eyes.

"Do you still have those ingredients Gatrielle and Esmond were finding for you?" I rushed out.

"Do I—well, yes, I saved them. Why?"

"Did I hear our names?" Esmond asked, coming around the corner of the nearest curtain.

"Yes!" I burst, looking between the three healers, excitement bubbling beneath my skin. "You collected *elements of sacred land*, correct? Rina was going to try to use them to get the poison from my arm."

"We did." Esmond crossed his arms, brows raised.

"I found what I could in our territory and the mountains," Gatrielle added, brushing his curls back from his face. "Mainly known sites of worship."

"And you thought they could be used to unwind the poison from my blood—what if it can be used to reverse the entire ritual?"

A stunned silence met my idea.

Then, a boisterous laugh burst from Barrett. "Reverse the ritual, and make my mother mortal." His smile widened. "So we can kill her."

"So we can kill her," I affirmed, returning his devilish grin.

"Ophelia!" Barrett picked me up, spinning me around. "This is ingenious!"

Perhaps not ingenious, but for the first time, I felt like I was counting on something besides my own desperation, my own vengeance. I was relying on a true plan that was concrete and discernible. It fed the hope I'd been afraid to let flourish.

When Barrett set me down, I whirled toward the Bodymelders and Rina who were discussing in hushed voices. "Do you think it will work?"

Esmond dragged a hand down his face. "I think it's possible, but we can't guarantee it. Not without knowing the proportions and how she prepared it exactly."

"But we can try?" I asked. I fought the optimistic smile that wanted to beam across my face.

"We can try," Rina confirmed. She brushed her hands on her apron, reaching for her notebook and turning to a blank page.

"Tell us everything you remember, and we'll work on it before you leave."

"Thank you, Rina." I scurried around the end of the table and hugged her. "Thank you."

This was a light in the darkness. A chance.

Vale cleared her throat. "Why am I here?"

"Because of this." I flipped through Lucidius's journal until I reached the entry on Starsearchers and shoved it at her. Her eyes widened as she read the familiar words.

"That's what I read during—"

"The interrogation, yes!" I couldn't help myself from smiling now. "Vale, this confirms that somehow, your readings are tied to this. This idea of living magic—I think Kakias has it somehow. Maybe it refers to her immortality, maybe there was something else Lucidius knew, but it all connects. How else could Lucidius have used the exact words your session gave to you? It's too big to be a coincidence."

"That doesn't tell us what it means, though," Barrett said. "Lucidius rambled on and on about living magic in those pages."

"It's about Kakias," I asserted, nodding. "I know it is."

Because I remembered what her power felt like tugging against my own. How that magic ate away at me like it was *alive*.

"What do you need from me?" Vale asked, decidedly snapping the journal closed.

"If there is anything else you remember," I nearly begged, "from that reading or any of the others, will you tell us while Santorina, Esmond, and Gatrielle prepare this? Every kernel of information could be imperative."

Vale hesitated, whether it was because she couldn't remember much or because she didn't know what to share, I wasn't sure. But finally, she lifted her chin and swore, "I'll tell you everything I can."

Gatrielle laid out a long leather roll, like one that might hold knives and daggers, only this one was stocked with an assortment of vials and pouches.

Esmond pulled a curtain around our space.

Santorina stepped up to the table. "Let's get to work."

CHAPTER FIFTY-SIX
TOLEK

"Ria?" I knocked on my sister's front door and peeked my head inside when I didn't hear an answer.

She was hunched over the table, rearranging sigils and muttering to herself. My steps were hollow in the empty cabin, and still she didn't look up. Bracing my hands on the back of a chair, I looked between her and the maps.

"What are you working on?"

Lyria's head snapped up. Her eyes were dazed for a moment, then they settled. She smiled at me, and I couldn't tell if it was forced or not. "Tolek. Hi." The smile quickly faltered as her gaze fell back to the maps. She chewed her lip, her eyes roving the table.

"What's happening here?" I asked, tentatively.

"Running all the numbers again. Making sure...making sure everyone is where they'll be the most useful. That we don't have too many units in unnecessary positions, and we're not leaving spaces open."

"Lyria," I said, placing my hands on her shoulders and turning her toward me, "you and your team have ensured these plans are strong."

"What if they're not? What if I'm overlooking something and I fail?"

I fail, she'd said. Not we. Not this army. *I.*

As her frazzled stare jumped between me and the board of war gracing her table, pieces clicked into place in my mind.

"You're *afraid* of failing." I knew the answer because it was the one driven into my bones by our father. I knew the lie she'd feed me, too.

"What? No, I'm worried for our people and allies and—" I raised my brows at her, stepping back and crossing my arms. "All right, fine, Tolek, I am afraid of failing, are you happy?"

My arms fell to my sides. "Why would I be happy about that?"

"Because I admitted it and now you win." Stress was turning her brutally honest. A harsh change from the sister who'd come to Damenal when I'd been captured, but I thought both sides of her were true.

"I win?" I echoed. I knew what she meant, but did she?

"Yes, you got me to admit I'm afraid of failing as the Master of Weapons and Warfare. Afraid I won't live up to those who came before me and people will look back on this war as the greatest failure of the Mystique Warriors. Afraid everyone will die because of some mistake I did not foresee. Now, if you do not mind, I have to run over these plans again to ensure that doesn't happen."

She turned back to the table, her attention falling to her figures. I contemplated my next words. Maybe it wasn't the right time, given I was about to leave and she was about to lead our army to battle, but if I didn't speak up, she might be distracted out there.

I took a deep breath and asked a question I wouldn't have been able to voice a few weeks ago: "Have you ever stopped to consider why you feel this way?"

Her big round eyes lifted to mine, but she didn't straighten.

I tried again. "Have you ever stopped to consider why you feel this need to be perfect?"

And right there, behind her eyes that mirrored my own, a shoddily-healed wound cracked open.

"What do you mean?"

The tremor of her voice confirmed I'd been wrong all these years. Lyria was not effortlessly perfect as she'd appeared to my younger self. She did not revel in that flawlessness. It was an act she was forced to uphold.

Fucking Angels, if only I'd opened my eyes sooner. Maybe I would have understood why she truly showed up in Damenal for me instead of being confused the entire Sunquist Ball. We may have been bred to compete, but there was a side of her that loved me.

I sighed, leaning against the table. How much should I unveil?

"I think you know how Father treated me growing up." I didn't think she was aware of the physical abuse, but she understood the emotional and mental games he played. How he felt after our mother almost died. He'd worked his magic on her as well, though in a different way. "He made sure I knew my...value to our family. How little it was. Because of that, I've spent a lot of time hiding my faults. Thinking they would push others away. I still do, but I'm trying to see otherwise."

Lyria sucked in a big breath, holding it for a moment. When she released it, her entire frame shrank. "His games made me believe perfection was the only option. The training exercises and implications that my value was in the rank I achieved for our family." She huffed a laugh and waved a hand over the table. "It worked, I suppose."

"It did not work if it beat you down," I corrected her.

"During the last war...something happened." Lyria's hands shook as she twirled an Engrossian marker. "Or nearly happened. I —I messed up."

My heart thudded, but I swallowed the fear her demeanor drew within me. Forced my voice to be steady when it appeared she couldn't. "You don't have to tell me the details."

"I will." She unfolded a story that made it really hard for me not to charge the Engrossian-Mindshaper line immediately. That anyone thought they could touch her...that she thought it was her own fault for making a reckless decision. Anger buzzed through my blood, but I shoved it down.

"I'm sorry, Ria." I sighed. "Spirits, I'm so fucking sorry that happened, but it wasn't an imperfection on your part. It was not because you aren't a good enough fighter or not strong enough. Damien's Spirit, you're so fucking strong to be here today." I waved a hand around the room at all she'd accomplished and built in the past few months. "You took a risk, yes, but what happened was a disgusting action of that warrior. And no one should ever have made you believe otherwise. I promise, I will be here for you for the rest of this war and beyond to remind you."

As I should have been as her brother all these years.

"Thank you, Tolek. I'd be happy to have you here." It was clear from her tone she didn't want to discuss what happened anymore. She wanted me to know, to hold that secret with her, and then she wanted to continue on together. Her brow crinkled as she considered me. "You know, Father made me think you were a competitor."

She said it as if this was the first time she was admitting it. Maybe the first time she was really realizing it.

"He made me think I'd never live up to you," I confessed. "And then I saw you as a competitor, too. I wanted so badly to resent you for it, and I did for a while, but that felt like another flaw. To hate the *perfect sister.*" I tilted my head to each side. "It's all very confusing."

"Yeah," she said thoughtfully, looking over her board. "It is."

"I didn't realize how much you cared until you showed up in Damenal."

Her head snapped up. "What?"

"Until then, I thought you resented me as I'd tried to you." Her jaw popped open, but I continued, "Think about it, Ria. We were never close. We only shared formalities, but how well did we truly know each other outside of that?"

She chewed over those words, looking at the figures and statistics lining the walls. "More people are going to die in this war, Tolek." Lyria met my eyes again. "I don't want to risk that with these bruises still between us."

"I'm letting mine go, Lyria." It was the truth. I'd been doing it bit by bit for a while now, and hearing her speak of how she felt growing up—how scarred she was—had released an immense amount.

"I'll do my best to." She evaluated me, deciding it was okay to share what she said next. "I was scared when you were...I was afraid you wouldn't wake up—and we'd always have the unaddressed rivalry between us."

"I'm here now," I promised.

No more. I wouldn't allow our father the power of building walls between his children any longer.

"She helps you see otherwise for yourself, doesn't she? Helps you see how wrong Father's thoughts are."

I didn't need to ask who she was asking about. I think my sister always knew how I felt, even before I'd admitted it to myself.

"Yeah." Unabashed, I flashed a lopsided grin. "She is helping me."

"I'm happy for you, Tolek." She didn't say more but I sensed there was something she was keeping in. Her fingers fluttered nervously over the table again, sinking back into that place of forced perfection. I wasn't sure what set it off, what had her taking her worth from these sigils, but I stepped to her side at the board of war.

"I've been a bad sister to you," she admitted.

"I have not been a great brother." I ran off in the night with her horse and a measly explanation of where we went, thinking she wouldn't care. "But let me help you now. Let me help you with this, Lyria." I searched her expression as she scanned the table. How was my sister as broken as I was and I never knew? "Please."

Her eyes glassed over. Finally, she nodded, and we sank into chairs around her war table, ready to play a much more dangerous game.

For once, we were on the same team.

Chapter Fifty-Seven
Ophelia

When I got back to the cabin, the elation I'd buzzed with in the infirmary quickly faded again. The inkling of hope replaced by the nagging that had persisted at the back of my brain since we arrived at camp

It pounded harder. Demanding. My fingers itched for something to do. Absently walking to the dresser, I opened a drawer, not wanting to pry into the owner's belongings if it was still full.

A rigorous tempo increased in my head as I stared down at the leathers folded in the top drawer. Three sets fashioned like my own official garb, stored here by Angels knew who.

Beat, beat, beat went that drum against my skull as I side-stepped to the second dresser and pulled. The loose handle rattled. Three more sets, these ones precisely the cut and style Tolek preferred.

And in the two drawers below each of those: tunics.

Rushing to the wardrobe, I threw it open. Cloaks of various weights weakened my knees. Heavy, lined ones for the harsh winter that was threatening the southern mountains. Lighter wool for a season that was months off when the snow may vanish from the tips of this camp but the stubborn cold still gripped the air. All finely-crafted and new.

As I stood there counting the garments and the boots lining the floor of the wardrobe, something cracked inside me. The drum beating against my skull reached its crescendo. This wasn't solely a camp. It wasn't made to be temporary and vacated after the battles. This place was a fortress established for as many days, weeks, months that this persisted.

And based on the reinforcements placed here for us, they were setting up for a long war.

Flashes of cobblestone city streets lined with bodies assaulted my vision. Smoke stung my nose and eyes. Rubble dug into my skin.

My fingers tightened around the wardrobe door until it cracked. Splinters sliced into my palm.

No, I swore, that shredding feeling inside of me splitting violently between my ribs. Warm vengeance pooled desperately in its crevices. This would not last that long. I took an oath for the Mystiques, and they would not spend another day in a war they did not deserve.

I wouldn't give Kakias the chance to string it out. We had a plan now. Remove the queen. Disable the forces. End this before anyone suffered anymore.

We were going after Kakias.

And this would be over.

Spice and citrus surrounded me. It took a few inhales of that steadying scent for my brain to catch up, to realize I was no longer before the wardrobe but cradled on the rumpled bed. I had not even noticed my hand being pried from the door or the arms supporting me.

"Tell me what's going on in that beautiful mind," Tol soothed.

Sucking in a ragged breath, I said, "She can't keep doing this."

"She won't." His thumb dragged across my jaw, gently tipping my face up to him. "This is ending."

I shook my head. "They're prepared for a long war, Tol. They can't suffer again. Not like last time." I looked into those chocolate eyes, counted the amber specks, and tension fell from my shoulders. "When I was inducted as Revered, I vowed to protect and guide the Mystiques. I won't fail them."

Tolek sighed, pressing his lips softly to my forehead. "And you won't, but you are only one warrior, Ophelia." I frowned up at him. His quiet laugh had me relaxing further. "You are one *magnificent* warrior; do not misunderstand my meaning. But even that vow cannot be upheld by one person. You can't control everything."

"I don't like that," I huffed.

A crooked grin spread across Tolek's face. "I know you don't. What you can do, though, is focus on what *is* in your control."

Running a hand over my necklace, I surveyed the room. The drawers hanging open, contents rifled through. The remnants of our weapons and things I'd spilled during my flurry.

I told him of everything I'd discovered and planned for in the infirmary, and Tolek was thrilled—confident—but when I finished, I said, "We need a contingency plan. We need to prepare for *every* move the queen might make and then expand our expectations beyond that." She had surprised us too many times already. I would not give her another chance.

"Let's find them, then." Tolek slid me off his lap and leaned over the side of the bed to grab his pack. Pulling out a worn journal, he flipped to an open page. "Tell me every worry you have, and we'll figure it out together."

I pursed my lips at all the doubts and fears that had poked through since leaving the infirmary and being hit once again with the force of this war. They plunged me toward a cliff's edge, poised to fall, but Tol's words pulled me back from the panic. He tempered me, somewhere between the buzzing euphoria of having a plan and the cold realization of the camp's permanence.

"Come on, Alabath," Tolek encouraged, shaking his journal at me. "Be a good girl and come plan the demise of your enemies with me."

I laughed, but it was a wicked smile that met his own. "Okay," I began. "Let's start with how we are going to destroy the queen."

Tolek's gaze ignited, and that fire curled my toes against the bedding. Perhaps it wasn't normal for us to react such a way to these murderous intentions, but I quite liked it. If I was to wield death blows, he'd smile as he placed the sharpened blade in my hand.

And I would take every weapon offered as we walked together into this darkest battle.

It was ending. Even if it killed *me*, Kakias would not live to wage another war.

~

BREATH OF LUNGS and threads of heart.

Vale's meditative words from the interrogation in the Labyrinth repeated through my head as we met our group on the western border of the war camp.

Night had fallen hours ago, true and deep, unlike the early hours of lingering dusk we'd had earlier. The army was settling in, extra guards on watch and all others stealing a few hours of rest, trysts, or peaceful stories before the fires.

From here, I could make out the highest peaks, where shadows stood resolute; I scanned the land beyond the vast ridges of the range. Bows in their hands, quivers on their backs.

"You're ready to join them?" I turned to Jezebel, trying to gauge her feelings.

Her emotions were guarded. "I'm as ready as I can be. Ricordan's rebels will arrive tomorrow and they'll be able to help me if anything goes..." Her words trailed off, and I swallowed past the pain of that possibility. A cool breeze whipped our hair around our faces.

"You are an incredible warrior, Jezzie." I placed both hands on her shoulders and turned her to me. "This power you hold is a gift. We are going to decipher what it's for—who it's from. But this is your purpose, and Father would be proud."

She nodded, a tear I knew she did not want to let go slipping down her cheek. "Thank you, Ophelia. I love you." She wrapped her arms around my waist and squeezed tightly. "Be safe."

"Stay true," I said, kissing the top of her head. Over her shoulder, I met Erista's resolute stare. The Soulguider nodded at me, and we exchanged a silent promise to help my sister. Erista tonight, and the both of us once this mess was cleared up. We'd discover the true reason behind Jezebel's powers.

When Jez pulled away, a shadow hovered over us. "Tolek," my sister muttered. Then, she was launching herself at him, too. Locking her arms around his waist. I thought I heard her mumble a "take care of her" into his leathers.

Thought maybe he replied, "With my dying breath" against her hair. He cleared his throat and added, "You be careful, baby Alabath."

Jezebel stepped back. "One day you'll realize I'm all grown up."

"Not today," Cypherion said, joining our group out of the darkness. He wore his brown leathers with the Mystique sigil stamped into the thick material and a band of knives strapped across his chest beneath his cloak. Intimidating to most, soft to Jez as he clapped a hand to her shoulder and smiled down at her. "You may be eighteen now, but you'll always be baby Alabath to us."

My sister rolled her eyes but smiled slightly. "Yes, well, I'll be fine here."

"She will be." Malakai stepped up and draped an arm over her shoulder, and that one small gesture inflated my heart. Watching my sister with these boys who had protected me—us—all our lives, the ones I would die and kill for, reminded me that despite the darkness we faced, there was a world in which it would all be okay. A future I could almost reach out and touch.

"Are you ready?" I asked Cypherion. Vale stood behind our group, whispering a low goodbye to Esmond and Gatrielle. Like Cyph, she carried weapons, though her lone short sword and pair of three-pointed daggers paled next to his cloak of blades.

"We are," Cyph said with a grim nod, gesturing Vale forward.

"Rina?" I asked, noticing she wasn't here yet.

"I went to the infirmary to say goodbye," he said.

"You two find what you need to fix the readings," I instructed, looking between them, "and then come home."

"Of course, Revered," Cyph said. "We'll be back before winter is thickest."

I hugged him tightly. "Thank you, Second."

He grumbled about still not wanting the title as he stepped away to say goodbye to Malakai and Tolek.

I turned to Vale, embracing her. She recoiled at first, surprised, but then her arms came around me.

"Get your answers, Vale," I whispered. "I know how it feels to think your gift is working against you. Stay true." I pulled back. "And keep an eye on him."

The Starsearcher held a longing silence after my words, nodding slightly.

Tolek, having come over to give Vale his own well wishes, added, "Maybe get him to relax again." His brows pulled together as he evaluated Cypherion.

"I will," Vale promised, her eyes locked on our friend. "We best be off."

When he was atop his horse, Cyph said, "Have fun killing a queen without me."

"Jealous?" Tolek asked.

Cypherion rolled his eyes, and that was that. They left together on two horses, and we looked after them until their forms melded into the night, my chest tightening.

"Shall we?" Barrett asked when they were gone. His wolf, Rebel, sat eagerly beside him.

"Before it gets too late," Dax advised. He stood at Barrett's shoulder wearing enough blades to rival Cyph and two gruesome axes on his back.

A lump was in my throat again as I faced those remaining behind. Malakai and the Bodymelders. Mila and Lyria.

"Wait!" Rina ran down the path, thank the Spirits. I would not leave without saying goodbye to her, though I'd been with her all afternoon and had the ingredients she carefully measured out stored in my pack.

But when she stopped before me, I looked her over—leathers sculpted perfectly to her lithe body in place of the skirts she normally preferred.

"Santorina?" I asked, gesturing to her clothing.

"I'm coming with you." Her brow set in determination.

A mixture of delight and terror raced through me. "What?" I looked at Esmond and Gatrielle, who nodded. "Aren't you needed here?"

"We can manage," Esmond confirmed.

Santorina waved a hand at the three men accompanying us and me. "You all injure yourselves so freely, it's only rational you have a healer in attendance."

They laughed, and a smile lifted my lips. "We don't do it on purpose," I said.

Rina shrugged. "Regardless." She pulled the straps of her pack tighter and assessed the different factions of our group. "They will be fine here with the extra Bodymelders Brigiet has sent. *You* need me, Ophelia. And I need to be with you."

She was right. We both really did need this.

Throwing my arms around one of my oldest friends, I exhaled. "Thank you."

"Of course." She squeezed me tightly.

Then, Lyria was hugging Tolek. "Be careful, baby brother. Don't do anything stupid."

"Now where's the fun in that," Tol quipped. But when Lyria stepped out of their embrace and glared at him, he swore, "I won't do anything unnecessarily reckless."

Lyria sighed. "I supposed that's the most I can ask for." She crossed her arms. "I love you, Tolek."

"Love you, too, Ria."

Hearing them exchange those words squeezed my chest. He'd told me of their conversation, how they worked on finalizing her plans together, though he knew they were already tight. How they discussed their father and the pain the man bestowed upon them both—the wall now coming down brick by brick.

Giving them a moment, I turned to Malakai. "Take care of yourself."

"Until the stars stop shining, Ophelia."

Where those six words may have stung before, they were a soothing balm to scars of my past now. A familiar, welcome reminder in the face of a precarious goodbye.

"Until the stars stop shining," I repeated. We both knew it didn't mean what it once had. I knew Tolek understood that, too. It was a promise. To keep ourselves safe, to keep fighting these battles, and to see the other side together.

PART FOUR
KRATOS

CHAPTER FIFTY-EIGHT
MALAKAI

"FIVE DAYS," LYRIA REPEATED. SHE TOSSED THE crumpled piece of parchment atop the table. "We have five days until their attack. The storm will hit by then."

Mila and Quilian had already begun muttering over the lists of legions pinned to the walls. Calculating who should be pulled back for the next few days to prepare for the charge on the front line. Who would remain on the second line for reinforcements. Which units of the infantry were best prepared for the fucking snow.

Jezebel and Erista were deep in conversation with Amara and Ricordan, discussing the lookout peaks. A small Mindshaper rebel force was prepared to stand with the Seawatchers in case Jezebel was able to tap into the warped power with their aid.

Lyria alone remained at the war board, fingers splayed across the wood as she scanned her map. In the two days since Ophelia and Tolek left, she'd spent most of her time here. She'd seemed a bit more relaxed until that mystique ink letter flared to life above the board, quick fingers snatching it.

I leaned across the table, snagging the note she'd tossed aside. It had those two words on it, but a series of symbols lined the bottom, whirls and triangles and slashes.

"Who sent this, Lyria?" I asked.

Her head snapped up as if only now noticing me. "One of my spies."

I flipped the paper over. "You're certain?" Her network had given us incorrect information before.

"Yes." She nodded. "Those symbols at the bottom are code. So we always know who's writing and where the intel is from. It's a system from the first war. We use the—"

"The what?"

Lyria sighed. "The wolves."

"*What?*"

Across the room, Mila laughed, and I tried to ignore the smile the sound brought to my face, meeting her eye quickly before going back to the matter at hand.

"The wild wolves." Lyria sank into her chair, leaning back. "The animals of our world are smart, Malakai. They're loyal to their God and gifted in return. The wolves scamper among the enemy and gather intel; then they direct it back to us."

"They talk to our army?"

"Not talk so much as lay their paws on a map and signal. It's incredible, really." A crooked smile lifted her lips. "They're our secret force of spies, communicating back to our soldiers hidden across the continent." Her head tilted, remembering. "And they're great comfort when you're lonely."

I guessed a furry companion wasn't the worst company, especially for a warrior stationed in isolation as a spy.

"So, wolves...like Rebel?" I asked.

"Yes, exactly like Rebel. Though he's a pup, so we've never used him formally, but he has the instincts. I told Barrett when he first brought him here. I was wary, but that wolf is attached to him, so I trust him."

"Okay," I relented, not because I understood or agreed, but because no matter how we'd received the intel, we had it. And Lyria remained frantic. "Then let's plan our strategy."

Those dark slashes of ink stared up at me. *Five days.*

∾

"FUCKING HELL," Ronders said, wiping his brow on his tunic as we dumped the next round of sand bags together and turned to gather more.

I heaved another from the wagon over my shoulder and carted it to its place. These things weighed forty pounds each. Sweat built along my shoulders and spine; I was finally combatting the fucking chill of these southern mountains. Up here on the archer lookouts, where the wind whipped at your flesh, it was even colder.

"Just a few more." I patted him on the shoulder, my eye catching a warrior behind him, who haphazardly tossed a sandbag to the floor. "Hey! Be sure you're stacking those as General Lovall instructed. Like laying bricks, three high around the edge."

"Got it, sir!" he called back. The formality zipped through me.

Ronders and I returned to the assembly line, hoisting the next bags over our shoulders. The wagon runner retreated down the mountains to fill her haul again. It was a tedious fucking job, but we had all been given them to prepare for siege. Some were laying sandbags to reinforce weaker points of the mountain walls between camp and the front line or they were up here with me, arranging them carefully around the edges of the Seawatchers' lookout points.

Once we were done, a new team would move in to ensure the catapults were tested after their last battle, flammable oils and rocks stocked. Archers were the first defense, Seawatchers the most accurate shot, but we were using all advantages.

Of course, there was only so much we could do now with the storm hitting soon. The planned attack was still three days away, and we were praying to the Angels for protection.

"Do you really think this is all worth it?" Ronders asked as we dropped the last haul.

"What's worth it?" My gaze swept across the line of bags again. I kicked one with my boot, satisfied when it didn't budge.

"This." The Turrenian Mystique waved a hand at the stream of warriors around us. "Will this matter? Stop them?"

My head snapped up. I often forgot how little the greater masses knew about the cause of this war. They saw an Engrossian siege, watched the death toll rise, and thought it was all Kakias vying for the mountains.

They did not know of her immortality ploy.

Had no concept of how she'd abused a deal with the dark pools or the havoc that magic could wreak on the continent should it be unleashed.

"It is worth it." I nodded, looking out over the landscape. From this vantage point, the view spanned for miles, snow-covered peaks seeming to ripple with power. Subtle trails dug along them, bare trees littering the dips into valleys and dotting the jutting tips sporadically until they stretched to the gray sky. "The Mystique manifesto rests in guarding these mountains. It's what we've been responsible for since Damien claimed this land. I do think we stand a chance against the queen's army, but even if I didn't..." I shrugged. "Are we not to try?"

Ronders opened his mouth to respond, but a slow clapping filled the silence instead.

From the shadows, Jezebel emerged, dressed head to toe in sleek black leathers that were definitely not her usual garb. She approached with a sly smile, hands not ceasing their drawling applause until she stood right before me.

"Said like a true leader," she teased.

Rolling my eyes, I turned back to Ronders and dismissed him. "I'll see you down at the mess."

Once he disappeared among the flood of warriors on this shift making their way to the dinner hall, Jezebel walked to the edge of the lookout. Aside from meetings, I'd barely seen her since Ophelia left. Jezebel and Erista had spent time prepping her magic in secluded areas—whatever that meant.

As she toed the sandbags, the next team fluttered around, restocking supplies. I scraped my hand through my hair, watching her test the defenses I'd purposely taken responsibility for, knowing she would be stationed up here.

"To your liking?" I finally asked, fingers ticking over the scar on my chin.

Jezebel flashed me a grin that didn't soothe me at all. It was too knowing, too accepting of the brutality waiting. "You've done everything you can, Malakai. I will be fine."

Fine was not a reassurance. Jezzie was so young. She may have harnessed some spirit power, but she was a little sister to me, barely eighteen years old. Perhaps it was hypocritical given that before I was her age I had signed a treaty taking responsibility for an entire war, but I had been raised with that pressure on my shoulders. Jez had always been free.

Ophelia and I had never talked about where our lives would lead if we were not first born, but I wondered sometimes what it was like not to live with the weight of a clan over your every decision. Jezebel deserved a choice.

"You will be safe. If there's a moment when you aren't, you retreat."

"Sure," Jezebel said.

"No, Jezzie." I stormed to her side and turned her to face me. Her shoulder guards were cold, even through my gloves. "You promise me you'll run if things get bad."

"I can't promise you that, Malakai." The resolve in her expression tightened my gut, and...was that pity softening her eyes?

"Why not?" I spat.

"Because you and my sister wouldn't."

My shoulders slumped. "That doesn't mean you can't—"

Jezebel took a step back so my arms fell at my sides. "I won't be a coward."

"It's not cowardly. It's self-preservation."

"And will you run?" she snapped, bracing both hands on her hips. There was the girl I knew, the challenge taking the shape of a warrior.

"No." I paused, surveying the drop below the lookout. "I won't run anymore."

"Then why do you expect me to?"

"Because," I sighed, "this is not your fault."

"And it's not yours."

I understood that—I did. Logically, I'd learned I did not have to absolve Lucidius's actions simply because his blood ran through my veins. Or at least, I reminded myself of it. If Mila of all people could believe such, who was I to argue? Still...

"I will do everything in my power to fix it, though."

"What did you tell Ronders?" Jezebel challenged. "This is *all of our* birthrights Malakai. It is what we sign up for in completing the Undertaking. This war started differently than some, but we will stand for the power buried in the mountains. We still carry out that cause."

I sighed, grumbling under my breath, and Jezebel smirked victoriously.

"I will be safe here with Amara and her team. The Mindshapers will reinforce my efforts. Erista won't leave my side in case I am distracted by my power. I have a constant guard at all times, even without you, Tolek, and Cypherion breathing down my neck."

"Fine," I conceded. "I'm still having Elektra readied below the lookout."

"That horse is always ready," Jez scoffed. "She would be waiting for me regardless. And besides—I have my own plans."

I wasn't sure what that cryptic ending implied, but as I watched her gaze over the mountains, I let it go. More warriors graced the lookout platforms on every side of us, their cheers and directives instilling the falling night with a bit of warmth.

Jezebel dropped her voice. "A lot of them have changed their opinions of you, you know?"

"Who?" I asked, eying a woman carting jugs of flammable oil, another tying a tarp over them.

Jezebel inclined her head to the warriors traipsing up and down the winding path to the lookout. "Ronders has been convinced for a while, but some were more hesitant when you first arrived. Quil was telling me of it."

The Soulguider would know how Mystique warriors felt toward us. The man's booming laugh and natural vivacity were revitalizing around camp. Many flocked to his company.

Ronders was a good man, though. He had always been patient as we trained and appreciative of my help. He did not fill the void of having Cypherion or Tolek, but he was a friend.

"Great to know they did not like me," I deadpanned. But I allowed Jezebel's words to sink in and tried not to shy away from the warmth in my chest.

"You've really returned to yourself here, Malakai. But you've become someone different, too. Someone content." For the first time, her grin turned sheepish. "It's good to have you back."

A slow smile spread over my face as I watched her toe a sand bag. "I missed you, too, Jezzie."

She breathed a laugh, and for a moment, as stars winked over the mountains, we were both quiet.

Until a horn sliced through the air.

CHAPTER FIFTY-NINE
OPHELIA

"You're certain this is everything, then?" I asked again as Santorina and Barrett poked through vials and jars for the umpteenth time since we'd stopped traveling.

We'd rode hard and fast through the first night, getting clear of the camp as quickly as possible and scouring our way across the mountains. Then, we took our pace more moderately. Malakai had written that they were expecting a siege a few days from now. Our best bet was to stall our plan until then when enough of the Engrossian-Mindshaper army would be occupied and the queen was hopefully more vulnerable.

We'd set up our own small fortress in a cave, the horses resting in here with us. Rebel curled up against Barrett's side, snoring peacefully, his little snout twitching as he dreamed. For the few remaining hours of daylight, we sheltered at the western border of the mountains, looking down on the Fraughten River running through the icy terrain. We'd stay here for a few hours, needing a reprieve after three days of travel.

Then, we'd descend into Mindshaper Territory, and we needed to be alert.

"It's a variation of each item we could recall," Barrett confirmed.

"And the ones Gatrielle had been gathering for me," Rina said, gesturing to the items the Bodymelders believed could count as elements of sacred lands.

Now, they formed our greatest hope. A way to potentially target, or reverse, *living magic.*

Breath of lungs and threads of heart.

With a grimace, Rina nudged the one jar she refused to open. One sealed with wax and wrapped in thick burlap, though I swore the tar-like magic within pulsed.

A last resort, Rina had made me swear when I asked her to bring it.

Even now, I remembered the way it had crawled through my blood, and agreed. I'd only use it if necessary.

I pursed my lips, thinking through our plan as I watched Tolek and Dax stand guard at the cave's mouth. The setting sun filtered around their forms and pooled across the rough rock of the cave, igniting snow banks blown in from recent storms. The golden highlights in Tol's hair shone as he tossed his head back with a laugh. Clouds fanned out on either side of the warriors, and something swam to mind.

"I've been thinking..."

"That's always a wonderful start to a sentence," Tolek called over his shoulder.

"You love my ideas," I responded.

"Adore them." He smirked, then turned back to the watch.

"Anyway," I said, facing Barrett and Rina again, "when we tested the Angellight to try to summon Damien, what did the light from Bant's ring look like?"

"It looked...well it looked similar to the light from Damien's emblem." Santorina tilted her head curiously, but that was exactly the answer I wanted.

"Yet Gaveny's was different. As was the light from Thorn's emblem in the pit. And I bet if I sliced my hand open and tested Ptholenix's right now, that would be unique in some way, too."

"No self-sacrificing," Tolek called.

"My point stands," I retorted louder. "The minor clan emblems emit a varied sort of power, whereas Damien's and Bant's remain similar. Perhaps because of the nature of their magic, I don't know, but I know the sensation of that power, and though your mother's looks different, both the one that squirmed through my body and the one poured forth from the ring *felt* the same.

"No two sources of magic are completely identical. But you said Damien and Bant were known to feud; maybe it was like-challenging-like. Power disputes among the reverent, once-mortal beings before they ascended." I twisted Barrett's ring around my finger. Considered the three minor clan emblems hidden in my pack. "The magic Kakias possesses is not natural born. We know it was gifted when she sacrificed her soul to the dark pools and in turn learned the immortality ritual."

"What exactly are you saying?" Barrett narrowed his eyes at me.

"I'm saying—what if that was not all she was given? What if there was something else?"

"Like what?" Rina asked.

I shook my head. "I don't know." The theory was budding in my mind, roots being planted, but nothing had sprouted yet. Tolek and I had categorized a number of ideas of what we may face if our plan to lure out the queen was successful—we'd set our own contingency plans, and he'd vehemently refused a few of my suggestions—but each still felt incomplete to me. "Vale recalled the Angels being prominent in each of her recent readings—as well as who she believes might be the gods—and she said she typically reads warriors, not higher powers. It's still only a theory, but what if Kakias also has Angelblood?"

"She can't." Barrett examined his hands, long pale fingers adorned with jewels. "That ring has been ours for centuries. We've all shed blood at one point or another, but nothing ignited it the way yours does."

I opened my mouth to argue, but it was Tolek who answered. "You can have Angelblood without it being active."

Dax swiveled around to face us, eyes landing on Barrett's ring on my finger. "Wouldn't he have at least felt something within that, though?"

"I never felt anything with Malakai's spear until well after he was gone, and he'd been training with it for years." I shrugged. "But it's only a theory."

And I was so tired of the queen being two steps ahead of us—so desperate for a modicum of revenge for what she'd taken from us—I would try anything. Angelborn's emblem warmed against my sternum as if in agreement.

"Speaking of the ring," Barrett said, taking out a journal and tossing it to me, "Dax and I have been recording every variation of Blackfyre lore we can recall."

I read their accounts quickly, then my eyes flashed up to his green ones. "Bant lost something?"

Barrett nodded, a smile twisting the mouth—a smile I'd once thought so cruel. "Even our renditions vary, as happens with folklore over time, but in every case, two facts remain the same: Bant was called there to battle a dark creature, and in the fight he lost a piece of himself."

"We don't know if it's literal, like a limb," Dax added. "But these things tend not to be."

"A piece of himself," I said thoughtfully, spinning the ring around my finger. "This wasn't voluntarily given, then? He did not sacrifice his fossilized power because he wanted to."

"Perhaps he did." Barrett lifted a shoulder. "Perhaps it wasn't about the ring at all, and that merely became the location later on. Either way, we have something to work with."

"Thank you." I sighed. It wasn't answers, but every piece, every theory, helped me gain a little more control.

"We'll keep thinking about it," Rina encouraged as she finished repacking the ingredients. My fidgeting fingers itched to snatch the vials from her and check them all again, but I took a length of rope from my own pack instead. "I'm going to rest until we have to move again."

Crossing to the back of the cave, Rina curled up, draped her cloak over her body, and rested her head against her pack.

"Tolek, I'll take over watch," Barrett offered. He joined his partner at the entrance, and the two began muttering.

Tol dropped down next to me, eyes catching on the rope in my hands.

"Yes?" I asked, slipping the thick cord around itself again. Did his eyes darken—or was it only the shadows of night beginning to fall?

"Ideas," he finally said.

When his gaze lifted, it burned with challenge.

My cheeks flushed as I looked between him and the rope. A thrill shot through me, but I gave him a small smile, tossing it aside. "Perhaps one day. If we ever stop running."

The fire in his eyes turned ice cold. Determined. He gripped the nape of my neck and stroked a thumb over my pulse. "A safe home and woven constellations," he promised. "I'm going to give you everything you deserve." Tolek pressed his lips to mine, and I allowed myself to hope for those vows to hold true. To allow this man to shelter me when I kept a guard up around everyone else.

Then, he pulled me toward him and leaned his back against the wall. "Let's get some rest before we enter enemy territory."

He joked, but the gravity of those words sank over me as I watched the sun slip lower behind the mountains, sleep evading me.

HOURS LATER, a deep purple sky was peppered with stars spelling unreadable fates. The seven warrior constellations were bright tonight.

"Let's get moving," I instructed the group as I finished preparing Sapphire. She nudged her nose against my shoulder, her presence a balm to my worries. "I want to make the descent by night and find a cave by the river for the day before we cross to the Thorentil side."

"I don't think that will be possible," Dax said from the entry-way. His hands were wrapped around his axes, shoulders tense.

We shuffled over to the general and Barrett, and my stomach dropped. A wave of dark-armored soldiers marched across the land in the distance, giving the snow-flecked mountains the appearance of a rippling ocean in the dead of night.

Flurries fell around them, picking up quickly.

They cut a track through our mountains, between us and the camp, fast approaching the southern boundary.

"It's their second legion," Dax said. "You can tell by the flags."

"And that means…" Tolek began.

My stomach turned over as I muttered, "The first legion is already near."

Chapter Sixty
Tolek

I threw Ophelia and Santorina onto their horses as quickly as possible, and we fled.

"We have to write to them!" Ophelia tried to argue as we flew down the western trails of the mountains.

"Alabath, you stay on that damn horse!" I roared back. "They are prepared and can take care of themselves—we have a job to do."

And for the sake of the fucking Angels, I needed her to worry about herself for once. We thought we had days to reach Thorentil, but apparently Kakias was ahead of us—again.

Luckily, Sapphire had a bit more self-preservation than her rider, and she did not stop. Not as we raced through forests and away from the mountains over the next hours. That horse was damn incredible, and smart, too.

Finally, a snaking, wide arc of ice was visible through breaks in the trees.

The Fraughten River.

Made passable only by a crumbling, snow-and-moss-covered bridge. The brick looked ready to collapse at any moment. We'd have to cross one at a time.

I held my breath until Sapphire's hooves met the icy shore, then Rina on her mare.

Right as Barrett's horse and Rebel cleared the brick, a roaring crumble cracked the night, the entire frame shuddering. Stone tumbled through the ice, chunks bobbing across the black current.

"Angel's tits," Dax swore, tugging his mare's reins.

He and I were left on the opposite shore as the Angel's-old structure collapsed, the weight too much for it. Astania paced the river's edge, and I watched the place where large red brick sank beneath the surface. Could practically feel the cold sting of the water in my lungs.

"Tolek!" Ophelia called, and my head snapped up, our eyes locking. The three of them stopped, lingering in the tree line. A soft snow was starting to fall, landing on her shoulders and the hood of her cloak, dusting her with the white of Angels' wings. Even from here it was hard to miss her fingers clenching around the reins.

"You three go ahead!" I called, and though it fucking ripped my heart out to send her on without me, I steeled my voice. "We'll find a way across."

She needed to go. She needed to lure out Kakias, and this river was thirty feet across. Though they were more powerful than regular horses, even a warrior mare wouldn't clear that with a jump.

Barrett and Ophelia watched Dax and I respectively. The prince's jaw ground as he and his general underwent some silent communication. She and I did the same, those magenta eyes not even trying to hide her fears anymore, baring every vicious thought she once would have hidden. They shredded through me, one by one.

And my nightmares played out behind my eyelids with each blink.

A knife to her heart.

Warm blood coating us both.

Her body falling limp as I failed to save her.

Panic tightened my throat, but I tried to picture her warm and vibrant against me. Hear the whispers she reassured me with, that consoling safety each night I woke screaming and the serenity her presence brought.

I would find her. Would do anything to or die trying. There was no doubt in my mind.

"We'll see you at the location," Santorina said when it was clear the rest of us weren't going to end this standoff. "Be careful."

"Always," I said, still not breaking my stare from Ophelia's.

Rina nodded and turned, nudging her horse so she picked up into a canter. Barrett inhaled a deep breath. When he released it, he said, "Deeper than the valleys, Dax. Deeper than the valleys."

Dax cleared his throat. "Brighter than his light." Though his voice was steady, whatever passed between the two across that vast river was as intimate as in a private chamber.

With that, the former prince left.

"Stay true," Ophelia shouted, so much hope and heartbreak in those two words.

I swallowed. "Guide by the Angels." I prayed those eternal fucking beings would guard their chosen. Otherwise, I would have to find a way to kill a deity locked in everlasting existence, and I'd rather spend the time after this war buried in Ophelia.

Right before she disappeared into the tree line, she turned back. Her eyes dragged over me like she was committing this moment to memory.

"I love you, Tolek Vincienzo," she called, and time stood still, across every realm and stretching to the Spirits. Hearing those three words from her lips for the first time since I had said them to her could have carried me over that damn water.

"Alabath..." I sighed. "You hang on to those words. Because the second I'm back to you, I'm worshiping you properly to remind you how much more *I* love you."

She rolled her eyes. "Always the competition, Vincienzo."

"For you? I'd win every game." I nodded toward the trees. "Go. I'll see you soon."

I watched until Sapphire's vibrant blue tail vanished between the trees.

"What do you suggest?" Dax asked when they were gone, a solemn sense of misdirection settling between us.

I blew out a breath. "I have no fucking idea."

The general assessed our surroundings, studied the trees and the route we'd taken down from the mountains. "I might know of something that can help."

CHAPTER SIXTY-ONE
MALAKAI

✷✶✷✶✷

THE ARMY EMERGED OUT OF THE DARKNESS LIKE A WAVE of rolling death, and my heart rioted in my chest.

"Jezebel!" I started.

"Go!" She nearly shoved me back toward the path to camp. "Go, Malakai! I'll be fine here."

I looked her over; her brow was set in grim determination. Erista and Amara charged up the path, a small troop of Seawatchers following them and falling into line around the lookout peaks. They ripped tarps off what had been secured and poured oil into wells, even as snow wafted around us.

"Go!" Jezebel yelled again.

Before I did, though, I crushed her to me.

"Be safe, Jezzie." Visions of the Battle of Damenal and the first war flashed through my memory. "Please be fucking safe."

She squirmed against my grasp. "You, too, Malakai. I love you."

"Love you, too."

Jez ran, then, scaling to the highest point of the lookout. Standing on a peak, clad in her black leathers against the star-flecked night, she sank into her power. And in that moment, I was certain she was right. As an eerie stillness overtook her, born of the mountains themselves and something else, Jezebel appeared the most formidable warrior I had ever witnessed.

With a breath of relief, I charged down the path, the wave of soldiers parting for me.

~

WHITE HAIR and shining silver armor caught my eye when I emerged from my tent what felt like minutes later. The camp blurred around me as a lower rank warrior secured the buckles of my own guards. My sword swung on one hip, Lucidius's dagger and an array of others on the opposite.

"Malakai!" Mila said, running up to me and taking over for the boy, sending him to help the next soldier. Her hands fluttered over my armor, checking the buckles. As I watched, a bit of that haunting from the Labyrinth fought to enter her eyes.

I gripped her hands, holding them to my chest. She wouldn't be able to feel my racing heart through the metal, but her eyes locked to mine, wide and concerned.

"Are you with us?" she asked, and I knew what she truly meant. Was I here? Was I prepared for what we were about to face?

"I'm with you," I swore to her. "I'm not going anywhere." Relief washed away her ghosts, and though we were about to face brutality, I sighed in agreement. She and I had overcome so much since we met. Tonight wouldn't be any different. "Now tell me what's happened? How are they already here?"

Mila swallowed. "Lyria's spies—someone betrayed us. We don't know who, but the information they fed us was false."

My blood chilled. "Let's go."

~

KAKIAS'S ARMY was thrice what we had been told to prepare for, and apparently there were more coming. I hoped Ophelia's group would not be in their way.

Their force marched toward where the border dipped across a low valley, wrapping further north than we had expected. They stretched well beyond our archers' range, providing a dangerous opportunity for them to surround us. And they'd been testing our weakest spots for weeks; they knew where their best chances were—where we'd likely reinforced our line, stretching ourselves thin.

A blood-chilling howl rang out through the night. They came mounted on *wolves*.

Giant beasts in a range of browns and grays and blacks, snarling and howling up to the moon. Their jaws snapped—not the docile creature Barrett had tamed these past months. No, these were creatures under Kakias's control.

The paws and boots created a haunting rhythm across the snow, ice crunching.

At the edge of our border, at the rim looking into the valley, they froze. Their presence instilled the night with a gentle, eerie hum.

Night breathed darkness into the land, the only light aside from the moon and stars was from the torches lining our outposts. Shadows seemed deeper around their force, like that dark rolling power of their queen.

Lyria sat atop Calista at the head of our legion, staring across the valley. Quilian and Mila were on either side of our commander, with me on Mila's other side. Cyren was sheltered behind us all, communing with the stars, but even they would join the charge when the time came.

"Why did they stop?" Mila whispered. "If they mean to cross the border anyway..."

"So we break first," Lyria answered. Her eyes flicked over the enemy, looking for weaknesses.

This was not how I envisioned an attack would strike. I thought it would be quick collisions and brutal charges. Not this silence stretching across the valley, crawling across my skin. I fidgeted in the saddle.

"Why are we waiting?" I asked.

"There will be a lot of death tonight," Quilian foretold, his eyes slightly glazed as his Soulguider magic spiked and relayed the ends of lives. "The Spirits are hungry."

"The Fates are singing," Cyren began, coming back to themself, "but I cannot tell of victory or destruction."

The prophetic words deepened the dragging sensation across my skin until my bones vibrated with it.

"Our war cries will sing with them," Lyria said. Raising a hand, she snapped, and an orb of mystlight shot to life above her palm. I jumped in the saddle, watching the swirling white glow.

With an inhale and a face set in grim destruction, the Master of Weapons and Warfare pulled her arm down.

And arrows rained across the sky.

More than I could count. They sank into the depths of the Engrossian army, met by distant shuffles as soldiers fell. But there were few cries at the impact.

Lyria flicked her hand up again, a second mystlight popping into existence.

But right as she was about to give the signal, a soldier stepped forward from their line. His movements were too graceful for a man of his size to be natural, even for a warrior.

And despite the distance, it was clear he had his eyes locked on one target: our commander.

A quiet gasp escaped Lyria as the man raised his fist, mimicking her motion. Her jaw ticked as she waited, braid whipping in the icy wind.

"That's Hughsten," Mila whispered to me, voice trembling. "It has to be. I'd heard he worked his way up the ranks."

"Who?" I asked.

"He was there when she..." She did not have to finish her sentence for me to understand the atrocities that man was guilty of. "She attacked him. He fled. We didn't pursue into their camp."

In an eerily timed motion, both Lyria and the Engrossian commander ripped their hands from the air. From our backs, arrows soared again, this time coated with flames.

At theirs, the wolves howled and snapped, brimming the edge of the valley.

"Stay true!" Lyria roared finally, her sword singing as she pulled it from its sheath.

Our army echoed her call.

And they charged, Lyria flying down the hill after them, Quilian beside her. Mila and I lingered behind, as instructed.

"Before we go," Mila whispered, eyes on her friend's disappearing form, "I have to ask…When?"

"When what?"

"When did you start to see me differently?" Her profile caught the moonlight, almond-shaped eyes narrowed. "Or am I a part of some savior complex for you because of Lucidius? If that's the case…"

Swords met axes, horses and wolves and warriors alike crying into the night. And yet she was the center of it all. The soothing voice that grounded me, reminding me I could do this.

"I don't remember when, if I'm being honest." Falling for Mila had been finding myself in the darkness. The two had happened in an intertwined pattern, one unavoidable with the other.

"It was gradual," I continued. "When I first saw your scars, I needed to know you. *Needed to.*" The clashes of battle and death grew louder, and a vice formed around my throat. Like I was running out of time, and if I did not tell her these things now, I might not get a chance to. "It was all I thought about whenever we were in the same room. How you got them, who was responsible, and whether or not they got what they deserved."

"They did." Even without looking, the satisfaction in her voice was evident.

I matched it. "I'm glad, although I wish I had been the one to do it."

Her sharp eyes glinted. "I've never had someone to protect me," she said. "Only Lyria."

"I will always protect you, Mila," I swore, a promise as easy as breathing. "I've been attracted to you since the day we met, but my head was too fucked to realize what it was." Deep in the valley, the screams began. "Then, when I came here, I realized how much I admired you. How strong and resilient you are." The whistle of the archers' arrows soared overhead, and the rest of my words came out hurriedly. "I was looking forward to training more and more every day, starting to feel like myself again because you showed me I could. And when we were in the Labyrinth, and you were gone, I missed you. I wanted to do anything to get you back. I guess that was the moment I finally realized it. I'm new to a lot of this. My whole life I've either been with Ophelia or been in a cage. I'm relearning what it feels like to be close to someone new. To trust someone new. To want someone new for more than a night."

Mila flinched as a particularly guttural roar spiraled up the mountains. We both watched for our signal.

"And that's me?" She sounded vulnerable in a way I hadn't heard before. It was different than when she spoke of being a prisoner. That had been a hardened kind of haunting. This was skeptical, as if she truly didn't believe I would want her despite the reasons I listed. "You want me for more than a night?"

"Mila, I want you for a hell of a lot longer than that." And because I needed to know before we charged into that battle, I asked, "When did it happen for you?"

"Back in Damenal," she said, without thinking, "when Ophelia was gone, and I saw how you tried to step up. I recognized something in you that I felt after the war. And as I watched that piece grow each day, I started to want to know it better. Started to fall."

Neither of us looked at the other as we spoke. We stared out over the valley, taking in the devastation and trying to mask it with words that felt at least a little hopeful.

"Thanks for waiting for me to catch up," I said.

It took a moment for my words to land, for my admission to sink in, but then her full lips split into a savage smile. "Best survive tonight, Warrior Prince."

She pulled her short swords from her back.

"I plan to, General." I unsheathed my own weapon.

A fire flared to life at the peak directly behind us, casting Mila's form in an array of warm hues. A signal bellowed. And together, we led the second charge into battle.

Chapter Sixty-Two
Ophelia

We raced around the edge of Thorentil, staying well out of reach of the guard towers lining the walls to the Mindshaper capital. Apparently, before I'd killed him, Aird had been a bit paranoid. The guilty usually were.

My hands were stiff from being locked around the reins in the freezing air, my entire body rigid, but all I could picture was Tolek's hard stare across the river; he'd tried so damn hard to pretend he was okay sending me off, though he knew I could defend myself.

His absence was like a phantom limb. I wished we had a Bind to communicate through.

"Ricordan said it's south of here," I called to Santorina and Barrett. I tried to focus on the task I was given as Tolek wanted me to.

We would find each other; I knew it.

Not long later, thanks to the mares' unrelenting pace, a looming shadow of walls came into view. Draped with ivy that persisted despite the winter air and miles away from the gates of the city, Ricordan's family property stood solo and resolute in the snowy night.

A base for our trap for Kakias.

We entered through the back gate as Ric advised, but it wouldn't have mattered if we came from the front. The property was abandoned. Anyone found here was fair to meet our blades, Ricordan had commanded.

Hooves pounded over snow as we pulled up to the back of the manor. Barrett hopped off his horse and pressed his face to one of the glass double doors, releasing a low whistle. Rebel perked up beside him. "Ric comes from wealth, then."

I followed him, cupping my hand around my eyes to peer through the chilled window. Though graced with layers of dust, the furniture was clearly finely made with gold trim on the couches and bronze and onyx frames decorating the walls. Over the stone hearth, a multi-generational family portrait hung proudly, their faces too morphed in the fogged glass to decipher who was whom. A grand piano sat in the corner and shelves lined with books and artwork covered one wall, moth-eaten curtains framing the windows.

The small details were what stood out, though. The blankets rumpled along the back of the couches. Candles half-burned. Volumes left messily stacked on the table beside the door and even a golden ring sitting delicately on top.

Despite the ivy and thick, black vines matting the manor's facade, it was clear this had once been a wealthy household, cared for and teeming with life. Now, it was an abandoned shell of a home, no one around for miles.

Before turning away, my eyes caught on that painting above the mantel, and my heart clenched in my chest.

"Yes, it seems he does." I turned away from the door before the sentimentality could grip me too deeply. There wasn't room for it right now, but a small ache dug behind my sternum, stinging my eyes.

Striding back to Sapphire, I forced it away. She pranced in place, restless.

"Hey, girl," I soothed, stroking down her nose until she settled; searching those deep-blue eyes, I reminded myself why I was here. "You're doing great so far, but we need to keep this up for a little bit longer." She'd been more skittish than usual lately, and it sent a twisting pain through my chest. "Rina, we need to find a place to prep—"

A clanking of metal echoed across the grounds. My horse and I both froze, our stares locked and alert.

The familiar scratch flitted on the wind again. It sounded like it was coming from the east, around the manor and toward the front gates.

"Ophelia?" Rina asked warily.

"Shh!" I looked at Barrett, knowing Santorina wouldn't have heard it. "Was that what I think it was?"

A deep, rumbling laugh that almost blended in with the riling storm drifted with the sharper metal scrapes. They were low, muffled as if through thick stone walls.

"Voices," Barrett said.

"And armor," I added.

They were getting closer now. Louder. Like a pair of careless guards on patrol.

"No..." The prince turned ghastly white.

"How in the everlasting Spirits?" I growled.

Go to my family's manor in Thorentil. He wouldn't have...

"What is it?" Santorina whispered, but I thought she already knew. Nerves had her eyes narrowed on the arched doorway leading into the manor.

"I think my mother's guards are already here," Barrett deadpanned, though his hands clenched at his sides.

Rina's eyes widened. Snow collected on our shoulders and layered the ground around us. We stood frozen as statues as the sharp clangs of metal drew closer, boots against stone accenting the pattern.

"Ricordan set us up."

CHAPTER SIXTY-THREE
TOLEK

> ✦

"WHAT EXACTLY ARE YOU LEADING US INTO, DAX?"

I squinted into the darkness. Even with our heightened vision, it was damn near impossible to see through the closely-packed trees, bare limbs jutting out at odd angles. Snow drifted down where it could force its way between the tangled canopy, flecks dotting the leaf-strewn ground here and there, turning it to soft mulch beneath the horses' hooves.

I didn't know how far off track we'd traveled, but I could feel myself getting farther away from Ophelia. Desperation was beginning to claw at my gut.

"Not much further," Dax said.

"*What* though, General?" Not where. I didn't much care where we were going if it was a way back to Ophelia, but I figured it was worth preparing myself.

"When I was in the army," he whispered, jerking his head to the side, "we had a number of camps in the woods. And there's one in Mindshaper Territory—near the Mystique Mountains and Thorentil—the queen was partial to. There's something there we can use."

I nudged Astania along quicker in the direction Dax had indicated. Around the ash-white cyphers and dark brown trunks, a white light pulsed.

Holding up a hand, Dax signaled to stop. I swung one leg over

473

my horse and landed lightly on the balls of my feet. Thank the Spirits for warriors being naturally swift-footed. Not much snow had snuck through the thick canopy overhead here, the ground free of prints, but I looked for fallen leaves that may crunch as I crept forward slowly; following Dax, I pulled my sword from my belt. I left my bow and quiver with Astania.

The general had an ax in hand, but his grip was loose. That glow pulsed around Dax's frame as he peered through the trees and exhaled quietly. "Abandoned. As I expected."

"*What* is?" I demanded. Impatience was eating at me.

"Kakias kept very few warriors at this camp. I never understood why. But they were her closest. The ones likely with her now."

Dax marched through the trees. Pushing past branches, I followed. Tents formed a ring around the clearing, surrounding something. The light was not from a lantern as I had expected. And as the general predicted, there were no warriors here.

Instead, only a slab of marble the size of a great table waited, illuminated and carved with—

"Is that Gallantia?" I asked, creeping closer.

"No," Dax said, determination solidifying his tone. "It's all of Ambrisk."

I observed the lines slicing through the ice-white sheet. A map of our entire world, delicately etched into a pristine granite surface like a work of art, valleys dipping and mountains jutting above.

"And we're going to use it to find a way back to them," Dax promised, walking around toward the southeast side and studying the Mindshaper Territory.

"Why is it here?" I asked. My spine tingled. It was too convenient, too random for the queen to store a map in the woods.

"I'm not sure." Dax shook his head. "But something about the strength of the mountains."

"Magic, then," I murmured. "The capitals are all marked. A few major cities, too..." The thought trailed off as I surveyed the locations flaring in the night. A small cluster of dunes in Soulguider Territory. An unnamed city in Mindshaper land. The Cliffs of Brontain. The list went on, the mountains being the brightest of them all with tiny *X*'s spotting their surface. A circle of them in the southern half. "There's no reason to it."

"Knowing the queen, I'm certain there is." Dax tightened his grip on his ax. "But she never told us."

There was an edge to his voice I suspected had to do with the queen's secrets from her son.

Stretching out a hand tentatively, I picked up one of the figures amassed around the southern mountains. Little shards of obsidian rock, no real shape to them, but they reminded me of infantry markers on Lyria's battle map, though less precise. More brutal and quickly fashioned. It rolled across my palm, almost seeming to vibrate in my hand.

"I wouldn't touch those," Dax warned. My eyes flicked to his heavy stare. I wasn't sure precisely where the marker had been before, but I set the sliver of rock among the pieces atop the mountains.

Dax inclined his head toward the top of the map where he stood. Creeping around the marble, I joined him.

There, staring up at us, was a bloody signature. The otherwise smooth surface had been scratched with what I thought was supposed to be the Engrossian sigil, a symbol Barrett's family had instilled many monarchs ago. It was lopsided and ridged, as if someone unskilled had carved it, but it was clear that it was a proud mark of ownership. Blood sprinkled the surface, filling in the hollows of the axes. My stomach turned over.

And around the trim of the map, there were grooves I recognized. "Endasi." I pointed to the words scrawled hastily into the marble. "That's the language of the Angels."

Like the axes, they were messy, impossible to fully translate, but I strolled along the edge of the slab, doing my best with my meager training. They seemed to resemble words of myths and burials and death.

"And those pieces likely represent her army."

As I expected. The longer we stood there, the more the map hypnotized me. I tracked circles through the dirt around it as I tried to work out the Endasi language.

"Do you think she's using it to track Ophelia? Is this how she's been finding her?"

Dax considered, but shook his head. "No, see there," he said, gesturing to the deserts west of the mountains, "you all weren't in Soulguider territory, and she has a number of spots alight there."

I nodded in agreement. "Hang on."

Jogging back through the trees, I found Astania and pulled a notebook from my pack. When I returned to the clearing, she and Dax's horse followed, evaluating the space with those equine minds. Quickly, I scribbled a messy rendition of Kakias's map as Dax searched for a route we could use to cross the river and get to Thorentil.

"I'm no cartographer," I mumbled, striking her 'X's through the mountains about where they appeared on the larger scale. "This will do, though, since we can't transport the larger one."

Anything we knew about the Engrossian Queen's plans was helpful, regardless of if we knew what it meant. We could figure that out later. Angels willing, she'd be dead tonight anyway.

At that thought, I shoved my journal into a pocket of my leathers and lifted my sword from where it leaned against the marble. Flipping it in my hand, I said, "All right, let's chart a route back to our partners before—"

My words were cut off by a scuffle over leaves and a grunt.

Whirling, I found Dax, his ax buried deep in the thigh of an Engrossian. A small dagger followed shortly into his neck, and the warrior crumpled to the dirt.

"Company?" I drawled, tightening my grip and picking apart the spaces between the branches. My heart pounded against my ribs.

"Appears so." Dax rubbed a hand across his neck where a deep red line was fading. "Jumped me from behind. Wasn't quick enough."

His voice was stonier than before. Flicking a glance over my shoulder, I caught his hooded eyes narrowing. A general's brain ticked away in his head, looking between the warrior bleeding on the floor and the rest of the clearing.

"Behind you!" he shouted.

I spun, raising my sword before I even saw the warrior. Two jagged blades crossed against my own. *Mindshaper weapons.*

Quickly, I slammed up every mental defense I could think to employ. Dragged up every memory with Ophelia or my friends, every sensation of calm serenity rather than the adrenaline I normally fed off during battle.

Mindshapers fought with different weapons, and I refused to be their prisoner again.

I leaned my weight against the stout warrior, pushing him back a step. My arms strained under the force of his knives, but this wasn't the grueling kind of pain—it was the kind that settled along my muscles and spurred me on. The kind that had me smiling wickedly down at this incompetent match of a fighter and knowing he wouldn't win. It was the spirit that awoke within all of our hearts as warriors, and I used it to meet my opponent's daggers again and again.

He spun them above his head as I swung to his left and dragged them in an X less than an inch from my face. He knew fancy maneuvers with the twin set—I'd give him that.

Frustration bubbled in my chest at fighting him with different weapons. That was the nature of a war among clans—within our own kind—but it was out of balance, unnatural.

Metal clashed repeatedly. Dax fought off his own warrior, and Astania reared up between the low-hanging branches, knocking some clean to the forest floor to trip up the man. *That's my girl.*

I ducked my opponent's blade and swung out, aiming for the sensitive back of his knee. A bit of a cheap shot, but when the opportunity was presented so carelessly, who was I to deny it?

He roared and lifted one of those over-sized daggers again. As it arched through the air, the map's glow fell on his vambrace—highlighted a series of broken buckles along his forearm.

Driving up hard as his arm dropped, I slashed my sword across his wrist. The clang of metal against metal rang through the forest, and the vambrace clattered to the ground.

My next strike went straight through his flesh, a satisfying grind of bone against blade. The Mindshaper's scream pierced the clearing as he fell to his knees, his hand severed beside him.

Dax and his own opponent did not stop their fight, but it was obvious who was winning. Our general had earned his title, anticipating every movement of an enemy and beating them to it.

As my own opponent cowered on the ground, clutching the bleeding stump of his hand to his chest, Dax took advantage of his other's slowed movement. He pinned him to a cypher with an ax through the shoulder.

When the tree took the impact, the whole forest seemed to rock. I shook my head, turning back to the bleeding warrior at my feet.

"This isn't usually how people end up on their knees before me." I circled him, tugging his hair to the side to force his gaze on Dax. "I wish you would have asked before your friend attacked mine."

"Why is that?" the Mindshaper forced out.

"Because I am a man of gambles, and I keep a long list of what I have traded, lost—though that list is rather short—or am owed. Debts don't go unpaid where I'm concerned." His teeth chattered, eyes dazed as my voice turned brutally, twistedly dark. "If you hurt him, I'm forced to repay the favor."

With his blood-loss, the warrior was slow to understand what I meant. That made it slightly less satisfying to pull my family dagger from my hip and slice it across his neck. The poor bastard barely had a chance to piss himself.

Sparing him no more thought, I kicked his bleeding body aside and turned to Dax. "Are you okay?"

"Fine."

I wiped the blade on my pants and returned my weapons to my belt. Stretching down, I tried to work some of the pain out of my right knee. According to Santorina, I'd continue to feel the ghost of my injuries despite magic, especially when in high intensity situations.

When I stood, I was face to face with the western half of Kakias's map, light ebbing along the surface like a moonlit midnight.

"By the fucking Angels," I breathed, whirling toward Dax and flexing my hand. "I have an idea."

Chapter Sixty-Four
Malakai

><

It was fucking carnage as we raced into the valley. A rush of adrenaline tapered the roars into a steady hum as I focused on my breathing and Ombratta's pace.

Our quickly-timed second attack was intended to break down what our first couldn't while they were distracted, creating a hole in their force. Everywhere I looked, weapons flashed, warriors screamed, and blood coated the night in murky streaks of crimson.

Ombratta held steady beneath me, a warrior horse to her core, and at our side, Mila sliced neck after neck of the Engrossian-Mindshaper army. Fucking Spirits, was she beautiful. An angel of vengeance with twin swords in her hands and the moon haloing her frame, blood arcing through the air after each kill.

All the motivation I needed to get through this battle was right there.

I shut out the pained outbursts, ignored the uneven ground and thoughts of bones trampled beneath hooves, and squeezed my thighs around Ombratta to hold myself up as we charged.

There was a gap in the warriors at the lowest point of the valley where the land leveled out. A crack in their foundation that, if we could keep pushing through, would segment their force. My vision tunneled around that point as I leaned forward, and everything around me blurred.

We had to break them. To carve their army into smaller groups. They outnumbered us, but we could surround them.

The further we raced down, the more vulnerability choked me. But for the clan that was ruined by my bloodline, I could do this. For the allies fighting by our side tonight, for the friends who were scattered across this battlefield and the rest, and for the general who survived atrocities and still returned, I could do this.

I braced my weapon as I sliced through an opponent, and Ombratta kept on; I focused on the tension in my muscles and where every strike landed. I wouldn't get injured again.

The deeper we drove, the heavier the air was with the stench of death. Blood coated the snowy floor of the valley, a deep crimson seeping across dirty white.

No one I know will join it, I swore to myself as I swung my sword across the back of an Engrossian whose cuirass had been knocked askew. It slashed clean down his spinal column, and Ombratta kept going.

"Malakai!" Mila shouted, and I pivoted in the saddle.

A buried but newly-awakened instinct had my sword raised before I saw the flash of the ax.

I met it, bracing my arm against the jolt of the collision, and forced the weapon aside. The man swayed on his wolf mount, fingers tangling in the animal's fur. Taking the chance, I shoved my sword between us. It was awkward atop our steeds, but the blade slid beneath his chin to claim his life.

It wasn't an explosion or valiant rescue. Not a roar of death, but a whisper. An eerie silence as a spirit left a body.

A dropping of his jaw and red bubbling between his lips.

A death no one would notice, not until this was over and the tallies were taken. Then, he'd be mourned. And the pain of this night would set in.

But I couldn't think about the possibilities of *after* the battle right now. Not if I wanted to stay present. Flexing my hand, I pulled my blade clean of the warrior. I rolled my shoulders, testing my muscles and centering myself in the present. Focusing on the new way Mila had taught me to fight, allowing everything I'd been through—survived—to culminate in strength rather than building a barrier around myself.

I dug in my heels, and Ombratta charged down their line, forging the gap we needed and scanning the valley as we went. Soldiers danced in front of and around us, and—

Lyria.

On foot, hair ripped free of her braid, and blood sticky across one side of her face. A barrage of axes and daggers flew at her from multiple angles.

"Not a fucking chance." Mila's voice was like a beacon as she raced past me. Ombratta immediately followed into the fray. After weeks of training under Mila's hand, I understood what she wanted me to do. From opposite directions, we circled our commander's attackers.

Lyria spit blood to the snow, but didn't acknowledge us, too focused on the man leading her opponents.

Hughsten.

I knew it was him without being told. Knew from the rage festering within Lyria and Mila, palpable amid the chaos.

Mila and I surrounded the band of warriors, pulling the attention of all but their leader. They were on foot and had dislodged many of their weapons, making them quick targets. Almost too easy. It took away most of the satisfaction. A muted high after having my enemy's blood on my blade.

Lyria continued to dodge knives until Hughsten only held one weapon: a brutal looking ax with scars decorating its double-edged blade.

Then, our commander launched herself at him.

She wasn't a coward—didn't wait until he was unarmed. She allowed him to walk directly into her trap.

Their blades flashed against each other. Mila and I circled his warriors, their attention diverted to their leader.

One Engrossian turned, running. But Ombratta followed.

He'd barely made it ten yards when my mare passed him and looped around. As we circled, I dragged my sword across his throat. He fell with a thud that was lost to the melee.

My attention snapped up in time to see Hughsten's ax raised above Lyria's head. My breath caught in my throat as it swung down.

But the commander dodged to the side.

And her sword ran through his ribs.

She shoved him to the ground and said something to him—something too quiet to be heard among the battle—but his eyes widened.

And then, Lyria brought her sword down again, decapitating him. Her attacker's life stained the snow, revenge painting Lyria's leathers and armor as she turned unremorseful, vengeful eyes on us.

And in that stare, a slice of freedom unlocked.

She buttoned up her emotions, though. Offered one nod to tell us she was all right—for now at least—and Lyria was back atop her horse, shouting at Mila and me to continue to push through their line.

A part of me wanted to follow Lyria, to make sure she was okay —thought Tolek would want me to—but those weren't my orders. I had to listen, to lead my forces as I'd been instructed, and deal with the emotions of battle afterward.

"Come on, girl," I said to Ombratta, and she was off, forcing her way through their infantry to make up any edge we'd lost by stopping.

"You okay?" Mila shouted from my side.

"You can't be worrying about me out here," I growled back. But she might have been asking more for herself than for me after watching what her best friend had done. They were an indestructible pair.

I honed that energy as my sword swiped soldier after soldier. Some were death blows, striking the neck faster than the mountains would heal them. Some were merely injuries sending them to their knees. Our troops would finish the warriors writhing on the snowy ground.

"I'm not worrying," Mila called as she took another life. It didn't sound like a lie. "I know better than you do that you're capable of being here."

Her words struck me like an arrow to the heart, sticking thick behind my ribs as I unraveled the sincerity, clear amid the carnage.

"Thank you, General."

Our horses picked up speed, widening the gap in their ranks.

"Make them bleed, Warrior Prince," Mila said as we broke their line. And I intended to.

Ombratta charged through the line, segmenting the legion while a stampede of the alliance followed.

Emerging on the other side of their force, we carved a path around the back, the troop I led surrounding this cluster of warriors. Success sang through my blood, mingling with adrenaline to form a dangerous combination.

Mila led the other half north, and though I'd lost sight of her, I knew in my bones she was slaying warriors without remorse. One for every mark placed upon her body.

Make them bleed, she'd said.

I would. For everything they'd done to the both of us, I vowed to make the Engrossian-Mindshaper army bleed.

With her scars and broken sobs echoing in my mind, I gritted my teeth and allowed that promise to fuel me. I still needed to memorize where each scar carved a story of her pain across her body, but I'd ensure my death count tonight was higher than them.

We were circling around the edge of the battle when Ombratta let out a pained whinny. One of the only sounds that could slice through the haze to me in that moment.

She reared up, and I clutched the reins to stay seated. Whipping my head around, sweat-soaked hair clinging to my face, I saw it: A Mindshaper's jagged dagger piercing my horse's flank.

No fucking way.

Stab me if you want, but touching my horse was a way to ensure you met the Spirit Realm.

I dismounted, and Ombratta spun in place. She would heal quickly—warrior horses benefited from Mystique magic the way we did—but that pain demanded punishment.

"That was a cowardly move," I spat, stalking toward the man. "We respect our animals in Mystique land."

I gripped him by the neck of his armor and swung the handle of my sword into his temple. Not hard enough to kill him, but enough to send him to the ground.

He didn't deserve a quick death.

I sheathed my weapon and crouched over him. "Don't." A blow to his jaw. "Touch." Another. "My." A third to the throat that left him gasping. "Fucking." One to the temple. "Horse." I beat until he didn't resemble a person anymore. Until his face was mottled, swollen, and streaked with blood.

His head lolled to the side as I threw the gutless warrior to the ground. My gloves dripped red, flicking to the snow as I shook out my hands.

I turned back to Ombratta to assess the wound, but it had already clotted. Should I remove her from the field?

No. I knew my horse. She had a heart like Sapphire or Erini or Astania. They'd been raised beside the rest of us to run toward fights, and if I was finally doing so, she'd want to be with me.

As I was finishing ensuring she was fine, the energy across the battlefield shifted.

In the distance, a small troop of about two dozen warriors scaled the highest lookout peak with impossible speed, as if they were puppets pulled by invisible strings. Up, up, up they went, trampling our army, running them through with daggers and axes alike. Wolves pounded toward the summit, tackling warriors as they landed.

Fire flickered atop the mountain, torches casting an orange glow across the battle. And even from this distance, I could see her shadow. Perched atop a rock in the center of the lookout, dark-armored frame gilded by flame, hair whipping around her face as enemies closed in.

And my heart jumped into my throat.

"*Jezebel.*"

From how still she remained, I could envision her with her eyes closed and face turned to the sky, drawing on her spirit power. Flashes of blades catching the light around her told me she was guarded, but it wasn't enough. Not with the unnaturally quick way those warriors scaled the craggy facade.

Maybe I hadn't fought for Jez before, and I'd hurt her when I left, but I'd dive into the Spirit Volcano before I left her in danger now.

I swung myself onto Ombratta's back and dug my heels in. "Let's get to the lookout, girl."

CHAPTER SIXTY-FIVE
OPHELIA

><><><><

THE GUARDS' VOICES DRIFTED THROUGH ONE OF THE stone archways leading into the interior of the manor. Two of them, based on the conversation and tempo of their gait.

I positioned myself behind a stone pillar on one side of the arch, Santorina beside me. Barrett hid across the way with Rebel sitting primly against the wall.

"Why are we the poor saps stuck in the snow?" one warrior complained. They were nearly to the exit now. I curled my fingers around my dagger at my thigh.

"Because she needs that woman more than either of us right now," the second reminded him.

Their steps froze.

"What *is* that?" the first growled.

Santorina's breath caught, but I suppressed a wicked smile.

"Is that a horse?"

"What in Bant's Spirit is it doing here?" They shuffled forward again. I could make out each of their exhales as they warily crept toward the grounds.

As they watched Sapphire straight ahead and twenty feet out, where I'd told her to wait. To steal their attention.

One of them gasped, gripping his ax. "Is it's mane blue?"

"Bant's fucking cock, it's her—"

But before the Engrossian could finish his observation, my

dagger lodged in his throat, his body crumpling to the ground like a limp doll.

The second whirled, his eyes widening. Barrett jumped him from behind before his ax was raised. The prince wrestled the soldier to the ground and tossed his weapon aside, pinning the Engrossian. Santorina retrieved the ax as I ran to the squirming pair.

"Your Royal Highness?" The warrior gaped up at his former prince, but Barrett only sneered, tightening his grip on his wrists.

I leaned over the man. "Where is she?"

He narrowed his eyes at me. "I knew it was you. That horse gave you away."

"That horse is the bait that got your careless friend killed," I hissed. "And you're next, unless you tell me where Kakias is."

"I won't betray my queen," he growled, his eyes flicking to Barrett. "Unlike some of you."

"Kill him," Barrett said.

The warrior bucked, but Barrett's weight pressed him harder into the snow.

"She's not on this side of the manor," I guessed. "You had no guards stationed here. Only one measly, useless patrol." He stilled, and I assessed that bouncing gaze. "So she's inside somewhere? Or..." I thought back to the layout Ricordan had drawn of his home, and I smiled. "She's in the inner courtyard isn't she?"

A protected space that still allowed access to the moonlight—a key ingredient we'd need to reverse the ritual. The reason Ricordan had recommended the location for our trap in the first place.

"I knew we shouldn't have trusted the information," the warrior spat. "The kid was brainless."

Barrett and I both froze. Behind me, Santorina inhaled sharply.

Trev.

Ricordan had not set us up. His son had.

Trevaneth had been lingering in the council all day as we planned, had asked a number of questions, and then disappeared. All the while, I'd thought him simply curious. He was too young for the gruesome realities of war.

But that was it—he was young. He was a boy who wanted his mother back, and though he made the wrong choice, I could not entirely fault him for that.

Now, though, we had to clean up his mess and hope losing the chance of surprise did not cost us the war. I bolted down the worries and aching sorrow that wrought within me, though.

"We're done here," I said, voice dry. Whipping Starfire from my belt, I swung her across the Engrossian's neck in one smooth motion.

I didn't watch him die. Instead, I strode around the side of the manor, reconstructing Ricordan's blueprint in my memory.

"Ophelia?" Santorina whispered, worry thick in her voice.

"We'll have to climb," I said, remaining emotionless. Scanning the ivy-wrapped side of the manor, I twirled my necklace around a finger.

This was no longer our trap to lure the queen in with my presence, to set up the ingredients we'd worked to gather on short notice and spin a web for her. No, now Kakias was the black widow, and we were the prey.

"Why climb?" Rina asked, eyeing me warily, but I kept my mask up.

"We can't very well walk through the front door," Barrett said. Briefly, I remembered when he first arrived in Damenal and scaled our gate when denied entrance. Now, he stretched up to grab a thick vine and planted his boot on another.

"Don't impale yourself again, Prince," I joked, tightening my hold.

"It only happened once," Barrett scoffed, surveying the high walls stretching toward the snowy gray sky. "This looks less problematic."

"And what about the ritual?" Santorina curled her fingers into the blackened plants. Her pack was slung across her back, supplies intact, but the plans for them burned away. There was no time for mixing potions—no time for establishing a carefully crafted boundary.

"We'll have to figure it out quickly," I said.

Backup plans. Tolek and I had worked them out for a reason.

But none of them involved us getting betrayed, by Trevaneth, nonetheless.

Sapphire released a low huff from directly behind me and nudged my shoulder.

Whirling, I tangled my fingers in her mane and held her face steady. She was warmer than usual, her breath fogging the air. "You were a beautiful distraction, girl," I whispered. "We'll be back soon. Wait here for me."

Without allowing myself to get emotional about parting with her, without acknowledging I was torn, leaving a piece of my soul behind, I turned back to Barrett and Santorina. Head to toe in leathers, with determination setting her features, the latter was a fierce predator, and Barrett's face was etched with vicious determination as he bid his wolf pup goodbye.

We all knew what we were scaling toward right now. The possibility of this not ending in our favor. And none of us would relent.

"Let's go," I said.

They nodded.

And we climbed.

I was grateful for my leather gloves, though I usually hated not feeling Starfire or Angelborn against my palms. Most times, that thin layer of flexible material made me feel like I had less control, but now, as thorns stabbed into my hands, I was glad they weren't piercing skin.

Up and up we went, silent but for the strained exhales and shifting of plants beneath our boots.

When I reached the roof, I dragged myself over the edge, careful not to let my weapons clank against the tile. It was flat, though, which was a blessing. Easier to scamper across.

Barrett pulled himself up next, only breathing a little heavier than usual. Rina came not long after, ponytail swinging behind her.

"You okay?" I checked.

She nodded, flushed cheeks burning in the chill air.

Then, an all-too recognizable voice drifted up to us, slicing through the empty night like a freshly-forged sword.

"It's been frantic, untamable..." The words were low mumbles.

We crept to the edge of the roof on silent feet. There was a gap of about two feet, and then a delicate edge of brick bordering a wide glass ceiling. Snow gathered along the iron panes. We wouldn't be able to jump across—couldn't know if it would hold our weight.

Through the skylight, the interior courtyard was visible.

Kakias paced within. My Angelblood heated upon seeing her.

The queen wove between thick stone columns engraved with images I couldn't decipher from here. Plants lined the perimeter, branches bare of greenery, and orbs of yellow mystlight decorated the top of each pillar, casting columns of illumination that melted into shadowed gaps.

"She should be here soon," the queen grumbled. My skin tingled. "It's been days already. How is she truly so slow?"

Indignation shot through me, hands clenching, but I clamped down any response.

The three of us lowered carefully onto our stomachs to peer over the space between our stretch of tile and the skylight. A narrow stone balcony surrounded the second story of the courtyard, mostly in shadow, though the gap gave perfect access to it. It was difficult to see the queen from this angle.

My pulses ticked away in my ears like alternating war drums as I swung my legs over the edge of the gap and dropped into the darkness of the balcony, landing in a silent crouch on the balls of my feet. The air shifted in the narrow space as Barrett and Santorina followed.

I ducked along the railing and took stock of the scene below. A second warrior stood resolute in the corner. With red-blonde hair braided back and dark armor cladding her frame, she would have been easy to mark as a soldier in the Engrossian army. But it was the vacant expression that gave her away. Not as addled as the prisoner I'd killed, but not entirely present either. A bruise bloomed across her cheek.

"May I—"

Kakias slapped her, the woman flinching but not crying out.

"I have told you many times you will be freed to your family once this plan works. You may have your entire manor back. I do not care for it."

Your family. The manor.

Trevaneth's mother. The sting of betrayal worked through me, softened by the reminder that this warrior had been taken from her family years ago.

Glancing at Barrett and Rina, I knew they understood, too.

Kakias continued pacing circles around the courtyard as if she hadn't just assaulted a warrior in her army. Her voice rang clear through the space. "She is unpredictable and powerful. Annellius warned of this happening."

I nearly stumbled, the world sweeping out from right beneath my feet.

*Annellius...*my ancestor. The first Angelcursed, the only other warrior we knew of who was tied to the emblems as I was. Who had died trying to complete this task.

I clenched my necklace, fighting off a fresh wave of deception. He'd *warned* Kakias.

About what? And how? I'd only spoken to him during the Undertaking, and she couldn't have done that.

Regardless, a deeper kind of treachery set into my bones. A curling need for answers and vengeance if he'd somehow aided her rather than me, his own descendant. The one who bore his own cursed blood and was plagued as he had been.

A gentle hand squeezed my shoulder, and I whipped my head around to meet the firm shake of Rina's. It was only then that I realized I had gasped at my ancestor's name. We froze, eyes locked, but Kakias did not react.

Swallowing the deception, dismissing the frustration stinging the back of my eyes, I nodded to assure Rina and Barrett I was steady. In control, though with every turn in this game of fate, the realization of how little control I truly held mounted.

Quietly, I stepped to the railing, biting back the cry of outrage I wanted to release at this queen and the Angels and Annellius and all of it. The heating in my blood that demanded my life stop being a toy to them all.

As Kakias rambled to herself, I unsheathed my dagger, letting her words bury the singing of the blade. I tipped the weapon toward Rina, knowing she had its twin strapped to her own body, the two a gift from Cypherion on my last birthday. The balcony swarmed with his strong, assured presence.

Flipping the weapon in my hand, I channeled that energy and hopped onto the railing.

I waited...waited...

And when Kakias prowled beneath my perch, I fell.

The queen's frame wasn't strong enough to catch my weight against her back. She crumpled beneath me as I wrapped my arms around her throat and legs around her hips. Together, we rolled across the floor, but I angled her to take the brunt of the impact.

Gripping Kakias's shoulders in her confused state, I forced her beneath me.

My legs came to either side of her hips, pinning her.

"Miss me?" I purred against her ear, every bead of betrayal and hurt and loss turning those two words into something wicked.

And I sheathed my dagger between her ribs.

Chapter Sixty-Six
Malakai

Ombratta and I flew around the outskirts of the troops we'd divided, cutting through clusters of dueling warriors faster than a lightning strike. She was driven, climbing the path to the lookout like it hardly took any energy. Her hooves clattered over broken pieces of armor and fallen soldiers, and still she remained focused, the way only warrior horses could.

Small fires burned across the valley, arrows raining down in sparks of orange and yellow, and across the vast battlefield, a shower of white-hot blues and a burst of screams.

By the time we emerged onto the platform, combat ringing below like a medley of living death, it was overcome with the Engrossian-Mindshaper force.

Jezebel hadn't revived from her stupor yet. Erista stood directly before her, guarding the girl she loved fiercely with a hooked sword in each hand and a scythe waiting across her back. As I dismounted and ran over, she swung one of those hooks through a warrior's gut—straight through the metal armor as if it was parting a stream —and tore out her guts.

My boots slugged over the remains. I sped to a stop beside her, catching my breath and facing the next attacker. A number of Mindshaper rebels circled the perch, as well, Ricordan standing at the very back.

"How long has she been like that?" I asked as I met an ax with my sword. My shoulder embraced the impact, jarring and sharp. I breathed through it, forcing the opponent back.

"Since the first horn," Erista said. There was no fear in her voice. Only calm rage and a hint of exhaustion. She and Jezebel were both too young to be in the heart of war. "She tunneled down and has been gone since."

A man danced around me, and I spun, dragging my sword across his ankle. He fell to a knee with a cry, spinning to raise his ax.

Above his head, I watched Jezebel. She didn't look *lost*, she looked *powerful*. Something born of another time, another world, when gods and Angels prowled the land. There was no visible sign of her power. Nothing that indicated if what she was doing had a tangible result.

Unless you knew where to look. She moved her arm in a graceful arc and a nearby dying Engrossian launched his ax at a fellow warrior.

She repeated the motion, and he did, too, never opening her eyes. It was as if she was seeing through the spirits instead.

Behind her, a shower of blue flames rained down, breaking my trance.

"What the fuck was that?" I asked.

But before Erista could say anything, more enemies crawled across the lookout like a swarm of ants, wolves snapping. They launched at our Seawatchers with claws and teeth. With a grunt, I turned away from those flames and drove my blade into the neck of the man before me.

"Get her!" I directed at Erista, ducking an ax and shooting back up. I rammed my sword beneath the man's arm and shoved his body to the ground, quickly spinning to meet the next. I ripped Lucidius's dagger from its sheath and sent it straight into the warrior's eye. "Wake her somehow, and get out of here—"

My words broke off with a strangled cry, sword nearly tumbling from my hand.

At first I thought I'd been stabbed, the pain in my chest was so sharp, but it cleared quickly, fluttering away with each beat.

"What's wrong?" Erista shouted over the clash of blades, but she was near Jez now.

"Nothing," I gasped. I pressed my hand to my chest and tried to focus on the fight—to find my next attacker.

A pair of Mindshaper rebels slid into place in front of me as I stumbled back, righting myself. My jaw ground against the echo of pain still stuttering behind my ribs.

"What—" Erista started, eyes dropping to my hand still against my chest and glazing over briefly.

She couldn't have a fucking vision now. Not in the center of the melee.

"Go!" I roared, gripping my weapon tighter.

There were shouts and a creaking whir of the catapult as our army launched boulders across the valley where the Engrossian-Mindshaper reserves waited. From here, the impact was barely audible, but it carved a crater among their ranks, and I sighed with relief.

Our Seawatchers and Mindshaper rebels formed a united front against the legion attacking the outlook, but blood rained down from either side. It sprinkled the dirt and snow, stained the souls of those wielding the weapons.

Every time one of theirs fell, a new warrior took their place in an endless flood.

My weapon met my opponents' again and again, the rush becoming a blur. Out of the corner of my eye, I saw an archer fire a flaming arrow, its fire painting the indigo sky orange. Then, beneath the arm of my opponent, I saw a Mindshaper ram his dagger through the Seawatcher's spine and kicked her body over the edge of the cliff. I roared as she fell, as the enemy's twisted focus turned on another.

Drawing that anger up within me, I swung my sword through the neck of my opponent and charged the next before their head hit the ground.

Quickly, I was coated in the blood of warriors. Everywhere I looked, we were all crawling through slaughter, trying to find the end of it. To *survive*. Sticky red coated my skin, dirt and gore and grime beneath my boots.

The battle moved in a haze of annihilation. Bodies piled up.

Weapons fell. Horses and wolves ran free of their riders. No sounds were discernible over the din of spirits being called to darkness.

Summoning what energy I had left, I whirled to meet another opponent. As Mila had taught me, I let the rhythmic memory of battle take me over my spinning mind.

War was not beautiful. It was not noble sacrifices, poetic retellings, or the romantic letters written home. It was not a place to laze about and indulge in your inner workings. War was base instinct and survival. It was contrived of greedy pursuits and desperation. It was strategy and strength, knowing that either could fail should fate strike when our backs were turned, but still we fought with every breath in our lungs.

As I drove my sword between the shoulders of a man who may have been innocent of any crime and simply in the army for the necessity of his family, the shame of battle and killing washed over me. I was proud to be a Mystique Warrior, born to protect, but I did not want to be a piece of the ceaseless puzzle of *this war*.

I wanted this fight to end.

Drawing back from the ledge, I returned to Jezebel's side to assess the raging battle.

Ricordan stepped up beside me. "I don't understand," he said beneath his breath. "How did they surprise us?"

"Someone betrayed us," I murmured.

"Someone who knew our plans," he answered.

"Dad?"

We both whirled, finding Trevaneth pale and wide-eyed at the back of the lookout where trees turned into thick forest.

"What are you doing here?" Ricordan demanded, storming over.

Trev only watched the slaughter, horror-stricken. I could practically see the scars forming behind his eyes.

"I didn't mean—"

And it clicked.

"You wrote to the queen didn't you?" I asked, and I wanted him to say no so badly.

But all he offered was, "I want my mother back." Ricordan

stared at his son with a mix of pity and shock. Behind us the cries continued.

"Son..." Ric stepped forward.

"I didn't know it would be...like this..." His voice broke, and I swallowed every reprimand I wanted to throw. This was not the time. Not when he was seeing lives being taken for which he felt responsible.

Putting a hand on his shoulder, I said, "I need you to tell me exactly how this happened."

"I talked to the intruder in the Labyrinth and he told me how to get a letter to the queen." Trev shook his head, eyes glued to the fight behind me. "She said if I gave her information and compromised the missive about when they'd arrive, she'd release the Mindshapers before the battle. That the battle wouldn't even be n-necessary," he stuttered, then met my stare. "I'm sorry, Malakai."

I took a deep breath. "You two should leave," I commanded, looking between the father and son. "Go back to camp. We'll discuss this with Ophelia after this ends."

If this ends.

Ricordan pulled his son along after him. Right before they were out of ear shot, Trev spun back toward me, his stare burning with regret. "She's waiting for her. The queen is waiting for Ophelia."

And then they were gone, that information echoing in my head.

There wasn't time to harp on it, though. Trevaneth's actions couldn't be undone.

Instead of allowing the familiar twist of betrayal to warp my mind, I jumped back into the fight.

Another ache struck my chest, two more following in quick succession, but I didn't let it stop me. I forced away the gruesome realities of war and treachery, sinking into the bloodshed. I became the warrior instincts I'd scorned for so long, the ones born in my blood, my only objective to protect.

At some point, Mila raced onto the platform, Lyria with her. The two had vengeance in their eyes. They fell into battle like two halves of a pair of legends brought to life.

As the wave of warriors continued to ascend the mountain, as their numbers drowned ours, I worried that we may not win.

That our alliance wasn't enough because they had abused power, unrelenting force, and treasonous intel on their side.

Nearly a dozen of the archers on this lookout alone had fallen. Across the peaks, less arrows flew.

We were being beaten.

But if they were unrelenting, then we would be, too, I swore, shoving my sword through another's side and slicing Lucidius's dagger across their throat.

I took up a spot on Mila's other side, slashing my way through the warriors who found a foothold over the ledge of the lookout. I stomped on the hand of one, sending her spiraling back toward the earth, and swiped across the ribs of another who had lost his chest-plate.

I stood heaving, peering over the edge of the cliff.

Mystiques stayed true until our dying breaths, and even if we lost this battle due to a well-intentioned letter written by a naive, hopeful hand, tonight would be no exception.

CHAPTER SIXTY-SEVEN
OPHELIA

KAKIAS SCREAMED AS I STABBED HER, HER POWER shooting outward in a blunt wind. It threw me back, stone and glass and starry sky blurring.

Darkness rimmed the courtyard, swirling like a dust storm of the Soulguider deserts. It clawed against my skin and stung my eyes.

Somewhere, Sapphire rioted, her whinny slicing through the night and my heart. But she was outside—safe, I reminded myself as I skidded across the hard floor, bones jarring.

That one stab wound wouldn't kill the queen—she'd made herself as close to immortal as possible on Daminius, unless she killed me—but it did deter her from attacking and riling up her magic. I wanted that power untamed within her. *Uncontrollable* and unceasing.

Power I'd once felt beneath my skin, that greeted me now like an unwelcome friend. It was more unruly than the sliver that had lived within me for months, like it had festered in the queen.

But it was undeniably *hers*. It tasted of her on my tongue, bitter and primal and greedy.

Pushing to my feet, I wiped my dagger clean of Kakias's blood. Tendrils of erratic magic pressed down on my body, but my second pulse beat wildly, pushing at the edges of my skin, like a beast longing to break free.

Use me, starry child of Angels.

Use it? I staggered under Kakias's power. How could I—

There was one thing that would light this courtyard with the essence of Angels. One weapon I had not planned to use tonight. But the power in my blood begged to be released.

So I trusted that instinct and did the one thing I knew would feed it.

I ripped my gloves off, swiped my dagger against my palm, and slammed the gash to my chest, right over Damien's emblem. I freed the ancient thing prowling beneath my skin.

Angellight burst from the shard and attacked Kakias's power.

That light wrapped itself around me, too. Warmth seeped along my skin like a tempered fever, but it was emboldening, not sickening. It was sovereignty and secrets wielded with the darkest intentions.

And looking down, I gasped, turning my hands over before me. They were radiating, gold.

"By the fucking Angels."

It was not merely a reflection of the Angellight swirling around me. Not a tint or an ethereal cast.

My flesh was *glowing*.

I was emitting a light I'd only seen from one other being before. A source of power that only the Angels could wield. One that stole the breath from my lungs and sent my world spinning.

But this light hummed in recognition of me...it was *mine*.

Somehow, I commanded the power of Angels.

Confusion blurred my thoughts, but I tightened my grasp on my surroundings. My Angellight continued to push at Kakias's untamed magic.

And I wondered, if this light was coming from *me*, would it also obey me? I focused on that source rather than wondering how in the fucking Spirits this was possible.

Inhaling, I pictured the Angellight expanding, ebbing, and becoming a solid force.

Exhaling, I let it seep along my skin. It was unnatural and natural all at once, to breathe with a power that manifested itself outside of my body.

But it wasn't wild like the queen's. It was peculiar but pulled at my bones with a deep understanding. It whispered along my skin, telling stories of things ancient and primal and trapped and living.

I tried to control it—pictured it before me—and breathed out. The Angellight pushed back harder against Kakias's power, forming a curtain between us. Protecting me, obeying me.

It was the same sensation from the induction, the same from the test I'd conducted in Gaveral, and from the fight at the trench. Each time, the flashes of Angellight I saw had been coming from *me*, not the emblems. And now I was taking control.

As the queen staggered to her feet, those dark whips collected around her.

Kakias growled at my veil. Blood-red lips pulling back against sharp white teeth, she pressed a hand to her slowly-healing wound.

Behind me, someone shifted, but I focused on maintaining my tenuous control on this newfound power. I gritted my teeth, trying to ignore how it already curled at the corners under my unpracticed hand.

Barrett's voice cut through the courtyard, over the gentle sizzle of the Angellight and the darkness pressing against it. "This seems familiar."

"Oh, you brought my son," Kakias ground out. "How lovely."

"The family reunion of my dreams, I assure you," Barrett deadpanned.

"Pity," Kakias said. "I did not want to fulfill any traitorous dreams of yours tonight."

Barrett rolled his eyes, but I caught the tightening of his jaw. The comment had struck deeper than he showed. "Then you will be pleased to hear you've been a disappointment since I was born."

Flicking a glance over my shoulder, I couldn't see Santorina, but I heard her moving in the shadows.

"Likewise." Kakias nodded. She lifted her chin, almost seeming pleased by her son's accusations. Her hand dropped from her side, fingers stained red.

As she spewed vitriol at him, I thought back to the version of her we'd battled on Daminius. The one I thought might have retained a sliver of something human, of the young girl who had mourned a child and went to unimaginable lengths to avenge that death.

Whatever had nearly stilled her hand then was gone now, absorbed as she committed crimes against the Angels to achieve eternal life.

Kakias tilted her head, and something glinted among her dark curls. I gasped—a broken diadem of thorns sat daintily atop her head.

Thorn's broken crown, the other half of his emblem. Ricordan had warned me not to wear it. That was how she'd been controlling the Mindshapers. Not secrets she'd won from Bant, but that twisted crown.

All this time, she'd had it.

"Where did you find that?" I asked, accusation burning in my words. Even now, warped as it was, that emblem called to me. It belonged to *me*.

"It's rather special, don't you think?"

I was tired of her games, her taunts. Fury burned along my veins, and I sent out another burst of Angellight to appease it, solidifying my shield.

Untethered, a tendril of power smacked against my veil. I gritted my teeth, the impact rocking down to my bones, an assault to my very being, but I didn't miss Kakias's wide eyes.

"Fascinating," Barrett breathed.

"What?" I muttered, straining against the pressure.

"Her power. It truly is like tar." He looked pointedly at me. "Like the Blackfyre."

The location where he thought Bant's ring came from. A direct tie to the Angel in the physical, visible form of Kakias's unnatural magic. Was that where she'd gotten it, then? Was I correct in my guess that the queen had Angelblood?

Before I could ask, a lash of power slipped against the veil, and Kakias released a surprised groan.

I smirked. "When did that happen?"

"What?" she hissed, recalling those tendrils to gather around the hem of her dress.

I gestured toward the slithering wisps. "When did you stop owning your dark magic? When did it stop listening to you?"

Kakias's face twisted minutely, but she remained firm.

"That will happen, you know," I said, trying to expand my shield. To get a handle on my own light. "Power takes over if you're weak."

"I am not weak."

"But you are weaker than what you harness." I thought of my claims to my friends back in the cave. Of Kakias's poison and my Angelblood dancing together in my veins for weeks. Of Bant's light mirroring Damien's. "Not everyone is made to handle the power of Angels, Kakias. What made you think you were strong enough?"

"He told me I was!" Kakias snapped. "As a piece of the deal, that Angel shed his own self into mine—shed his *power* into my veins."

"Were you ever going to tell me we had Angelblood?" Barrett asked.

Kakias laughed. Barrett and I exchanged a wary glance. "You think you know so much."

"You just admitted it," Barrett accused. "He shed himself into your veins, and you would have passed that power on to me— though I can't use it." He gestured his sword at the Angellight protecting us from his mother.

Kakias's eyes flicked around the gold curtain, a gleeful confidence in that dark gaze. Her cheekbones were more pronounced than before, her curls bigger and wilder and that scar across her face starker. The heaving of her chest looked like more effort as she stretched her magic toward my Angellight.

I thought back to what she'd been musing over while we listened from the balcony. Who she'd been talking about.

"You called on Annellius," I said. Her power slashed at mine, but I dragged in a ragged breath and continued. "You summoned his spirit...how?"

"No." She grinned a sharp-toothed smile. "I did not."

She did not call my ancestor's spirit, but—

"How old are you, Kakias?" I forced my Angellight out further. "How long have you been playing these games?"

And if it was possible, that smile widened.

No. There was no way. Annellius had lived and died *centuries* before us. Centuries before Kakias and Lucidius and all their schemes began.

"Parts of me have been indulging in this feud longer than you could imagine, little Angel child."

Barrett stilled beside me, but his stunned gaze was hot against my cheek.

Behind us, boots shuffled over rock. A low chime like metal against stone echoed a few feet away, quiet enough that the queen couldn't hear it. My second pulse beat wildly.

"Whatever power you think you have, you're making a mistake. You were not born with it," I sneered, but kept the queen's attention on me as Barrett sank into the shadows. "Your body is not adept to it. And now you've put your blood and bones through too much. They cannot contain the power—a mortal body too frail."

"I am not mortal!"

"As long as I breathe, you are not immortal either." She lingered somewhere between the two. I didn't consider what that meant as I took small steps backward until my boot met those small metal items I'd heard rolling across the floor. "And here's what you have not considered, Kakias: I am not immortal, but I *am* kissed by the Angels. I am born of myth and legend."

Tossing my dagger in the air, I caught it by the blade, reopening the healing slice to my palm. Blood poured through my fingers.

"I thought by now you would have stopped underestimating me."

Dropping my dagger into my other hand and sheathing it, I swiped up the three minor clan Angel emblems Santorina had dropped for me. Held tightly to them despite the shining pain of the open wound.

But nothing hurt when light exploded from me, and shock widened the queen's eyes.

Three different channels of Angellight sprung up in the court-yard, feeding into the veil. Kakias's tar-like power drifted to them, tugging against her like they were being siphoned, pulling at the lines of her frame. She roared against it.

One beam of Angellight floated across the stone surfaces of the courtyard, turquoise tinged gold that I knew in my Angelcursed bones belonged to Gaveny.

A second spotted the air with the silver, sparking clouds of Thorn's magic.

And the third—this one I was sure was Ptholenix's. It burned orange and yellow, licking across the floor like flames, circling the queen.

My own Angellight from Damien's emblem surrounded the entire scene, scorching and iridescent.

Shock marred Kakias's features—that twisted outrage an expression I'd never forget. Hooves sounded on cobblestone as Sapphire tore through the entrance to the courtyard, riled and frantic, headed straight for the veil.

Kakias lashed her power out at mine, battering my combined force of four Angel emblems.

Fissures formed along the veil's edges, like an icy lake fracturing. Angellight rippled across the scene, a shimmering masquerade of slumbering power and awakened magic. It licked at stones and danced like starlight.

And the power was so new to me, so entirely overwhelming, I nearly cracked beneath her unrelenting strength, but I forced my knees not to buckle. Forced my eyes to stay on Kakias.

Channeling through my bones and blood and all I was made of, the light tethered strings to my very spirit. It dug down within me until roots of ether wound through my soul, and I siphoned its power in return.

I breathed when it breathed—moved when it moved.

As I installed that shield against the queen, I thought of each trial I'd survived so far. Each way we'd earned these emblems that somehow dragged a power out of me and planted it in me all at once.

I thought of the relentless courage required to battle the alpheous amid a warring sea and how nature thrashed in challenge. Of Malakai's account of recreating a celestial event and the planning and sacrifice it required. And of grasping my fortitude within the pit to remain conscious against the luring darkness.

I pulled each of those strings to me—each of those learnings—and stole my body and mind against the magic warring around me. I focused on strength and cunning and determination. Brute force balanced by thoughtfulness and patience. Within me, the strings of Angellight separated among their respective lines and morphed back together to form a discernible but unanimous teaching of power. They were each a greater part of a whole.

I wove those lessons into my bones, and the magic seemed to settle. *Worthy*, it purred. *Chosen*.

And in a strange way, those threads of ancient magic filled the empty spots I had not known existed within me.

Kakias roared, and her power battered my shield so forcefully, my knees almost buckled.

Sapphire pranced around the courtyard, but her presence empowered me as I called on the strength of my second pulse. As I summoned the power of Angels living within me.

It answered with wild beats of feathered wings.

"One more," I said through gritted teeth. One more and I was sure I'd be able to push back Kakias's magic.

The only emblem I had yet to ignite.

I removed Bant's ring from the pocket of my leathers and slipped it onto my thumb. Dried blood crusted my hand. I'd have to slice it one last time. One last time, and I believed I could over-power her.

But as my dagger hovered over the wound, the wall behind the queen burst apart with ground-shaking force.

Debris flew across the courtyard, dust coating the space. I squinted into the cloud before the new entrance.

And through it stepped two shadows, with pointed ears.

CHAPTER SIXTY-EIGHT
OPHELIA

THE QUEEN SPAT AN ENRAGED ROAR, AND THAT GENUINE shock was the most delicious source of encouragement. I stilled my hand with the dagger pointed at my palm and crept closer to the veil, squatting through the glow.

Those shadowed beings stepped clear of the swirling dust, dressed in fine tunics and leathers, foreign blades decorating their person.

"Lancaster?" I blurted, as the fae male assessed the scene with that familiar disinterest. And the woman beside him, smiling savagely—"*Mora?*"

I'd met her once before, all those months ago. Before Daminius and the emblems. Before Kakias revealed her immortal scheme. When I was resting in an inn, on a hunt for the man I love.

But then she had been a wife fleeing the bruising hand of her husband. Then, when she'd smiled at me, she did not do so with the flash of elongated canines that greeted me now. The pointed ears peeking between her long, cinnamon-colored curls had not revealed her true lineage.

"Lovely to see you again, Mystique." The *fae female* grinned wider, indulging in my confusion like it was her own little game.

"What are you two creatures doing here?" Kakias spat. Tendrils whipped around her, as if suddenly unsure where to aim their power—my Angellight or these new opponents. It lashed at the veil, and the pain of that strike slid along my bones. It rattled my skull.

I groaned under the pressure, and Kakias smiled. Fucking Angels, I shouldn't have let that weakness show.

Lancaster and Mora flicked controlled gazes across the scene, cataloging the blood spilled around me and the magic roaring through the air. "Interesting," he said, glancing at the female.

"Lancaster," I gasped as another stream of darkness slammed into my Angellight, and Kakias shifted her attention between me and the fae, "not the time for nonchalant observations."

"There she is." A voice that sounded like home rose from behind me, and my heart stuttered in my chest.

There was no way—

But I whirled, and Tolek was there.

He emerged from the shadows of the courtyard with Dax beside him. Blood and dirt crusted their skin and leathers, but both held weapons at their sides, Tol's bow and quiver across his back.

My Angellight flared brighter as he crossed to me. Kakias growled in response, and I flicked a glare back over my shoulder to catch the fae sinking into predatory stances. They circled the queen, her ire cracking, hints of nerves slipping through. Her tendrils pulled toward my light again.

Quickly, I returned my attention to Tolek, looking him over to be sure he was okay. "How did you get here?"

"Called in a bargain." He flashed his ring at me with a crooked smirk, and the pieces clicked together.

"You summoned the fae?"

He had done this. He had called Lancaster—and somehow Mora—to come to my aid—used his deal with the tricksters for *this*. He had found his way here and not alone, but with reinforcements to see our mission through and ensure Kakias's demise. *He'd come for me* as he had time and time again in my darkest hours.

"Don't you know by now there's no tool at my disposal I wouldn't weaponize for you, Alabath? No line I wouldn't cross if it meant helping you."

Those words stretched out to my scarred and Angel-burning

soul, the deep tenor of his voice wrapping around us with reverent, eternal vows.

"By the fucking Angels, I love you, Vincienzo."

His eyes darkened. "Say that to me again when we're alone so I can make good on my promise." Heat rivaling the Angellight burned through me. I turned to face the queen before I could get carried away, but Tol's hand wrapped around my wrist and tugged me back. "One second."

His lips slammed against mine, so warm and familiar I nearly crumbled against him, but he bolstered me. I could feel my Angellight burning brighter, tingling along my bones. I was so much stronger with him around, like our spirits really were one. Tol's hand came to the side of my neck, fingers tangling in my hair as he tilted my chin up with his thumb to kiss me deeper.

"I love you, too, Alabath," he whispered against my lips, eyes flicking between mine.

Those words set me alight.

Spirits I wanted to sink into this moment, to let the Angellight burn through the queen and circle around this spot so it only embraced the two of us—shut us off from the world.

But Kakias's animalistic snarl crashed through the bliss as the fae prowled around her. The walls they had blown open shivered, cracks reaching to the glass ceiling.

"Beautiful display of affection," Dax said. "Now remove your tongue from her throat, Tolek, and let's end this."

Kakias cackled, the sound spiraling and unhinged, bouncing against the stone pillars and glass doors that still stood. "I should not be surprised to see you, Lieutenant Goverick."

Dax's eyes subtly flicked about the scene, clearly looking for his prince.

"It's General Goverick now." His hand tightened on his ax.

"How lovely—a promotion." Kakias's voice was as chilling as ever, but her eyes flickered around her, keeping track of her predators. "Too bad it is for the wrong side. Rank means nothing in death."

I stepped back to the veil of Angellight and in turn sank back into *my* most predatory place. Tolek followed, his eyes dropping over my bloodied hand and the emblems I'd released to the floor. He nodded, and stepped sideways toward Dax. They exchanged low whispers before taking positions flanking me.

I assessed the queen—the harsh lines of her sharp face deepening as she tried to work a way out of this. The flutters of her fingers trying to contort her wild magic. The working of her throat as Mora slunk behind her and vanished from view for a blink.

Taking it all in, I channeled a place of calm cool even as a whip of magic pummeled my light.

"Lancaster, as I said, this reunion is a pleasant surprise." *Keep talking*, I thought as the queen's eyes darted around. The conversation unsettled her, and we needed time.

Behind her, Ricordan's wife stood still. Was Kakias's focus not honed enough to keep her mobile right now?

"Spit it out, Mystique," Lancaster snapped, fingers inching toward his blades.

"Tell me you're here for a purpose," I argued back. I wasn't sure what aid the fae could provide—what depths their magic ran against something like Kakias's, but I knew the fae held secrets, likely power unfathomable to us warriors.

"It appears you can do something we've never considered." Lancaster said it as if it were a golden secret, a knowing smirk tilting his lips and canines poking through.

The queen launched another bout of blows to me, her attacks growing sporadic. Each ricocheted through my frame, but I wouldn't give her the satisfaction of showing that jarring pain again.

Just as I couldn't let the confusion over how or why I was commanding Angellight slip through. I'd never controlled the light of the emblems before. My blood had caused it, but it was their own. Not something I directed.

Yet when I exhaled, the light seemed to expand with it. When it sputtered, my own pulse did as well. I processed Lancaster's words.

I'd seen Kakias use her own power. Seen the way she ordered it with a touch or a thought or a flick of her fingers.

This light was different, though. Hers had been traded to her to own and control. *He shed his power*, she'd said.

Mine had grown within me, was nurtured by the Angels. I thought it was still *theirs*, though, even if it was in me.

Which meant if I wanted to use it, I had to do so in their manner. I dug inside of myself and found each Angel's tether to their magic.

The flaming light licking across the floor ebbed as I watched it. This light belonged to Ptholenix, a creature of bodily connection. With an inhale, I closed my eyes and imagined those flames flooding my muscles right down to every nerve ending. I envisioned them growing, taking form of actual flame and slithering across the ground to wrap tendrils of light around the queen's darkness and burn through it.

"What are you doing?" Kakias gasped.

Cracking open my eyes, I bore down on the sporadic control as the Angellight from Ptholenix's gilded petal poured across the floor and swallowed one tendril at a time. The smaller ones went easily, the larger putting up a stronger fight.

Kakias's magic was Angel in origin, if my theories were correct. We may have come into it differently, but hers was not so different from mine.

Intent of power could have drastic effects, and the queen's was rotten. Kakias's face twisted in a sneer, and she flung an arm out.

Mora shrieked as a thick stream of darkness banded around her waist and hurled her through the air.

"No!" I screamed.

Before she hit the ground, Lancaster waved a hand in her direction and a large cushion appeared.

"I suggest you keep your dirty power off of my sister," he spat at the queen.

Sister? I mouthed over my shoulder at Tolek who shrugged. That would be something to inquire about later, as would that trick he had performed.

Mora regained her breath and stepped back to her brother, shoulders heaving. "If she does not fight with blades..."

"Magic it is," Lancaster finished.

And the two vanished.

My jaw dropped open. Behind me, Tolek and Dax both swore.

The queen spun, searching for them. Tendrils whipped around her, searching the air. As she was distracted, I pushed Ptholenix's fiery Angellight tighter toward her.

Then, Kakias gasped, and a blade was at her throat. Lancaster winked back into existence, breathing down the queen's neck as he once had Santorina's.

But there was a darker promise in his eye now.

Kakias stretched a hand out, and a wisp of power wrapped around Lancaster's throat. The two struggled, each strangling the other. A second tendril snapped out and latched around Mora's neck, pulling her form back into sight. How it had found her, I didn't understand. The female raised a wicked looking sword, glinting in the night, and aimed it at Kakias's chest.

"Ophelia, you need to drop the veil," Dax said, hand tightening on his ax.

"It's the only thing protecting us!" But he was right. I couldn't keep trying to shield them.

"Those weapons won't work on her!"

From the background, Rina's voice said, "Do it, Ophelia." And there was a firm conviction in her tone.

She had had enough time. She and Barrett were ready.

"Say the word, Mystique," Lancaster ground out as Kakias tightened her hold on his throat. Both of the fae watched me, waiting for me to give a signal of what to do. Deferring to me in a warrior matter so their kind could not be blamed.

But they did not realize she was near-immortal. Those weapons alone would not end her.

Over the fae's shoulder, a movement as subtle as the wind rippled through the darkness.

Lancaster tilted his head, hearing it, too. His nostrils flared, scenting who it was, and when I dipped my chin minutely, he nodded.

And I let the light fall.

It happened over staggered seconds, Damien's emblem light retreating under my summons first. My head spun as it slammed back into me. Gaveny's and Ptholenix's came next, Thorn's wild clouds evaporating into the night until the courtyard was once again bathed only by mystlight and the moon streaking through the glass overhead.

But the moment the last of the light came back to me, Kakias sent a desperate spear of darkness shooting across the courtyard.

And it sank deep into Dax's gut.

"NO!" Barrett's voice echoed from where he hid in the shadows behind Kakias and the fae. And with a ragged cry, he pounced on his mother.

Tolek caught Dax as he fell.

Lancaster and Mora held Kakias's arms, ignoring the lashes of her power as it struck them. Barrett wrenched her head back, widening her jaw. I ran to them, gripping her hair and taking the tonic from the prince's shaking hands.

The one Santorina had been brewing in the shadows since we arrived. The one meant to reverse the queen's immortality ritual if it was made correctly.

The blood of the Chosen, transformed under the light of midnight, stirred with elements of sacred land...

We'd been shooting arrows blindly into the dark, but we tipped it down her throat now and slammed her mouth shut, forcing her to swallow.

Her dark magic whipped at my back and hands. It stung, sliced, and bled.

And it *grew.*

A mighty shadow roared from the queen, sweeping over the courtyard, mystlight barely fighting through it. It breathed like a wind and dripped like the tarred substance that created her power. Like the essence of Bant's Blackfyre.

The ethereal being tunneled through the doors and windows. Glass shattered, rock crumbled, and Kakias screamed in a voice not entirely her own, *"The army must stand! Feuds long-fought prevail!"*

The army.

"No," I gasped under the whips against my skin. My gut churned, but I forced myself to stand as my flesh tore and wind pummeled us. "She's sending it to the mountains!"

Kakias was using what little control she retained over her magic to cast it away from her body—to attack our army and fortify her own.

I was vaguely aware of Barrett charging across the stones to his consort, sobbing as he sank to his side. But I couldn't focus over the bubbling sensation in my stomach. It boiled through my chest and extended along my limbs.

I screamed, staggering back, and falling to my knees. Sapphire echoed the noise.

My blood. My blood had been in that tonic. It had been the key to her wicked schemes. It was the answer to her undoing.

And now it was boiling beneath my skin as it worked to reverse unnatural abuses and ancient secrets. It pulled at the frayed edges of my being, at my scorned and healing heart, and the Angel-tainted life source beating through my veins.

Soft, cooling touches brushed my forehead, Santorina whispering over me, "It will end soon."

It will end soon.

I only had to endure it a little longer, scrape up the dregs of my fortitude to survive this pain, because it would kill the queen. *It had to kill the queen.*

And it would ensure that everyone else lived, that the Mystiques saw the dawn.

It will end soon, sorrida, my father's voice echoed in my head. A sob scratched out of my throat. I tried to picture him beside me, encouraging me. My skin stung where her tendrils had lashed at me.

It will end soon.

Through hazy vision, hunched over my knees and peeking between the sweat-coated strands of my hair, I saw Kakias crumple to the ground, power continuing to pour out of her and race away.

But even from here, the rise and fall of her chest was evident. And my heart sank through my twisted body at the sight.

"She's not—" I choked out. "She's not—it didn't—work."

The queen was still alive. The tonic had not stolen her immortal life, it was clear from the breath still in her lungs. Our plan to remove her immortality had failed, and she'd responded with a strike worse than what I'd imagined.

I'd thought if we lured her away from the army, they'd be more protected. Not safe. Not with her own infantry battering the border. But they'd be spared *her* wrath. Her power.

I'd been wrong. Miscalculated somewhere along the way, whether it was with her or the Angel power in her veins, I didn't quite understand.

I cast my fractured thoughts back to the night of Daminius, trying to determine what I'd missed as people moved around me. Lancaster crossed to where Barrett held Dax and relieved Tolek's position so he could come to me. Mora bound the queen in ropes I hadn't seen her acquire.

The blood of the Chosen, transformed under the light of midnight, stirred with elements of sacred land...

Had there been something else? An ingredient I'd forgotten?

I'd been on the brink of unconsciousness when she recited the potion. I was certain we had it all, but I could have forgotten something.

"There's one more—ah!" I gasped as my stomach flipped. Tolek held me steady. "One more—thing to try."

I met Rina's eyes, wide and uncertain. "Ophelia—"

"Please, Rina—I have to try it. I'm the *Revered*." I'd sworn a vow dating back to the Prime Mystique. I'd promised to protect each warrior under my jurisdiction until my spirit was called away.

And as Angel power ravaged my blood, there was one string I had not yet pulled.

Shaking her head, Rina reluctantly raced to her pack.

"Ophelia," Tolek said, turning my face to his, holding my cheeks so tenderly in his sure hands. Hands that were a refuge I now needed to say goodbye to. Tears streaked beneath my eyes at the pain worming through my body, at the way I did not want to do what I was about to. "Don't do it, love. Please, don't."

"I don't have a choice," I said. It killed us both, this inevitable task.

All along, a part of each of us knew it would come to this.

When he'd saved me at the trench, none of it had felt over. It had only been another step toward this fate. Another mark on the list of horrific things we knew we'd have to do before this ended.

It was why we'd both been so frightened, so desperate to salvage the other's life, even if it meant untangling ourselves along the way. When we'd fought afterward, and he'd sworn my safety was all that mattered to him, there was always a lingering shadow hanging over those words. A frenzy that screamed we both knew it wasn't the end of our pain.

A promise I knew he might not be able to keep, even if he'd see his grave because of it—a fate *I'd* face death to avoid.

Because the vow I took outweighed my life, and if I had to suffer for it, I would. But I would not let him.

Rina appeared again, unwrapping that burlap package we swore was a last resort. Tolek's eyes burned with the desire to shove it away. To tell me there was no way he'd let me do this. To insist on another answer.

Any other answer.

But there wasn't one. Not now. Not as Kakias's magic speared toward the mountains, our camp.

And it was in the silver lining his eyes, the slow blinks to keep emotion at bay, that I knew he'd let me do what I needed.

"I'll be right here," he promised, voice strong for the both of us as he took the jar from Rina with one hand, the other holding my cheek, and flicked off the cap. "Right here, *apeagna*."

As I looked at the magic inside, its depths toxic and tarred, I promised I'd return to Tolek.

"I love you, Tolek," I said, fear rattling my words, cracking his resolved stare. "Infinitely."

"Come back," he pleaded.

And I tossed the sticky, sour remnants of Kakias's power we'd cut from my arm down my throat, throwing myself into a void of warring Angel ether.

Chapter Sixty-Nine
Malakai

"What is that?" Mila gasped, guarding my back.

I whirled as the Engrossian before me fell over the edge of the lookout.

Clouds formed on the horizon, thunder booming through the air. But snow already coated the ground, crunching beneath my boots as I brought my sword down again.

Death hung over the valley. Soulguiders shouted at the pressures of departing lives, many of them fleeing as their visions took over, making them vulnerable. Erista and Quil stayed before Jezebel.

Below the lookout, the battle raged. Forms ascended the cliff face as we beat them down.

"We'll deal with it," I promised, but my skin itched at the rolling darkness, spreading too quickly toward the mountains.

From the direction of the Mindshaper capital. Where—

"Oh fucking, Angels," I panted.

And I knew from the wide eyes in her dirt-streaked face: Mila recognized it, too.

The thick, breaching darkness that had clung to the canopy of the Gennium Forest while we were in Firebird's Field. The same that flooded the Fytar Trench as we raced to our friends, and whipped around, untamed, as Tolek sliced open Ophelia's arm and the queen collapsed.

It was that roiling, congealed source of power.

"What the fuck is that?" Lyria growled, joining us at the cliff edge. Winds whipped around us. Across the valley, the Engrossians swarmed one of the peaks, drowning the league of Seawatchers and Soulguiders stationed there.

"A gift from the queen," I murmured, dread solid in my gut.

Soaring toward the battlefield, like a being with wings extending into the night, it came.

And as it reached the valley, it rained upon her soldiers, instilling them with more energy.

"Jezebel?!" Erista shrieked behind us.

And I spun—

To find Jezzie sprawled on the ground.

Chapter Seventy
Ophelia

I WAS BEING SHREDDED IN HALF.

Gray light filtered through the air around me, thick and heavy as I writhed. I levitated in this chasm, no ground or sky, nothing but endless gray iridescence stinging everywhere it touched my skin, like it wasn't sure I was supposed to be in this realm and needed to test me.

I'd thought my autonomy was stolen when Kakias's poison built in my arm, but this was worse than the queen. This was my ribs being pried open, my spirit being disentangled from my body, the void filled with an unrecognizable power.

No—*two* powers.

There was the one from Kakias, that tainted opponent. The thing jerking through my body as it fought to vacate my spirit.

But there was also Angellight, the substance only those seven Prime Warriors were supposed to ascend to. The one that somehow was *mine*, pouring through my body. It pierced the gray in sporadic places, and I swam toward it through this murky plane. Desperate for its comfort and strength.

One endless beam of golden light sliced through the air, feet away. Squeezing my eyes tight against the pounding it sent through my head, I stretched toward it. Heat radiated all around me as my fingers brushed against the warmth.

But a spiral of darker power speared toward the light, and the

519

sensation shot through my body like an anchor in my gut. My feet met solid ground I hadn't realized had formed, but it took every bit of strength within me to remain standing.

"*No.*" The word left me in a growled plea, melting into the gray.

"Ophelia?!" A voice tore through the void, desperate, and a flash of white-blue illumination followed.

I whirled toward it. "*Jezebel?*"

The two powers collided behind me, the dark piercing the light, and the impact rocked through my body, sending me to my knees. A clap of thunder vibrated along my bones and throughout the void. Warring, incohesive, a rivalry.

It mirrored the battle occurring in my body between Daminius and cutting the queen's power from my arm. Played it out physically for me to relive, as if I could forget it.

Wherever we were, it was bringing that feud to life.

And I was at the center of the cataclysmic undoing. A battle seeped through the air, as mighty as the Angels.

"Jez—" I gasped. My arms wrapped around my torso, my words tight. "What are you doing here?"

"I—I don't know." Jezebel shook her head, her hands gripping my arms to keep me upright. "I was on the lookout. I was using the departing spirits. And then I was here."

Angellight cracked like lightning. Pressure mounted in the air. Jezebel's frame glowed with white-blue light, like the heart of a fire.

"Ophelia, how did you get here? Where are we?"

"Kakias was winning," I gritted out. "We reversed the ritual. It didn't work. She sent her power to the mountains—ah!" My chest ached like it was being flayed open. "I used the power Rina cut from my arm."

"You used it..."

The gray surrounding us shifted. Winged forms paraded across the sky in a dazzling and horrifying caravan, bodies like humans, horses, and things much larger. Stars burst around their heads, and slowly—in the distance—two tumbled to the earth. It was graceful and mesmerizing as they cascaded like shooting stars, legends whispered in their wake.

"What's happening?" I asked.

"I don't..." Jezebel looked from those flying beasts to her own hands, the blue glow flaring. Her gaze snapped to mine, eyes wide and excited. "Ophelia, where are you now?"

"What?"

"Where are you outside of here? Your corporeal form."

"My corporeal...Jez, do you think we're in the Spirit Realm right now?" The plane between worlds where Spirits went to rest. Where Soulguiders led them home after their death and they spent eternity.

I looked around. Angellight forked through the sky and creatures soared above. The dark mass of power swarmed in the distance.

"There or somewhere else, I don't know." My sister shook her head. Her illumination called to my own Angellight, soothing it. "But I have an idea of how to help in our world."

"We're at Ricordan's manor," I explained. Pressure squeezed me tighter. "Trevaneth set us up. Kakias was waiting for us."

Shocked sadness cracked across her features, but she wiped it away. "I'm going to go back, but hurry and get out of here."

"Be careful, Jezzie," I said, pulling her to me.

"You, too."

Then, she was gone. The flying forms in the sky, their burning constellations, and the comforting blue glow went with her.

And in her place, as if it had been waiting for me to be here alone again, the pressure mounting in the air popped. I cried out as it shattered my hearing, my knees weak again.

The sky exploded with a scene like a mural gifted with movement. Two forms painted the vast gray expanse, both radiating golden light, but one had something like black ink seeping from his skin.

Glorious wings beat at their backs in time with the heated accusations they hurled. I couldn't hear them, could only see the rage lining their features, but I was certain who they were. This was the feud that echoed through millennia—the one our mortal warriors were still fighting.

Damien and Bant.

The inky substance swirled around Bant, and he lashed out, whipping into the void. Like Kakias's stolen power but sharper and deadlier.

Then, the mural swirled, their forms blurring and fading into the cloud-streaked sky.

Three different forms stood in a field of wildflowers. The space between cracks of lightning dimmed the scene, and when it flashed again, four more joined them. Wings undulated at their backs, light burning along the feathers, unique to each of them.

The Ascension played out before my eyes, sacrifices made, unheard words spoken.

Heat ripped down my back with each Angel's contribution, shredding along my spine. My vision spotted, and when it returned, that legendary scene was gone. Replaced by wind whipping around a warrior as he kneeled on a cliff before a winged form.

As he bled and bled and bled.

And the Angel did nothing to stop it.

Darkness swallowed up the mountain—*my mountains*, I realized. Exactly as they were today. And in this realm with the powers of eternal beings consuming me, I could see Kakias's power burning toward the war camp.

It swallowed up the moving mural, flooded the air, and even descended on me. It ate at that hollow spot where I thought my spirit belonged, and I screamed out against it. It seemed to smile in return.

Unnatural—it was so fucking unnatural; the battle of Damien's and Bant's powers obliterating my senses. Mine and Kakias's—two warriors born of warring Angels.

No one was meant to withstand the assault ripping through me. I wasn't meant to contain it, wouldn't survive it.

But as I watched Kakias's power flood toward my mountains, I knew I had to stop it—I had come here to stop it. To save my people who didn't even know what madness soared toward them.

So as the realm unspooled with feuds of eternal beings, I fought. The war was within my blood and bones, it had been all this time. I pulled the threads of power I'd gathered from each emblem, their light within me, and wove them together as I had against the queen. I sewed them through the hollows and voids I'd earned from a tarnished spirit and desperately *pushed*.

If I'd conducted power on our plane, it reasoned that here, among magic and myth, wherever it was I'd been transported, I could do more. That I could defy and destroy the darkness shooting around me, the one I'd ingested, and wreck Kakias's magic on the mountains as well.

And that unwelcome presence—I needed it out of me. I needed to obliterate it.

I had to go back to Gallantia.

I had to go back. Pressure hit my limbs, a tightness in my chest. I'd *promised*. I'd promised I'd go back.

Promised someone with chocolate eyes and hands that knew my body like his own. Someone who was my soothing sanctuary, who would tear the stars from the sky and rearrange the constellations if I broke my promise. Who was *home*.

And this love between us could withstand any storm—would uphold any promise.

My vow as Revered meant I'd tied my life and spirit to the protection of the Mystiques and the cause of our clan. But if I was shredded by pure ether, would I truly be a help to them? Surely I could do more, I could *be* more for my people by beating this power, ensuring the end of the queen, and unraveling the rest of the Angelcurse.

And—selfishly—I had only recently realized what it was to *live*. And that was because of Tolek. I'd been lost for so long; I was only learning to balance my responsibilities as ruler with my personal joys and desires. I wasn't done living with the man I loved.

It was the thought of him, of all of them waiting for me, that drove me as I tunneled into the Angellight deeper than I thought possible. As I ripped up the threads of each Prime Warrior from within myself. Siphoned the ethereal power from every particle of air in this gray realm until the plane held no light, but *I* did.

I contained it all, fed from the source. It was in each expansion of my lungs and flex of my muscles. It was a part of me waiting to wake.

And I had been waiting to let it burn.

Angellight twirled along my limbs in strands of scorching gold as I fell to my knees. Murals blurred across the sky, the darkness fading with each pulse of light I emitted. Like I was swallowing up the threat, eating away at it before it could reach its destination.

And then, I exploded with searing light, and scorched the plane to ashes.

Chapter Seventy-One
Malakai

"Jezebel!" I'd said it so many times, I knew she wouldn't answer, but I was lost. I'd carried her into the trees what felt like ages ago, and she hadn't stirred. "Jezebel, please wake up."

I begged and begged. Didn't care who heard. The battle still boomed through the valley, screams echoing along the mountains.

Erista was beside me, quiet with Jezebel's hand wrapped between hers. She hadn't given up, and with her being a Soulguider, that promised me more than anything.

"Come on, Jezebel," I pleaded.

Finally, she stirred.

Her eyes blinked open slowly, assessing us. "Malakai..." Then, she was standing, much steadier than I'd expected. "E, we need to go!" Grabbing Erista's hand, she darted through the trees before I could speak.

"What in the fucking Angels?" I growled, and ran after them. Bare branches jutted across the path. I ducked and wove as they did, following their scampering forms. No one who was just unconscious should be that fast. "Jezebel!"

"I'm sorry, Malakai!" she called back to me. "Go back to the lookout. We aren't done with this fight yet!"

Go back to the lookout? She'd been out, for Damien's sake. She needed a healer.

We rounded a bend, emerging into a clearing, and I blurted, "What's going—"

But my words died under a rush of wings.

"What in the fucking Spirits is that thing?" I yelled. Jezebel whirled to face me, but backed toward the beast.

Wings. Large, leathery wings and a body three times the size of Ombratta.

Jezebel sighed as if I was the ridiculous one. "Malakai, I do not have time to explain this right now."

A second one of those creatures emerged from a high cave in the mountainside, assessing us all. It opened its maw and a column of white-blue flame shot toward the sky.

The first one laid its wing against the ground, and Jezebel scrambled onto its back.

"What are you doing?" I gaped.

"Trust me." And it was in her solid stare that I felt her assurance. She'd been planning for this all along. Ophelia had her contingencies, Lyria had hers, and Jezebel...well, Jezzie clearly had secrets no one knew about. Plans to save our asses in this battle.

"Let's go," Erista said. I hadn't noticed her mounting the second beast, but she sat comfortably astride it now.

With a confused nod from me, Jezebel kicked her feet and the beast rose into the air.

I raced back to the lookout in time to see them clearing the far end of the battlefield. They soared through the night, clear over the armies, faster than any creature I'd ever seen, and disappeared.

Forcing myself into action, I rejoined the fight with Mila and Lyria.

I didn't know how much time had passed when light exploded in the sky. Dazzling strikes beating through the rolling darkness.

Again and again, they burst on the horizon, forking toward the ground in a shower of golden lightning.

Though the bolts didn't hit them, the Engrossian-Mindshaper army *screamed*. Torturous, blood-curdling echoes against the rocky mountain facades, like life was being torn from their bodies.

They remained standing, continued to fight, but the darkness receded. It had fueled their movements briefly, turning them faster. Harsher. Deadlier.

Now, as the shadows were chased away, their army slowed.
And we struck.

CHAPTER SEVENTY-TWO
TOLEK

"WE DON'T FUCKING KNOW WHEN SHE'LL WAKE UP!" Santorina shouted at Lancaster, a savage edge to her words I rarely heard. "She's trying to save our entire army, and it's kill—"

Rina's words cut off as Ophelia writhed in my arms.

Again.

Whatever that toxin she'd swallowed did, it was brutally abusing her. Sweat dripped down her face and neck, but aside from the squirming and wrinkle of her brow, she appeared fine, which was even worse.

They were attacking her internally, and I knew how much that fucking hurt. How much I *couldn't* do anything about it. All I could do was guard her here.

The cuts Kakias's power left across her skin were healing, but her agony clenched my chest as if it was my own.

"The queen's power has gone," Lancaster reminded us. How he thought we could forget the way it had inexplicably incinerated, swallowed in a snap of golden light, was beyond my consideration as Ophelia writhed again. "That was her purpose."

Angels, I was regretting calling on this damn fae.

"The power is gone from here," I growled, "but clearly Ophelia's battle is not over."

I took her hand in mine and held her closer, wishing I could

528

kill whatever was doing this to her. Protect her, that was my promise. And I was breaking it.

Sapphire nervously nudged my shoulder. I didn't know how I knew it was nerves, but I somehow did. This horse was the only one who may love the girl in my arms as much as I did.

"She'll be okay," I encouraged.

She would come back. She had to.

My throat tightened at the consideration of any other result.

"What I meant," Lancaster retorted, "is that if the power is gone, Ophelia is likely dealing with the after effects of it."

"We understand," Rina snapped, barely looking up from monitoring Ophelia to cast the fae a gruesome look. "Just because we are not pompous immortals does not mean we are dense."

Mora snickered, gliding over to us, but Lancaster was properly chastised enough to remain silent. He returned to assisting Barrett and Dax. The general was unconscious from his wound, teetering on the edge of death. Barrett kept mumbling about how Dax couldn't die. The fae male's reassurances that he would save his consort did nothing to appease the prince. Spirits, I understood that sort of desperation.

Mora squatted next to me, extending a hand. "May I?"

I nodded, frantic for any kind of answers. Mora assessed Ophelia, with what fae power, I didn't know. But she pressed her hands gently to Ophelia's body and closed her eyes.

"She's burning up," the fae finally said. "She'll likely be in pain. But her heart is strong, Mystique. Do not fret."

She left us then, returning to where Kakias was tied, her body limp but very much alive. Mortal, immortal, I did not give an Angel's fuck about it now.

Not as Ophelia's temperature spiked, heat burning through her leathers. My heart thudded painfully, each beat audible as I watched the crease between Ophelia's brows deepen, her lips trembling.

"Come on, Alabath," I whispered. "You can beat it. You can beat these damn Angels, or whatever it is in there." I dropped my forehead to hers. "I came back to you. Don't leave me now."

"Tolek," Rina said softly. "We need to get her—"

But her words were cut off by a shadow blocking out the moon. Long, scaled legs and razor-sharp claws shattered the glass ceiling. Shards rained around us, so small they were practically dust misting the air.

With them a sprinkle of crimson liquid so dark it was nearly black coated us all. Then, four things happened at once.

Sapphire whinnied—a pained, strangled sound that had Ophelia crying out, too. She writhed like they shared that pain, her eyes flying open.

The shadow lowered to the ground, a great wind gusting through the courtyard.

And Kakias released a bloodcurdling shriek that echoed like the end of a thousand lives.

CHAPTER SEVENTY-THREE
MALAKAI

✂≻⊱≺✂

THEY FELL. ONE BY ONE, KAKIAS'S ARMY OF Engrossians and Mindshapers collapsed to their knees.

"What's happening?" Mila breathed, disbelief making her words airy. She adjusted her grip on her swords, eyes flicking across the valley below.

But they were not rising. Some fell on daggers or axes, impaling themselves. Some tumbled to the ground, a daze on their faces. Some were entirely unconscious. But almost every soldier in the queen's army bowed before us.

It wasn't only the searing light that had punctured the darkness. This was something more. Some final cord of Kakias's reign being snapped.

This was a lifting of a dizzying air, spiraling dark and hazy above them, like dust being spread through the sky in a storm. It drifted apart into small bits until it was swallowed up entirely by the clouds over the mountains.

"I think they did it." I turned to Mila, beaming, a surge of knee-shaking relief mixing with desperation and lust in me. Wrapping my arms around her waist, I spun her. Her swords clattered to the ground with a ringing that echoed like victory bells.

Mila's eyes widened, but she gripped my shoulders and dared to let a smile show.

Gripping the back of her neck, I kissed her as hard as I fucking could. I melded us together, leaning her against the side of the cliff, and memorized the feel of her against me. Earlier tonight, I hadn't been sure I'd get to do this again, and I had only done it once so far. Not nearly enough.

Her sinfully sweet taste danced across my tongue, and I instantly was hard at the thought of tasting her elsewhere, wanting to experience this woman in every fucking way I could now that the battle was over, fear becoming a heady rush.

"You really think they got her?" Mila asked when she pulled back, eyes sparkling and cheeks flushed.

"Mila," I said, cupping her cheek, and dragging up the two words I knew would mean more to her than anything else, "we survived."

Chapter Seventy-Four
Ophelia

Blinding pain exploded through my back, and it *burned*.

"Aoiflyn's holy tits," Mora gasped.

"Ophelia!" Tolek's voice was a beacon in the night. "Ophelia, what is it?"

I couldn't answer, though. This was worse than the Angellight I'd manipulated on the plane, worse than the heat of the emblems. This seared along my muscles, stretching them.

My horse's pounding hooves and distressed whinny stood out among a riot of cries, an alluring call to steady me.

"Sapphire," I mumbled.

"She's—"

"Need to see her," I panted. Light still flared before my vision, but strong hands helped me up. Blindly, I followed my instincts to find Sapphire. I needed to feel her, to help her.

My hands fumbled through the air, finally meeting something soft. Downy and decadent, almost like layers of cascading velvet. Whatever it was, it wasn't Sapphire, but running my touch across it soothed my frantic nerve-endings, dulling the sparks shooting through my body.

Spots of reality pushed back into my vision, and I took stock of the different sensations to ground myself. The pain in my spine solidified along my shoulders. An arm draped around my waist, supporting me. Citrus and spice and all that was good, beautiful moonlight remaining my tether as it had on that plane.

Spirits, my head was heavy on my neck. Around me, voices were loud and in frantic discussion. The ground seemed to sway.

I made out flashes of stone floors strewn with glittering dust. My boots were coated with it, too, a deep black liquid dotting the leather. Where moonlight hit the drops, an eerily-beautiful, hypnotizing crimson sheen reflected up at me.

I braced one hand against the velvet and wiggled my toes to ensure I had feeling through my entire body. The plane hadn't affected my physical form, then. Sapphire huffed softly nearby.

"Ophelia," Tolek whispered, his thumb slowly stroking my hip. His voice was not wary as I'd expected. It was awestruck. "Look, love."

I staggered against him, but tilted my face up to meet his gaze.

"Welcome back," he said, eyes misty and relief turning the words into a sigh. *I wouldn't have lived without you*, that breath said.

I blinked against the pain in my head. "Is my beauty really that devastating?"

He laughed as I repeated the words he'd said when he first woke. Then, he kissed me like he couldn't resist any longer, a kiss burning with passion that awoke all of my senses and scattered them in a much more satisfying way.

When he pulled back, his fingers slid down my arm. "Yes," he said. "But I hadn't meant look at me." Lifting my hand, he placed it back against that velvety material. "Look at Sapphire."

There was something in his voice that had me wrenching my eyes away from his. I met Sapphire's crystal blue ones, but—

"*What in Damien's name?*" I breathed. The ground rumbled, but I couldn't take my eyes off her.

A pair of snow-white wings extended from Sapphire's body. With the tips tinged crimson from the sticky substance still dripping across us all, she looked like a blood-streaked legend. She flared them, meeting my stunned gaze with a proud one.

I looked between her eyes and the wings. Through that inexplicable connection we always shared, she seemed to communicate something to me. I was not sure exactly what words she sought, but she and I were based on instinct. It was a confirmation, an assurance that she had been waiting for this day her entire life.

The shadow of Sapphire's wings fluttered across me as she slowly beat them. Power poured off her, misty in the air.

"You're a *pegasus*?" I gasped. Tears stung my eyes.

My warrior horse was not only a fearsome mare to ride into battle—she was a being of myths. A creature I thought only existed in fables.

Unable to fight the smile on my face, I whirled to Tolek, who grinned and shook his head with disbelief and excitement. "It seems she is. But there's also..." He gestured behind him, and rage solidified in my gut at what I saw.

One of those ghastly beasts, with leathery, scaled wings, that we'd fought in the forest on our way to the Undertaking. The one that attacked Jezebel, whose spirit she had communicated with.

Every blissful feeling Sapphire had spurred in my heart was replaced with hot fury. I lunged for the beast, unsheathing Starfire from my hip.

But Tolek's arm banded around my waist before I took a step.

"Let me go, Vincienzo!" I struggled against him, and nearly broke his hold. Now that I was awake, I felt stronger than ever.

Tolek only let out a low, infuriating snicker in my ear.

"Relax, sister." Jezebel stepped around the creature, her hand resting affectionately on its snout. As docile as my horse—pegasus —that thing nudged her shoulder. "He won't harm us."

"Jez." I wilted against Tolek. Starfire dropped at my side, blade clattering against stone. My sister and I locked gazes, and everything that had happened on the other plane flashed before me. "Jez, are you okay?"

"I'm fine," she said confidently. But the lack of explanation for that realm and the burning desire to understand how we'd ended up there solidified between us.

"I'll explain what I have answers to," she assured me. The frame of Ricordan's manor shuddered again. "But we need to get out of here before the courtyard collapses."

Snapping back to the moment, I swept the scene. Mora held a

limp but breathing Kakias. Her gaze filtered in and out of consciousness, one moment widening at the beasts, the next clouding over.

Lancaster held Dax, Barrett watching cautiously. Santorina glared at the fae male, her hands clenching at her sides, and I remembered her promise to kill him the next time she saw him. She was determined enough to do it, I knew for certain, but she'd confront him when he wasn't helping one of our friends.

Mora gazed at Sapphire and the scaled creature with starry-eyed adoration. Then, a second winged beast swept through the now-open ceiling.

Atop its back, Erista grinned her feline smile down at us. "We should go quickly." There was a tightness in that smile that unsettled me.

"Did you fly those things here?" I shot at Jezebel, my jaw dropping open. "What about the border?"

"Yes, they're impossibly fast, and we need to ride them out," Jezebel said urgently, ignoring my second question. "Lancaster—not sure it's a pleasure to see you again, but I'll let your presence pass given that you appear to be on our side. You, Dax, and Barrett are with me." Rina's shoulders sank in relief. "Santorina, you and…"

"Mora," the female fae provided with a wide smile. She tossed her brown curls over her shoulder and secured her weapons in her belt, listening attentively.

"Rina, you and Mora take Kakias with Erista. Take that one, too." Jezebel gestured to Ricordan's unconscious wife.

Everyone filed toward the mounts she directed, not willing to argue. Dax would have had questions, his general's mind picking apart any potential threat, but he rested silently in the fae's arms, too much blood staining his leathers, and Barrett obviously didn't have a thought beyond the man he loved.

Mora bounced over to Erista's beast and threw Kakias's body roughly over the back, quickly scaling the creature's side to settle behind her. They were much larger than our horses, easily able to accommodate four or five riders.

"It's been centuries since I've seen one of these!" Mora gushed.

Leaning forward, she patted the beast's side right above its wing, and I thought it might have purred.

"You've seen these?" I gasped.

Lancaster hopped up with my sister and the Engrossians. "She is very old," he answered, shrugging as if that were a simple explanation.

Mora nodded. "If you must know," she said, holding her hand out to Rina who appeared the only wary one of them all, "they are called khrysaor."

"Khrysaor," Jezebel breathed, like it was a word she'd been longing for. The beast nudged her fondly, and I tried my best to see past the threat. Still, Jezebel had a lot of explaining to do.

It would have to wait, though. The courtyard trembled again, walls unsteady from both the fae entrance and the explosive escape of Kakias's power. Pieces of rock crumbled to the ground, splitting with an echo. A large crack speared up the side to where Jezebel and Erista had crashed through the ceiling. The khrysaor and Sapphire stomped their hooves—claws.

"Let's go!" Jez roared.

"Well, where are we going?" I argued, gesturing at Tolek and myself.

"Isn't that part obvious?" Jezebel's knowing smirk had my eyes narrowing.

She jerked her chin, and when I turned, Tolek was no longer behind me. He was seated on Sapphire, with the emblems repacked and his satchel slung over his shoulder. My horse's old saddle was destroyed on the ground now that it no longer accommodated her wings. Tolek held his hand out to me.

Wind gusted around me as the khrysaor took off into the sky, whipping my hair in my face. They soared into the distance, shrinking to a dark speck. Like a shadowed star blasting through the night.

Chewing my lip, I looked between Tolek and my horse—pegasus. Sapphire's stare seared me with a promise: no matter how frightened I was, she was here. Sapphire had *always* been there. Perhaps the only one I could rely on to steady me as much as the man now atop her, ready to explore this new legend with me.

That, combined with Tolek taunting, "Well, if you're too afraid perhaps she can walk," had me quickly fitting myself in front of him. My knees tucked above Sapphire's wings, a more awkward position than I was used to, but those muscular extensions on either side were reassuring.

"There's no reins," I argued.

Sapphire shook her head in response, and I understood what she wanted. I tangled my fingers in her mane, indulging in that new, direct connection, and Tolek's arms wrapped around my waist. "Just like old times," he muttered, pressing a kiss to my neck.

"Don't unseat us, girl," I said, a little breathless already.

Sapphire's huff almost sounded offended, and I laughed at that.

Then, she was galloping. Straight through the back entrance to the courtyard and quickly out of that tunnel. Across the grounds, those strong wings extending on either side as she picked up speed.

They flapped once, and the wall at the edge of the property loomed closer. A second beat, and the vines crawling across the brick were individually visible.

No, no, no, a voice in my head echoed. Fear tumbled through my throat.

But my stomach dropped, and the snow-covered earth sank away from us. Sapphire's hooves skimmed the top of the wall expertly, as if she had been doing this for centuries and knew exactly how much room she needed.

She banked softly around a copse of trees with limbs bare to the calm snowfall. Then, we were climbing, chasing the shadows of the khrysaor making haste for the mountains. From here, the rocky peaks stretched to the stars, fitting against the clouds like they were pieces of a puzzle long ago sketched.

Curling my fingers tighter in Sapphire's mane, I dared a look down. Trees were the size of berries and a blanket of white stretched upon the land, the storm ceasing. It was so serene, not a hint of warfare able to reach us up here. No cries of pain, no shrieks of rage. The only sounds were the secrets between the three of us. The most alone I thought we'd ever be and the most together I had ever felt.

Up here, the air smelled of midnight stars and the burgeoning promises made beneath them. Tasted of possibilities and hopeful dreams.

We coasted over a pocket of air, bobbing slightly, but my stomach didn't flip over as I'd expected. Instead, the wind slapping my cheeks awoke something in me, the rhythm of flight as natural as breathing. Because Sapphire was made for this, and I was made for her. The easy coast of her skillful flying was a lullaby rocking every fear I'd ever had.

The flap of her wings every so often became a song in the wild night.

I looked closely at those new extremities. The way the feathers had a faint golden sheen when the moonlight hit them just right. How they layered over each other in a seamless pattern. I couldn't wait to spend days exploring these new traits, counting the streaks of gold and memorizing them like I had each deep-blue speck in her crystal eyes. The thought sent a thrill through me.

Tolek's arms squeezed around my waist, but he didn't need to say anything. A silent agreement sealed between us that this experience was beyond our wildest dreams, so full of magic that words didn't fit it.

And that stitched a sense of untethered freedom inside of me. One I had not known I was searching for amid the decisions I'd been forced into recently. One that had me clenching my knees against Sapphire and stretching an arm to the heavens. One that had a wild cry pouring from my lips, given to the stars.

At the sound, Tolek whooped over my shoulder.

As we coasted toward our mountains, I knew, no matter what waited, I was precisely where I belonged. And this new freedom was one I would nurture.

CHAPTER SEVENTY-FIVE
MALAKAI

LYRIA HAD CALLED US TO HER CABIN UPON OPHELIA AND her party's immediate return to the mountains for a debrief from both sides. I'd be lying if I said my heart hadn't pounded in my chest until I saw everyone was safe. Everyone but Dax—but he was healing, thanks to the fae.

Ophelia had spoken with Ricordan and let him leave with his son and wife. Trevaneth may have set us up, but he had not understood what he was doing. She wouldn't punish a child.

We'd won—at least for now. The surviving Engrossians disappeared in the chaos. With their queen in our custody, we didn't know what their next actions would be. They needed a leader. Would they accept their exiled prince back? Or would war continue to rage?

Regardless, those who had been under Kakias's control were free. Mindshaper rebels and Bodymelders were gathering the ones who were not injured in battle and assessing their faculties. No doubt some had been in that army willingly and would be a problem to deal with.

My chest tightened at the thought. Beside me on the couch in the commander's cabin, as if sensing my discomfort, Mila placed a hand on my knee. I gave her a small smile in return.

Everyone had disbanded—the Bodymelders and Rina to the

infirmary, Lyria and the minor clan generals making rounds—but Jezebel and Erista had asked Ophelia, Tolek, Mila, and me to stay.

"According to Mora, they're called khrysaor," Jez explained of the winged creatures she and Erista had flown off on and returned with after the battle.

"And they haven't been seen in thousands of years," Erista added.

"Mora said she saw one," Tolek interjected.

"One," Jezebel confirmed, taking a seat on the ledge of the fireplace and brushing her hands down her thighs. "A rogue one. Herdless. A few centuries back in Vercuella. We don't know how or why."

So, one of these stray beasts had been on the fae continent. I wasn't sure what to make of that. It didn't seem like anyone knew.

"Where did you find it, Jez?" Ophelia asked, leaning forward. She and her sister both seemed different since the battle, more so now that everyone else's adrenaline was settling. They seemed to have ignited in a way I couldn't explain.

"I didn't find them," Jezebel said, twisting her fingers. Behind her, the fire flickered, casting dancing shadows across her frame. "Once we got back to the mountains, they found me."

"That's where you'd been disappearing to," I said, and Jezebel nodded. She and Erista had been gone for long stretches of the days after Ophelia left. The khrysaor had called to her.

"I can communicate with them instinctually."

"I thought the one we saw months ago spoke to you?" Tolek asked. He crossed one ankle over his knee, sitting back to take in all of this information.

"He did, but the connection is frayed. I think I only heard him then because he was frantic and had recently woken. He hasn't been able to tell me anything, yet."

"And that's all we know?" Mila asked.

"It is," Jezebel said, nodding.

"Well, that," Ophelia began, "and we saw them flying on the plane." She explained how she used the poison from Kakias's scar to traverse her spiritual form to a different plane. How she had somehow called Jezebel there, too, and that was where Jez had been when she'd fallen unconscious. "The pegasus were there and some other creatures, I believe." Her lips pursed as she considered it, and Tolek whispered something in her ear that soothed her.

I dragged my hand down my face, taking in all of these unfathomable developments and trying to make sense of them. There were so many unknowns on top of everything still left untied with the Angelcurse. Stress writhed in my chest. Spirits, the Alabath sisters would kill me, wouldn't they?

"I suppose we have some digging to do," Erista said.

"And some magic to explore," Jezebel added, locking her hand with her partner's and sharing an excited grin.

And though the uncertainty worried me, at least that was a place to start.

~

ONCE THE OTHERS had left and it was only Mila and me back upstairs, I looked around her temporary room. One that would no longer be hers.

"Are you going back to Damenal?" I asked.

She spun toward me, removing her ivy wrist cuffs and placing them on the dresser. "I don't know what's next," she said.

And there was a question there. An open breath at the end of her sentence.

I took it. "Come with me."

"Where?"

"Wherever." I crossed the room and placed a hand on either side of her waist against the dresser, caging her in. "When the camp cleans up and the village is returned to its former residents, come with me, Mila. I don't know what's next. I don't know if we'll go back to Damenal or somewhere else, but come with me."

Her eyes flicked between mine, considering. "I'm a general. Even while the army is disbanded, I might be needed."

She wouldn't abandon Lyria.

"You'll keep the title." I didn't have to check with Ophelia to know it was true. "I'm sure there will be negotiations to be had with the Engrossians, possibly the alliance clans, too. The

Engrossians will need a leader, and who knows what Barrett will try to do there. I'm sure Ophelia will welcome your and Lyria's experience."

Mila's gaze held mine as her tongue flicked across her bottom lip, and I nearly groaned. She let out a small laugh, like she knew exactly what she was doing.

"Is that a yes?" I asked.

Mila nodded. "Yes, Warrior Prince. I'll go on this next adventure with you."

Leaning down, I came so close to kissing her that our lips brushed as I said, "Let's make it one worthy of legends, General."

Chapter Seventy-Six
Ophelia

THE CELLS AT THE NORTHERN BORDER OF CAMP WERE where Lyria had taken prisoners since the summer. It was under a constant guard that had been tripled in the last hours, though the lone prisoner was too weak to fight anyone off. She barely held on to life at all.

Barrett stood outside, his black hair absorbing the pale sunlight, like some stark relief painted in pools of watercolor, the hues undulating as the wind lifted his curls. His green eyes were hard, sharp features stony.

Rebel sat at attention at his side, tense as his warrior. He'd apparently been waiting for Jezebel's khrysaor outside Ricordan's estate. He hadn't left Barrett's side since. Everyone else's horses would return soon, knowing the trek to the mountains better than even we did.

"Are you sure?" I asked. He made this request once, but I wouldn't hold him to it.

Barrett's fingers curled in the fur along his wolf's neck. The animal nudged his leg in response.

"I am."

Lyria had set up the holding cells in a network of caves. Manacles were welded to the walls and iron doors secured them. All were gaping chasms now but one.

"Leave us," I said to the guards at her door. "Get some rest."

We didn't need an audience.

Once their footsteps faded into complete silence, I swung the door open for Barrett. Kakias slumped against the back wall, dress torn and frame seeming smaller than ever, but she was more alert than I'd expected.

"Did he live?" she asked.

"Yes," Barrett spat. Dax was currently sleeping with the aid of a tonic. He would have died were it not for Lancaster's healing expertise. Even Esmond would not have been able to restore an injury of that magnitude.

"Shame." Nothing human of the queen remained in that response.

Barrett clenched his dagger tighter. Rebel released a deep growl, hackles rising, and my own rose with it. Angelborn burned across my back, but we needed answers first.

"You need to tell us of Annellius," I demanded, and those dark, soulless eyes flicked to mine.

"What of your treasure-hiding ancestor, oh child of wings?"

I picked apart her poetic way of speaking. "Annellius is responsible for hiding the emblems, then?" It was something I'd been considering. That the previous carrier of the Angelcurse had found the emblems and taken to hiding them. Only, I could not decipher why. "And you knew of this?"

I gripped my necklace, but Kakias watched my other hand. The one bearing her family ring.

"Annellius was a fool," she said, dragging out each word. "He had so much power at his fingertips; if only he had stretched out and seized it."

"Annellius had been greedy. He did take that power, and it drew his death." That was what he had said during the Undertaking. It was what the files on his life and death had confirmed.

"You are as delusional as he was." Kakias laughed. "History is written by the survivors, girl." I wasn't sure how that mattered here, but I tucked it away for later. "Annellius's life held so much possibility, and all he cared about was getting rid of it. Doing what was *right*." Disgust twisted her features, and the scar across her face that normally looked painted on moved with it.

Annellius hid the emblems because he thought it was right?

Kakias was veering away from my questions, stare glazing over. There was not much awareness left in her. I needed to be blunt.

"How did you know him? Annellius lived long before your time."

Kakias sighed, an exhausted sound, and she finally gave us an answer as if it would take too much energy to hold things in any longer. "I was not alive when your ancestor was, but my power was. Before it was shed unto me, this magic saw many millennia. It lived in another until the day I was called. When I made a desperate deal and was needed for a fate—when an Angel attempted to turn me into something I could never be."

Barrett and I exchanged a confused glance, but we'd have to untangle the cryptic hints in that explanation later. Energy was slipping for the queen with every word.

"Why did you need me? Was it only Angelblood?"

She inhaled and exhaled heavily. "The agent that activates it"—another breath—"confirmed the ritual."

"What is it?" I urged, desperation dry in my throat and tingling in my fingertips.

Kakias's voice croaked through cracked lips. "You are not asking the right questions, little Angel child."

My mind raced, but I wouldn't show how clueless I was. Instead, I pulled another thread.

"How did you get the crown?" I asked.

"Found it to control the armies. I did not know what it was."

"Why did you not go after the emblems sooner? Surely something so powerful could have given you the immortality you sought."

"They could not," she breathed. "But I learned at Daminius they could be used against me. I wanted them then, but only you could find them." She took another large inhale, the sound ragged. "I was supposed to. But it did not work as the Angel hoped."

I was needed for a fate. An Angel attempted to turn me into something I could never be.

Bant had tried to turn her into a chosen. He had tried to turn her into *me* when he shed his power into her.

Perhaps after Annellius failed, the Angel's vengeful desire against Damien rose. He wanted the pride of having an Engrossian be the Angelcursed. Wanted one of his own to fulfill the task.

But it didn't work. Kakias had never been able to locate the emblems, and even if she had, she clearly was not interested. When she gave up her soul to receive the keys to immortality, she lost that desire.

Kakias's eyes slipped closed for a moment, and it was clear she was done speaking.

And if she was done being helpful, we were done with her.

Whatever had happened when the khrysaor crashed through the glass ceiling of Ricordan's courtyard and Sapphire transformed into her pegasus had ignited the final piece of the reversal ritual. We needed to decipher what it was. But for now, Kakias no longer claimed immortality, and the magic she had conducted was quickly taking a toll on her body.

With only a blade, the queen was killable.

"I'm done," I said. "It has been a pleasure being your undoing, Kakias."

I nodded at Barrett, handing the control to him.

He took two slow steps forward and crouched before his weakened mother. The woman who had trapped him—the one who had tried to turn him into a monster. But Barrett had fought back. He had retained the good naturally born in his heart, despite the malice nurturing him.

Kakias's lids lifted slightly, giving her son a dead look. "You may as well do it," she said. "There is nothing left of me. I can go be with my child now."

My heart stuttered. Barrett's frame trembled with a ragged breath.

"This is for every life taken on your battlefields. For every family now in mourning. For every time," Barrett muttered through clenched teeth, his voice shaking as his fingers did around his dagger, "that you were a tyrant instead of a mother. That you tried to beat the kindness, the compassion, and dreams out of me." He lifted the blade and stilled his grip. "This is for my brother whom you tortured. It's for the woman behind me now. It's for me." He swallowed, gripped her shoulder. "And it's for Dax."

And Barrett drove the dagger into his mother's heart.

Kakias gasped a small, pained sound that did not capture the severity of a knife through the heart but somehow seemed to make the moment all the more fragile. It hung on the air until her eyes closed.

Between the two of them, it seemed like a shared release of so much animosity, of so much pain felt throughout both lives, and a sense of closure.

Barrett was still for a minute, watching the place metal sank into flesh and blood dripped around it.

Where he took his mother's life with his own hand.

I thought a sob might have slipped past his lips, though she'd been nothing but cruel to him. But before I could offer any reassurance, Barrett took a deep breath, squared his shoulders, and wrenched the knife from her chest.

And light poured forth from the wound.

Similar to the burning intensity of the light I invoked from the emblems, it erupted like a beast kept caged for far too long. Alive and sentient, pulsing as if it breathed. Blinding, the light filled the cell, scorched rock and melted earth with its tendrils of golden threads. It pushed against the walls, an ancient pressure wrapping around my frame. A caress to my cheek.

Hello, child.

That presence grew and grew, taking a humanoid form with two large protrusions extending from its back that morphed into a fluttering pair of feathered wings.

The frame seeped through the cracked rock walls, absorbed into their surfaces. There was a whisper of understanding, a familiarity in that sentience—

"Bant's Spirit," I gasped.

"I know," Barrett exclaimed lowly, still in shock over what he'd done.

"No, Barrett." I gripped his arm and pointed at the disappearing golden glow. "Bant's Spirit."

The queen contained *living magic.*

We had been working to undo it, but I didn't think about what it was beyond the immortality ritual. Didn't consider what had allowed Kakias to speak to Annellius, conduct the dark magic, or survive after sacrificing her soul.

The spirit of the Engrossian Angel, the Prime Warrior, had been trapped within the queen since the day they made that deal.

It was shed unto me. This magic saw many millennia.

"Bant tried to turn Kakias into a chosen—into the one able to find the emblems." The pieces slid into place, and Barrett watched me with wide eyes. "Bant and Damien feuded for centuries; you said it yourself. Bant *lost a piece of himself* at the Blackfyre, Barrett! He left his ring there in the battle, and centuries later gave up his spirit there, as well." I gripped his arm.

"He tried to turn your mother into his weapon—to replace Annellius after he failed and make me unnecessary down the line. It had not been Angelblood Bant had shed into the queen. It had been his fucking spirit itself.

"That's why her power felt like it was warring with my own in my blood. Because mine is tied to Damien, and those two Angels left a legacy of feuds." I had seen them on the plane. The answer had been right there. "It's why there was a weird tie between your mother and me in that scar, why she fed off my power and fainted at the trench when it was disconnected."

Breath of lungs and threads of heart. A living spirit. Had Lucidius known, too?

Barrett gaped between the dagger in his hand and the bleeding wound on Kakias's chest.

"What does that mean?" he asked.

I shook my head and clenched my fist around the Engrossian emblem, letting the burning familiarity steady me. It felt less potent, the pulse not as strong now that the Angelic Spirit of its predecessor had returned to wherever it belonged.

"I don't know," I admitted.

For the Angel, for us, for the next steps in this aimless hunt—I did not know.

THE RANGE WAS peaceful from the highest peak looking down on camp. Far below, warriors scurried to-and-fro, carting supplies, packing tents, some simply relaxing. It was a necessary reprieve after the constant battles of the past few months.

Tolek and I sat on a blanket beneath one of the few cyphers that had somehow retained its leaves, though there were only a few, sporadically dotting the branches. The storm had cleared, the sky a gray lilac though it was the middle of the day. Tol had pulled me up here after long hours tending to the injured, and I'd told him of Kakias's confessions and Bant's spirit releasing from her body.

"Where did it go?" Tol asked, drawing shapeless designs in the snow with a stick.

"Disappeared into the mountains." I shrugged, watching my hand as a thin thread of Angellight danced between my fingers. "I think it's all connected."

Tolek raised a brow, and I dismissed the light, turning toward him.

"Kakias practically admitted Annellius hid the emblems." I pushed onto my knees, anticipation bubbling within me. "It would make sense with what Vale has seen. Annellius found the tokens and hid them."

"Why, though?" Concern was etched in Tolek's face.

"Because..." I gripped my shard necklace, almost afraid to admit the next idea. "Because he didn't like what he was meant to do with them."

"If that's the case, Alabath, we need to be even more careful than before." Chills spread down my arms. "Remember how Annellius's story ended. We don't know what these things are capable of."

He was right, but the thought stuck to my mind, a theory I needed to continue to work on. I sagged back against the tree, lifting my hand again to summon Angellight. It burned in a bright snap for a moment, and I concentrated on that orb, willing it to dim.

Once it did, and it was nothing but a thin film wafting around my palm again, Tolek laughed and reached up to brush my hair from my face.

"It's amazing," he said.

"I don't have much control over it," I sighed, watching this new power ebb on its own will.

It is clear to me that your spirit sits differently on the plane among us, Missyneth had said to me before we left Damenal. I had not realized how right she'd been until I visited whatever realm Jezebel and I had been in, but was there more to her warning still?

And how did it connect to Annellius?

"You have more control than you did a few days ago," Tolek reminded me, pulling me from my thoughts. "You'll learn it as you have everything else."

I dropped my hand and crawled to him, straddling his lap and locking my arms around his neck, relishing in that easy confidence he carried about every endeavor I faced.

"Thank you for believing in me so fiercely," I whispered, and I dropped my lips to his. It was a languorous kiss, exploring each other lazily, like we hadn't had the time to before. A brush of my lips against his jaw, down his neck. Him sighing into me before turning us, pressing my back into the blanket and hovering over me to steal control back.

I could kiss him forever. Even if the Angels rose around us, I'd choose him over it all as I had on that plane.

When Tol pulled back, he rolled onto his side next to me and brushed my hair behind my ear. His steady hand cupped my cheek, eyes searching my face. "Tell me what happened there."

There. The plane.

I told him all of it, every sensation I could recall, every pain and power surge. How Jezebel appeared and the winged constellations fell. How when the light exploded around me at the end, an excruciating burning shot through my body, and the gray murky world was obliterated. How we assumed that was what defeated Kakias's power on the battlefield. How I was left tunneling through white light, trying to get back to him, my whole body scorching.

When I was done, he lifted my hand, and I knew what he wanted. Focusing on the shard at my neck and the tether it left in my soul, I willed a bead of Angellight between my fingers.

"Whatever happened there...it unlocked this," Tolek mused. I nodded. "Another mystery to figure out." He kissed my fingers and tucked them into my palm, holding the light within my clenched fist.

We fell into one of our comfortable silences after that, breezes coasting across our skin. Tolek wrote in one of his journals, slamming it shut every time I asked what he was working on. I constructed a crown of weeds that pushed through the icy ground up here, looping one over the other in an intricate fashion.

"It's like the halo," Tol observed. It did resemble the symbol a Revered was inducted with.

"I hope we'll return to Damenal soon so I can see it again," I said, setting the fake adornment atop his head.

He laughed, removing it and crowned me instead. "That's where it belongs." Closing his journal and wrapping the leather strap around it, he pulled me to him, and together we looked over the jagged mountain range. "Where to next, Revered?"

I considered. "We have two emblems left to find. Two more pieces to unlock before we can fulfill this Angelcurse."

"Soulguiders and Starsearchers," Tolek said, and I could tell he buried his worry.

I tracked the clouds drifting across the sky, and though my heart longed to return north to Damenal, I said, "Looks like we're heading west."

Back into this search for tokens. We had no indication of the final two locations, but we'd uncovered many secrets of the Angels in the hunt thus far. Though it may hold death and dismay, a piece of me wanted to uncover the next steps.

"I miss CK," Tolek sighed.

I laughed. "It's only been a week since you've seen him."

"Yes, but I was worried about him before he left. I hope this mission with Vale works in more ways than one." Tolek rested his chin on top of my head.

"I hope so, too." Not only did I want them to find answers to healing Vale's sessions and deciphering why they malfunctioned around the emblems, but I hoped, for their sakes, they could work out what was between them.

I trusted they would, once they finally spoke about it. With that assurance, I allowed myself to relax.

Until a deep voice behind us barked, "Revered."

Lancaster and Mora emerged over the ridge of the mountain, and the harsh look on the fae male's face twisted my stomach. Tolek and I both immediately pushed to standing, his hand bracing my back.

"Yes?" I asked, donning my mask of Revered. Both fae had been given clean tunics and places to wash, their warrior leathers looking out of place on their bodies.

"We won't be staying." Lancaster's canines caught the light, peeking over his lips. I supposed the fae could not make themselves comfortable in our camp. Most warriors would not understand this tentative peace.

"I understand," I said. "We appreciate you coming to our aid."

Mora grinned, but where her brother's smile was tight, hers was gleeful. I couldn't decide if it was friendly or unsettling. "We will be back."

I stilled. "What?"

"Our queen is calling in debts." Lancaster's eyes fell to our bargain charm resting against my chest. "From the both of you."

"What do you mean?" I asked.

Lancaster gestured to Tolek. "When he used your charm to summon me, the indefinite bargain tied the two of you together." Foreboding tightened my gut. "It is now not only your life indebted to mine, but it is both of yours. And last I counted, I have fulfilled three requests so far."

And Tolek and I had completed none. Now, the queen was summoning Lancaster to call in debts *she* requested. I swallowed the fear stirring in my gut.

"And if one of us breaks the bargain?" I asked, already searching for a way to get Tolek out of this.

A cocky smirk twisted the fae's lips. "If one of you fails, the other suffers the consequences."

"Consequences?" Tolek asked.

"Death," Lancaster said, darkly.

Dread tingled through my limbs, my heart pounding in my ears. Beside me, Tolek stilled.

We were tied together, our lives and fates, by the promises of the trickster fae. If one of us failed—the other died.

"I'm making the first request of the bargain by order of my queen," Lancaster continued as if he had not just twisted my world. "She and her court are on their way. We will be in touch to establish details of where you'd like to host her."

The Queen of the Fae was coming to Gallantia.

The hands that bled with tricks and secrets would be on our shores due to the bargains Tolek and I had made with Lancaster. The ruler who slaughtered humans, who despised warriors due to our domain of magical land. My mind spun, already slipping away from the tentative peace I'd held with Tol moments ago.

But I did not let the dismay break my facade.

"We'll be waiting," I confirmed.

"Until we meet again," Tolek said, a mock friendliness in his voice.

Lancaster and Mora left, and it wasn't until their shadows had faded to specks in the distance that I looked at Tol.

Despite the distress cascading through my body at the new turn of the bargain, the warmth in his eyes assured me it would be okay. That we'd faced curses and queens and war before and we would continue to do so, fighting for that safety only we provided for one another.

"I never wanted my bargain to threaten you," I said. "It was supposed to save you, not force a tether between us."

"I was already infinitely yours, Alabath. We'll survive it together." There was such a hardened steel in his voice—a guarantee that he would do anything to protect me—that I wanted to believe it.

But I couldn't ward off the apprehension.

Tolek pulled me into his arms and tucked me beneath his chin until our breathing synchronized. As I fought my racing heart, I promised myself we would not only face whatever the future held —we could overcome it.

And if a bargain claimed our lives, then we would conquer the Spirit Realm *together*.

The glimpses of Sapphire and the khrysaor soaring high above the clouds in the distance eased my worries further. I could not help but smile, knowing instinctively how free they felt and wanting to grasp that feeling again.

As I looked out over my mountains, I thought of the legends of this fabled, bloody queen sailing toward our shores and the bargains she spun. I remembered the stories shared of pegasuses claiming the skies and recounted the tales of Angels I'd always thought were nothing more than lore exaggerated through the centuries.

And for the first time, I considered: perhaps all the myths were alive.

EPILOGUE
DAMIEN

BANT'S BODY FLARED AS THAT OUTLINE OF LIVING power merged with the shallow husk of his body. As the spirit he had long ago shed returned and fate—so torn by the Angel's path —rioted through his frame. He writhed as senseless decisions took their toll, fluttering along eternal bone after empty centuries.

But our master watched the shattered Angelglass. One burning image lingered.

A spiral of stars ripped from the sky, their wings flaring. They fell among the land and breathed life to legends and things long dead. A twisted fate not even he had predicted. An army ready to rise on the backs of two young myth-born girls.

"It has been millennia."

And he smiled.

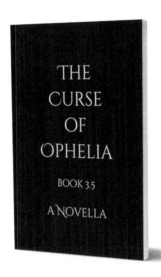

**THE
CURSE
OF
OPHELIA**

BOOK 3.5

A NOVELLA

Don't miss Cypherion's and Vale's story, coming 2024
Preorder now so you're ready for release day!

Did you enjoy *The Trials of Ophelia*? Please consider leaving a
review on Goodreads, Amazon, your favorite retailers, or social
media.

I'd also love to have you join my newsletter to be the first to get
updates, join The Cub's Tavern on Discord, or subscribe to
Patreon for monthly bonus content from the TCOO world.

ACKNOWLEDGMENTS

This book was an entirely different beast to tackle than the last two. In a lot of ways, writing Trials felt like kicking off a new leg of the series. Not to say the first two books weren't as important, only that so many things had been building to moments in this book. I'd been waiting to take you to new parts of the world, share more warrior cultures, dive further into the Angels, and of course, feature the romances (that cave scene lived in my head for way too long).

But none of those would have been possible on my own, so here we go.

Every day I consider myself incredibly lucky to be supported by family and friends who may not even be romantasy readers but still scream about my books as if they are. To my parents, thank you for quite literally being the reason I can keep pursuing this endeavor. To my brother, for continuing to make everyone you know buy these books, even if you refuse to pronounce the characters' names correctly. To my friends (both those living near and far) who are my rocks every day, believe in me way more than I do, and remind me that every small milestone is worth celebrating—and that I need a break now and then.

This book wouldn't be half of what it is without the fantastic team behind it. Thank you to Kelley, for wrangling that early draft. To Friel, for cleaning up the mess and giving me the confidence in my story and characters to put this book into the world. And to Kayla, for not only proofreading but also being such a champion of the series. Finally, to Fran for yet another stunning cover. In my totally unbiased opinion, this series has the best covers *ever*.

To my indie author friends: I cannot even attempt to name all of you—which is a very fortunate position to be in if you ask me—but thank you for everything. I always say the best part about being an indie author is the community, and I'll die on that hill. To Liz, for being there since day one and believing in this story on the days I don't. To the Coven, the writer chat, the indie goddesses, the awesome author group...truly every group chat that has formed, welcomed me in, and supported each other. And to the countless, incredibly talented individual authors I talk to every day, thank you for just *getting it*.

To Chey, Carmen, and Lynn, for being you (there's no better way to say it). To my beta readers, for sacrificing your time to read this manuscript in its unfinished state and providing such helpful feedback. And to my ARC readers and all of my reader friends for the support getting to launch day. The texts, DMs, and tags all make my heart want to burst.

To my Street Team, my Angels, for screaming your hearts out about these books—you are why this series continues to find new readers every day. I can promote my books all I want, but it's you who are really helping authors make leaps and bounds in such a tough industry. And on that note, to every bookstagrammer and booktoker—I am forever grateful to each of you for taking a chance on Ophelia and crew.

To Ophelia, for letting me continue your story. I hope I do you justice. Even on the hard days, thank you for always being there as my escape.

And last but certainly not least: to you, reader. Thank you for reading. This is beyond my wildest dreams.

Infinitely yours,

Nicole

Nicole Platania was born and raised in Los Angeles and completed her B.A. in Communications at the University of California, Santa Barbara. After two years of working in social media marketing, she traded Santa Barbara beaches for the rainy magic of London, where she completed her Masters in Creative Writing at Birkbeck, University of London. Nicole harbors a love for broken and twisty characters, stories that feel like puzzles, and all things romance. She can always be found with a cup of coffee or glass of wine in hand, ready to discuss everything from celebrity gossip to your latest book theories.

Connect with her on Instagram and TikTok as @bynicoleplatania or on nicoleplatania.com.